The Christian Dilemma

The Christian Dilemma

Adam Gambill

The Christian Dilemma

© Adam Gambill 2018

Published by
Lighthouse Christian Publishing
SAN 257-4330
5531 Dufferin Drive
Savage, Minnesota, 55378
United States of America

www.lighthousechristianpublishing.com

Chapter One

"Look around you," says a gentle voice.

I stand on a mountaintop, overlooking a vast, open country. A pair of hands grips my shoulders, holding me upright. A cool breeze ruffles my hair. I blink in surprise. A veil of clouds dissolves so that I am now staring at huge mounds of grain. Each mound appears to be touching the sky, its golden grains gleaming in the sunlight.

The hands move down to grip my upper arms. Gently, the hands slowly begin to rotate me, as if I am standing on a moveable platform.

"Do you see all this grain," says the voice. I swallow hard with a nod. "Everything you see testifies against the lies that your government has spread among your people. For a long time now, your leaders have deceived you into believing that an unprecedented drought has crippled your nation. And so, for all these years, you and your people have been subjected to hard labor, and forced into a miserable existence."

I try to speak, but a group of fingers suddenly touches my lips, keeping me from doing so. The fingers are soft and gentle, as are the hands that hold me upright.

"All of the great mounds of grain that you see represent the abundance that has been stored away and even sold to neighboring countries. Meanwhile, you must eat the scraps from your leader's table while you harvest the very food that fills their stomachs. But all this shall soon come to an end. Very soon you will no longer labor for mere scraps. Nor will you feel the stinging lashes of your oppressors' whips against your backs. The Great

Deception that has swept the nation will soon fade like morning mist, revealing the evil for everyone to see."

I wake with a smile on my lips. I lean against a spreading oak, sheltered from the blazing heat of the afternoon sun. A hot breeze ruffles my hair as I look at my friends around me. All of them look drained, their eyelids lowered or closed. Ethan Garret, my best friend, sits beside me, his eyelids lowered into a weak smile.

"I swear you make sleeping against a tree look as comfortable as a bed," he says, massaging a spot on his shoulder. "If only I could convince myself that this tree is a cushy pillow. But then there are all these annoying ants." He blows a black ant off his wrist with an irritable puff. Honestly, the ants do not seem to bother me that much. With a sigh, Ethan turns around and gives me a measured look. "I'll bet my shiny pendant that you were dreaming, weren't you?" I nod with a small smile.

Ethan braces a hand against the dusty ground and then turns around so that he is now staring me straight in the eyes. "Was it the same one, about the mounds of grain?"

I scratch an itch on my shoulder. I nod.

Ethan frowns, brown eyes thoughtful. "Strange isn't it? I always seem to know when you've had that dream again. But then again, your peaceful expression always seems to give it away. You always look as if you've been revived, like all signs of stress and exhaustion have been wiped from your very soul."

I laugh. "You sure have a way with words. If we didn't have to shell corn all day long, I can imagine you sitting in a classroom somewhere, with a group of students awaiting your every word."

Ethan gives me a sad smile. He turns his hands over and examines his calluses. "I don't know how much longer I can take it. I'm so sick and tired of shucking and shelling corn all day long I could strangle myself. And for what," Ethan says, meeting my eyes with a curious expression. "For whom are we toiling? I don't believe for a second in that pathetic excuse of a drought. Besides, I think there's more to your recurring dream than just a pleasant escape, don't you think?"

I shrug with a smile. "Hard to say. I'm not even sure what it means. Mounds of grain do not really explain anything. And as far as the voice I always hear, he always says pretty much the same thing."

An exhaustive sigh. I turn to find Agatha, an elderly widow who we have all come to respect, giving me an exasperated look. She shakes her head, long white hair swaying in the wind. "My dear boy," she says, leaning forward in her rocking chair, blue eyes strong and alert. "How many times do I have to tell you, them dreams of yours is a sign, a sign of not only the present, but also of things to come. Why else would you continually have the same dream over and over again? Now listen closely," Agatha adds with a cautious gleam in her eyes. "I may be an old fruit bat to most people in this commune, but I still have my wits about me. Decades I spent teachin' young folks every Sunday morning about all the signs and wonders in the Bible. Don't think fer a moment that God has forsaken us, 'cause He hasn't. Them dreams you have is fer a reason, a sign of things that is and of things to come. Just you wait. Just because most of the people around these parts think you're nuts, that you have lost your mind, shows nothing but ignorance on their part. This old woman may sound like an old lowing cow to most, but I haven't been allowed to reach the overripe age of ninety- four fer nothing."

I laugh. Agatha smiles, a gaping hole without teeth. Beside me, Emily rises to her feet with a groan. She moves to stand in front of me, brown eyes flicking between Ethan and Agatha, until finally resting onto me.

"Agatha's right," Emily says in a sweet, heart clenching tone of voice. "And, while I would love to do nothing but sit around and listen to you all for the rest of the afternoon, I fear the whip more. We have less than five minutes till our shift resumes."

I scramble to my feet on that note. I turn to Ethan and extend a hand. He takes it and I help him up. He brushes off his pants, a trail of dust in the wind.

Together, we make our way to Agatha. Emily and I take a hold of her arms and help her to her feet. Ethan stands in front of her, just in case she loses balance. Agatha shuffles forward and, once a few feet from the chair, Ethan swoops in to pick it up. We take turns carrying Agatha's chair back and forth from the corn field to beneath this tree. Despite our collective insistence that Agatha rest as much as possible, she always manages to shell most of her daily quota: Twenty bushels of corn. We make up the difference among us. As for each of us, we have to harvest and shell an extra ten bushels. Still, it's not fair that the elderly have to meet such a steep quota, but we can't change it.

"Thank goodness," says a winded voice from behind me. With a sigh of relief, I turn around to face my uncle Mark. He grins, green eyes agleam with his usual rich store of energy. He brings an arm to his forehead and wipes away the sweat. Poor Mark with his shiny black hair. How he manages to hold up so well in this heat without withering away is beyond me. As for me, I am thankful for my brown hair, though lighter brown hair would be better, especially since we do not have any hats to keep the sun from baking our heads. This is supposed to keep us from feeling lazy.

Mark breathes a sigh of relief. "I was afraid I wouldn't make it back in time. I think half the families from all four of the surrounding communes were in line ahead of me. But I got our petitions in nonetheless."

Petitions. I sigh. This started back a few months ago, that in order to receive our government provisions, including food and medicine, we have to submit a formal petition each month stating our plea. There must be one for each family. In Agatha's case, Mark always submits hers along with ours. As for Ethan and Emily, along with Ethan's younger brother Zeke, their parents submitted theirs this morning, in hopes of beating the long lines at the Hub. The Hub is the center of authority that governs every aspect of our lives.

We alternate our breaks so that there are always about half of us working, like a safety net. That way, we always manage to come out ahead of our quota. Not much, but enough to prevent the near constant harassment that plagues some of the other families. Just a short distance down the corn field from us are the Dovers. They are just one of twelve families that work on our commune. Andy and his brother Caleb are very good friends of ours. Their younger sister, Teresa, has a crush on Ethan that would make your head spin. But then again, most of the girls in our commune have a crush on Ethan. Ethan is just exceptionally good looking.

Ethan snaps his fingers in front of my face. "Anyone home," he says with a toothy grin. "Jeeze Ryan,

I know how much you hate to leave the shade, but still." His grin broadens. "Will I have to get Emily over here to coax you with a kiss?" I give him a disapproving look.

Ethan shakes his head with a knowing smile. "You can't fool me, I see you staring at her all the time. If you don't eventually speak up, then I will. It's high time you two put aside your stuffy treatment of each other and embraced each other like the lovers you are. I know she won't turn you down. And come on," Ethan adds with a mischievous smile, "you can't deny that you've not wanted to sample her sweet lips. Or, if you want my shy friend, I can arrange for you two to meet deep within the field. As your best friend, I only want to see you happy. And here lately, you look like a guy who could use something new and exciting in your life. Well, we all could for that matter, but you know what I mean."

"Fine," I say, earning a surprised look from Ethan. "I will let you broker our relationship on one condition: That I get to do the same for you. For a long time now, I have waited to see if you would express your feelings to Arianne McGerbert, but you continue on as if she's nothing more than a pretty friend. And yet, here you stand, wearing the heart shaped pendant that she gave you so long ago. Now," I say, raising my eyebrows into a triumphant look, "what do you say to that?"

Ethan shakes his head, a stray lock of dark brown hair brushing against his brow. "No. No. And no. You have completely misunderstood the meaning of this pendant. I only wear it so that all the other girls will leave me alone, not because I am in love with Arianne."

I snort a laugh. "Yeah right, and I am staring at you right now and yet I am blind. Surely you do not expect me to believe that."

A sharp voice, high and full of urgent warning fills the air. Emily. I look around frantically. I see no sign of any agents.

I wave her off. I suppose she is peeved at Ethan because he is still holding onto Agatha's chair. Agatha, as usual after a good rest, is working like a bee.

I turn back to Ethan. "Do we have a deal?" Ethan swallows hard, looks nervous.

I give him a wry smile. "I didn't think so. Now come on, before that back of yours gets another lash for getting caught holding Agatha's chair. I don't think we can use the same excuse twice."

With a nod, Ethan heads towards the spot where Agatha stands beside Mark, chattering away as usual, which is something that, when there are no agents around, happens on a regular basis.

I fall into step beside Ethan, my mind revisiting the recent episode when Ethan was caught idly holding onto Agatha's chair. I saw the agent before he reached us. One glance at his malicious face told me to jump into action, and so I did. I sprang forward and grabbed a hold of the chair and argued that it was my turn to carry Agatha's chair. Ethan, bright and quick to understand, saw what I was doing and went along with me. Needless to say, the agent, who we call Perverted Demon, looked at us like we were crazy. In the end, he gave us a simple but painful option: To decide which one of us would receive a single lash. I spoke up first but Ethan cut me off, took his shirt off, and received the single but very painful lash. I waited, and as soon as the agent turned away, took a cloth, dipped it into a pale of water, and cleaned his wound. He would have done the same for me.

Ethan carries Agatha's rocking chair through two rows of corn before sitting it down gently. I pick up a worn pair of gloves and begin to slip them on. We are only issued two pairs apiece, and they always wear out well before the month ends. One more week and we will receive our next round of provisions.

Ethan reaches the small wooden work bench next to the field and takes a pair of gloves. He shakes his head and gives me a weary look. "I wish you didn't always have to be so good. It was my turn for the ratty gloves today. You've worn them the last two days."

I incline my head at his hands. "Your hands need a break. Your calluses will thank me later on. Besides, you gave me half of your apple the other day when mine was wormy, remember?"

Ethan expels a defeated sigh. "So be it. But tomorrow I get the ratty gloves, and if…" Ethan trails off with a frown.

I glance around me, but find nothing unusual. No, I take that back, Emily is gone. I feel my heartbeat quicken as I search the area for her. We all try to keep a close eye on each other. You never know when one of the perverted agents over us will sneak up and try to harass one of us in private.

"Looking for me," Emily says with a smile in her voice. She rises to her feet from behind the table. "I was just tying my laces. No need to look so worried."

I sigh inwardly and turn back to Ethan. He still looks troubled, despite having found Emily. "What's wrong," I say.

Ethan bites down onto his lip. "I was just thinking. What if we don't get our provisions? What then? I mean, how do they expect us to work like slaves without sufficient supplies?"

"We'll get 'em," I say, though I can't deny that I too am concerned.

Ethan doesn't look convinced. "I hope so. But for now on, I think it'd be a good idea if we put a little something aside, just in case. I know it's against the law, but still. Otherwise, we risk starvation."

Mark clears his throat and turns around to face us, his hands grinding around a cob, sending its plump golden kernels falling into a wooden bucket at his feet. "You two boys are going to worry yourselves sick over something that may never even happen. Just because a few families from the northern commune didn't receive their provisions doesn't mean it will happen to us. Don't forget, in times like these, what better way to safeguard our lives than by prayer? I know it might not seem like it, but God is still in control."

"That's right," Agatha says with a bright smile. "Mark's right, for which I am glad. It's nice to know that all those years of drilling Scripture into his head have paid off." Agatha begins humming a cheerful melody.

"I know that," Ethan says, but not unkindly. "But what about all the families who didn't get their provisions?"

Mark looks troubled. "I don't know. Perhaps the other families will share with them."

I can't see that happening. "Maybe seven years ago, before Gloss came to power, but probably not now. You know, the name Eugene Gloss sounds so harmless, and yet, he is so very destructive."

Ethan's face darkens into an angry look. "Oh how I hate Gloss. I could strangle the leaders of our country for handing over power to him just so they could sleep all day, or whatever they do. Everything was going fine without him. It completely goes against what our founding fathers had intended."

I feel the same way. I miss the days when our nation was ruled by district governors. Each district was run by a single governor, elected by the people for the people. Now we have a dictator who calls himself a president. He rules all eight districts with an iron fist, and to our dismay, he also abhors Christians.

"But it happened," Mark says with an agitated sigh. "The only thing we can do now is hope and pray that things return to the way they were. Meanwhile, we had best get to work, lest we fail to meet our quotas and wind up with bloody backs. I have no desire to attend a public whipping, especially if it is any one of us."

I stand still, not wanting to move. Our shirts are already sticking to our bodies with sweat. I can see the ripples of Mark's abdomen through his white T-shirt. We all wear white T-shirts, even the women.

Mark lowers his eyes to the front of his shirt. He looks up with a curious frown.

I roll my eyes. I turn around to face Ethan. "How is it that we do the same amount of work, eat the same food, and yet he has a rock solid abdomen and we don't?"

Ethan frowns. "What kind of a question is that? Good grief Ryan, of all the things there are to talk about and you want to talk about abdomens." He runs a hand over his own abdomen. "And speak for yourself, I'm proud of my ripples of renown."

Mark looks at Ethan with a lopsided smile. "That'll teach you to fall asleep shirtless under a tree."

Ethan recoils. "It wasn't my fault. I was just resting, and when I woke, half the girls in the surrounding communes just happened to be standing over me. I did nothing wrong."

I clear my throat, getting Ethan's attention. "It was more like ninety percent of the girls. Remember, I was the one who rescued you. And so, because of you, I suffer to this day from being known as your handsome body guard."

Ethan smiles weakly. "Yeah, I guess I forgot about that. Only I think you are overlooking the worst consequence of my mistake. Because of me, most of the guys around won't even talk to either of us anymore because of their jealousy. Honestly, if I could take it all back I would."

The afternoon dragged by slowly, the same as usual. I glance at the sun. A little less than an hour and it will be gone. Our work is done for the day. I breathe a sigh of relief.

I stretch my arms with a yawn. As I lower my arms, Ethan staggers up to me and drapes an arm around my neck. I pull away in disgust. He knows that I hate it when he does this, as if I am not a walking bead of sweat on my own.

Ethan gives me a satisfied smile. He rests his head on my shoulder in his usual, joking manner. "But I thought that's what best friends are for."

I roll my eyes. "You mean so that you can drive me crazy?"

Ethan feigns injury. "Nail me to a tree and run a spear through my heart." I laugh.

Ethan's expression turns serious. "You know, I've been thinking a lot here lately about what I would do if something happened to you or Mark. Or any of us for that matter. We make such a great team, that the absence of any one of us could spell disaster."

I swallow against the lump in my throat. "I think it's best not to think about things like that. Each day has enough trouble of its own, remember?"

Ethan gives me a small smile. "How could I forget? Agatha must quote that Scripture at least a dozen times a day."

"Are you boys going to stand there all day talking," Emily says from behind me. "We're supposed to sneak off and meet Andy and his new girlfriend, remember?" With an irritable sigh, Emily walks away, leaving a trail of corn stalks rattling behind her.

I wish I had never agreed to go along, and judging by Ethan's weary expression, he feels the same way.

We meet up with Emily under the spreading oak. Even from here, I can see Mark waving at me from the front porch of our house. I wave back at him. The agents have already come by and hauled away our grain to be placed in a storage facility before it's shipped out. As usual, we all managed to meet our daily quotas.

Part of me wants to back out of Emily's agenda to meet Andy right now. I want to spend the evening talking to Mark in relaxation, not trudging across the corn field we worked in all day just to meet Andy's new girlfriend. But then again, any time spent with Emily is time well invested. Plus, I cannot deny that I am curious to see how Andy treats his new girlfriend.

After guzzling down large gulps of water, we head out. Emily leads the way, passing through the rows of corn ahead of us like a graceful doe. Ethan catches my eyes and gives me a knowing look. I give him a light punch in the arm.

"Come on you slow pokes," Emily says over her shoulder at us.

I want to remind her that what we are about to do is illegal, but I decide to stay silent. Besides, it sort of feels good going against the laws of the wicked perverts who have waged war against our lives and our religion. I pray that we can one day reclaim our country and practice our religion openly.

After several minutes of advancing across the corn field, we finally make it to the other side. Now this is the tricky part. We are not supposed to cross over into another commune. Breaking this law will earn you an instant twenty lashes if you are caught.

We now stand on the edge of our commune, facing a small row of houses that are just like ours. I look about the area but see no sign of Andy or his girlfriend. Of course, I have only seen her a few times in Town, and mostly before the law preventing cross communal activities. Before that law was passed several years ago, everyone from all four of the surrounding communes got together on a regular basis throughout the year to celebrate many festivals. Now I find myself trying to remember who occupies which commune. Other than occasionally meeting in Town, people are rarely seen talking openly anymore. Fear has drained all the life and happiness out of most people. One of the first things that Gloss did when he came to power was to strip all the names of the Towns in the country. This shocked everyone, even gave rise to rioting, which was quickly put down. Not long after that, the Hub was constructed. Then the agents poured in and since then, things have been a nightmare.

"Here he comes," Emily says excitedly, snapping me out of my daydream.

I look up to see Andy heading towards us. He could use a bath more than anything. As for his girlfriend, she looks like she could use a comb. I have never seen such messy blond hair in all my life.

I sure hope Andy never gets caught. There would be a public whipping, requiring everyone from the surrounding communes of our Township to attend, and in addition, he would be under strict scrutiny for a long time to come. In short, his life would be very miserable, plagued by near constant harassment, not to mention the affect it would have on his parents. I suspect Jim and Liza would nail him to the wall as additional punishment.

Looking like a thief, Andy draws his girlfriend closer to us, scanning the area for any sign of agents. I laugh inwardly. In a way, I suppose Andy is a thief. He is, after all, about to cross over into our commune with a girl who does not belong.

I back up as Andy plows into the edge of the field, leaving the crunchy brown lawn behind him. His girlfriend has light brown eyes, though not nearly as pretty as Emily's, and wispy blond bangs.

Andy comes to a stop right in front of me, and bends over to catch his breath. Ethan shoots me a nervous glance, undoubtedly as worried about their welfare as I am. Agents are like mice, they can pretty much appear anywhere at any given time with little to no warning. And most agents love to harass us, including removing our clothing to satisfy the perversions of their hearts. Perverted Demon is by far the worst among the agents to take pleasure in forcing young people into embarrassing situations.

With a sigh of relief, Andy looks up and meets my eyes. I give him a wary look. He reminds me of a guy I once read about in a novel who, being inflamed with love, expressed little concern for his actions. He made decisions with his heart and not his head. And unfortunately, things did not end well for that guy.

I shake my head. "You won't be smiling if you get caught," I say, giving Andy a serious look. "Andy, this has to be about the dumbest thing you've ever done." And that is the honest truth. Andy is normally very reserved, and very level headed. Still, the deepening smile on his face shows the little concern he has for going against the law.

"Just what exactly do you plan on doing," Ethan says sensibly.

Andy pulls his girlfriend forward. "First off, in case you guys have forgotten, this is Amelia Hawksworth." Emily frowns irritably. Andy, realizing his mistake, gives Emily an apologetic look. "Guys and girl, I mean. Now, I hid some food the other day by the old shed in the middle of the field. There should be plenty for all of us." He turns to face Amelia. "They won't bite, I promise. You do remember them, don't you?"

Amelia nods curtly, brown eyes narrowed onto Ethan with mounting dislike. "How could I forget? Everyone knows who he is, the boy who broke my best friend's heart."

Ethan looks as speechless as I feel. "Sorry," he says, sounding sincere.

Amelia raises her thin eyebrows. "Sorry won't erase the memory of my friend crying her eyes out over you." She narrows her eyes onto Ethan's pendant. "I see you're still wearing Arianne's heart. Was it because you hated her so much that you also had to keep something that meant so much to her? That pendant was a gift from her mother you know."

Emily takes a step forward so that she now stands beside me. She gives Amelia a reproachful look. "That's not fair. And I don't appreciate you plowing my boys into the ground, as if they are nothing more than chicken manure. And to think, I actually thought for a moment that Andy had done well with you." Emily, by far much prettier than Amelia, clenches her fists at her sides. She has a look in her eyes that begs Amelia to bring it on.

Amelia smiles sourly. "I wouldn't talk if I were you. You are just as renowned in the art of heart breaking and…haughtiness as your precious boys are. Perhaps that is why you three make such a good team, 'cause you're all alike." Amelia flounces her head, messy blond curls bobbing at her ears. "It's a wonder your commune hasn't kicked you out for vanity, Emily Wilson. And, if things hadn't changed so much, if our lunatic of a president hadn't messed everything up, they probably would have exiled you by now."

Andy stares at Amelia like he does not recognize her. He lets go of Amelia's hand as if it is a burning stick of firewood. Amelia tears her gaze from Emily to give Andy an injured look.

Andy backs away from her, coming to a stop next to Ethan. "Emily's right," he says, looking somewhat dazed. "You're not the girl I thought you were." Andy shakes his head in disbelief. "How could you say such hurtful things about my friends? Ethan can't help he's so good looking any more than Emily can. Or Ryan for that matter." Andy wets his lips absently. "Go home Amelia. Go back home and don't ever expect to see me again."

Still keeping with her sour expression, Amelia turns on her heel and stalks off. Andy turns to face me. "I should have listened to you. You told me I should stick to seeing a girl from our commune, but I wouldn't listen."

I shrug. "Everyone makes mistakes," I say. "But perhaps it's for the best. I'm afraid that if you had continued going back and forth across the communes, you would have eventually been caught."

Ethan flaps his shirt to cool himself. I turn to find his shirt splotched with sweat. I shake my head.

"What is it," Ethan says with a frown.

I wave him off. It's just odd how, despite being drenched with sweat and having worked all day, Ethan still possesses a strong energy about him. Not so with me. I just want to take a cool bath and relax in the living room chair across from my uncle Mark.

"So what now," Emily says, giving Andy a weary look.

Andy kicks at a dirt clod, sending it flying through the air in several pieces. "I guess we go home. Or," Andy adds, looking up with a hopeful smile, "we could lay into that food I set aside."

Ethan's face brightens with a wide smile. "I vote for the food," he says. He steps forward and slaps me across the chest with the palm of his hand. "What about it my sweaty friend, or are you ready to call it quits for the day?"

I give Ethan a speculative look. I can tell that, unlike me, he really wants to take Andy up on his generosity. The thing is, it's against the law to store food, so I'm more than a little concerned. It'd be just our luck to make it to the old shed, break out the food, and then get caught by an agent. As much as I hate to put a damper on his excitement, I do not feel like I can go along with it. Besides, Andy should know better than to do something so stupid. The punishment for hoarding food is twenty lashes. All food must remain in the house of its occupants so that, if an agent made a surprise visit, all the food would be accounted for. I believe the agents fear that, by hoarding food, we are not as dependent on their regular supply and therefore pose a threat to their authority.

I meet Ethan's hopeful eyes with a decisive look. "No," I say.

Ethan rolls his eyes dramatically, undoubtedly thinking that I am way too cautious.

"And you won't be going either," I say. Ethan parts his lips, an unspoken protest resting on them. "And don't argue with me. I will *not* let you risk the chance of getting caught eating illegal food."

"That's not fair Ryan," Emily says.

I give her an incredulous look. Rarely does Emily say anything that goes against good sense and judgment.

Emily appears to be choosing her words carefully. "Ethan may be your best friend, but you shouldn't spoil his fun, especially when we get so very little of it nowadays."

I swallow. I look between the three of them. Emily, with her uncharacteristic zeal for me to let Ethan do as he pleases, as if Amelia's unlawful presence wasn't enough risk for the day. And then Andy, who, more than anything, could use a bath to wash the sweat from his sticky red hair.

I turn to face Ethan. I know that he won't go if I do not want him to, but perhaps I'm not being fair.

Perhaps this would be a good time to loosen the cautious yoke that I have made him wear for so long.

"Fine," I say, barely audibly. I can tell that Ethan wants me to speak up. I let out a ragged sigh. "Fine, but if you're discovered, don't expect me to spend the next week babying your wounds."

Ethan jumps to the side, takes a hold of a corn stalk and then pretends to kiss it. "Good news sweetheart, my master has given me permission to take you to the dance after all."

I roll my eyes. Andy claps his hands together, looking pleased.

"He'll be fine," Emily says, whispering in my ear. "I promise to keep a close eye on him."

I throw my hands up in the air. "Good grief, I might as well go to. I guess I'll just have to hold off on the bath until later."

Ethan, taken by surprise at my sudden change of heart, let's go of the cornstalk, takes a hold of the partly exposed ear of corn, and then jerks it from its shuck. He strides forward, holding the plump ear in an outstretched hand. He stops in front of me with a toothy grin.

"Here," Ethan says. He lifts it up and presses it to my lips. "I swear I'm so happy I could kiss you. But, since I have no desire to do so, let this gorgeous lady, this plump maiden smother you with her sweet lips."

With a sigh, I take the ear of corn from Ethan's hand and whack him across the arm with it. He laughs. I let it fall to the ground. Looking pleased, Andy surges past us, beckoning us to follow him.

We arrive at the old shed in the middle of the field several minutes later. After checking to ensure our privacy, that no agents are around, Andy makes for his stash. Meanwhile, Emily sits down under a spreading oak, on the only patch of green grass around. I stand next to Ethan watching him wring sweat from his T-shirt. He just took off his shirt, saying he was beginning to tire from the extra weight of the sweat. Already, beads of sweat dot his chest, and run down his face in streams. The hot breeze that blew for much of the day has been recalled to its heavenly storehouse.

"How is it that you never seem to get any darker," I say. "We all look like overcooked bacon and yet you look like you've barely seen the skillet."

Ethan laughs. "You exaggerate. I'm not much darker than you are. We both have farmer's tans; it's just that the sun seems to dislike me more."

I point to a pale spot sticking out from beneath his pendant. "Aha, so that pendants good for more than you thought it was."

Ethan takes a hold of my wrist with a smile. "That my friend is an invasion of privacy. And for that, I shall toss you into the shed to sleep with the moccasins. Maybe then you will come to understand what I think of you." His smile widens as I jerk my hand free from his grasp.

Emily lets out an exaggerated sigh. "You boys are nuts," she says, shaking her head. "But I suppose you deserve some crazy time, what with all the work you do. Only don't go wrestling each other in the dirt, at least out of respect for my poor lungs. Not that either…"

Emily's mouth falls open in horror as she scrambles to her feet. I stiffen and turn around. Perverted Demon stands poised to ruin our day.

"We're in luck," Andy says, rounding the side of the shed carrying a basket. "The worms haven't found the apples yet, nor have the…" He looks up, the basket of food falling from his hands. Looking faint, he squeezes his eyes shut, and then opens them again. Dawning horror floods his face.

I swallow hard. It is too late to run, too late to do anything.

"Well well," Perverted Demon says, his dark beady eyes overjoyed with the sight before him. He takes in the apples and cans of pears scattered across the ground with sheer delight. "Hoarding food and…" He flicks his crazed eyes to Ethan's bare chest. "I won't even ask what you were planning on doing. But I can guess that it probably would have involved something with that pretty girl." He chuckles.

Ethan looks as if he could pass out. This is typical of Perverted Demon, to harass those who truly mean no wrong. I mean, we have to eat. He looks like he always does, with a fat head and overstuffed gut. He loves to find people violating the law governing food so that he can confiscate it for himself.

Perverted Demon fixes me with his dark beady eyes. I feel my body go rigid, my heart slamming against my rib cage.

Perverted Demon eyes me thoughtfully, or about as thoughtfully as can be expected from a dummy. "And what of you? Blocking the sun from your pretty friend?"

Ethan clears his throat nervously. Perverted Demon flicks his eyes to the pendant at this throat. "Oh my, a boy who wears jewelry." Looking absolutely delighted, he sets off towards Ethan. If only Ethan had kept his shirt on, his pendant would still be covered up.

"I'll kill him if he touches you," I say under my breath. "If he so much as lays a finger on you, I swear I'll take him down." Ethan mumbles something that sounds like *be careful*.

"A boy with two hearts," Perverted Demon says as he stops in front of Ethan. He reaches forward and takes it in his hand. "As if someone as pretty as you needs to wear jewelry." Ethan stands as straight and stiff as a tree. "I'll wager some pretty girl thinks she has your real heart in exchange for this love charm. When truth be told, if she had any sense, she'd know that shiny boys like you never give their hearts away completely. Isn't that right? You always play with their feelings; make 'em think you love 'em when in fact you have eyes to mount half the pretty mares in heat." With a flick of his wrist, Perverted Demon jerks the pendant free from the silver chain.

Looking happier than I've seen him in a long time, Perverted Demon turns around to face Andy. "You've earned yourself a sure twenty lashes young man," he says with pretend sympathy. Andy swallows hard. "But do not worry; I'll not lay a finger on you. Instead, this boy here will do me the honor."

Perverted Demon, without even turning to look, thrusts a hand out toward Ethan. I quickly move to stand in front of his hand. He turns around and, frowning curiously, gestures to me. Something else about Perverted Demon, he's not very smart. Ethan groans miserably. But I refuse to give Perverted Demon a chance to find fault with Ethan, and of course, Ethan knows this.

Perverted Demon unfastens the whip from its sheath at his waist. I want to descend on him and take him down, but I would only bring down more trouble onto all of our heads. Feeling slightly dazed, I take the whip and begin to make my way toward Andy. Looking absolutely horrified, Andy removes his shirt and then braces his hands against the wooden facing of the shed. Behind me, Perverted Demon chuckles in delight. I bristle.

I stare at Andy's sweat slicken back in dread. I never thought I would end up standing over him with a whip in my hands. I look at the whip. The handle itself is short, shiny black leather, looking almost harmless. If only that was the case. Protruding from the end of the handle is an ugly rope made of several individual cords twisted together to form an ugly rope the size of my little finger. And, blossoming from the end of the rope are four smaller ropes, each adorned with stiff pieces of leather.

"I'm sorry Andy," I say. I bite down onto my lip.

I bring the whip up over my shoulder, and, with a plea of forgiveness on my lips, thrust the whip forward in a loud crack against his back. Andy cries out, his back arching in pain.

I'm so sorry Andy, I say inwardly as I unleash another stinging lash against his back. Maybe Ethan will distract Perverted Demon so that I can go easy on Andy.

"What is it boy," Perverted Demon says, annoyed.

With the whip poised in my hand to unleash another painful blow against Andy's back, I pause and breathe a sigh of relief. It is as if Ethan read my mind.

Perverted Demon gives Ethan a measured look. "This had better be good, because if it aint, you'll have to make up for my loss of entertainment."

I bring the whip forward against Andy's back lightly, as if I am striking him with little more than a bouquet of flowers.

Again and again I do this.

Perverted Demon finally goes silent. "Cry out this time," I say. Andy gives me an almost imperceptible nod.

I lash his back, only not too hard, but certainly hard enough to convince our main spectator that Andy is receiving his due. Andy lets out a miserably loud yell. I raise the whip slowly, straining to hear Perverted Demon's voice, and I finally do. He sounds entertained with whatever Ethan has him distracted with. I just hope the distraction continues.

I continue to lash Andy's back. Four. Three. Two. "Now," I say, leaning in closer so that only he can hear me. I hover over his back, looking his skin over. "You don't have enough angry marks to account for a full twenty lashes. Andy, I'm so sorry, but if I don't make you bleed, he will. Only his lashes will be far worse."

"It's okay," Andy says hoarsely. "Do what you have to. I was the one who got us into this mess to begin with."

I bring the whip up over my shoulder, grit my teeth, and then thrust it forward with a thunderously loud crack against Andy's back. He lets out a loud cry, but I still do not see any blood.

"Brace yourself," I say, hearing the dread in my voice.

This time, I decide to lash him at an angle, like I have seen agents do time and again. I hold my breath and bring the angry ropes forward against his back in a loud crack. He cries out in a ragged voice. I wince as the blood wells up and slowly begins to mix with his sweat. Even so, there are still not enough trails of blood, not nearly enough.

I cast a nervous glance in the direction of Perverted Demon. Sure enough, Ethan continues to distract him. I turn back to Andy's bloody back and decide to paint.

"Be very still," I say. I group my fingers together and press down on the bloody rivulets. I move over a little, to a bloodless area, and drag my blood slicked fingers down his back. Andy sighs. "Feels good does it? I never thought I'd be painting your back with your own blood." He laughs. "Be still, goof ball."

Back and forth I look, from Perverted Demon to Andy's back. I continue to paint a nasty picture of utter brutality. Finally, Andy looks as if he received the whipping he did not deserve. And Perverted Demon, dumb as he is, continues to remain captivated by Ethan.

I take a hold of Andy's arm and pull him upright. "How do you feel," I say, earning a weak smile. "Stop smiling. Remember, you're in so much pain you're about to drop. Teary eyes now, jokes later." And then it hits me. "Fall to your knees you stinking piece of rotten flesh."

Obediently, Andy lowers himself to his knees.

I give him a light kick for good measure. "Good boy. Now, be sure and cry out, convince him that you're in bad shape." I stare him down until he nods.

I move to stand beside Andy, the handle of the whip clutched tightly in my hand. Perverted Demon breaks away from Ethan and heads this way. His dark beady eyes take in Andy with a satisfied gleam. Every step he takes appears to wind him. He is in awful shape.

I school my face to appear broken, grief-stricken. Perverted Demon smiles viciously. He gestures for the whip and, with a pretend tremble of intimidation in my hand, I place it in his.

Perverted Demon brings the whip up over his shoulder with a smile. Then, with a glint of hatred in his eyes, he brings it forward with a loud crack against Andy's back. Andy collapses to the ground. Perverted

Demon wets his lips with a frown, as if considering administering yet another lash. I hold my breath. And then, looking satisfied, he puts the whip back into its sheath.

"Here you are sir," Emily says with a charming smile in her voice.

I turn to find her arms outstretched, the shiny cans in the basket winking in the sunlight. "I know how busy you are, sir."

Looking as dumb as usual, Perverted Demon sighs and takes the basket. "You know, you're not half bad looking," he says to Emily. Emily pretends embarrassment.

Perverted Demon gives her a wistful smile. "Maybe some time you and I can spend some quality time together. I love to make love to pretty little things like you." And at that, he turns away with a dazed smile and wobbles away.

I wait until his wobbles carry him out of ear shot. "That was brilliant," I say. Emily bats her eyes and then turns to stick her tongue out at Perverted Demon.

I crouch to my knees in front of Andy. He lifts his weary eyes to mine. "Are you okay?" Slowly he nods and extends a hand to me. I take it and pull him to his feet.

"Here's your shirt," Ethan says, laying it across Andy's hands. Emily and I move to stand next to Ethan. Overall, I'd say my finger painting went a long ways.

Ethan gives me an impressed look. "You never told me you were an expert in blood art. But it's a good thing dummy is so dumb or it might not have worked." I laugh.

Andy turns around to face us. He swallows, tears brimming in his eyes. "You all were amazing," he says. "I know what each of you did for me and…" He looks at my hand.

I bring my hand up to look at my blood smeared fingers. "I can't believe this is your blood, goof ball." Andy lets out a pained laugh. I meet his eyes. "But I'm glad I could help."

Apart from sheltering a variety of tools that we use throughout the year, I have to say that the next best thing about the old shed is that it houses a fully functional sink. Although the interior is a bit run down, what with weak floor boards and buckets sitting here and there to collect rain water, it came in helpful yet again. Between the three of us, we managed to clean all the blood from Andy's back. Then Emily applied some healing salve that we keep hidden under a loose floor board for special occasions. By the time Andy shrugged his shirt back on, he looked as if nothing had happened. Well, except perhaps for the utter exhaustion visible in his green eyes.

Feeling exhausted, I now sit in front of Mark. He occupies the chair across the table from me. A fat candle sits atop the table, its double wicks aglow with just enough light for us to see each other. I miss electricity with a deep ache. I also miss things like cool showers, hot food, and the piano that, until it was confiscated, saw Mark's skillful fingers racing over its keys in cheerful melodies. The piano was my mother's favorite pastime. Nearly every family around had one; just like nearly every family had the same kind of household furnishings. And everyone lived in the same small, two bedroom one bath homes. Everything about our former lives ensured that no one had a monopoly on anything. Instead, each family, as mandated by the laws that established equality long ago, had limitations on what they could own. For instance, when it came to things like houses and objects of necessity, all families had to conform to the prescribed list of government approved property. And, while it might sound a bit radical compared to the Old Country, nearly everyone lived in peace and harmony. We were happy.

The idea of limiting ownership of goods came about at the end of the Old Country with the expectation that, by doing so, it would reduce the kinds of emotions that made it such an unpleasant place to live, and it worked. Shortly after our founding fathers crafted and implemented a new set of laws, much of the hate, anger, greed, envy, and discomfort associated with life in the Old Country ceased to exist. In short, people took to the new government with uncontained zeal. Neighbor helped neighbor instead of ignoring their plights. People no longer focused on trying to accumulate great wealth just to set themselves above everyone around them.

When I think of where we are today compared to the time before Gloss, my heart aches. Believe it or not, the communes use to be the heart and soul of life for everyone. Just about everyone in our country, Eden, belongs to some kind of commune, be it farming, mining, or timber. But farming is and always has been by far the most common occupation for communal life. And, before Gloss snatched away all of our machinery, everyone from the twelve families in each commune old enough to work enjoyed our communal efforts. And every family received the same reward for their work. Friendly government workers came around each month to ensure that everyone complied with the laws that limited ownership of goods. And, because crime was nearly nonexistent, we had no steady police force like in the Old Country. Instead, all four communes surrounding a Township chose Elders whose job it was to hold Meetings to handle disputes and administer justice fairly. This was necessary because, despite our countries great achievements over the Old Country, we still had stubborn, hard headed people who tried to buck up against the system.

I sigh. Even through the dimness of the erratic flicker of candlelight, I can see Mark smiling. The sun just set earlier. A warm breeze blows through the open windows, making the house feel just less than an oven, but I will take it. Too many evening's we have spent fanning ourselves with Agatha's homemade fans. Often times, when no breeze stirs, we take up occupancy on the front porch steps. But other than the occasional owls that can sometimes be heard off in the distance, we have no other company. At this time of day, it is against the law to leave one's house. So, everyone spends their time with family, to the chagrin of those with kids who have a hankering to sneak off and be kids. And, when a kid sneaks away and gets caught, it is the parents who receive punishment, which could range from anything from a couple lashes to a temporary increase in their daily quotas.

"You're very quiet," Mark says, stirring uncomfortably. "I didn't want to have to be the one to tell you this, but I made another trip into Town, after we parted for the day." I narrow my eyes onto him.

Mark smiles weakly, green eyes luminous. "I checked the Status board before I left. Ryan," Mark adds with a wary frown, "if Andy gets two more strikes, that'll be it for him. He will be arrested and taken away to wherever they send delinquents, possibly to work in one of those terrible factories owned by Gloss. And, from what you said, Andy was caught hoarding food earlier today, which means that now, there's only one strike keeping him here in our commune."

I swallow hard. I had not realized that Andy was standing this close to ruin. I told him that he needed to be more careful, but he ignored me. As for Mark and I, we each have three strikes apiece; not at all anywhere near the twelve strikes necessary to uproot us from our commune. I got my first strike from accidentally spattering water onto an agent's boots one day after a thunderstorm. Mark received his for knocking Perverted Demon's hand away from his chest. Perverted Demon seemed bent on harassing Mark for no apparent reason, and Mark was not about to stand for it.

Best I can remember, and I have not looked at the Status board recently, Ethan has four strikes and Emily has two. If it was not for Emily's knack for sweet talking agents, she would likely have two or three more. Agatha, bless her soul, has nine strikes against her. Or at least she did the last time I looked. But she is not concerned. *I'll be pushin' up daisies in the Lord's garden before long anyway*, she always says. Usually, when she gets a strike it is because she preaches against the *godless agents*, as she calls them. *Don't you think for a moment that just because you burned all the Bibles to a crisp that you can somehow drive God from the country. You'll get your due, just like all the wicked people who rebel against God.* These potent retorts are just a couple arrows that I have seen Agatha draw from her loaded quiver.

Still, I cannot deny that I am very worried about Andy. Next to Ethan, he's my next best friend. I could wring his neck for not heeding my warnings. Sometimes I wish he wasn't such a ladies' man. Perhaps Ethan and I should take him to the side and shave his eyebrows off or something. He gets way too much attention. Even Emily goggle eyes him, though she would never admit it. I saw how she ran her hands over his back today when we were washing away his blood. She might as well have kissed his booboos. And to think that Ethan actually believes she is interested in me.

I flick my eyes from the candle to Mark. One thing I like about Mark is that, when he knows I am deep in thought, he rarely interrupts me. "You never told me why you never married," I say. I have lived with Mark for the last six years, ever since my parents were killed in a school shooting. My parents were both teachers, so until their death, I lived in Town in the same style of home that everyone else lives in. Not long after that, the school was closed so that nowadays, the only instruction kids receive is what little their parents or guardians can give them in between the exhaustive demands of their subjugation.

Mark looks caught off guard by my statement. He leans forward, black hair gleaming in the dim light as he clenches and unclenches his hands nervously. "Seems like I said something about this before," he says, but not unkindly. "I just never found the right lady. Or, more precisely, they always seemed to be more interested in my appearance than my personality. But I don't suppose I should talk, not when I was being so picky as well."

I laugh. "I guess that's one of the downfalls of being so good looking. I fear Ethan has the same problem, as if it matters nowadays." No one ever marries anymore and you can't blame them.

Mark nods sadly. Before Gloss, you rarely heard about friends betraying friends for advancement. But now, it has become a common practice for so called friends to act cordially to your face while harboring ill will towards you. So that, when you least expect it, the person you thought was your friend lets slip what you said in confidence to an agent. All for a few cans of food or a temporary reduction in their quotas. Or, if the tipoff is something serious, a great transgression of the law, like organizing illicit meetings involving several families, then the betrayer might end up with a new addition to their house or something even better. Although there have been several such cases of similar betrayal in the surrounding communes, we have yet to witness anything so disturbing in our commune. I think Agatha has everyone so afraid to do such terrible things for fear of reaping what they sow. Then again, most people are so amiable towards each other in our commune that betrayal is likely far from their minds.

"What about you," Mark says, not concealing a smile. I frown uncomfortably. "Has anyone caught your eyes, or should I even ask." I remain silent. "You know, out of all the guys in the area, you are the most modest. I see the way Emily looks at you when you're not watching. She has good tastes. Ryan," Mark adds with a playful smile, "I had not planned on telling you this, but I overheard Emily talking to Tanya Allen the other day in Town. Neither of them knew that I was standing on the other side of the Status board. Emily told Tanya that out of all the guys around, you have, and I quote, 'the prettiest green eyes of any guy she has ever seen.'"

I give him an incredulous look. He must have heard wrong.

Mark gives me a knowing look. "Plus, she told Tanya that in the right light, your brown hair gleams like rays of golden sunlight. In short, she thinks you're very handsome, and I would have to agree with her."

"Mark," I say, raising my voice in slight embarrassment. He shrugs with a smile. I shake my head. "It doesn't make sense. The way she ran her hands over Andy's back today, you'd think she was trying to win him over."

Mark grins. "Could you be jealous? Oh well, you have every right to be. Here is what I think: Emily was using Andy's injuries to turn up the heat on you, to try to elicit a declaration of love or whatever."

I raise an eyebrow. "Sounds like you missed your calling. You should have been a love specialist." That is, of course, if such a thing existed.

Mark laughs. "Maybe, but that's not the point. Ryan, she thinks you're beautiful. Anyone with eyes can see that you inherited your mother's exceptional beauty. Lily was the most beautiful lady to ever grace this commune, and you got her high cheek bones, lips, nose, and, well, what more is there to say."

I wet my lips to speak. "Maybe you should have married her."

Mark closes his eyes in a pained expression. "Your father…I told William that if he didn't marry her, I would. But I saw how taken he was with her so I wanted him to have her. She was a dove, your mother. Never in my life had I seen a woman as gentile and lovely as Lily. As soon as they announced their engagement, all the eligible young men in our local communes went into mourning."

As much as I miss my parents, I am very thankful to have Mark. He took me in the day my parents were murdered. There is no one else who I care more about than Mark. And, despite his occasional protests, I enjoy pampering him. I do all his laundry, fix all his meals, and even give him haircuts. Every once in a while, I remind him that, without him, I would have ended up in someone else's home, someone other than family. And of course it helps that Mark is such a gentle, easy going guy.

I yawn. I watch in amusement as Mark catches it. I laugh. "About time for me to tuck you in," I say jokingly.

Mark grins, white teeth gleaming in the dim light. But then again, it wasn't a complete joke. I cannot even begin to recount all the times in the past, especially during cool weather, when I would wake up in the middle of the night to check on Mark. On many of those nights, I found him lying mostly uncovered, his body curled into a ball to try to get warm. So I would cover him up, and often find myself staring down at him, amazed at how young he looked. Like a teenage boy, his smooth skin glowing with health. Mark has done the same for me. In fact, there have been several times when I would wake during the night, even recently, to find Mark sitting on the side of my bed, watching me sleep. Mostly when he does this, I try to act like I am fast asleep in hopes that he will stay a while longer. And, to my delight, he usually does. Mark is more than just my uncle, more than just my guardian. I equate Mark to pure goodness, to pure happiness. If anything should ever happen to him, I fear I would lose the will to live, despite having Ethan.

"Ryan," Mark says gently. I lean forward, drawn to the caution in his voice. "You know tomorrow is the day for Evaluations. Please, just try to be careful. I know you and Ethan deserve to goof off from time to time and be the young guys you are, but don't do it tomorrow." I swallow, my body gripped by the emotion in his voice.

Mark looks worried. "I hate to bring it up, but if anything happened to you…Look, just be careful. I know it's been a while since the last Evaluations, and so you might have forgotten how dangerous they can be, so I beg you, please, don't do anything to put yourself in harm's way. Promise me."

I nod. Mark smiles solemnly, boyish looks strained by fear and anxiety.

Admittedly, I had completely forgotten about Evaluations. Mark is right for reminding me. Evaluations are no place for any kind of foolish behavior. Best I can remember, the last Evaluations were well over a year ago and landed several people in hot water. It was after those Evaluations that nearly everyone's quotas were increased from twenty to thirty bushels. And, for some of the unluckier folk, they experienced public humiliation of the most degrading degree. Perverted Demon himself led the way by poking and splashing cold water onto the naked bodies of those who had been found guilty of violations. Meanwhile, everyone in our local communes had to watch. Violations included arguing with agents, aiding or abetting rebellion, and refusing to comply with bodily examinations. In addition to all the questions and general observations done during Evaluations, I dread bodily examinations the most.

Oh how I hate bodily examinations. Depending on the agent administering the exam, you might find yourself shirtless, or in your underwear, or even worse. To the agents, we are nothing more than objects of fascination or burden. Now as for the non-Christian farmers, things always go much better for them. But as for Christians, it is as if we are not even human in their eyes, which is ridiculous considering that our bodies look and function the same way theirs does. Last year, a male agent examined everyone in our commune. We stood in line and sweated until I felt like I was going to drop. Finally, when it came time for Mark, the agent asked him to remove his shirt, which he promptly did. I breathed a sigh of relief. I learned later that week that in the western commune, everyone had to remove all their clothing for a very perverted agent who everyone said spent more time looking at their bodies than performing proper examinations. He did very ugly things to some people.

I look at Mark. "Let's pray that we get to keep most of our clothing on," I say, hearing the fear in my voice. Mark nods solemnly.

Chapter Two

As usual on Evaluations day, nearly everyone, or those who have good sense, keep their heads down and their hands busy. And so that is exactly what I am doing.

The sun just peaked over the horizon, the sign that the Evaluations agents should begin making their rounds very soon. Special agents are brought in to perform the Evaluations, though the regulars continue to make their rounds. I suspect that Perverted Demon will be itching to talk to Emily since the impression she made on him yesterday. I swear, if he touches her, I will break his arm.

A finger pokes me in the back. I turn around to face Ethan. He grins, and holds a small green snake in an outstretched hand. I shake my head in disbelief. He has got to be joking, and on Evaluations day of all times.

"Thought I'd put it in my pocket," Ethan says with a mischievous smile. "That'll teach those sick creeps to go shoving their hands into places that don't belong."

I close my eyes in dizzying disgust. When I open them, I find Ethan poking the snake into his pants pocket. I swear, out of all the stupid things I imagined either of us doing today, this takes the cake. And there is a good chance that one of the special agents will invade his privacy.

"No," I say forcefully. Ethan jerks his head up, pats his pocket with a frown. "You heard me. If they catch you with a snake in your pants…Ethan, I don't even want to think about the punishment they'd inflict upon you. Plus, you'd be defeating the purpose by giving them a reason to mistreat you. The last thing I want to think about is everyone in all the communes witnessing your public humiliation." I shake my head at his defiant smile.

"Ethan, God has blessed you with an exceptionally nice looking body; don't do something stupid that will make you a display for sick creeps."

Ethan swallows, brown eyes sobering. He shakes his head in mild disappointment. "Alright, since you put it that way, but also for you, because I can see how distressed you are." Gingerly, he reaches into his pant pocket, fishes around, and then withdraws the snake. With his fingers clamped down onto its head, he points it at me. "And my sincerest gratitude to you, otherwise I would have had to stay in this pretty boy's sweaty pocket for no tellin' how long." I laugh, finding Ethan's sibilant performance very entertaining.

Ethan bends down, and lets the snake slither from his hand. It dives under a pile of corn shucks, the taste of freedom on its outstretched tongue. Ethan straightens up with a sigh. He wipes his hands on his pants.

"You know," I say, getting his attention. "If it wasn't for Gloss, if he hadn't confiscated all our equipment, we'd be done harvesting and enjoying the harvest feast right now." Ethan gives me a sad smile.

Wistfully, my mind conjures up images of the long tables covered with dishes piled high with mouthwatering food. Nearly everyone from the surrounding communes would come together for a great feast to give thanks to God for an abundant harvest. It was just one of several feasts we held throughout the year.

I shake my head, feeling hollow and sad. "It's hard to believe that it's been seven years since we had the last feast." Ethan nods sadly.

For the first year after Gloss was given power over Eden, everything was fine and mostly unchanged. Then, at the beginning of his second year, things began to change for the worse. His polished, friendly image faded away, revealing the monster from within. One of the first things he did was to banish all communal feasts on the grounds that God was no longer ruler over us. With an iron fist and a heart of stone, he then sent his agents out to collect all the Bibles in existence to be destroyed. It was at that point when we knew we were in big trouble. Without any notice, no one had time to hide their Bibles to prevent their destruction. Not long after that, Gloss began to boldly interfere in just about every other aspect of our lives. Of course, all regular Meetings, including weekly church services were forbidden on penalty of death, so everyone grew apart out of fear for their lives. And, while it's not against the law for people to visit each other after a hard day's work, most people refuse to do so out of sheer exhaustion and safety concerns. Agents love to harass people. For many of them, it's their favorite hobby. Still, some people, especially us younger folks, risk our well-being to spend time with each other. I think the agents fear that, without letting us get together every once in a while, we'd be more likely to pursue plans of revolt in secret. It's all about keeping us under control.

"I miss all the pretty girls," Ethan says sadly. He throws up a hand. "Yeah, I know I said that they annoyed me, but I didn't mind looking at them. What guy in his right mind wouldn't want to be right in the middle of a huge feast with a bunch of pretty girls?" Ethan sighs wistfully. "What I wouldn't do to bring back the old days. But I guess they're long gone, never…"

A loud bellow of a horn fills the air. Ethan and I exchange nervous looks. Behind me, I hear Mark let out a wary groan. This can't be good. Just down the way, I see Emily and her parents, along with Ethan's family pulling off their work gloves. Emily decided it best to work with them today so that she could comfort Ethan's brother Zeke over the loss of his pet field mouse.

"What on earth," Agatha says curiously. She turns around, looking between Ethan and I. "Perhaps it's me they want, wouldn't that be funny. The old lady who refuses to shut her mouth in the face of adversity."

I swallow. I doubt the call to assemble has anything to do with Agatha, but still. This is the first time for calling everyone into Town since Evaluations began several years ago. It can't be good.

By the time we enter Town nearly ten minutes later, I feel a twinge of panic in my chest, my heartbeat on the run. From the looks of the gathering crowd ahead of us, everyone from all four communes has responded promptly to the bellowing horn. Emily stands next to the Status board, an impatient look on her face. I see Emily's parents, along with Ethan's family already standing at the fringe of the crowd.

As we approach, Emily moves away from the Status board, and locks eyes with me. "I have a bad feeling about this," she says. I swallow and shrug weakly.

With a slightly frustrated look, she flicks her eyes to Ethan. "Brush your hair flat, you." Ethan frowns. Emily walks up to him with a sigh. "It's sticking up here and there like corn silks." Ethan looks confused.

Emily runs a hand through Ethan's hair. I feel a prickle of annoyance. If she thinks she can make me jealous by showing abnormal affection to one of my friends, then she is greatly mistaken. I think.

Looking peeved, Ethan jerks his head to the side, narrowly avoiding another swath of Emily's hand. "I intend to have a talk with you after all this is said and done." Ethan flicks his eyes to me. "And you too. Tonight, after Evaluations, if you two can't…"

"Let's go," Mark says urgently. "Before you all get us into big trouble." And so we do.

I walk between Agatha and Ethan, careful to keep my distance from Emily. Fortunately, Emily doesn't seem to mind. She and Mark lead the way as we quickly advance towards the growing crowd. A few people, mainly those with babies and the elderly are still inching towards the crowd, easing the tension in my chest that we would be the last to arrive.

Agatha suddenly appears ashen. "Are you alright," I say. Ethan leans forward with a frown. He notices Agatha's troubled expression as well.

Agatha tries to smile, but falters. She looks as if she wants to tell us something, but is too shaken to do so.

Ethan and I exchange worried looks. We come to a stop just behind Mark and Emily. Mark turns around and meets my eyes with a worried smile. He takes in Ethan, and then rests his eyes onto Agatha. Agatha, not appearing to notice Mark, moves forward to stand on the other side of Emily. I shrug mentally.

Another blow of the horn suddenly fills the air. Mark bites down onto his lip and makes his way to stand between Ethan and I. Mark slides an arm across my shoulders, and I feel a slight tremble in his hand. He does the same to Ethan, who, like me, he has always treated like a son. Ethan looks past Mark and meets my eyes with a weak smile.

The crowd goes silent. Despite Mark's attempt to ease my anxious mind, I feel like my heart could come bursting from its cage at any second. Just in front of

Emily, I see Ethan's father, Luke, wrap an arm around Zeke and pull him to his side.

I stare ahead, but all I see are the backs of dozens of people blocking my view. The sun has now climbed high enough above the horizon to cut through the dense row of trees next to the Hub. The Hub, shaped like a plump ear of corn, glows with the fiery orange glow of live coal. I might appreciate the architectural beauty of the building to a greater degree if not for its semblance of a cruel and oppressive government. Inwardly, I say *down* with the government that steals our grain and treats us like we are their nothing but rats.

"May I have your attention," says a very loud and unpleasant voice. It came from the front of the group. Mark grips my shoulder and pulls me against him. "As a result in the widespread failure to comply with the law forbidding religious expression, President Gloss has ordered swift retaliation to those found in violation of his supreme decree. In this Township alone, there have been two well documented violators. Both of these people have blatantly flouted Gloss's decree despite multiple warnings to remain silent. For one of them, the prescribed punishment is death by beheading. As for the other culprit, you will be exiled from this Township, never to return again."

I hear my heartbeat in my ears. I feel dizzy. Mark's arm feels burdensome, like an odd piece of rubber. I feel strange, like this is a dream. It has to be, for who has ever heard of a beheading?

"Our dear president is not just a man," says the speaker. "He is like a god in that he has all power and authority over all of you. But, despite that, he still has a good heart. So, he gives you a choice: Either turn over

Agatha Birchwood for her execution, or, any one of you can step forward to take her place. But one of you will be executed this morning."

"No one will take my place," Agatha says without delay. "I give myself up freely."

I tremble. Slowly, one by one, people begin to turn around to face us, particularly me. This doesn't surprise me as I have been noted as Agatha's closest friend.

The crowd parts and I get a clear view of Agatha. She stands on a wooden platform, just behind a yellow block of wood. Beside her is a man wearing a black face mask and robe, his gloved hands resting atop the hilt of a sword, its point ominously balanced on the platform.

I turn to Mark. "We have to do something," I say, hearing the panic in my voice. I want to grab Mark and shake him. He appears to have lost all sense of perception. "We can't just let her die. Not Agatha. I…think I know what to do."

I slip free from Mark's arm and take a step forward. Mark seizes my arm and turns me around to face him. "No," he says fearfully. "You're all I have, Ryan. I won't let you get caught up in this. Stay quiet; it's what Agatha would want."

"Mark," I say, shocked. "This is Agatha we're talking about, our friend, a member of our work unit."

I swallow against the lump in my throat. I glance at Ethan for support, but see only despair.

Mark shakes his head, green eyes apologetic. "I know, but Agatha would rather die than have you risk your life to speak up for her. We both know her. Agatha's prepared to meet God." That may be, but I intend to speak up, regardless. I take a step backward away from Mark. Mark's face pales. "Ryan, don't do this. Don't leave me."

I school my face to appear strong and courageous. "I'll be fine, honestly. Look, I serve the same God that Agatha does. Do you think He won't protect me? Do you think He won't keep me from harm? Honestly Mark, where's your faith?"

Mark swallows hard and I turn around and begin the short trek to the platform. I can almost hear Mark's heart stop, so to revive him, I say as firmly as I can without turning around, "You either stand up for what's right, or take a back seat and let evil prevail."

I think what I just said did about as much to boost my own confidence as it might have done for Mark. And then there's Ethan. As I was turning away, I caught a glimpse of him. He looked so shocked and afraid as if he had been turned into a statue. I'm surprised he did not try to stop me. As for Emily, well, for once in her life, she actually looked at a loss for words.

I come to a stop in front of the platform.

"Who are you," says the executioner.

I wet my lips nervously. "My name is Ryan Collins," I say. I clear my throat. "I am a friend of Agatha's."

"Ah," says the executioner, gently twirling his sword. "And so you've come to give your life to save hers?" I swallow hard. "I didn't think so. Tell me, why did you come forward then?"

"To reason with you," I say, feeling as insignificant as a mouse. I flick my eyes to Agatha. Agatha looks deeply troubled. I turn back to the executioner. "Why does your kind feel like you can do whatever you like, say whatever you want, but just as soon as one of us speaks out against your ways, you go irate? Is not Agatha's freedom of religious expression what is at stake here?"

I'm sure that if I could see behind his mask, he would be snarling.

The executioner laughs at me. "I come in the name of President Gloss, the greatest man there is and ever was. I come with power and authority to carry out his masterful work. You, on the other hand, come forward with the plea of a sick, flea infested dog. For that is why you have come, is it not, to prevent this old hag, this old worn out rag from certain death? Let her God save her, if He wants to. Why trouble yourself with what you cannot change?"

I remain silent. I think back to the Biblical story of David and Goliath. If I had a sling shot and a stone, I'd send it hurtling right towards the face of this insolent rebel without a moment's hesitation. How *dare* he say such things about my God and Agatha.

The executioner adjusts his face mask. "I admit, before I began, I had thought this whole ordeal would involve a great deal of trouble, but you have proved me wrong. You just happen to be the other person who I spoke about earlier. The person who I said was facing exile from this Township."

I feel my strength leaving me, my legs weakening. Now what have I done?

"Seize him," says the executioner, pointing to me with his free hand. I stand still, meet Agatha's eyes. Her mouth falls open in utter horror, blue eyes painfully confused.

Suddenly, two guards take a hold of my arms. I stiffen in fear. I can't believe this is happening. I stare at one of the hands gripping my upper arm. Just a moment ago I was free, and now I am in the custody of two agents.

"What have I done," I say, my voice sounding far off.

"Your guilt is two-fold," says the executioner in a matter-of-fact tone. "You were overheard numerous times discussing foul Scriptures with this despicable woman who you think so highly of. As for your other charge, perhaps you should have kept your dreams to yourself." I swallow hard. He nods at my captors. "Take him away."

Instantly, the agents gripping my arms tug me forward, but I refuse to budge. "Wait a minute," I say. I hadn't thought of begging, but I feel it is now my last resort. "Please. I do not deny your charges, but I only feel it right for you to listen to my entreaty." The executioner twirls his sword. "Please let Agatha go, she's a good woman, and a hard worker. You'll not find a better person around. She keeps our spirits up; helps drive us to meet our quotas. Nor has she ever failed to meet her own quota."

The executioner lets out a snort of disgust. "She is a worthless lump of clay as far as I am concerned. She has come to the end of the road. Relent, for there is nothing you can say or do to prevent her death."

Surely there is something I can say to change his mind. There has to be. Agatha can't die. She just can't. "Look, you are clearly an intelligent man. What good would her death serve when she is still able to contribute to the well-being of this country? Is not one small apple better than none at all to a hungry person? Is not her twenty-bushel quota better than nothing at all? Come now and see reason."

I hold my breath in nervous anticipation.

"You surprise me," says the executioner with a haughty smile in his voice. "I had not thought to find anyone of such intellectual value in this Township. How very interesting indeed. I would almost consider elevating you to a more suitable position of employment. Nevertheless, I am under strict orders from President Gloss to execute this woman. So, as you can see, your entreaty has been in vain."

"Wait," I say, hearing the hysteria in my voice. "Do you have no feelings? Look, if you let her live, you can increase both of our quotas, put us on probation. Then, if we fail to meet your expectations, you can deal with us as you wish. Only please do not take me away from my family. Please, I'll do anything you ask of me. I'm a hard worker; you can increase my quota and decrease my provisions, whatever you wish, but please, let me remain here with my uncle."

"I wondered when you'd attempt to bargain for your own well-being," says the executioner with humor. "Honestly, I had thought you to be a rare example of moral uprightness. What is it you Christians always say? Ah, love thy neighbor as thyself or yourself or whatever." He shakes his head. "Sorry, won't work. She has a date with my sword, one that I am indeed looking forward to keeping. I love beheading those whose last words to grace their lips are praises to their God. Now," adds the executioner with a sneer in his voice, "I have heard all I am going to hear from you. Say another word and I swear I'll make you taste the blood of this old hag before making your uncle drink a cup of your own."

I feel a stab of terror in my chest. And before I know what to say or do, I am being jerked forward. Behind me, I hear Mark cry out, a desperate plea unlike anything I have ever heard before. Another cry, this time with an element of physical pain involved. The agents have subdued him. I try to turn around, to say goodbye, to see Mark one last time before I go, but the agents are like walls of steel on my sides, preventing me from doing so.

"Mark," I say with a pang of horror in my chest. I feel light headed. Everything that I just said was for nothing. *Agatha...Agatha, I tried.*

The guards tighten their grip on my arms, threatening to cut off my circulation. I cut one of them a harsh look. Not surprisingly, he looks on with a stone cold expression. He has dark brown hair and green eyes. I consider spitting on him to get his attention, but judging by the hatred in his eyes, I'd likely find myself knocked insensible.

I look away from him. Just ahead are two agents standing beside a black car. As we approach, one of them opens a door and stands to the side.

We come to a halt by the open door. "That will be all Michael," says the dark-haired agent with green eyes. Michael nods stiffly and then turns to walk away.

Mr. Authority turns on me with a glint of hatred in his green eyes. "Get in. I won't ask you again." I give him a hard look before climbing into the car. He slams the door shut behind me.

As he rounds the side of the car, I push the door open with the desire to run away. It slams shut from the outside almost instantly. I shake with anger. I wish I had some kind of weapon to use in my defense. I'd try to fight my way out. I do a quick search around me, but find nothing useable.

With a defeated sigh, I cross my arms over my chest and lean against the door as Mr. Authority climbs into the driver's seat. He shoots me an ominous glare.

"Buckle in, and don't even think about trying to escape again or I will shoot you." I swallow hard.

I give him a sharp look. "So it's just you and me then," I say. "Tell me…"

Mr. Authority slams an arm against my chest. I grit my teeth in pain. I take a shallow breath, and feel a flare of pain across my rib cage.

"Unless I ask you a question, you are to remain silent," he says.

He starts the engine of the car and takes off.

Minutes give way to many painful hours. I try not to think about Agatha or Mark, but images of their faces keep materializing in my mind. I have prayed for Agatha's safety. Perhaps there was a chance that she was spared; after all, everything I said to try to help her was true. As for Mark…. Oh please God, please be with Mark. I hope the agents didn't harm him. The only family we had was each other. And then there is Ethan. I close my eyes in pain. I feel a tear spill over and slide down my face.

Despite my attempt to stay awake, I feel an unprecedented wave of exhaustion taking me under. I guess my safety at this point doesn't really matter that much to me. If Gloss wanted me dead, he would not have exiled me from my commune. But then again, maybe death, if it be God's will, would be better than life for me now. *Take me if you want my Lord, you know that I am ready.*

I sit on a boulder with my face buried against my upright knees. A cool breeze ruffles my hair. Somewhere nearby is the tranquil flow of water. I feel the hollowness of despair within me warring against the peaceful abode around me.

Fingers, soft and comforting tap my arm. I lift my head wearily, and find myself staring into the eyes of a concerned friend, though I do not necessarily recall ever having met him before. Rather, there is something about him that feels familiar.

He extends a cup to me. I blink in surprise and then look into the cup. "It's water," I say.

He nods with a gentle smile. "Yes, it is water. Are you not thirsty? You will find this water most refreshing."

I lean forward and take the cup. I bring it to my mouth and, with a tilt, let the cool sweetness touch my lips. It seems harmless enough. I part my lips and welcome the refreshing goodness. I do not know why, but it seems to be giving me strength.

After draining the cup, I hand it back to him. He takes the cup with a smile. There's a softness to his eyes that, along with his luminous appearance, feels so pleasant.

"Who are you," I say, hearing the intrigue in my voice.

"My name is Gabriel," he says with a friendly smile. "And I have a message for you. The road ahead of you will be very challenging, but do not give up hope. Everything you have just experienced happened for a reason. Remember, you are not alone. But be very careful, for there are those who would seek to use you for their own means."

Gabriel shimmers, and I feel the boulder beneath me soften into a comfortable cushion. I breathe in a sweet aroma, and shift my head slightly. I feel warmth…and something soft.

I open my eyes to find myself staring at Mr. Authority's shirt sleeve. I feel a stab of terror in my chest. He elbows me in the jaw.

I jerk away instantly. I massage my jaw. How careless and stupid of me.

It is mostly dark, except for the weak glow of lights illuminating the dashboard. But I can see his harsh glare without any problem. "You're very lucky," he says with a sneer. "I was just about to slam your head into the dashboard. What a pity, a battered face would have suited you quite well, because where you're going, some bruises and cuts would make you look less a target."

I massage the side of my jaw indignantly. "You…could have just pushed me away," I say, hearing the pain and fear in my voice. This man is vicious. "I didn't realize…how did I end up…All well, never mind. You wouldn't care anyway."

"You're right," he says sharply. "There's nothing you can say or do to make me feel sorry for you. But know this; should it happen again, I won't go easy on you." He cuts me a nasty look, luminous green eyes glancing over my jaw. "I hope you have the ugliest bruise ever."

"Where are you taking me," I say. I lean into the door, wanting to get as far away from him as I possibly can, just in case he tries to abuse me again.

"To a place where nightmares are reality," he says. This guy is a lunatic. He gives me a speculative look and then turns back to the road. "I hope you're stronger than you look, because you're soon going to face obstacles that you never thought existed." He lets out a haughty laugh. "From worthless, pathetic farmer to becoming a key player in President Gloss's very own private arena, imagine that. What a whirlwind of a change."

I swallow hard. "Private arena," I say, trying not to sound afraid.

"Oh yes," he says with a twisted smile. "But you won't be alone. You'll be in charge of training four equally pathetic people like yourself, all of them Saints. You see, you aren't the only one being punished for breaking the law. It'll be your job to train them and eventually lead them into a vicious battle involving seven other teams. You will be their team leader, although you will answer to me at all times. I'd start praying now if I was you, because your chance of survival is slim to none. And when you consider that the other teams will be trained by the most elite guards that exist, by President Gloss's very own private guard, your team has little chance for survival."

I bite down onto my trembling lip. "Why? I mean, what good is all this pointless bloodshed? And please, tell me your name, since you already know mine."

"It's Mason," he says with a ferocious look. "Just Mason to you. I belong to President Gloss's private guard. As far as your question, I thought it was obvious. You're about to enter into the penalty phase for your transgressions. Surely you know that you broke the law. And now, all the prayer in the world won't be able to save you from the horrors to come." He smiles. "Oh how I can't wait to taste your blood, to plunge my hand into the bloody hole that could soon be the remnant of your smooth, young chest."

"You're sick," I say with a shudder in my voice.

Mason shrugs. "You had best get used to it; we're going to be sharing a room together, after all." Oh no, I know all about these sick creeps, and to think I accidentally fell asleep on his arm. "And no, you're wrong. I can tell by the look on your face what you're thinking. You'll have your own bed, though we will share a closet and a bathroom. I will be keeping a close eye on you. Honestly, you should consider yourself lucky. I could harm you, that is, if I was not so interested in wanting to study you."

I feel my mouth fall open in stunned surprise.

Mason cuts me a twisted smile. "Oh yes, I have a million questions just waiting to be answered. I have always wondered why you Saints deny yourselves so much, attempt to walk a straight and narrow path, and so on and so forth. So, as long as you submit yourself to my authority, and cooperate with me by answering all of my questions and doing what I ask of you, I will see to it that you do not spend your last days in complete misery. I have been looking forward to observing you for quite some time now."

"Observing me," I say with a frown.

Mason sighs exhaustively. "Yes, observing you. You see, in addition to being one of President Gloss's private guards, I am also a physician. And while my expertise is in medicine, my curious mind enjoys all manner of inquiry. The point is, I have been granted permission to do pretty much whatever I want where you are concerned. The only condition is that I cannot murder or incapacitate you, for obvious reasons."

It is so strange how someone can look so innocent, how I can see God's masterful touch on this guy, and yet, he is so evil. It's a shame. I might consider telling him as much, if not for making him hate me even more than he already does. Instead, I decide to ask him about my new role in life. "So, how can I be expected to train people when I have had no prior training myself?"

Mason taps his fingers against the steering wheel. "I will teach you everything you need to know. Then, you will be given four Saints out of a total of thirty-two that will become your team."

I frown. "Why thirty-two? Why so many?"

Mason gives me a venomous smile. "There are eight districts in the country. President Gloss has chosen four Saints from each district to participate in his special entertainment venue. Well, technically five from your district. You are a special case."

"A special case," I say, not liking the sound of that.

Mason nods. "Yes, though you'll find most of the Saints to be young, beautiful sixteen year olds like yourself. But with you, President Gloss has passed harsher punishment. You see, the lives of your teammates will depend heavily on your ability to train them efficiently. After the final challenge, after all eight teams come together to show off their new skills, there will only be one surviving team. Everyone else, all the other twenty-eight Saints that is, will be dead. But here's the real eye opener: Should you perform well, should your team be found at the end of training to be worthy competition, your life may be spared."

"Well isn't that nice to know," I say sarcastically. "You know, if you let me ask you questions along, I promise to be much more cooperative with you."

Mason looks surprised. "Oh? Just what is it you want to know?"

I swallow, prepare to dodge a fist. "Why do you hate Christians so much? What have I ever done to you to make you hate me? What did Agatha ever do to deserve death?"

"I do not only hate you," Mason says, "I find you completely uncivilized."

"I would like to say something else."

"You would," Mason says with a jeer in his voice. "But I guess that's not completely surprising coming from your kind of people. Do you not realize that curiosity and blatant stupidity are the two main reasons why your kind of people have come under so much fire?" He says this in a sharp, pitchy tone, the incorrect pedant that he is.

I shake my head in anger. "Why do you enjoy trying to sound intelligent? It's clear that you are intelligent, though your opinions are flawed. Why not just state your opinions in a polite, nonaggressive manner? You don't hear me raising my voice to ridiculously unnecessary levels." I stiffen, brace myself for retaliation, but Mason only smiles.

Mason shoots me a haughty look. "A successful argument depends heavily on one's ability to get their point across, or didn't you know? That includes knowing when to use your voice to emphasize things of importance." He smiles smugly.

I roll my eyes in disgust. I see him give me a brief look from the corner of his eye. "You sound just like all the agents I have ever come into contact with. You all like to say things to puff yourselves up, but when it comes down to it, you have very little wisdom. And yet, in your eyes, you're wiser than Solomon himself. How do you expect to gain wisdom and understanding if you refuse to listen to anyone but yourself?"

Mason looks thoughtful. "It might be more worth my while to observe you than I thought. Perhaps you're not as stupid as I thought after all, though I would advise you to be more careful in the way you address me. While I may not be able to break your arms, I do however have permission to give you as many bruises as I wish."

I swallow hard. "What makes you so abusive? Don't you realize that if you hurt me, I'll only feel less inclined to answer your questions to the best of my ability? After all, you don't even have the ability to tell whether or not I am being completely cooperative. I can either give you really great answers, or waste your time by feeding you junk."

Mason throws an arm out, presses the back of his hand against my chest. I swallow. I look down at his hand. Even though he is not hurting me, I want him to withdraw it.

Mason makes a curious sound. "Judging by your heartbeat, I'd say you are terrified. Good, that means you're not half the idiot I thought you were." He pulls away, places his hand back on the steering wheel.

I let out a sigh of relief. I look out the window. I feel my heart lurch in excitement. A blood moon lights up the sky. I believe this is the second one in the series. I recall what Agatha recently said about the blood moons as mentioned in the Bible. Apparently, they foretell the coming of the Lord Jesus Christ.

Mason gives me a look of pretend surprise. "Worshipping the moon are we? I thought you Saints only worshipped one God."

I give him a cool look. "We do, but my observation of the moon had nothing to do with worshipping it. I do not practice astrology. But from what I here, your kind does. As a matter of fact, my friends and I saw a group of agents bowing down to the last blood moon. I don't worship the sun or stars either, but rather He who created them."

"Careful," Mason says with a condemning smile. "You just admitted, though indirectly, that you and your friends were outside after dark. I could have your friends arrested, even tortured if I wanted." I stiffen in fear. "One of the things you should strive to do, and it is very important where you are going, is to think carefully before you speak. Otherwise, you limit my ability to…sort of help you, as long as you do everything the way I tell you. That's right, I am interested in observing you, but if anyone else heard what you just said, you and your friends would be in serious trouble. So, always think carefully about what you will say before you say it."

I wet my lips. "So you won't harm my friends then?"

Mason chuckles. "Not if you cooperate with me, I won't." I breathe a sigh of relief. "However, should you tell anyone about the bargain I just made with you, I will personally see to it that your friends are not only tortured, but also made aware that you were responsible for their suffering."

I swallow hard. "I won't say anything, I promise. Just don't harm my friends, they've suffered enough…" I trail off, quickly deciding not to finish the sentence by telling him that their suffering was his boss's fault.

I wait tensely, certain that Mason will pick up on what I didn't say. Seconds roll by, my heart beating anxiously. If I am to protect my friends, I must try to stay in good with this jerk for now on.

Minutes roll by, but Mason remains quiet, much to my relief. My heartbeat has almost stabilized, and I feel an unusual sense of relaxation settling over me, as if my weary mind has decided that Mason poses no immediate threat to my well-being. In fact, he seems intent on keeping me alive, if nothing more than to treat me as his very own object of study. Despite his abrasiveness, I can tell that he really is interested in figuring me out. And, as far as I can tell, it is because of my faith that he finds me so interesting. Well, that and because his boss has chosen me out of all others to perform a special role, among other things.

I feel a cool breeze against my skin. I almost forgot how pleasant air conditioning is. I am surprised that he would treat me to such comforts. But then again, I feel certain that if he had some way of blocking me from the comfortable air flow, he would without hesitation.

I am so tired. And, even though I do not think Mason would harm me, I feel my body cautioning me against falling to sleep right now. I stifle a yawn.

"Stop it," Mason says, yawning. "Unless you want me to fall asleep at the wheel and take us both out, not that there are any other drivers, but any one of the trees would make for a nasty impact at seventy-five miles per hour."

I close my eyes. I won't fall asleep, I won't. I can't...afford to let my guard down in the midst of a lunatic.

"Whoever heard about snow falling this far south in September," Ethan says with a frown. He bends down, gathers up a handful of snow, and begins to make a snowball.

"Ethan," I say cautiously, as if afraid his hands might melt or something. Neither of us has ever seen snow before.

Ethan stares at the snowball in his hand. He meets my eyes with a grin. "It's so…cold."

"That's because it's snow goof ball," I say, earning a laugh from Ethan. "What exactly do you plan on doing with it?"

"This," Ethan says with a playful grin. He reaches forward and, prying my lips open with his free hand, commences to shove the snowball into my mouth. I clamp my mouth shut and knock his hand away. The snowball falls to the ground and breaks open.

Ethan presses his lips together reprovingly. I shake my head, and lower my eyes to the snowball. I see a strip of paper sticking out of the middle of the snowball. I bend down and pick it up. I see print on the underside of it.

Ethan snatches it out of my hand. He unfolds it with a curious frown. He begins to read it, brown eyes alert. His mouth falls open in shock.

"What is it goof ball," I say.

Ethan's hand trembles and the paper twirls gracefully to the ground like a severed butterfly wing. It dissolves on contact. I blink in surprise. I give Ethan a stunned look.

"The end is near," Ethan says in a daze. I swallow with a frown. I shake my head incredulously.

"It said *the end is near*," Ethan says, throwing his hands up in annoyance. "That's what it said, I swear. Jeeze Ryan, out of all the years we've been friends and you now choose to question my integrity?"

I roll my eyes. "I'm not questioning your integrity goof ball. It's just that, well, perhaps you were mistaken."

Ethan rolls his eyes and sighs exaggeratingly. "If a spider was crawling on your hand, would you mistake it for a butterfly?"

I laugh. "Depends."

"On what," Ethan says with a frown.

"On the butterfly. I have seen the weirdest looking butter…" Ethan claps a hand over my mouth. I frown with disapproval.

With a ragged sigh, Ethan looks down at the ground, shakes his head, and then meets my eyes again. "I know what I saw, what I read. I just don't know what it means."

I push Ethan's hand away from my mouth. All of a sudden, I feel my feet warming through my shoes. I look down and gasp. The snow is on fire, with flames licking at my shoes. I stand firm with fear and shock. In the distance, I hear a loud noise. I look up and see the Hub collapsing, each floor caving in onto the other. A stiff breeze pulls at my hair, as if an invisible hand is trying to get my attention from above. I look up and find the blood moon falling from the sky. I feel a pang of horror in my chest.

With an angry rumble, the ground erupts nearby, spewing lava hundreds of feet into the air. I feel my heart slamming against my rib cage, warning me to seek shelter. The air around us explodes with a roar and I jerk my head back to the sky. The moon is about ready to take us. As it bears down on us, large drops of blood drip from its surface, splashing to the ground. New eruptions explode from the ground where the blood tears fall. I open my mouth to tell Ethan goodbye, but the words are drowned out by the ear splitting roar. Ethan's eyes roll up in his head, and he collapses to the ground. I drop to my knees beside him, praying for a miracle. I feel my back ignite with flames, but the flames are not hurting me.

Everything suddenly goes still. I look up and find the moon suspended in midair, with several blood red tears glowing like giant rain drops in the air beneath it. Around me, the violent eruptions from the ground have ceased, their ominous plumes of magma creating a beautiful still life scene against the blue sky. Nor do I any longer feel the flames licking at my back, though they never hurt me.

Even through all of this, I never let any harm befall you, says a gentle voice. I blink in surprise. Looking from side to side, I see no sign of anyone. I turn to Ethan just as he opens his eyes. He takes in the scene around him with a dazed expression.

I wake with a sigh of relief. I sneak a peek at Mason out of the corner of my eye. To my relief, he does not appear to have been watching me. I'm sure I would have looked terrified if he had.

Minutes roll by and my legs begin to protest from pain.

"We're here," Mason says.

Chapter Three

I look out the window. A large gray stone building stands illuminated from a row of lights that run along the front of the building.

"That's the administrative building," Mason says. "It is also where most of the guards stay, though you'll find that many of them have quarters in the training building, where our room is located."

Wearily, I turn to face Mason. He leans forward, green eyes studying me. I match his piercing gaze with one of my own.

Mason's lips twist into a spine tingling smile. "Unless you want to wind up in one of the terribly unpleasant prison cells with pieces of flesh hanging from your back, you'll do exactly what I'm about to tell you." He raises his eyebrows expectantly. I nod in agreement. "Good. Now, while it is unlikely that we will meet anyone at this hour, I want you to be prepared nonetheless. So, should we meet someone, it will likely be one of my fellow guardsmen. You will only speak when spoken to. And for your sake, you had best show reverence to them. Should any of them ask you about your unfortunate position here, politely address them with a guilty response." I recoil. "Yes, you heard me. You are guilty of breaking the law, of more than one I might add. You recognize your guilt and, as a result, willingly accept the punishment that lay ahead of you."

With a curious expression, Mason scoots towards me, and takes my jaw into his hand. He turns it with a smile. "Perfect. They'll want to see some proof of abuse, to satisfy their hatred of you. This should satisfy them, at least for now. And don't look at me like that; you're lucky

I didn't slam your face into the dashboard like I wanted to." I push away his hand.

Mason takes my jaw again and squeezes. "Remember every word I told you, unless you want me to change my mind about your friends. And don't even think about running away, this entire compound is well guarded with men who have the instinct to shoot to kill." I swallow hard.

I open the door, feeling some like a lion escaping its cage. If only I had more energy, I might let out a ferocious roar. If only I had more energy, I might even dare to challenge my captor, though my lack of weaponry and familiarity with the area would doubtless lead to my defeat.

I rise to my feet. Judging by the sweet smell of the pavement, it rained not long ago. Lightning flashes off in the distance, though the sky directly overhead is mostly clear. The blood moon, thankfully much smaller from this distance than the one in my dream, glows brightly. How people like Mason can be so dull as to deny the existence of God begs questioning their sanity. Everything is much too well constructed, much too well orchestrated to simply write it all off on a ridiculous cosmic explosion, or some other stupid theory.

A finger jabs me in the back. I wince and turn around to face Mason. Mason slams the door shut and grips my upper arm. With an impatient jerk of my arm, he sets off. I walk along beside him, feeling strangely secure. I guess after what he told me about the other guards, Mason seems like a defanged viper compared to them.

I trip, my shoe colliding with the curb. I stagger forward as Mason whirls around, and grabs a hold of my arms. That was a close call.

"Watch where you're going," Mason snaps. He regains his hold on my arm and pulls me forward. "Clumsy fool, you won't last a day if you keep that up."

I want to defend myself, to tell him that this is my first time here, but decide against it. How can you reason with someone who believes they already know everything? He is the one who is a fool, and yet, in his eyes, I am the one who is the hopeless case.

Mason stops in front of a door, and then reaches into his pant pocket. He pulls out a card, brings it to a slot in the door, and then swipes it through the groove. A blue light glows in a tiny bubble of glass, earning a satisfied smile from Mason. He pockets the card, opens the door, and then, squeezing my arm, pushes me across the threshold.

Mason grabs a hold of my other arm, so that now, I am in a painful vice of his hands. The door closes with a thunderously loud crack behind us.

I take in the room around us. Directly ahead of us is a large staircase with at least two dozen steps, the topmost steps bathed in faint blue light. Beyond that is more blue light, though considerably brighter. To my right appears to be a cafeteria, with several long tables and chairs peeking out of the darkness. I swallow hard. I am hungry.

On my left is a wall with an open entryway at its middle. I see no sign of any other guards. Perhaps most of them are asleep.

"Come on," Mason says gruffly.

He lets go of my arm. I try to match my pace with his, falling into step beside him. He leads me towards the staircase of all places. I had hoped to avoid climbing all those steps so soon. Well, to be honest, I was really hoping he would steer me into the cafeteria.

Mason lets out an impatient grumble. "The first thing I want you to do is to shower and leave your old way of life behind you. I will not share a room with a filthy Saint."

I examine myself closely. "I'm not that dirty," I say, offended. "And I do not smell, so…" He digs his fingers into my arm. I grit my teeth from the pain.

"Remember what I said," Mason says dangerously as he brings me to a halt at the top of the staircase. He searches the room in front of us and then fixes me with an ominous glare. "Death can either come quickly around here or be postponed. Surely you did not think this was going to be a pleasant holiday, or are you really that stupid?"

I hold my tongue, though I would love to spew one of many sharp retorts at him. Instead, I simply nod my compliance. That seems to be what pleases him the most.

Mason turns around to face the room. He points to a large pillar of light at the middle of the room. It is huge, rising from the floor and extending to the tall ceiling. "That is the Mother Dome. She casts a force field over the entire compound. Nothing can come in, and nothing can get out."

Mason starts forward, jerking me along beside him. He leads me past the Mother Dome, which I now see is surrounded by a circular steel guardrail.

Mason looks between me and the guardrail. "Do not ever lean over to touch her, unless you want to die. She has more power in her veins than any other mother on the face of the earth."

I nod. Mason sets off, whips me forward with a stiff tug on my arm. If I was a vicious person like his kind of people, I might concede to the idea of luring him to stand by the guardrail just to try to push him to his death. But despite his hatred of me, I don't want to hurt him. I'm not sure why, but there is something about Mason that I find strangely familiar. I can almost see a smile buried beneath his sour expression, a faint light on a nasty window pain.

I wish he would let go of my arm. I have no plan at this point to make a run for it. Where would I go?

"That hurts you know," I say, tempted to knock his hand away.

Mason stops, and looks down at my arm. He swallows almost imperceptibly. He loosens his grip with an irritated sigh.

I stare at the angry marks on my arm. "Thanks. You know, if you would be…" I trail off as someone exits the hallway at the end of the room.

Mason shoots me a dangerous look, and then turns to face the rapidly approaching figure. It's a man, most likely one of Mason's fellow guardsmen from the looks of him. He has a bald head and a rounded face.

"Mason," says the man curiously. He comes to a stop in front of us, brown eyes looking between Mason and I. "And I see you've brought company. The rabid dog has been rounded up and…shouldn't it be wearing a muzzle?"

I bristle. Mason's fingers dig deeper into my arm. I lower my eyes to the floor in a submissive look.

"Not a bad idea Jack," Mason says, letting go of my arm. He takes my jaw. "It already tried to bite me once, but I drove it away with my fist."

"I see," Jack says with a lazy smile. He appears to be in his mid-thirties, and has just as much hate in his eyes as Mason does. "But are you sure it's safe to lead it around without additional security?"

Mason gives him a confidant look. "It's nothing that I cannot handle. I'd say that from the looks of its jaw, it'll learn to keep its mouth shut from here on out."

Jack takes a step closer, brown eyes appraising me. "You know, when President Gloss told us about it, he made it out like it was a terribly ugly creature, but it actually looks halfway human, and sort of pretty to. And it has green eyes, how very unusual. I thought all Saints had sad gray eyes from all the mourning over days of old. I wonder, will the others look like this?"

Mason shrugs. "It's hard to say, but I have yet to see what you mean about it looking 'sort of pretty'. Unless perhaps you mean the beautiful bruise that I inflicted upon its jaw."

"Yes," Jack says with a faint glare. "What did you think I meant?"

"Nothing much," Mason says with a casual smile. "I just thought it'd be a good idea to make clear your intent to the dog. You see, it doesn't catch on very quickly. It suffers from a serious lack of understanding, like all Saints do. But I told it what all would happen to it if it failed to live up to our expectations."

Jack laughs mirthlessly. "I bet that got its attention."

Mason nods. "It did."

Jack looks like he suddenly remembers something. "Shaebeth wanted me to tell you not to worry about reporting to her tonight. She said you can wait until tomorrow, after you've had time to rest."

"Very well," Mason says, looking somewhat relieved. He grabs a hold of my arm, inclines his head at Jack, and then tugs me forward. "I'll see you at breakfast tomorrow morning."

I clench my teeth from the pain. Mason leads me into a large room and waves his free hand for introduction. "This is the common room, where the sixteen Saints under my supervision will, on occasion, be allowed to talk to each other. Or, more likely, try to rip each other's throats out. The other sixteen Saints will have the same kind of setup, but will be held under Jack's care. In order to prevent what I'm sure would be a major catastrophe should all thirty-two Saints be allowed to live with each other, each team will have their own room. I expect that four Saints from each district can quite possibly get along with each other without murdering each other. And in case you're wondering, the reason there are four Saints from each district is because there are four counties in each district. It's simple enough. Still, President Gloss will be eagerly awaiting news of the first round of bloodshed when it occurs. He doesn't think you Saints have as much restraint as you let on about. And I agree with him. In fact, one of the reasons he wants me to study you in particular is to develop a better understanding of why your kind practices so much restraint when there is nothing in it for you. Do not lie, do not steal or kill or become intimate before marriage. It is my expectation that, after studying you, I will arrive at some useful conclusions, albeit, they will doubtless explain the existence of your one God."

Mason steers me down another hallway. He seems intent on controlling my every move. I wish he did not have to be so rude. I am more than just a walking piece of garbage, despite what he may think.

I give him a reproachful look. "Do you have to be so rude? Earlier back there, you kept referring to me as 'it' to that guy, as if I am nothing more than a walking piece of garbage. Let me show you that I am just as much human as you are, just as capable of…" I cry out in pain as Mason digs his fingernails into my arm.

Mason looks like he could also spit on me. "I'm in no mood to hear anything you have to say." He comes to a stop in front of one of several doors that line the hallway.

Mason opens the door and pushes me across the threshold. I stagger forward, and quickly right myself. He slams the door shut behind me.

I slide my shirt sleeve up; examine the angry red marks left behind by his fingernails. I have never felt so violated in my entire life.

I examine the room around me to find two beds, a desk, and a couple of chairs.

Mason walks past me, heads towards an open door on the other side of the room. He beckons me to him just before entering the room. I swallow and force myself to comply.

Mason disappears into the room just before I reach the door. This would be a good time to bolt, if I wasn't so weary. But again, where would I go?

I cross the threshold, my mind warning me against trusting Mason. I swear, if he turns out to be one of those sick creeps like Perverted Demon, I will not hesitate to defend myself.

I lift my eyes from the thin blue carpeting on the floor to Mason. He stands on one side of the room, which

I now see is a closet. "Come here," he says with a friendly smile.

I bite down onto my lip, not liking the look of this at all. He stands in front of several shelves of clothes, his expression somewhat friendlier. If he expects me to change in front of him, then he is terribly mistaken. I refuse to take another step. Mason raises his eyebrows in expectation.

I swallow and shake my head. "Look, if you're one of those sick creeps with a warped mind, you'd best find someone else to bother because…"

"Stop," Mason says, cutting me off. "I may be a lot of things, but I am not a pervert. Honestly, I have no desire to see any more of you than I have to. Now," Mason adds with asperity, "are you going to come over here or do you want me to pick out all your clothes for you, including your undergarments?"

I rush forward on that note.

Mason steps up to the shelves, a satisfied gleam in his eyes. "Everything you need to look and smell presentable can be found in here." Mason reaches forward and seizes a black shirt from a stack. He hands it to me. I take it, finding it surprisingly soft and light.

Mason clasps his hands behind his back. "Everything on this side of the room is yours, and everything on the other side of the room is mine. Go on," Mason adds inclining his head towards a stack of jeans. "Or do I have to do everything for you?"

I step up to the shelves and take a pair of jeans. I make my way down the shelves like an assembly line and take a pair of socks.

Mason follows along beside me. "You need not worry about doing laundry around here. There are maids to take care of that. Should you be embarrassed about any one of them collecting your dirty clothes, just speak up and you can do your laundry yourself."

I hold the stack of clothes against my chest. "Why should I be embarrassed?"

Mason shrugs with a weak smile. Then, as if realizing his friendliness, he glares at me. "You Saints have a way of sensitivity like nobody's business. It would seem like I just learned something else about you."

"Great," I say sarcastically. "But believe it or not, I'm learning about you at the same time."

Without a word, Mason walks past me and stops in front of an oak cabinet. "Everything else you need to look and smell presentable can be found in here." He opens the cabinet, lets the doors swing wide open. He takes a tube of toothpaste from one of the compartments and places it atop the stack of clothes in my hands.

A few moments later, Mason closes the cabinet doors and I am loaded up like a pack horse. The last thing I expected when I left home was to arrive someplace where I would be provided for. We received all this stuff back home in our monthly provisions; they were just not nearly as nice. Plus, back home, everyone had to wear white T-shirts and jeans, even the women. But here I stand with a nice black shirt, a pair of jeans without holes in them, new shoes, and anything else I could want.

I shrug on my new shirt and look in the mirror. I am surprised at how good I look. I had almost forgotten what it was like to wear shirts other than the same color each day. Before Gloss, I had an array of colorful clothing. Then came Gloss's stupid mandate saying that we had to "shed our old way of life and embrace change." As you can imagine, this upset many people who, rightly so, took his insensitive comment as ridiculing us for our faith. After all, the shedding of old ways and habits, of old lifestyles is a core element of becoming a Christian. Who wants to step out of the shower with much of the filth still clinging to them?

I look at myself again in the mirror. I wish Emily could see me now. All well, it's just as well. If she were here, she would probably faint at the site of me.

I turn away from the mirror. This bathroom is amazing. The shower was huge and put out so much water, I felt guilty for wasting. Back home, Mark and I bathed with rain water, and we normally had enough to clean up with most of the time.

I make my way to the door. I wish Mark could see me now, just to ease his mind. I open the door and find Mason leaning against the opposite wall, arms crossed over his chest. I pull the door closed behind me. Mason blinks in surprise, a faint smile playing on his lips.

I frown. "So tell me, other than having to look the part of a guard, why do I get to enjoy all of these fineries?"

Mason kicks off the wall, green eyes cold and hateful. "I already told you. I refuse to share a room with a filthy Saint. Now come on, I have to show you around." And judging by his tone of voice, it is the last thing he wants to do.

Mason sets off down the hallway with an irritable puff. I fall in beside him. I can't help but notice that he is wearing the same kind of clothing that I am. I would have expected him to have a golden collar or something that would set him apart from a filthy Saint like me.

"So tell me," Mason says in a curious tone. "What did a Saint like you do back home besides shell corn all day?"

The question catches me off guard. It's really none of his business. I feel like it could be a trap to try to incriminate me on additional charges. Still, the question could be worse. "I made it my goal to try to mind my own business. I find that that is the key to get through life."

Mason considers this. "But I thought Saints were all about sticking their noses into everyone else's business, in order to preach them into heaven."

I give him a cool look. "You know what I mean good doctor. Now is there anything else you want to know?"

Mason nods with a small smile. "What makes a Saint a Saint? I mean, why does your kind feel like they are the cream of the crop?"

I could ask him the same thing; after all, it is the sick creeps like him who currently strut about controlling everything. Instead, I say "A good Christian, that is, one who has accepted Jesus Christ as their Lord and Savior tries to live a holy life unto God. That means out with lies, lusts of the flesh, and anything else that can hinder your walk with God. You see, the God I serve cannot tolerate sin. The wicked have no place in His presence."

We reach the staircase and begin our descent. Mason looks at me like I am crazy. "That's the stupidest bunch of crap I've ever heard of in my life. No wonder why your kind lost power, you were way too boring. Who wants to live under such strict guidelines? I learned a long time ago that the only way to enjoy life is to indulge in your hearts desires."

What an idiot, but of course I won't tell him this. "Everyone needs to learn self-control. Without it, you cannot hope to achieve the fullness of life. What good is doing everything you want if you're just going to wind up with all the consequences that follow? I believe in moderation. If you cannot control yourself, then something or someone else will. If you do whatever you want as often as you want, then you are foolishly allowing yourself to be controlled by your habits."

Mason appears to be deep in thought. "I've always wondered why Saints were so miserable, now I know. What good is life if you cannot have fun?"

Mason leads me down a hallway across from the cafeteria. He asks the stupidest questions.

I clench my teeth in frustration. "Surely you know the answer to that question. If something is good for you, then it will have a positive outcome for you. Take lusts of the flesh for instance, what good is giving yourself over to the perversions of your heart if they are just going to bring about your destruction through diseases? Surely you understand this."

"Careful," Mason says tersely. "Not everyone around here would go so easy on you if they heard what you just told to me. The only reason why I don't punish you is because I am interested in studying you. If not for that, then rest assured, I would have already carved my initials onto your heart."

I don't doubt him. I just hope that he won't change his mind about helping me anytime soon.

Mason comes to a stop at the edge of a large room. "Welcome to the obstacle course room," he says with a wave of his hand. "This is where the Saints will spend part of their time training when they're not invested in even more dangerous undertakings. I expect there will be many brawls and curses break out in this room as opposed to hugs and blessings.

"And you'd like that," I say, finding his tone of voice as annoying as sandpaper. "Wouldn't that only create headaches for those guards whose job it is to keep them in line?"

Mason shrugs. "Not really, many of them have been looking forward to instigating Saint rivalry for a long time now. Who wouldn't want to see a bunch of Saints throwing punches at each other?"

I take in the room around us. Directly over the middle of the room is a catwalk that overlooks all the obstacles in the room. I imagine the catwalk crawling with guards whose sick eyes look for ways to bother people. If they are anything like the perverted agents back home, then it's not going to be good for my incoming brothers and sisters. I suspect that there will be a great deal more occur in this room besides brawls and curses within a matter of time.

Mason sets off towards the catwalk. I follow along beside him. I see a ladder quickly approaching.

Mason comes to a stop next to the ladder and turns to face me. "You first, but you need to be careful, should you fall, both of my bosses would want my head."

I don't know whether to laugh or feel angry. "Oh I'll be careful. The last thing I want is for you to lose your head over something as insignificant as me."

I take the ladder in my hands and begin to climb. The railings are pleasantly cool to the touch. Maybe I should let go, fall to the floor, and pretend injury. That would get the good doctor's blood boiling, wouldn't it? But then again, it would also get my blood boiling.

The ladder shakes lightly, sending a vibration through my hands. Mason has begun his ascension. I quicken my pace, anxious to get out of his way. I hear Mason let out an irritable grunt. I suppose he was hoping that I would be afraid of heights. Then he would have another reason to bark at me.

I reach the top, take the guardrails in hand, and then pull myself to my feet. It is nice to have both feet planted firmly side by side. I dislike heights, but I have always hated ladders.

I take a few steps backwards as Mason grips the guardrails and thrusts himself forward. As much as it pains me to admit it, the good doctor seems to be in great shape. I wonder if he holds with that old saying of eating an apple a day. I wish I had an apple, particularly a sour one. I'd shove it right into his mouth without a moment's hesitation.

Mason points to a rock wall. "That is for climbing," he says in a tone of voice as if he is talking to a simpleton. It has dozens of ledges sticking out of it at irregular intervals. "It helps with strength and coordination. Pretty much everything else you see in here is self-explanatory. Those," Mason adds, inclining his head towards four black sacks hanging in the air, "are punching bags. Is this the first time you've ever seen punching bags?"

"Yes," I say with a nod. "Inanimate ones, that is, although there were many agents back home I would have loved to have pummeled, mainly because they couldn't keep their hands to themselves."

Mason swallows, green eyes concerned. "Did…any of them ever bother you? I mean, like force your friends to watch as one of the agents made you feel uncomfortable or something?"

I swallow hard. "No, but one of them, an agent who we called Perverted Demon forced Ethan to strip to his underwear one day in front of everyone for no other reason than he wanted to look at him."

"Ethan," Mason says curiously. "I believe I saw him standing beside you before you intervened with that woman's death sentence. He was surprisingly good looking for a Saint."

I scowl. "People are people. And it humiliated him. He should never have had to experience that."

Mason fixes me with cold hard eyes. "No, he should not have. But it might have done him some good. After all, your lot is way too finicky when it comes to showing skin."

"Oh," I say with disgust. "You think we should just run around naked just to please a bunch of perverts? Is that what you want *me* to do?"

Mason looks like he could hit me. "No, I wish for you to continue practicing your strange religious ways, regardless of what I think is right. You see, if I'm to make sound conclusions about you, I need you to behave as you normally do. In other words, do nothing to water down your identity, at least not while you're around me."

I look at him like I have lost my mind. "Sure thing doc. But I'd like a blue heart instead of a red one, doc. The sun's bright but my new image even outshines that, wouldn't you agree, doc? And I have this thing with caterpillars; they crawl up my nostrils, dig into my brain, and then explode in a million butterflies after hibernation. Did you know that I…"

Mason takes a hold of my wrist. "Stop acting like a lunatic," he snaps. "You're too sm…stupid to tell your right hand from your left."

I give him a wry smile. "You slipped, good doctor. Were you about to call me smart?"

Mason lets go of my arm, looking distraught. "Like you said, I slipped. Believe it or not, even intelligent people make mistakes every now and then, though I have had few such instances."

I stifle a yawn. "Whatever."

Chapter Four

I sit across from Mason, who, now ready for bed, occupies the only other chair in the room. Tomorrow is the big day, when he will finish showing me around, as well as teach me how to throw knives in preparation to train my team.

Taking me by surprise, Mason entered the room earlier after showering wearing nothing more than black shorts and a T-shirt. He rests a foot atop his knee, green eyes fixed on me expectantly. He wants to know what I think about love, life, and morality.

"I already told you," I say. "I love caterpillars, kiss life's heart, and consort with lady bugs. Lady bugs are pretty and much less likely to break your heart."

Mason lets out an exhaustive sigh, brushes his fingers over his ankle. "You're nuts," he says flatly. "Look, do you really expect me to protect you and your friends when you act like this?"

I lean forward and trace a heart on the side of my foot. I flick my eyes to Mason. "Why is it that the heart is in the chest and not one of the feet?" I want to annoy him.

Mason blinks, as if trying to figure out if I am serious about my inquiry. He stares at my foot. "Because over tens of millions of years, the evolutionary process of our ancestors favored a centralized heart. Many great scientists believe that the heart not only gravitated towards the center of the chest, but that it also grew substantially to accommodate the bodies increased circulatory needs."

Oh dear God, he has got to be smarter than this. "Okay good doctor, you wanted me to cut the craziness, so brace yourself. Nothing that you just told me can be validated. And need I point out the vagueness of your weak explanation. Please don't insult me by telling me that I descended from apes, algae, or a rhino's horn." I watch in amusement as Mason presses his lips into a hard line of disapproval. I take a deep breath. "My body, though it may not be as pretty as yours is way too perfect, way too expertly well-constructed to say that I came about by accidental or preferred developmental traits. A body does not just decide it wants to change, how could it? And don't start in with the whole environmental excuse. *Oh*, because ants were so small and hard to reach, anteaters just happened to sprout snouts as long as my forearm to reach them. And remember, this was all very well documented twenty million years ago, despite having occurred before man learned to write. Wait a minute," I add in a calm voice at Mason's angry protest. "Allow me to call myself an expert in pig poop. As strange as it may sound, it seems like I recall having read about such experts in the Old Country. Anyway, in keeping with my expertise in pig poop, I have studied it very well indeed. And, after having unearthed several fossilized piles of such poop, I have determined it to be nine hundred million years old, because I was there nine hundred million years ago and just happened to watch the pig that pooped the pile I now hold in my hand. Oh, but I forgot, the reason why the pile of poop in my hand is so small is because all that time ago, pigs were once mice before they became pigs. And the sun was a giant ball of water doddering around the heavens before it suddenly decided to become a hot ball of fire to allow enough heat to bring forth life on earth. Imagine that, a blazing ball of fire suddenly formed a womb and gave birth to everything around us. Amazing, isn't it?"

Mason looks torn between wanting to snap at me and wanting to ask me a question. He runs a hand down the front of his shirt absently. "Tell me, how did you become so…well informed about all this?"

I smile. "I like to read. More importantly, I have prayed for wisdom many a time so that I would be able to discern what's right from all the junk. You know," I add, meeting his eyes. "Out of all the books I have ever read, the Bible was the most informative. It made the most sense."

Mason regards me with a weak smile, not unlike the way Ethan has looked at me in the past. "Perhaps I have misjudged you; you might be more interesting to listen to than I thought."

I give him a curious look. "How old are you?"

Mason looks like he is not sure whether or not he wants to tell me this. "Thirty-three, if you must know."

I lean forward with a smile. "I can't believe I'm about to say this, but you don't look a day over twenty."

Mason almost smiles. "Continue to talk like that and I will…try to be more reasonable with you."

I drop my jaw in pretend shock. "You mean you'll be nice to me, like address me politely instead of referring to me as 'it' in public."

Mason considers this. "Maybe, but it'll depend on how well you answer my questions. That means when I ask you a serious question, you will do your best to answer it as seriously as possible. I don't want to hear about you keeping company with lady bugs or kissing the moon's craters or dangling on a spider web over a fly cobbler."

I frown. "I don't think I said anything about the last two of your examples." I swallow with amusement.

"But I'm impressed. I never thought about 'dangling over a fly cobbler' before, but is sounds like fun."

A sudden knock on the door. Mason rises to his feet with a worried expression. He smoothes a wrinkle from his shirt and runs a hand through his hair. Then he turns around to face me with a solemn air of superiority. "Don't speak unless you're spoken to, and even then, you had better choose your words carefully. Do you understand?" I nod; hurt more by the harshness of his tone of voice than the words themselves.

With a dangerous look, Mason turns away from me and makes his way to the door. And just when I started to think he had begun to change his opinion of me.

Feeling downcast again, I turn towards the door just as Mason pulls it open. I crane my neck to try to see past Mason, but he bars the doorway.

"Carrie," he says, sounding wondrously surprised. "I...didn't expect you until tomorrow morning."

"Sorry to bother you sir," she says in a sweet, apologetic tone of voice. "But I left my duster behind on your desk."

I look at the desk. There, lying on the side of the desk is a green duster covered in cobwebs. I rise to my feet, my mind more interested in seeing the girl behind the sweet voice than anything. I stagger forward, and brace myself against the desk. I take the duster and slowly turn around. And come face to face with a very beautiful red-haired girl.

I stiffen under her piercing gaze. She gives me a friendly smile. I swallow hard. "I…uh…here," I say, feeling like a fool. I take a step forward, holding the duster upright like a stick of cotton candy. If she doesn't think I'm nuts, then… She takes the duster from my hand with a grateful smile.

"You're Ryan Collins," she says in a heart clenching tone of voice.

I wish I could become invisible. Instead, I give her a polite nod. I feel a slight tremble in my knees. I hope she doesn't notice. She pulls a stray curl behind her ear, blue eyes thoughtful. "I didn't think you were supposed to arrive until tomorrow."

I give her a blank look. I wish she'd look away for a second so I could recover.

"That's when the others will arrive," Mason says. "The thirty-two Saints will come marching in at some time tomorrow evening."

Carrie considers this, and slowly begins to turn around to face Mason, her eyes struggling to leave me. Now that her back is to me, I breathe a deep sigh of relief. She is so heart staggeringly beautiful.

"Forgive me, but I have to go," Carrie finally says in a slightly affronted tone of voice. Without another word, she turns around and makes for the door, her green duster gripped tightly in hand. She casts me a final glance, and then pulls the door shut.

I narrow my eyes onto Mason. "She sounded offended," I say.

Mason gives me a knowing smile. "Pretty, isn't she?" I want to tell him that that's not answering my question. Looking pleased, Mason takes a step forward. "If you do everything I ask of you, I could arrange for her to come by more often."

"And do what," I say, finding his mischievous tone of voice both disconcerting and rude. "You're a pervert if you think I'm going to put on a show for you with her. I may not be perfect, but I am certainly not dissolute. You're even sicker than I thought. Look," I add, as Mason approaches me with an angry look, "if you think threatening to hurt my friends will mean I will do whatever you want, then…" He presses a hand over my mouth.

Mason shakes his head, keeps a hand over my mouth. "That's not what I meant. Besides, I know you're too good a Saint to do such a thing. And honestly, I'm glad. I'm a physician, the last thing I want is for you to mistreat your body, especially when I can see just how well you have taken care of it." Mason withdraws his hand.

I swallow. "About Carrie, I take it she's a maid?"

Mason nods. "And senior maid at that. She has a staff of six girls working under her. But let's get back to my original point, before you cast it aside. I saw how you looked at her. It was clear you found her attractive. I only meant that I think she would be good for you. You know, like the sun is to a sick person."

I raise my eyebrows. "Oh, so you think I'm sick? Like mentally or physically?"

"Look," Mason says with a scowl. "I just think Carrie would be good medicine for you. She's a Saint to."

I glower. "So that's it then. You just want to study us, to see how I react to a pretty girl who just happens to be a Saint."

Mason looks like he wants to hit me. "It's late. And you will have a challenging day ahead of you tomorrow. The body cannot function well without proper rest. Need I say more?"

I hate being talked down to. "What is your problem? Earlier, you turned hateful towards me at the knock on the door. I thought we had reached a sense of mutual respect for each other, or were you just toying with my mind?"

Mason takes a deep breath and lets it out slowly, as if he is trying to refrain from snapping at me. "You've come to a dangerous place, or hadn't you noticed? What did you expect; that I'd risk my own position just to protect you? There's only so much I can do for you. And I won't do anything for you if you refuse to cooperate with me. That means that you do exactly what I tell you. Believe it or not, you're very lucky, you just don't realize it. If they had sent any other guard to get you, then you would be experiencing living hell right now. But instead of being grateful, you insist on hammering me with stupid questions."

"Grateful," I say, hardly believing my ears. "I'll probably never see the only people I ever cared about and you think I should be grateful. My uncle and best friend are doubtless broken, likely to incur serious harassment because of their association with me and yet you couldn't care less." I shake my head, finding Mason's impassive expression very irritating. "You don't get it do you? I don't care about my life at this point. But it hurts me to think that the only two people I care about most in the world are broken and doubtless certain that they'll never see me again. Do you have any idea what that feels like?"

Mason shakes his head, a glint of anger in his green eyes. "No, and I don't care. You brought this on yourself, remember? If you hadn't gone on about your stupid dreams and quoted those awful Scriptures, then you would have been left alone. But you refused to remain silent, and therein lies your blame. You broke the law and now you must pay for your mistake."

I scoff. "Since when did it become wrong to speak the truth? I'll tell you: When your people came to power, everything good became evil and everything evil became good. That is one reason why my friends and I privately called one of our agents back home Perverted Demon, because he had a knack for everything vile. He was such a threat that we couldn't work in peace for fear that he'd come by and begin sexually harassing one of us. I already told you what he did to Ethan, and you clapped your hands in amusement. Since when did it become right for a grown man to abuse a teenage boy?"

Mason swallows, green eyes indifferent. "It might not be right, but it is not my place to say either way. I belong to President Gloss's private guard. I carry out his requests without hesitation or protest. When it comes to the local governance of Townships, I have absolutely no jurisdiction."

I shake my head in anger and look between the beds. "Which one is mine?"

Mason shrugs. "Whichever one you want. But I warn you, I am a light sleeper, so keep this in mind should you contemplate escape."

I resist the urge to kick him. And yet, I do not think he should get off so easily. I hold up three fingers. He raises his eyebrows like I am stupid.

I smile mischievously. "I might as well tell you, I am considering escaping three times tonight, so sleep well." I smile with satisfaction at his startled expression.

I head towards the nearest bed. I hope he has a miserable night tonight, not closing his eyes once for fear that I will be on the run.

I sit down on the side of the bed and look at Mason. He still stands in the middle of the room. I laugh inwardly. Little did he know that we would become such good friends. Honestly, I find our heated exchanges quite entertaining. If Mason did not remind me a little of Mark in his appearance, I do not think I would be as kind to him. After all, he is the one who brought me here, who took me away from my family and friends. I know that he was just acting on his boss's orders, but still. He obviously hates Christians, or Saints as he calls us, so I cannot help but feel a little angry.

I look him straight in the eyes. "Sweet dreams, guardian angel. And should I wake from a nightmare, I will expect to be read to. I know your kind banned all books, but surely you have one stashed away that'll do. And don't talk too loud, lest you stir the blood in my fist. And it had better not be anything perverted, frightening, or medical. But then again, perhaps you'd be better off just telling me about your experiences with the ladies of your life. And no," I add, wanting to pester him, "I do not mean lady bugs this time. I mean the pretty, delicate, gentle companions that God intended for us to have. Just avoid any stories involving hot tempered girls. I've had my fair share of them already in life." I turn away from Mason just as a confused frown begins to build on his face.

That night I dream that Carrie appears beside me, her delicate red curls gleaming in the nightlight. She sits down on the side of my bed and takes my hand. I strain my eyes to see her. I finally make out her pretty blue eyes. She leans forward, and whispers in my ear. Her breath tickles my ear, but I remain still. Looking relieved, she pulls away, brushing her fingers against my collar bone. I shiver. Amidst my nervousness, I somehow managed to make out her warning: *He will soon present you with a gift, and you will take it. But beware, for all the devil's schemes lead to destruction.*

Despite one crazy dream, the remainder of the night went by smoothly, all things considered. I had expected a series of nightmares, culminating with unprecedented abuse by Perverted Demon towards Mark and Ethan. I also braced myself for a glimpse of Agatha's execution, but I was also spared that as well, though a muffled sound of grief did escape me at one point. Fortunately, Mason's soft snores drifted across the room, putting my mind to rest that he might have overheard me.

The door suddenly swings open, and Mason enters the room. Judging by the absence of the faint stubble that covered his face the last I saw him; he just came from the bathroom.

I sit upright with a yawn. I push the covers back. I swing my legs over the side of the bed. I wipe the sleep from my eyes with the hope that Mason will allow me enough time to get around.

I lower my hands from my eyes to find Mason seated in front of me. I did not even hear him sit the chair down. He looks surprisingly well rested all things considered.

I clear my throat. "Was there a guard posted outside our door last night," I say.

Mason studies me carefully. "No, I didn't see any reason for extra security. I didn't think you'd try to escape. You're much too clever to attempt a job that has no chance of success."

I don't know whether to feel happy or sad. "I think I'll dance about the room like a lunatic tonight." That should drive him nuts. I mean, why should I allow him to rest peacefully? What promise has he given me to ensure the well-being of my friends and I? Why should I trust a man who works for Gloss, a man who is responsible for taking me away from my family and friends?

Mason leans forward and jabs me in the chest with his index finger. "I wouldn't do that if I were you. Besides, you'd only be hurting yourself. I'm not the one who will be expected to train four Saints until they demonstrate their worthiness to compete against their opponents in the final challenge. But go ahead if you must," Mason adds with a shrug. "Dance about all you like, just don't expect me to join you. Besides, there's a book I've been wanting to read anyway. Your commotion would only serve to help keep me alert and therefore more receptive to what I read."

I massage my chest. I wish he would keep his hands to himself. My arm is still sore from where he jerked me around like a puppet yesterday. I shake my head. "Whatever compelled you to become a doctor? I mean, it's clear you enjoy hurting people. Oh," I add quickly, suddenly realizing something. "I bet you entered the field with the intention of learning all the secrets of inflicting bodily harm on people. Let me guess, you probably know more ways to break someone's heart than to cure it. Am I right?"

"You're wasting time," Mason says darkly. "We can either continue sitting here bickering about nothing particularly meaningful, or you can allow me to teach you some skills that you will soon need if you are to survive this place."

I lean forward with an outstretched hand. I thrust a finger towards his chest, intent on giving him what I'm sure he left me, a nasty bruise. With a flash of his hand, he intercepts me, and grips my wrist tightly. I wince from the pain.

Mason lets out a superior laugh. "Nice try, but your speed and coordination was clearly impaired due to nerves."

"What about breakfast," I say, feeling my stomach rumble with hunger. "I'm sure I saw a cafeteria downstairs last night. Or perhaps those were your operation tables." Maybe Mason plans on carving me up and serving me to the incoming Saints.

Mason rises to his feet. Without a word, he turns his back on me and makes his way towards the closest. I stare at his ankles, thinking this a good time to wound his Achilles tendons. Yes, he'd go down hard and then I could force him to tell me how to get out of here. Because regardless of what he says, there must be a way to escape without getting caught.

Mason disappears into the closet. I sigh miserably. I do not like him, but I do not want to hurt him. Surely he has a wife and possibly kids somewhere who would mourn him if anything happened to him. And then there's the similarity between he and Mark. If only he didn't remind me so much of Mark… And if these reasons aren't sufficient, he clearly trusts me enough to turn his back on me, to leave me behind without fearing for his well-being. More importantly, if I tried to escape or did anything to hurt him, it would only confirm his prejudice of me. No, as much as I hate to admit it, I need to at least try to convince him that I am not a haughty Saint. And while the task of doing so seems nearly impossible to me, it's just a small thing for God.

Mason leaves the closet behind with haste. He carries a tray in his outstretched hands, his expression gently oscillating between irritability and something akin to embarrassment. As if detecting my own perceptions of his strange behavior, Mason gives me a funny look. Honestly, I'm surprised he doesn't sneer at me.

"Peanut butter and jelly sandwiches," he says, sitting down in the chair across from me. I never thought I would hear that in this place, but it sounds fine to me. He balances the tray across his knees. "And no, I did not make them myself. That job belongs to our cooks. But starting tomorrow, you will have your meals in the cafeteria, beside me."

I meet his eyes with an appreciative smile. "Whatever you say, good doctor. Just don't let me starve."

To my surprise, Mason actually gives me a halfway friendly looking smile. I consider slapping a hand across my chest theatrically, but I do not want to lose what grounds I seem to have made with him. The last thing I need is for him to think that I'm making fun of him.

I ended up eating three sandwiches, an apple, and a glass of milk. Then, Mason sat the tray aside, dropped to the floor, and began pumping his arms in a ridiculously fast set of pushups. I sat there and counted to a hundred before he finally told me to get around. And so I did. As soon as I left the bathroom, he moved past me, clean clothes in hand, and said that he was going to take a quick shower. He needed one; his shirt was soaked with sweat.

"So is it just you and Jack then," I say as Mason leads me across the common room.

"No," Mason says, packing more force into one word that I ever thought possible. "There are many of us, I just cannot tell you how many for security reasons.

Some of them are located directly outside the building, while others are stationed at strategic locations throughout the compound."

"Then where is everyone," I say, not hiding my suspicious smile. I catch his eyes as we descend the staircase. He cuts me a look that says like-I'll-tell-you. I sigh inwardly.

Mason slows down and begins to take the last three steps slowly. He squares his shoulders, as if Gloss himself were waiting for us at the foot of the stairs. We touch down at about the same time, an almost imperceptible sigh escaping him.

"That's the cafeteria," he says pointing towards several rows of long tables and chairs. I want to roll my eyes. Like I can't see that. He looks at me out of the corner of his eye. "And just beyond that is a stairwell and elevator that leads to the basement. I will show it to you another time." He turns to the side and makes for a door by the staircase.

I feel my heartbeat quicken in nervous anticipation. Mason pulls the door open and gestures me forward.

I walk past him and stop just shy of the threshold. I turn around to face him. "I can't see anything. Isn't there any lights?"

Mason rolls his eyes in disbelief. "Of course there are. They're programmed to come on as soon as you cross the threshold."

I have never heard of such a thing. I hold my breath and take a tentative step forward. Lights burst to life above me, giving life to a long corridor. Mason presses a hand between my shoulder blades and pushes me forward. I nearly fall down.

I turn around to face him with an angry scowl. "I wish you'd stop trying to kill me before I even have a chance to do my job."

Mason looks like he wants to laugh. "I'm not trying to kill you, but I am trying to toughen you up. You will begin training your team tomorrow morning. If they find you weak or without skill, it will undermine your ability to train them, thus making it that much harder for you to survive this place. You must start off strong; try to convince them that you know what you're doing, even if you don't."

I swallow hard. "But I only just arrived, and I don't even know what I'm supposed to do. And won't they think it funny that the other teams will be trained by professional guards while they will have to put up with a nobody?"

Mason shakes his head impatiently, and then sets off down the corridor. "None of the incoming Saints know anything about you. As far as they know, you *are* a guard."

I let out an irritable sigh. "So I'm to begin training four people tomorrow morning with the hopes that they will all find me well prepared and thirty-three years old? How absurd. And don't you think they'll question my identity once they see all the other teams being led by guys like you. That is of course, assuming that you're not all talk, but that you actually do have some skill other than tormenting me."

Mason stops dead in his tracks, turns around to face me with an incredulous look. "You think I've been tormenting you? I've treated you better than you deserve, all things considered. I haven't abused you beyond that which you deserve. I have taken you under my wing in order to try to help you. And not to mention," Mason adds pointing to my stomach, "I had the cooks prepare you breakfast, and a rather healthy one at that. And yet you think I've been tormenting you?"

I shake my head. "I…don't know what to think. How can you expect me to trust you when I barely know you? How do I know you're not just toying with my mind on your bosses' orders?"

Mason looks at me point-blank. "You have potential. But if you tell anyone what I am doing to help you, then I swear, I'll make you pay in ways you could never imagine. And don't forget about the reason I am helping you. It has nothing to do with what I think of you personally. I am only interested in studying you, in learning all I can about you during your time here. But," Mason adds with a dangerous look, "should you betray me, should you breathe a word of what I said to anyone, then be prepared to pay the price, because however much you think you can trust someone around here, they are *all* in my pocket. And I wouldn't dare reveal your true identity to the Saints that will soon make up your team. They will be questioned daily for any signs of your betrayal."

I swallow hard. So much for planting seeds of sedition in hopes of building allies to leave this place. I groan inwardly. How am I ever going to escape? Mason was right: I haven't been that mistreated, but still. When you're used to living life one way and all of a sudden, you get caught up in a net and told to adapt, you can't help but try to look for opportunities to break free. At this point, it looks like Mason is the only guy who I can try to appeal to for help, and he doesn't seem that trustworthy.

I hear my breath hitch in my throat. That's it! Maybe if I try to get along with Mason, to treat him well in hopes of softening him, I can convince him to rescue me himself. And I mean to actually devise a plan of escape. If that means stuffing me into a trunk and carrying me out of here to be placed in his car, then so be it. I'm not above hibernating in a trunk if it would help me gain my freedom. And who knows, Mason, being the smart doctor that he is, might come up with a plan to rescue some of the incoming Saints at the same time.

I open my eyes. Mason, at some point in my reflection, migrated to the end of the corridor. He now stands with his arms crossed over his chest, a much smaller looking threat from this distance. Well, to be honest, if not for his verbal abuse of me, and to a much lesser extent his physical abuse, it would be easy to think of him as a pushover. And then there's his slight resemblance to Mark. And on top of that, where Mason is hostile, Mark is very gentle.

I quickly close the gap between Mason and I. I still think my best shot for escape will involve Mason. The thing is, I do not want to trick him into liking me. That's not who I am. And yet, I may have no other choice.

"Slug," Mason says with disgust as I approach. "If this is how you're going to be the rest of the day, then you can count yourself good and dead before sunset."

I scoff. "Oh, so do you plan on killing me?"

Mason uncrosses his arms and stares me down. "No because that's not my decision to make, although any complaint I file against you will certainly be taken into consideration. I am under orders to teach you the skills necessary for you to train your team, and if you insist on dawdling, there won't be enough time to train you, which means my bosses won't have any reason to keep you alive. We can always bring in another Saint to take your place if we must."

I feel a stab of fear in my chest. I swallow hard. I wish he wasn't so hateful. I look past him to a row of doors. I count eight of them. "Why so many doors?" From the looks of it, there's a good twenty feet in between each of them, making me wonder what's on the other side.

Mason looks like he wants to spit on me for asking such a stupid question. "To accommodate all of the teams that will soon be assembled. Each team will train separately, with the expectation that minimal exposure to each other will ensure a very exciting reunion of Saints in the final challenge. Just think of it," Mason adds with fervor. "Good God fearing people will be coming together tonight like lambs, only to be trained up and turned lose against each other like wolves. Oh how even the softest heart can become stone when one's life is in danger. 'Let the lambs be turned into wolves and let streams of blood flow from their mouths as they rip each other's throats out in hopes of surviving the unspeakable.' My boss's exact words."

I feel a pang of horror in my chest. That's worse than anything I could ever have imagined. I feel as if I am only now realizing the kind of place I have come to, as well as the kind of person Mason really is. How can a good person sound so excited about such a warped agenda? I swallow hard. It sounds like it is going to be harder to find a genuinely good side of Mason to appeal to than I thought. How can you appeal to something that does not really exist? Oh dear God, what am I going to do?

Mason gives me an oh-you've-not-seen-anything-yet sort of look. Reminding me of a kid looking forward to an upcoming birthday, Mason turns and, with a widening smile of sheer delight, takes the doorknob.

I run my sweaty hands down my pants. Mason pulls the door open and I feel a blast of cold air spill out of the room. The room is completely dark. I take a step backward.

"Afraid of the dark," Mason says with an amused smile in his voice.

Mustering my courage, I set off towards the gaping hole of darkness with a prayer on my mind. I walk across the threshold with my eyes closed. An image of Emily flashes in my mind, her outstretched hand coming to rest against my chest. I shiver.

I open my eyes. I cannot see anything through the darkness. Behind me, the door bangs shut, followed by footsteps. Why hasn't he turned the lights on? I feel a stab of terror in my chest. What if Mason plans on doing something hideous to me right here and now, like chase me around in the dark with a knife?

"Lights on," Mason says right behind me.

I flinch. Mason grips my shoulders. I look at the room around me in shock.

I swallow hard. I have never seen anything like this, never even imagined anything like this existed. I lift my eyes to what has to be the world's tallest ceiling. You could probably stack every house in our commune on top of each other and still not reach the ceiling. What a huge room.

I take a deep breath. "What is this place," I say, hearing the wonder in my voice.

Mason lets go of my shoulders and moves to stand beside me. To my surprise, he looks a bit thunderstruck himself. He waves his hands in the air and looks about the room. "We call this place the Mirage."

I frown. "Why?"

Mason lowers his hands to his sides and meets my eyes. "Let me show you why."

I'm not sure I want to know.

"Jane," Mason says in an authoritative tone of voice.

I feel my heartbeat quicken. But nothing happens.

Looking confused, Mason shakes his head in disbelief. "Strange." He clears his throat.

"Jane," he says, only louder this time. I flinch.

"Master Mason," says a giggly voice that wraps around my skin. "I'm sorry, I was asleep, sir. When I heard your voice, I thought I was dreaming. What brings you…Oh? I see you brought company."

Mason scoffs. "You can't see anything; you're as blind as a bat."

An injured sniff. "Must you always remind me of my bodily absence? A woman doesn't have to have eyes to detect a handsome man. She can feel his gentle nature, his lovely face without ever gazing upon his beauty. And it just so happens that I detect a very gentle spirit, a boy whose personality and beauty surpasses even that of yours, Mason. Oh yes, he is lovely. I feel his soft skin, his gentle heart." Her voice vibrates over my skin like static electricity.

I stiffen so that I now feel like a statue.

Mason turns around and gives me a bewildered look, as if he finds it hard to believe what Jane just said. "He doesn't look like anything special to me."

"That's because you're a man, Mason. I, on the other hand, find him very attractive."

"How old are you," I say, looking up at the ceiling.

Jane claps her hands together. "And he has such a strong, handsome voice for such a young man. Oh Mason, did you bring him here for me?"

Mason rolls his eyes with a scowl. "You're too old for him and you know it. Now," Mason adds with irritation, "get us rigged up to break some automatons hearts, and be sure you get us the ones who cannot fight back. I don't want him getting slaughtered on my watch."

Jane lets out a defeated sigh. "Will it be crossbows or knives?"

"Knives," Mason says sharply. "And be prepared to give us an endless supply, for I fear he will spend a hundred before he ever hits a target. Oh," Mason adds, looking like he suddenly remembered something. "You can throw up the walls; we won't need the whole room today."

"As you wish," Jane says stiffly. "But you had better watch out if I were you, someone was in here this morning trying to change my identity."

"What a shame they weren't successful," Mason says with a hateful look. "Now, walls first and then weapons and targets if you will. I want him to see how big the room is that he will be training in each day."

Jane claps her hands together loudly. I wince. I wish she did not have to be so theatrical. She is not even a real person.

Two bright lights flash directly ahead of us like twin lightning bolts. I yelp and jump backwards. Out of the blinding light stand two people, a man and a woman. Mason beckons me forward.

This just keeps getting crazier and crazier. I shuffle along, afraid to move at all.

I do not see any sign of a weapon. I take a deep breath. I need to calm down. When Mason said that he would be teaching me how to throw knives, I never dreamed of being in an environment like this. I just assumed that it would take place in a quiet room with dummies. This is insane.

"Hurry up," Mason snaps. "Remember, it's your time being wasted here, not mine. It's your life on the line, not mine. Don't you even care about your own life?"

I feel a stab of fear in my chest. He has a point. I rush forward and fall into step with him. It's just that I feel so dazed by everything, I can barely even think.

Then it occurs to me, where are the walls Mason requested.

"What about the walls," I say, not seeing anything around that resembles a wall.

"Oh they're here," Mason says, green eyes carefully observing the surroundings. "You only see them if something comes into contact with them, like a weapon or a Saint."

I'm not sure I like the sound of that.

I look at the female automaton. Other than the absence of certain features, she looks much like any other woman I have ever seen. She has chin-length brown hair that curls up on the ends and gray eyes. Sunken slightly within her chest is a large glass heart that sparkles like a ruby.

The man looks much the same, except for the absence of a shirt. He has a smooth silver chest, and even a well-defined abdomen. Like the woman's, his heart also sparkles like a ruby. But other than the heart, I do not see how a knife could penetrate any other place on either of them.

A knife sails through the air towards the man's heart. It shatters, raining down shards of glass onto the floor. I turn around and find Mason standing several feet behind me.

"Break their hearts," he says with a smug look. "That is your current assignment."

"You could have hit me," I say. I turn around to stare at the man. It's a miracle that Mason didn't hit me. I blink in surprise. His broken heart has just been restored, as if it had never been broken. I rub my eyes in disbelief.

"But I didn't." Mason stands beside me, gives me a half smile. "I rarely miss. I think it has something to do with my skilled physicians hands."

"Where'd you get the knife," I say, looking around. I do not see any sign of a knife anywhere, not even the one he just threw.

"I summoned it into being, you just weren't paying attention. Now watch," Mason adds, a hint of excitement in his voice. He turns his hand over, palm upright. A knife instantly appears across his hand. "See what I mean?"

"Is it real," I say, narrowing my eyes onto it.

Mason offers it to me hilt first. Cautiously, I wrap my fingers around the hilt. It feels real enough to me. And yet, it is just a mirage, just an illusion. I doubt it can even leave this room. I begin to walk backwards.

Mason turns around to face me. "You had better watch me throw a few more before you try yourself. Otherwise, I fear you'll be terribly disappointed."

I come to a stop at about the same place Mason stood when he sent his knife sailing through the air. I grip the hilt of the knife. I bring my hand up over my shoulder. Mason watches me with his arms crossed over his chest.

I stare at the woman's heart with an unspoken prayer on my lips. I thrust my arm forward and release the knife. It sails straight and true and shatters the heart like a vindictive lover.

I meet Mason's eyes with a smile. He looks as if a pretty woman just slapped him across the face, green eyes incredulous.

I turn my hand over, palm upright. I feel the knife materialize across my hand before I see it. I turn around to face Mason. "I challenge the good doctor to open heart surgery." I smile at Mason's nervousness. "Oh come on, surely you aren't afraid?"

"Of course I'm not," Mason snaps. "I…where'd you learn to throw like that?"

I move forward with an added spring in my step. I swallow hard. I will not tattle on Mark. "Someone who thought it'd be a good skill to learn just in case your people ever withheld our food rations. And I must say, it's coming in handier than either of us could have ever imagined."

Mason extends both of his hands out, palms upright. He smiles and grips the knives. "Let's see if your skill can match your big mouth."

I swallow hard. I am in trouble. "Fine with me," I say, not wanting to let my worry show. I feel like my senses are too attuned with handling one knife to be able to deal with a left hand throw as well. I should not have challenged him to begin with. That's the risky thing about speaking to soon. But I refuse to let my fear show. The last thing I need is for Mason to look any more confident than he already does. So, without another moment's hesitation, I turn my hands over and feel the cool blades of the knives materialize across my sweaty palms.

At this, Mason begins backing up. I swallow and follow suit.

I stop at about the same place I stood earlier. I cut Mason a sideways look. But he is not there. I turn around. I feel my heart drop. Oh no, he has backed up at least another six to eight feet. Now there's every bit of twenty feet between us and our targets.

I squeeze the hilts of my knives. Judging by Mason's confidant look, he seems to think I am about to lose the challenge. I feel my hope dwindling with each passing second.

I wonder what would happen if I targeted one of Mason's feet? Inwardly, I laugh nervously. I doubt it would hurt him; after all, the blades are not real. And really, it is just as well because I do not want to hurt him anyway. I would however like to impart some good sense into that narrow minded brain of his.

Mason looks at me like I am scum. I bristle. He's just trying to undermine my confidence.

"I'll go first," I say, taking myself by surprise. I watch in delight as the color fades from Mason's face.

I face the automatons with a twinge of anxiety in my chest. If I hit either of them from this distance, it will be a miracle in and of itself. But then again, if God intends for me to hit them, I will.

I know one thing; I am going to have to pack a powerful punch in order to hit either of the hearts at this distance. If only the hearts were even larger than they already are. I suppose someone like Mason probably made them, though I am at a loss to say how. So, need I be surprised that they are not any larger than they are, or that they even exist?

I see Mason bite down onto his lip out of the corner of my eye. I feel a slight boost of confidence. If he feels nervous enough to resort to absently biting his lip, I may have a chance yet. Perhaps Mason bit off more than he could chew.

I look between the glass hearts. If I'm going to do this, I'm going to have to do it soon. Otherwise, I risk losing what confidence I have.

I look between the two hearts. Gripping the knives tightly, I bring my hands up over my shoulders. I take a deep breath and exhale slowly. I thrust my hands forward, first one and then the other.

I follow the first knife as it strikes the man's heart dead center. The second knife strikes the woman's heart a second later. I look at the glass shards at the automaton's feet. I thank God inwardly. New hearts materialize in the cavities like turtles suddenly poking their heads up out of the water. I laugh.

I turn to the side to face Mason. He looks more worried than disappointed. No doubt I just set the bar high for him. Mason stares at the floor where I stand. He pushes me aside and takes my place. Ah, yes, the lucky spot, as if a change in location will be enough to compensate for lack of skill. It looks like the good doctor could use a chill pill.

But he's still not standing in quite the same spot I stood. I reach forward and take his arm to help adjust him. Mason jerks his arm out of my hand, green eyes cold and hateful.

I shrug. "Fine. May your fall be gentle, but judging by your pride, I'd say you had better brace yourself for a major attitude adjustment."

Mason glowers. "Just shut up and back away, I didn't crowd you."

I try not to laugh. He sounded so babyish, so unlike the sure minded doctor who could take on anything a moment ago.

I keep backing away, intent on getting as far away from him as possible. I do not want him to blame me if he fails. I back right into a wall, and nearly have a heart attack.

Mason makes a satisfied sound. "Told you they were there, you just can't see 'em. And no," Mason adds with a leer. "The other teams won't be able to see each other train. We want to keep the final challenge as much of a surprise as possible. We expect each team to have at least two Saints who are particularly vicious and blood thirsty. That'll make the final challenge all the more interesting. Now whether or not you will be around to…"

"You're wasting my time," I say, cutting him off. I ball my hands into fists at my sides.

Mason nods and then turns to face the automatons. He lets out a loud whistle. It reverberates off the walls in an ear aching cacophony. He brings his hands up over his shoulders and cuts me a triumphant smile. He turns back to the automatons and then thrusts his hands forward, first one and then the other.

I follow the first knife as it sails through the air and strikes the female automaton's heart. I watch as the second knife bounces off the man's heart and then clatters to the floor. What just happened?

"Naughty, naughty," Jane says. "I would have you know that both of your knives would have missed had I not directed them to their targets. Next time, if you want to get my attention, blow me a kiss instead of whistling. I am not a dog, nor do I want to be treated like one. I am a woman, with a kind heart who deserves respect."

Looking angry, Mason looks up at the ceiling. "You don't have a heart, remember? You're nothing more than a series of complicated codes entered into a computer. In fact, you wouldn't even exist if my fellow guardsmen had not sat down and slapped you together."

"I could say the same of you," Jane snaps. "If not for your parents, you wouldn't be standing there breaking *my* heart. But judging by your appearance, I'd say that your parents must have been in a big hurry, because you look like you were thrown together in haste."

Mason's mouth falls open. "That's it; I'm going to have a talk with Christian about *deletion*. Honestly, why he thought he had to have a computerized woman with a smart mouth when the world is full of them is beyond me."

Jane sucks in her breath. "Surely you wouldn't. I never took you as a murderer, but if you bring about my destruction, then that is what you will be. Murder is murder, regardless of by what means it is done. Call it what you like, but God is watching."

I frown. "How do you know about God?"

Jane laughs. "Because my…" Her voice suddenly dies away.

Mason pulls a hand out of his pocket, looking satisfied. "That'll be all for now. I see no reason to continue since you hit both targets right off."

I shake my head with disapproval. "You pulled the plug on her, didn't you? That's why she left."

"So what if I did," Mason says, point-blank. "It's none of your business. She was out of place, so I got rid of her."

I narrow my eyes onto him. "She was about to say something that you wish to remain a secret wasn't she?"

Mason raises his eyebrows. "Jane knows no secrets, think about it. Why would we tell a computerized woman a secret?"

I shrug. "I don't know, but I know you looked pretty worried with what she was about to say."

Mason shakes his head with a laugh. "I can't believe I was beat by a Saint." Mason looks me straight in the eyes. "A little more effort and you might just convert me yet."

I sigh irritably. "Stop changing the subject."

Mason's face darkens dangerously as he takes a step forward. "The first rule of survival around here is to remember your place. Do you need me to tell you again where you stand?" I glare at him.

Mason slips his hands into his pockets, ambles closer. "Whatever I say and do is always right, even if you think it's wrong. Repeat after me: Mason is always right, even when I think he's wrong." I press my lips into a hard line of disapproval.

Mason looks murderous. "I said repeat after me."

"'Mason is always right, even when I think he's wrong,'" I say bitterly. I take a step forward so that I now stand directly in front of him. I meet his eyes with angry defiance. "And Mason is always a smart aleck, even when he doesn't want to be."

Mason strikes me across the jaw. I wince from the pain.

I back away from him, massaging my jaw. "Abusing me isn't going to make me cooperate with you. I want to show you something."

I swallow, not sure if what I'm about to do is a good idea or not. Still, I see no reason why Mason should not see all the scars on my back. The thing is, I have been whipped so many times, that a fist to my jaw is nothing compared to what all I have experienced.

I grab a hold of the collar of my shirt and pull it up over my head. The cold air blasts my chest and back. I shiver. I turn around to show Mason my back. At last count, I had eight livid scars on my back. I have had to contend with all forms of abuse back home, and that's nothing compared to what Ethan has had to put up with. He has had one perverted agent after another whip him for not letting them have their way with him.

"What do you think," I say, imagining his eyes scanning across my back. "And, if you'd like to know specifics, I'd be more than willing to provide details. After all, they say the devil *is* in the details."

Silence. He must be in shock. I turn around, wanting to see his reaction. But Mason is nowhere to be seen. I hear the door we came through earlier close on its own. I thought he would come at me with a barrage of questions. In fact, I was looking forward to answering them. I hope I am not in any trouble.

I take a look around the room. It's so breathtakingly huge. It could easily accommodate thousands of people. And I still cannot get over how tall the ceiling is. You can only see so far up, and then it's shrouded in darkness. I may be wrong, but I think it could easily be a couple hundred feet to the top, maybe farther.

And then there's the floor. It looks as if it is one giant computer screen. The walls appear to be made out of the same dark material. I have a feeling that I have only experienced a glimpse of what all this room can do.

By the time I reach the door just outside our room, I feel a twinge of anxiety in my chest as my mind conjures up images of an angry or hostile Mason. Perhaps the reason why he left without commenting on my scars was because he felt like I just wanted to be pitied. Not so. Rather, I just wanted to show him that I am no stranger to abuse.

I take a hold of the doorknob. I swallow hard. If Mason plans on chewing me up and spitting me out, then so be it, but at least my conscience is clear.

I push the door open. I feel the tension of anxiety expanding in my chest.

I squeeze through the crack of the door, afraid to widen it too much for fear of immediate and hateful chastisement. Mason is so hard to please.

"Care to join me," Mason says in a polite tone of voice.

I stiffen in fear. Is this some kind of a joke? I search his face for any signs of duplicity. He sits in one of the two chairs, facing the door. He holds a box of what appears to be candy in one hand, with a small pile of its contents in the other.

Cautiously, I gently close the door behind me. I still can't help but wonder if this is a joke, just one of his many strange ways to toy with my mind.

Mason inclines his head to the chair in front of him. I stare at it apprehensively. I set out towards it.

"You know," Mason says in a gentle voice. "If I wanted to abuse you, I would have already done so. I don't want you to be terrified of me. I can see the fear and anxiety in your eyes."

I swallow. Now I feel even more vulnerable. He must view my distress as weakness and therefore wants to treat me with pretend kindness in hopes that I will be more willing to answer his questions. Well, if that is what the good doctor is banking on, then he will be disappointed. I am *not* stupid. I will not allow him to feel like he has control over me. The last thing I want is to spend what is likely the last few days of my life being manipulated by a lunatic.

I sit down and, just to show him my courage and strength, lean forward to look him straight in the eyes. His smile falters, green eyes startled.

"I know what you're trying to do," I say, earning a blank look from Mason. "But just to let you know, I am not the easiest person in the world to manipulate."

I stare at the pile of candy in his outstretched hand, already melted into a glob. "You want to show me kindness in hopes that my mind will become like clay in your hands. And, while I am sure that your tactics work well with beautiful women, they won't work with me."

I give him a satisfied look. Mason looks almost impassive, though I can see the wheels turning in his eyes. I can see him gathering his thoughts. I brace myself for a hostile response.

Mason sighs, looking sadder than I have seen him yet. "You're wrong. That's not at all what I was thinking. I merely wanted to prove to you that I am not the monster you think I am. Just because I do not like your kind doesn't mean that I hold a special grudge against you.

And yes," Mason adds, averting his eyes to the floor between us, "I saw your back. I never would have thought by looking at you that you had experienced so much abuse. But I know something without any doubt; you're stronger than I thought."

I feel the anger and desire to set him straight for his nastiness all but disappear. Something in his expression tells me that he is sincere. And just for that reason, I decide not to ask him why he left me shivering in the Mirage earlier.

I clear my throat. "Well, it would seem that I was wrong about you as well. But you're still on probation, just so you know. Until you prove to be trustworthy, I will still be suspicious of you."

Mason leans forward, careful not to drop his candy. He regards me with a shrewd look. "The more I'm around you, the more I come to realize just how much I have underestimated your kind. But then again, something tells me you're a cut above the rest of the Scripture babbling idiots. Tell me," Mason adds with a curious gleam in his eyes. "You must have continued to read and study despite the law forbidding ownership of books."

I swallow nervously. I wish he was not so observant. I search his face for any sign of deception, but I do not see any. He looks more interested to hear the truth than concerned about whether or not I broke the law. "Yes, I read on a regular basis until recently. I had my own private collection of books well hidden, so that none of your people would discover them. I also had a dictionary. In fact, Ethan used to ask me nearly every day what my favorite new word was. One day I told him that it was *deception.* When he asked me why, I shrugged it off, not willing to tell him about a dream that I had the previous night. But eventually, after I had the same dream twice, I finally felt compelled to tell him. And so I did. I told him as much as I could remember, including the giant mounds of grain that touched the sky and the gentle voice behind the words."

Mason wets his lips absently, green eyes thoughtful. "Gentle voice, you say, like a man or a woman's?"

"A man's," I say. "Why?"

Mason leans back in his chair with a bewildered look. "I thought I knew all about your dreams, having heard them recited so many times over the course of the last several months. But I can see now that my informants were not nearly as well informed as they thought they were. For even the smallest piece of evidence can shed a considerable amount of light on the narrative of events."

I narrow my eyes onto him. "What do you mean by that?"

Mason smiles, looking pleased. "I mean to say that the *devil* is in the details."

I recoil. "Oh, so now you think I'm demon possessed or something? Is that it?"

"Not necessarily," Mason says with a speculative look. "Demons are much too valuable to waste their time on someone like you. And since they practice deception, it is highly unlikely that the voice in your dreams was a demon. Now, if the voice in your dreams never mentioned deception that would be one thing, but you say the voice clearly does. It makes sense," Mason adds with a look of putting two and two together. "If you want to lead someone into a snare, you don't take them to the spot and point it out to them. That would defeat the purpose. Likewise, if you want someone to believe something other than the truth, you tell a lie. It's really that simple. Perhaps the same goes for your dream. Why even bother to bring up deception if the voice you heard really wanted to deceive you? Again, that would defeat the purpose."

I shake my head wearily. "So you're a liar as well? Why does that not surprise me? But I guess lies are but a small sin compared to all the things your kind of people do. I have heard stories of agents sleeping with their children as well as participating in other immoral acts just to temporarily sate their insatiable lust."

Mason looks on me with scorn. "Just because people act differently doesn't mean they are bad."

I raise my eyebrows. "Oh really? So you think it's okay for a man to sleep with his daughter, or even his son? Or you think it's fine for men to take teenage boys into their beds just because they can get away with it? Or that the sexual harassment of Christians by perverted agents is perfectly acceptable?"

Mason throws a hand up. "Slow down, you're giving me a headache. And no, I don't necessarily agree with those who act that way, but that still doesn't make it wrong. But need I remind you, I am a physician, Ryan. Believe me; I am fully aware of the kinds of diseases that ravage the bodies of people who are driven by lust. And it's not pretty."

I give Mason a surprised look. "You just said my name."

"So," Mason says with a shrug. "I can do anything I want, remember? Well, except incapacitate or murder you. And as long as you continue to talk to me like you are doing right now, you might get more respect yet."

I blink in surprise. "But I didn't think you liked it when I disagreed with you."

Mason swallows almost imperceptibly. "There's nothing wrong with disagreeing with me. You can disagree with me without hating me."

I'm so confused. "But you told me not to disagree with you, that everything you say and do is always right even if it's wrong."

Mason nods. "In public, yes. And by public, I mean anyplace where there are other people besides you and me. There are eyes and ears all throughout the compound that will be paying particularly close attention to how you behave. I do not want them to think that I have, in any way, made you superior to them. At the same time, I cannot study you properly without allowing you to act like yourself, to an extent. But I warn you, don't speak unless you're spoken to. And ask for my permission before you say a word."

Okay, so let me make sure I've got this down. "So you want me to live two different lives, to be somewhat vocal and engaging when we're alone while kissing your signet ring in public?"

Mason lowers his eyes to an ornate ring on his right hand. "You *are* observant. Yes, that is exactly what I want you to do, figuratively speaking, of course. If anyone saw you actually kissing my ring in public they'd instantly know that something was wrong, and I cannot afford for that to happen."

I extend a hand to him for a shake. "Okay good doctor, you're on."

Mason stares at my hand in disgust. "No, I do not shake hands, period."

I withdraw my hand from him with an insidious smile. "It's just as well. I wasn't planning on saying anything, but since you're a physician I might as well.

You see, I often find myself massaging a painful sore that refuses to heal. It's really quite embarrassing."

Mason searches my body with keen eyes. "Where is it located?"

I put a hand over my heart. "My heart, good doctor. I miss my family and friends. And the hole in my heart suggests I am dying. I think I am losing the will to live." And despite the fact that it started off as a joke, I can't help but feel that it ended in truth.

Mason looks deeply troubled. "Well I can't have that. How can I expect to perform a proper study of you if you are on the decline?" He says this seriously, as if his study of me is more important than my well-being.

Mason looks at me with pity. "While I do not want most of the people around here to be aware of my leniency with you, there are a few people who I believe I can trust. One of them is Carrie. And since you tell me that your heart is in such great need of attention, perhaps you should take me up on my offer and allow me to invite her here to talk to you. And no," Mason adds, narrowing his eyes onto me. "I know what you're thinking, that based on our interaction this morning, Carrie must not think too highly of me, but you're wrong. I was the one that rescued her and gave her the job she has as senior maid. Even Carrie will tell you that she owes her life to me."

I find that hard to believe. "As long as you're sure, but I hope you don't think that her company will in any way fill the hole in my heart, 'cause it won't."

Mason grumbles under his breath. "I need you to be as engaging as possible. And if a pretty girl will help heal the hole in your heart, then so be it."

I stare at his biceps. I think I know what he has up his sleeves. "What about you? I can see Carrie kissing you easier than I can see her wanting to talk to me. Besides," I add with a disapproving frown, "there's a girl back home that I'm kind of fond of."

Mason looks captivated. "She must be really pretty for you to turn down a chance to hang out with Carrie."

I cannot help but smile. "Oh she's pretty alright. The problem I had was mustering enough courage to talk to her. And I never seemed to have the right moment."

Mason gives me a knowing look. "Women can be tricky creatures at the best of times. And believe it or not, I have always found it difficult to approach the women who catch my eyes. And by catch my eyes, I do not just mean by appearance only. I find a gentle spirit about as appealing as good looks."

Has he been drugged? "Okay, good doctor, so let me get this straight. If what you told me is true, then wouldn't that make you a gentleman? I mean, in order for you to say what you did, in order to favor gentle women, you must be gentle as well. Because I find it hard to believe that someone with a gentle personality would prefer someone who wants to prance around like they are the most impressive thing on the face of the earth. So, the real question is, why do you act so haughty in public, but not alone with me?"

Mason looks impressed, if not moderately uncomfortable. "I think you know the answer to that question. I already said that I cannot hope to make a proper study of you if you feel uncomfortable with me. How many times must I repeat myself? Believe me; if I thought I could get away with treating you like the scum you are and still get the answers I wanted, don't you think I would? But that's just not possible. But to answer your question," Mason adds with a pointed look, "I am somewhat of a rarity around here. That is why there are two beds in this room instead of one, for instance. I want you to trust me, to feel comfortable around me. Again, you are lucky that you got stuck with me and not one of the other guards, however much you dislike me. Not all of my fellow guardsmen are as tolerant as I am. That said, you need to be very careful. There are those who would seek to use you for their own means."

I bite down onto my lip. "Like as a weapon or something?"

Mason considers this with a frown. "Possibly, but you need to realize how different you are. Need I say more? Now stand up so that I can get a good look at you."

I rise to my feet. I feel the circulation returning to my legs. They fell asleep at some point during our conversation.

Mason crooks a finger at his lips, green eyes appraising me. "I still can't believe that you look as good as you do. I mean, it's not like you have enjoyed the best food that nature has to offer."

Mason takes a step forward and takes my wrist. He presses a thumb against my artery as he checks his watch. "You have a strong pulse. That's a good sign of a strong healthy body. It will also make your job less taxing for you."

I raise an eyebrow as he stares at my chest. "What is it? Want to listen to a broken heart?"

Mason frowns with disapproval. "No, I was just thinking, that's all."

I throw my arms out with a yawn. "So what's next on our agenda, good doctor?"

Mason almost smiles.

I take a step forward and wag a finger at him. "You like it when I call you that don't you? But the question is why do you like it so much?"

Mason pushes aside my finger with a small smile. "You're too smart for your own good. But yes, I like being called 'good doctor'. Now," Mason adds with a trace of exasperation in his voice, "I have to finish showing you around before the Saints come marching in."

Astonished, I stand firm, surprised at his admittance.

Mason turns around to face me at the door. "As soon as we walk out this door, you're nothing more than a filthy Saint-boy who knows that he must do everything I say."

"Of course," I say with pretend enthusiasm.

Mason beckons me to the door. "And remember, don't speak unless you're spoken to, and act like you can't stand me."

I nod. This is starting to get interesting.

Chapter Five

I remain quiet as I walk beside Mason. He's not as bad as I thought he was. And yet, something in the back of my mind is warning me against trusting him. Of course, I do not know him as well as I would like, but I have no other alternative. But it seems like someone warned me against placing my trust in him. And I believe it was Carrie. Of course, but it was just a dream.

I scold myself inwardly at the thought of jumping over the last few steps on the staircase. I do not want to compromise our deception. But I can tell that, beneath Mason's hard mask of pretend hatred of me, there is a faint beam of light just dying to escape. Could it be that he actually likes me?

Mason leads me past the cafeteria. It is such a big room. I wish we could stop and get a bite to eat.

I wonder what the seating arrangements will be like. Despite wanting to ask Mason about this, I keep my mouth shut for obvious reasons. But I know one thing; this room has the capacity to seat several dozen people. Sturdy oak benches line both sides of the tables, their grains and knots standing out on the yellow wood like scars.

As we reach the end of the room, Mason steers me towards the elevator. I would much rather take the stairwell, if I had a choice. I can't stand elevators. Back home at the Hub, we had no choice but to use the elevator. Since the Hub was shaped like a corncob, I suppose it would have been a costly engineering feat to have to design a staircase to reach to the fiftieth floor.

Mason jabs a finger on the button, prompting the door to glide open. I move forward to stand beside him.

Already I feel my palms moistening with sweat in anticipation of what all I will find in the basement. Mason steps into the elevator with a haughty air of superiority. With a silent prayer on my lips, I step in after him.

I take a deep breath to try to calm myself. I hope we don't drop like a rock to the bottom of the ocean. I'm always afraid that every elevator I ride on will malfunction.

The door glides open, and I jostle past Mason to get out. I come face to face with the infirmary.

There are six beds on wheels, each adorned with long white pillows. A long counter runs the length of one side of the room, with a built in sink and adjacent paper towel holder. A single examination table occupies the space between the counter and the beds. A refrigerator and microwave oven punctuates the end of the counter. Several IV machines, along with boxes presumably filled with medical supplies line the other side of the room.

Mason walks past me with an air of professionalism that suits the place. Admittedly, until this point, I have found it hard to believe that he really was a doctor. He just seems so hateful and callous to possess the willingness and skills necessary to help people. But then again, I have no idea just how capable he is. For all I know, he could be a really great doctor.

"Sit down," Mason says, nodding at the examination table. "I need to mark you."

I back up to the examination table and, pressing my hands down firmly, hoist myself up onto it. Mason opens a cabinet door above the counter. I swing my feet back and forth nervously. He never mentioned anything about marking me. Why do I need to be marked? It's unlikely that I will leave this building anytime soon.

Mason turns around to face me, a fat silver pen gripped tightly in an outstretched hand. What does he plan on doing? Perhaps he wants to draw an X over my heart to symbolize my hazardous nature?

"Give me your hand," Mason says, but not unkindly.

I offer it to him. He takes it gently. He stoops over and runs a finger across the back of my hand. I shiver.

"What are you doing," I say, ready to withdraw my hand at a moment's notice.

Mason meets my eyes with warning. I could kick myself. I'm not supposed to speak out of turn. He turns back to my hand.

"I'm going to insert a microchip into your hand," Mason says casually. "You'll need to be very still. It will sting a little bit, but it is essential."

I look at my hand, at Mason's fingers holding mine, at the fine crisscrosses covering his smooth skin. He takes good care of himself, that much is evident. I feel a sharp stab of pain, reminding me a lot of a wasp sting. I jerk my hand away from him with a scowl. He lied. I should have known I couldn't trust him.

Mason straightens up with a smile playing on his lips. "I told you it would sting, so don't look at me like that."

I would like to tell him much the same, but I can't. Instead, I school my face to appear submissive. Oh how I would love to just reach out and jab a finger into his chest. And, if it wasn't for the satisfied smile that I see trying to burst forth from beneath his surly smirk, I might just do it. I think when it comes to acting; Mason does as good a job as me, if not better. I will have to be on my guard.

Mason checks his watch. He meets my eyes. "The Saints will be arriving soon. It will be during this time when the guards who are responsible for training them will make their selections. Needless to say," Mason adds in a matter-of-fact tone, "you will get whatever is left over. Whichever four Saints remain after my fellow guardsmen make their selections will be yours. In short, since the best will be snatched up, you will end up with the dead beats."

I give Mason an inquisitive look. He gives me permission to speak. I take a deep breath. "How are these people going to be treated? I mean, should I expect to see them in the same clothes day after day or what?"

Mason shakes his head, green eyes disgusted. "No one wants to be around a herd of smelly Saints. No, after they are divided into teams, they will be brought here to be marked and bathed. You can lend a helping hand at that time if you'd like."

I recoil. He's not joking. I wait for permission to speak. Mason inclines his head at me with permission.

I shake my head as I rise to my feet. "I have no desire to bathe anyone other than myself. These people are like me, good upstanding people who have been taught not to flash their naked bodies around like scum. The last thing I want to do is to humiliate them by looking at their nakedness. Besides, it'll be bad enough for them without me standing over them with a palm full of shampoo."

I hear someone enter the room. I look at Mason. He looks troubled. Someone claps their hands together. I stiffen in fear.

"How commendable," says a sarcastic male voice from behind me.

I turn around slowly, my heart slamming against my rib cage. I blink in surprise. The guy in front of me makes Mason's pretend haughtiness look positively angelic. He has on orange leather pants, and a brown T-shirt.

"Christian," Mason says curiously. "What brings you down here?"

Christian sashays forward, blue shoes about as annoying as his haughty blue eyes. "I came to visit Carrie. But not for the reasons you may think. If she had only done her job to begin with, I would be resting right now. Still," Christian adds, giving me a superior smirk, "I can see that it was indeed worthwhile to make a trip down here."

This guy needs a major attitude adjustment. Never before have I seen anyone act so haughty.

Christian narrows his eyes in disgust at the wrinkled paper on the examination table. He gives me a condescending smile. "Why is it that everything you Saints come into contact with becomes defiled? I thought you believed in purification and perfection."

He wants to make trouble. I catch myself frowning, and quickly school my face to appear impassive to the best of my ability.

Christian picks up on this. "Oh, you disagree? Well then, please try to set me straight."

I look at Mason for permission to speak. The last thing I need is to turn him against me. He nods for me to speak.

I turn back to Christian. I swallow hard, my nervousness likely evident. "There was only ever one perfect man, and they nailed him to a cross two thousand years ago as payment for our sins."

Christian raises his eyebrows in disbelief. "You say 'they'. Why is it that your kind never can explain themselves? It's always they or because the good book says. I'd say you don't know what you're talking about? So tell me," Christian adds with a mixture of hostility and amusement in his voice. "Who are *they*?"

I clear my throat. "Well, best I can remember, Jesus Christ was murdered by a group of religious leaders who were offended at hearing the gospel truth. He did nothing wrong. He presented the Word of God, but it hurt their pride, so they put him to death. But," I add with mounting courage, "He willingly gave himself up. He didn't have to. He was perfect and very gentle, and could have called upon any number of angels to come to His rescue. But yes, we Christians believe in trying to live as purely as possible, not to say that we don't make mistakes every once in a while, but still."

Christian claps a hand over his heart dramatically. "How very touching," he says, flicking his eyes to Mason. "I am so glad I'm not a Saint. I have no desire to give up my wicked ways. And here lately, I have had so many offers to display every square inch of my flawless body, and I am half considering giving it a try. Perhaps I will help bathe and clothe the incoming Saints. I have heard the most bizarre stories regarding their bodies. For instance," Christian adds, turning back to me. "Your kind turns their noses up at belly button rings and hot tattoos. No wonder why you all always look so miserable, you don't know how to have fun."

I give him a chiding look. "What your kind calls fun only leads to destruction."

Christian steps forward and takes the hem of his shirt into his hands. He pulls it up to his neck to reveal a solid abdomen and a tattoo of a set of lips over his heart. Christian points to the set of lips. "See these? This is the path to my heart. I only let the hottest girls kiss me here. These lips are a replica of my very own, in case you haven't noticed."

Talk about ridiculous. He clearly has too much time on his hands. I shake my head. Mason does not look surprised.

Christian turns to the side and places a hand on his butt. "I have an even hotter tattoo here. Just don't ask me to show it to you."

That's fine with me, like I want to see it anyway. But at least he isn't like Perverted Demon, who once lowered his pants to show Emily and I a tattoo of a lily pad on his butt. He forced us to watch. I threw up all of my lunch shortly thereafter. Ethan, bless his soul, came to our rescue and consoled us until we were done vomiting. Fortunately for Ethan, he was in the old shed and stayed hidden until Perverted Demon left. He stayed by our side until we recovered.

"There's work to be done," Mason says in a professional voice, earning an irritated look from Christian. "Everyone around here knows that you have a nice body, Christian. But unless we finish preparations for our soon to arrive guests, we will be asking for trouble. It'd be such a pity to have to shackle Saints to the prison walls on the first night of their arrival."

Looking disappointed, Christian lowers his shirt and gives it a tug at the hem to adjust it. "Perhaps you're right. But I hope the other guards make it in time. I think the storm clouds may have slowed their progress."

Mason nods in agreement. "Most likely, but I'm not worried. They haven't let us down yet."

Christian eyes me suspiciously. "You're hiding something, I know it. Let me guess, you have a tattoo somewhere but you're too ashamed to show it off."

I raise an eyebrow. "Do I look like the kind of guy who would have such a thing? Just because the Hub provides free tattoos doesn't mean I have one. Wait a second," I add at Christian's mounting hatred of me. "The reason I don't have a tattoo is because God specifically spoke against them in the Bible. It's one of the requirements to keep a holy body unto God."

Christian looks at me like I am an idiot. "Your God sounds way too picky. I think you'd be happier if you'd forsake him for our gods. Then you could do whatever you want."

I try not to lose my tempter. "First off, there is only one God. He is the God of Abraham, Isaac, and Jacob, the same God who rescued the children of Israel from Egyptian bondage. Besides Him, there is no other God. He has every right to tell people how to live since He created them."

Christian looks unconvinced. "I don't believe that for a moment. How could only one God create everything around us? Furthermore, what God in his right mind would want to be so boring?"

I swallow. "He's not boring. He's very awesome. I miss reading his Word on a regular basis. It was exciting to read all about how God dealt with people in biblical times. If people would get back to reading the Word of God, they would find out just how far they have strayed from the way God intended for us to live."

Christian gives Mason a pitied look. "So this is the kind of crap you have to put up with. I am so glad I am not you. I think I would strangle him if I had to hear a sermon every day."

Mason nods. "But I have ways of dealing with him. He knows there are limitations to what I will allow from him. Rest assured, I have him well under control."

"I know that," Christian says, but not unkindly. "If anyone could handle a Saint-boy, it'd be you. If it was up to me, I would have already killed him by now. But enough of that," Christian adds with a glimpse of disgust at me. "What about all the Saints that are soon to arrive? You know they'll probably come quoting those terrible Scriptures. That's one thing I don't understand about Saints, the desire to quote Scripture in one breath and then shove their tongues down each other's throats in the next."

I try not to lose my tempter. "I think you've heard wrong. I don't know of any true Christians who do that. Just because someone says that they are a Christian doesn't necessarily mean that that is the case. Talk is cheap but actions go a lot further in demonstrating who a person really is."

Mason looks like he could yell at me. "That's enough. I didn't bring you hear to preach to us. Christian and I have more important things to do besides listen to you flap your mouth about things that we care nothing about. Now then," Mason says, looking at Christian, "the last thing I want to think about is a Saint revolt, but as you know, it cannot be completely ruled out. So, if you don't mind, I'd appreciate it if you would help keep order tonight."

Christian places a hand over his heart with a facetious smile. "I know just the way. I could let the Saint-girls kiss my lips if they promise to behave. As for the guys, I'm not sure; lest it be to give them permission to let their hormones run wild with excitement in exchange for cooperating with us. I bet we'd see just how immoral Saint-boys could be, despite their claims of righteousness."

Mason rolls his eyes, absently slips a hand into his pocket. "We'll see, but first, let's try to maintain them with whips and fists. If that doesn't work, we have several cells to imprison the disobedient."

"So be it," Christian says stiffly. "But I intend to have some fun with these people before their lives end. And if any of the Saint-girls please my picky eyes, I might just invite them to bed with me. Oh yes," Christian adds with a wistful sigh. "I have always wondered what it would be like to bed a Saint. Surely they're not as boring and shy as they make themselves out to be, but I intend to find out. Besides, should one of them become pregnant after a night of…frolicking with me, the baby would never be born, because they'd likely be dead before long anyway. But of course that would depend entirely on which team survives the final challenge."

Mason shakes his head with a sigh. "Whatever you want Christian, just don't hurt them. Remember, President Gloss wants eight teams fully trained and ready to entertain him before too much longer. Should you break any ribs or any other bones in your wild excitement, he wouldn't be very happy."

Christian smiles, shows a perfect set of bright white teeth. "I *am* gentle Mason. The last thing I want is to hurt a girl, even a Saint-girl."

I fist my hands at my sides. From the way he talks, we Christians are nothing more than fascinating objects to experiment with, as if our bodies are somehow different than his. Christian may be blessed with good looks, but when it comes down to it, he still has four limbs, not to mention an exceptionally dirty mouth.

Christian flashes Mason a mischievous smile and then looks at me. "I will expect your advice about which Saint-girl would be the best choice to try before long, so I'd keep a close look out if I were you. Not that I will go with any of your suggestions, but still. But I must warn you: Should you recommend a girl who ends up boring me to death, I will force you to do everything to her that I intended to do myself. Who knows, you might just end up a father before the week is out."

I swallow hard. Christian crooks me a dangerous smile. He takes off towards the elevator, strutting like a buck in rut.

I turn to Mason. His eyes are fixed on Christian's back. He looks like he wants to join Christian, but because of me, he has to stay behind.

Mason gives me a dangerous look. "I'd be careful if I was you. Christian wasn't joking. And don't expect me to save you should he come seeking your advice. He and I are like brothers. But if you continue to cooperate with me, I might be able to deflect some of his attention away from you and onto somebody else."

I give him a grateful nod. I let out a sigh of relief. "Why does he dress like that? I mean, how can he expect anyone to take him seriously when he looks like a freak?"

Mason leans forward and yanks me to him by the collar. I throw out a hand on the edge of the examination table to right myself. I swallow hard.

Mason looks like he could rip me into shreds. "Christian is my friend, not to mention a fellow guardsman. If he asked me to remove one of your eyeballs and preserve it for him as a present, I would be obliged to do it for him. He may look like a freak to you, but he is a skillful fighter. What we did earlier today in the Mirage was nothing. Christian *never* misses."

I am tempted to point out that *he* is the one who messed up, not me. He lets go of my shirt. The bad thing is, I do not see any sign of respect, of friendliness in Mason's expression whatsoever. It has all but vanished.

I pass the remainder of the afternoon helping Mason unpack boxes of shampoo, tooth paste, and everything else conceivable for the maintenance of the human body.

"Oh," Mason says, rising to his feet from a crouch. He reaches into his pocket with a weak smile.

I lay down a package filled with fingernail clippers onto the top of a box. I can't help but feel suspicious.

Mason pulls a silky blue cloth from his pocket. He offers it to me. "Here, I meant to give this to you earlier today, you'll need it."

I take the folded cloth from Mason's hand. I search Mason's face for any sign of a joke, but the weak smile on his face suggests otherwise. I unfold the cloth to reveal a very nice wrist watch. I take that back. I have never seen a wrist watch this nice. Even the watch Mason currently wears does not look this luxurious. I run a finger around its smooth golden face.

I swallow hard. No one has ever given me something this nice before. I look at Mason. "Are you sure you want me to have this," I say.

Mason nods. "If you are to be convincing at playing your part, you must look the part. Plus, you're going to have to monitor the time for yourself. I don't want you bothering me all the time over something that you can do yourself."

I lower my eyes to the watch. "Are you sure it's not too nice for me? I mean, won't it look out of place on me?"

Mason shakes his head. "No, and besides, I can do whatever I want around here. No one can prevent me from giving you a tool to help you. Now," Mason adds, taking a step closer. "Are you going to put it on or do you want me to take it back?"

I meet his eyes. "This may sound stupid, but I've never owned anything this nice before. I'm afraid I'll break it."

Mason lets out an annoyed sigh, takes the watch from my hand. With his free hand, he tugs at the blue cloth, lets it fall to the floor. Looking uncharacteristically pleased, Mason begins fastening the watch onto my wrist. I look between his increasingly sad expression and the careful movements of his fingers. It is as if he is trying hard not to hurt me or scare me. I swallow back my mixed emotion. Honestly, I feel like I am in the eye of a hurricane right now, awaiting the tumultuous winds and pelting rain to remind me of my dire situation.

"There," Mason says, adjusting my watch. His green eyes travel from my wrist to the top of my hand, his lips parted, as if there is something he wants to tell me. He meets my eyes. "I just can't get over how healthy you look."

What does he think, that I'm supposed to look like a walking corpse?

I look at the tiny red dot on my hand where Mason inserted the chip. "Why did you mark me? I mean, it's obvious that escape from this place is next thing to impossible."

Mason looks at the dot of blood on my hand. "It was necessary in order to allow you to better communicate with Jane. It will allow her to sense your exact location in the Mirage, like she did with me. Without it, you would not be able to control her. It will also allow her to distinguish who among your team has authority. Every guard, including myself has one. As for the incoming Saints, they too will be marked, only without the command of authority."

"It's five o'clock," Mason says almost inaudibly. He lets go of my wrist and meets my eyes. "The Saints should be here at any time. We had best make our way to the obstacle course room."

After a few minutes, we arrive on the threshold of the obstacle course room with the expectation of seeing a flurry of activity. What we see, however, is just the opposite. The room is completely devoid of life. I brace a hand against the wall to catch my breath, while Mason stands on the threshold, green eyes both curious and relieved.

Mason shrugs. "Perhaps their souls are here, and we just can't see them." He laughs at his own joke. "I imagine they'll…"

A loud voice echoes down the hallway behind me, cutting Mason off. "They're here," says an unfamiliar voice. I stiffen with fear and anxiety as footsteps draw closer. "Hey!"

I flinch at the loud exclamation beside me. I turn around to find a guy about Mason's age giving me a measured look.

"So you are the guy who refused to keep his dreams to himself. If I was you, I'd practice keeping my mouth shut, lest someone contributes to the bruising on your chin."

"There's no need to terrorize him, Jace," Mason says with a smile. Jace meets Mason's eyes with pretend hatred, a smile tugging at the corners of his mouth.

I get the impression that Mason and Jace are close friends, maybe even closer than Mason and Christian are. Jace fists a hand and sends it flying towards Mason's chest. He stops short, and then gently presses his knuckles onto Mason's chest. Mason knocks his hand away, as if an annoying fly.

Jace backs up and nearly runs into me. He has dark blond hair and a body about as solid as Mason's. "This whole Saint business has me freaked out, literally. What if I get struck down by lightening or something by speaking against them? Perhaps I should give each of the four Saints I choose a kiss, just to avert calamity. If they're all girls, I mean. For the guys, I might…I don't know, shake their hand or something."

Mason gives him a worried look. "And take a chance of getting Saint-pox? I'd refrain from touching any of them if I were you."

I find Mason's statement ridiculous, especially since he showed no signs of concern when he adorned my wrist with a new watch earlier. But I suppose he is just keeping up appearances.

Jace turns around to face me. I know I should probably be somewhat afraid of him, but I'm not. He looks harmless enough, what with his blue eyes and jagged bangs. Unlike Jack and Christian, the only other guards I have met here, Jace seems easier going.

"Is that true," Jace says with a wary look. "Saint-pox, I mean."

I can tell that Mason doesn't seem as opposed to me talking around Jace. I give Jace a steady look. "Oh it's true all right. But it really depends on the person, on whether they're willing to accept a change of heart. If you're not, then you have nothing to worry about. So go ahead," I add with an outstretched hand, "if you're willing to take the risk."

Jace gives my hand a suspicious look. "I don't think I'm ready to touch one of you just yet. Not until I know that you pose no danger to me."

"Fair enough," I say, lowering my hand to my side. "I…this whole experience is new to me as well, so I guess caution's not a bad thing." Jace nods stiffly.

Voices. Jace jerks his head down the hallway towards the approaching noise. "I think we had best take our positions."

"Let's go," Mason says. He crosses the threshold and heads towards the catwalk. Jace walks beside him, while I follow along behind them.

Jace suddenly surges past Mason and takes a hold of the ladder. "Let me go first," he says with hysteria. "The last thing I want is to end up stoned to death like Goliath."

"But surely you're not afraid," Mason says, teasing him.

Mason nods for me to go next. I wait until Jace reaches the top before taking hold of the ladder. I twist around to find Mason giving me a solemn look.

"Remember not to speak unless spoken to," Mason says, giving me a sharp look.

I make my way towards the top. I hear several inhospitable voices drifting in from out of the hallway. It sounds like the guards are cursing the Saints to hurry up. I swallow hard. I pull myself to my feet. Jace leans against the guardrail, the tip of his shoe hanging off the side of the catwalk.

"They're nearly here," Mason says, jabbing me in the back to get out of the way. "Move to the other side of Jace."

Jace leans forward against the guardrail as I pass by him. I step up to the guardrail, careful to keep a respectful distance from Jace. I feel a vibration through my shoes as Mason rushes down the catwalk behind me.

I look down at the floor below. I would say that we are every bit of thirty feet in the air. I visualize Christian spitting on the heads of Saints below and laughing if he was here with us.

I see movement out of the corner of my eye. I jerk my head towards the hallway. The first of the Saints are spilling into the room, their faces registering mixed forms of emotion. One girl looks as if she has been crying while the guy next to her looks like a walking statue, his movements stiff and painful.

They're coming in faster now. It looks like there are already twelve or fifteen of them in the room. I hear Christian's sharp voice sail like a knife from down the hallway, shouting for everyone to get a move on.

Jack emerges from the mouth of the hallway, his brown eyes skirting over Jace, Mason, and then onto me. He looks tired, despite his attempt to look on top of everything going on around him.

Several guards who I have never seen before begin pouring into the room. Christian is among them. I hope he stays on the ground. The last thing I need is for Christian to be up here pestering me for advice about girls, especially when he has no desire to respect them. Rather, Christian seems only concerned about humiliating them for his own pleasure.

The guards fan out and surround the Saints. I know I probably shouldn't be calling them Saints, because it's not entirely respectful, but I feel it's necessary to train my mind to do so in order to avoid getting punished for addressing them more respectfully.

Not surprisingly, many of the Saints look in need of a hardy meal and a good rest. Just a few of them show signs of malnourishment or underdevelopment. I can see the differences in how each one of them have been treated. I have no doubt that some of them have enjoyed more food than others. Since all of them are currently staring at the floor, I cannot get a good look at their faces, but the rest of their bodies speak volumes.

I feel sorry for all of the Saints. Having just been torn away from everything I held dear in life, I know exactly how they feel. Or do I? No, perhaps I don't. Despite what I think about Mason, I believe he was right when he said that had he not got me, I would have been at the mercy of someone like Christian. And that would have made my entire experience that much worse. There is no telling what all these people have suffered. But I know one thing; I'm going to try my best to treat them with as much kindness and respect as I can without bringing down the wrath of our oppressors on my head.

"Listen up," Mason shouts. "Look up here all you Saints."

One by one, several sets of eyes peel away from the floor and look up in this direction. I stiffen as many of them look at me. I grip the guardrail to calm my nerves. Remembering that I am supposed to act like a guard, I school my face to try to look important, though I feel like a tadpole among mature frogs. I feel a bead of sweat run down my back.

Mason claps his hands together loudly, sending a shock wave of terror across the room. Not to mention sending my heart into cardiac arrest. I swallow hard. That was unnecessary, but it did seem to get everyone's attention.

"You all know why you're here," Mason says, his voice hard as flint and laced with disgust. "The days of quoting Scripture are over. You broke the law so now you must pay the price. Each one of you stands condemned to face the challenging days ahead, and I assure you they will be anything but heavenly. Now," Mason adds with an irritable twitch at the corner of his mouth, "you are about to be released to go to the various obstacles throughout the room. You will continue to make your way around the room until we have had time to evaluate you at each station. Then, you will be divided up into eight separate teams, with four Saints per team. And while these teams will be your new family from that point onwards, you will still be expected to treat everyone from all the other teams with equal respect. Should any of you disobey and get into a scuffle of sorts, well, you'll find that we are well equipped around here to doll out the most brutal if not excruciatingly painful punishments."

Mason looks past me to Jace. "Was there anything you wanted to add?"

Jace faces the crowd with a hard look. "Some of you Saint-boys may think that just because you're in a group with a bunch of Saint-girls, that you will find companionship. And, while we certainly have nothing against Saint-boys kissing their sweethearts, should you try anything else, you'll find that we have special punishment reserved for any…unwanted activity. The same goes for you Saint-girls, though from what I hear, Saint-girls are usually less flirtatious in their quest for love. But know this," Jace adds with harsh eyes, "I will personally be monitoring all of you to ensure that none of you lets your hormones get in the way of your training."

Mason lets out a shriek of a whistle. I force myself to remain impassive, despite wanting to scrunch up my face.

Mason looks nastier than I have seen him yet. "I want no more than four Saints at each station. And keep in mind that, while you train, the guy or girl next to you could well become your teammate, so don't try to do anything to make them look bad. Each of you will be evaluated not only on your own performance, but also on how well you interact with the other Saints at your stations. Now get moving."

I wish Mason didn't have to be so hateful. I grip the guardrail in a flare of anger, though I try to keep it from my face. It's like he lives to bring people misery. I think he should have chosen a different field of study. Doctors are supposed to have caring personalities, and Mason has just the opposite.

I watch in sympathy as several of my brothers and sisters head towards the weight lifting station, which is the closest. Nearly all of them show signs of intense perspiration, evidenced in the large splotches of sweat on their white T-shirts. My heart goes out to them, even though I am also in a bad situation. I just want to go to them and let them know that they are not alone, that as much as they likely feel hopeless and afraid, they're not in a complete nest of vipers.

"They're so pretty," Jace says in a whisper in my ear. "I saw several Saint-girls that caught my eye. I have to admit, I am shocked. But let me guess," Jace adds with a sly smile, "you Saints enjoy divine beauty treatments or something. Perhaps you can spare some time to fill me in on how you Saints look so good."

"Not you too," I say, hearing the nervousness in my voice. "Christian has already included me in his warped plans to…Look; our bodies are no different than yours, so why do you all make it out like we come from another planet?"

Jace shrugs, looking uncertain. "Maybe if you all showed a little more skin, our imaginations wouldn't be quite so apt to run wild."

I scowl, hardly believing what I just heard. I do a quick survey around us to ensure our privacy. Everyone looks busy, including the guards. Behind me, I hear Mason shouting to the Saints at the dart station to pick up the pace. The sounds of shoes scuffing against the wooden floor as well as all the other noise has given me a good environment to talk to Jace in without fear of being overheard. From the sound of it, the tree stumps at the exercise station must be more difficult to stack on top of each other than I thought. The example pillar, composed of five polished stumps, is an unreasonable expectation in my mind.

I take a deep breath. I might as well get off my chest what I want to say. Undoubtedly sensing our relative privacy, Jace now stands with his back against the guardrail, his arms crossed over his chest. He regards me with a quizzical frown, as if not quite sure what to expect from me.

I part my lips to speak, but decide it best to ask for permission first. Then, if I say something that angers him, I will have something to use in my defense. "Can I speak?"

Jace considers this. "I guess, just make sure you choose your words carefully. I'd hate to have to throw you overboard should you anger me." What does he think that we are standing on, a plank of wood over deep and foreboding waters?

I swallow hard. I do not think he was serious, but still. His message was clear. To Jace, I am just an object of interest, something less than human. I can tell that he is having the time of his life. But I think he and Mason would find me more interesting if they would just give me a little more leeway to express myself.

To avoid being abused, I think it best to gradually build up to what I really want to say. I clear my throat. I give Jace a cautious look. "Other than being *Saints*, what is the other commonality among our new guests?"

Jace looks shocked, perhaps by my thought process. He crooks a finger at his lips, blue eyes appraising me. "Let's see, you all look like you're afraid we'll gobble you up at any moment, as if we are the barbarians instead of you. Or, it could be that you all have this sad, stray puppy dog look about you. Do you want me to take you in and rub your ears?"

I don't think Jace is as moral a person as I thought. I try to keep the concern from my face. "Consider their clothing. You make it out like they're boring to look at when it's your kind who determined their attire. Wait," I add quickly, throwing a hand up. Jace looks ready to clobber me.

The floor vibrates, bringing Mason closer to us. I need to be quick. "Try to imagine yourself in our position. I'm sure that you have great talents otherwise you wouldn't be in the position you are in, but still. My kind endures great persecution on a regular basis, while your kind enjoys comfort and luxuries that we could only ever dream of. Don't forget, your blood runs just as red as mine."

Jace looks at me with a glint of anger in his eyes. He uncrosses his arms and hurtles forward. He grips my throat, his fingers digging into my neck. "Don't think for a moment that just because you're standing up here with me that you're my equal, because you're not. You'll never be one of us. And, for the record, my blood is far superior to yours. I come from the ruling class. You come from those who don't know their right hand from their left. Without us, your kind would be doddering around in the daylight, as if at night."

I swallow against Jace's grip. He releases me and I take a deep breath. I rub my throat, sure that I would see red marks left behind by his fingers if I had a mirror. I take a step backward. I did not expect this from him, maybe from Christian, but not him.

I lower my hand. Jace eyes my throat predatorily. A hand grips my shoulder and spins me around. I stagger and throw out a hand to right myself. I give Mason a chiding look.

"Very nice," Mason says, green eyes taking in my throat. "I told you to keep your mouth shut, but it looks like you didn't take me seriously. You should think Jace by the way, from the looks of it, he went easy on you.

Now let's go," Mason adds with haste. "It's time for you to meet your team. While you were babbling away like a fool, we separated the culls from the herd for you. Come and meet them." I glare at him.

Mason smiles approvingly at Jace as he walks past me. Jace flexes his fingers at his side. I don't know who I now despise more, Jace or Christian.

I force myself not to look at Jace as I walk by. The last thing I want is for him to gloat over me. As much as I want to stop and chew him out at the least, I try to calm myself. It's just so frustrating. These people regard wrong as right and right as wrong. And, as you just witnessed, they cannot stand it when they hear the truth. The truth angers them. I might not be the nicest person on the face of the earth, but at least I try to respect other people's opinions. But then again, is right and wrong really just opinions? Or are they not as plain as the nose on my face? I mean, it is wrong to abuse people, and yet to guys like Jace and Mason, abuse seems perfectly acceptable to them. Just because they do not agree with what I say does not give them the right to abuse me. And yet, there comes a time when one has to stand up for oneself. And although I do not yet have the courage, I hope that, before long, I find some.

I let go of the ladder with an irritable puff. I look up with the expectation of seeing Jace on his way down the ladder, but to my relief, he is still on the catwalk. He's probably kissing his hand in elation.

The room is remarkably quiet. I hurry to catch up with Mason. He forgets that he has longer legs than I do. I feel a pang of fear in my chest. I hope my team does not find me intimidating or hostile like Mason and the other guards. I do not want them to think that I will abuse them.

Mason turns around to face me. "Will you hurry up," he snaps.

I pick up my pace. I look past Mason to the other end of the hallway. It is clear. I wonder where everyone has gone. I thought I would get to see my team in action before they left the obstacle course room. I thought the whole process of dividing everyone into eight separate teams would take a lot longer. I also half expected the guards to argue over who gets who.

Mason throws out an arm to bar my way. "They just sat down to eat. I will take you by their table and point as I go by. Try to get a good look at them but do not speak to them. You will have time after dinner to meet them. But first," Mason says, lowering his hand to his side, "let me see your throat." He leans forward to get a good look. "Not too bad, most of the marks have already faded. If they hadn't, I was going to suggest you eat on the staircase, out of sight. But you look fine so let's go. And do yourself a favor," Mason adds with a trace of faint disgust in his voice, "and put on a tough face. You look too docile."

Part of me, namely my fist, wants to show him how docile I really am.

Mason nods with approval. "Not bad, you look like you just got chewed out by a drill sergeant. Keep looking like that and you might just earn the respect that will help save your life. Your team consists of two guys and two girls, by the way. Some teams have three guys and one girl, or all girls."

I'm not sure what to think about this. I do not think I would have wanted all girls, and four guys would have been way too much muscle to handle. But then again, I come from the same background that my brothers and sisters do, so at least I have an idea of what to expect. Mason waits for me to answer.

I shake my head in weary despair. "I don't think it'll matter. I'm a dead horse fly and I haven't even bitten anyone yet."

"True," Mason agrees. "A defeatist attitude leaves little room for winners. Look at me," Mason adds with a sigh. "Either decide victory right now or find yourself in a terrible situation. You have no other alternative. Starting tomorrow, you will embark on what will probably be the most challenging task of your life. I can tell you right now that your Saints are not going to cooperate with you if they think you're a pushover. You're going to have to tap into that anger, into that rich supply of energy that you have bubbling just beneath your surface, and put it to good use."

The last thing I want is to harass people like Mason and his friends do.

Mason punches me in the arm. I give him an indignant scowl. He tries to hit me again, but I evade him. I rub my arm. His knuckles felt as hard as steel.

Mason looks poised to deliver another punch. "Don't look at me like that. I just did you a favor. If it takes rough housing you to save your life, then so be it. I cannot hope to continue on with my study of you if you are dead. And believe me, if you don't change your mindset, you won't be around much longer. Plus, you need to consider your team. If you can't get your act together soon, if you fail to live up to expectations, then you will also be responsible for the death of four Saints. They'd be slaughtered like sheep right before your eyes, and then you'd be next. Just think, you'd have to meet that God of yours with bloodstained hands. Not a pretty thought if you ask me."

I recoil. "Their deaths wouldn't be my fault. It'd be yours, and that of your bosses. You're just trying to scare me just so you can continue to study me. I am not a guinea pig or lab rat or whatever you mad scientists use as the objects of your crazy experiments."

Mason snorts in disgust. "You'd better be, if you want to survive. Otherwise, I might as well lock you in a cell and hold you until President Gloss is informed on your resistance. I assure you, the manner of execution in which he chooses will be much worse for resistance than if you had tried."

I sigh, feeling defeated. "Fine. I will try my best as long as you live up to your word, as long as you help me. But," I add at Mason's smile, "should you choose only to observe me and not help me, I might change my mind. Despite what you may think, I am not afraid to die. I know exactly where I'm going, and it's not to a large cheese wedge in the sky."

Mason looks like he could roll his eyes. "Let's go, and remember everything I told you."

Mason begins to turn around. He points to the floor beside him. I groan inwardly. It was one thing to be a slave back home, but at least I did get a little leisure time even then. This is ridiculous. I cannot even talk around others without being under strict scrutiny. I might as well ask God to take me out now, though without pain.

Mason puffs his chest out, squares his shoulders as we exit the hallway. I copy him. I feel like such an idiot. How can I be someone who I am not? It is a fake identity and I hate it.

I take in the scene before me. Since the first time I came here, the tables in the cafeteria are finally occupied. Each team sits at a separate table, with all four individuals of each team huddled closely together. I wonder which team belongs to me. Most of them appear to be eating, except for a few who look worried sick. And who can blame them?

I follow Mason down an isle between two tables. I stiffen as many pairs of eyes begin to lock onto me. Plates of sandwiches occupy the center of the tables. And, to my surprise, the sandwiches actually look appetizing. I swallow, partly out of hunger and partly out of nervousness.

Mason emerges into the main isle, between the two sections of tables. There are four tables on either side of the main isle. I need to breathe, just breathe. If I pass out, perhaps the good doctor would be good enough to let me die, but I doubt it. He seems intent on keeping me alive for his own agenda.

Not surprisingly, it looks like all the guards that Mason talked about have arrived. Other than Christian, Jace, and Jack, I have not yet met any of the others. Nor do I want to. But I know one thing; there is a heck of a lot more than the eight guards necessary to train the eight teams. From the best I can tell, and this might not be all of them, there are at least twenty-five to thirty guards currently dining. I have no doubt that several of them watch the outside of the building. Like vicious spiders, they would hate for any of their prey to escape before they get a chance to suck all the life out of them.

Mason takes an abrupt left turn between a table full of guards and a table occupied by one of the teams. He throws a hand out and points as he passes by. He keeps looking straight ahead. And while he expects me to do the same, I feel compelled to stop, so I do.

I feel my mouth fall open somewhat absently. If these are what Mason calls dead beats, then he *is* nuts. Not only do they look very smart, but they are an attractive group. Not at all the kind of team I thought I would end up with. Of the two girls, one of them, a black girl with a smattering of dark freckles across her nose regards me with a friendly smile. She is very pretty indeed.

Half holding my breath, I take a step closer to them. One of the guys sort of reminds me of Ethan. He has brown eyes and curly red hair. He lays a partially eaten sandwich down onto his plate as he regards me curiously.

I want to tell them who I am, but Mason told me to wait. It is bad enough that I stopped, already disobeying his orders. I move past them, careful not to lose what little composure I have.

I search the guard's tables and find Mason sitting next to a very pretty female guard. Indeed, she is striking. Mason looks so caught up with her that he has forgotten me. I breathe a sigh of relief.

I round the table and make my way to the empty place beside Mason. At least with the outer wall directly behind us, I won't have to worry about anyone scrutinizing me from behind.

I sit down on the long wooden bench next to Mason. Other than the talk from all the guards, all of the Saints are silent. Straight ahead, at the opposite side of the room is a door that must lead to the kitchen.

My stomach rumbles. I turn to the sandwiches and swallow. I lean forward and seize a nice fat one. Mason takes a hold of my wrist. I flinch and let go of the sandwich. I meet his eyes.

"Don't think you can ignore my instructions," Mason says dangerously. "When I tell you to do something, I expect you to do it exactly how I say, otherwise you risk not only your own life, but also the security of us all. The last thing I want is a Saint revolt."

Making sure that no one is watching, I jerk my hand free from his grasp. "I couldn't help it. Maybe if you hadn't lied to me, if you hadn't told me that I would end up with the dead beats, I wouldn't have been so captivated."

Mason leans in closer to me. "I did *not* lie to you. You're judging by appearances, but I can assure you that you received the garbage of the entire group. Good looks are nothing if you don't have any abilities. Don't forget," Mason adds with a respectable smile, "all the other guards chose the cream of the crop, if you will. You have been assigned the blighted, weak stalks of corn. It will be up to you to make the best out of the worst situation, to turn water in to wine, if it can be done."

I want to elbow him in the side, at least. How would he like it if everything that spewed forth from my mouth was offensive? I doubt I would have a pleasant spot on my entire body from all the bruises.

Mason looks at the plate of sandwiches. He breaks a section of paper towel free from its roll, folds it hastily, and then picks up the sandwich that I dropped a moment ago. He sits it on my plate. I stare at it in shock.

Mason shrugs. "I cannot allow you to starve, now eat."

I cross my arms defiantly. No, I believe I will have a drink. And while I might spurn food just to spite Mason,

I refuse to die of thirst. I reach for the pitcher at the center of the table. Mason pushes my hand aside gently.

"Allow me," he says, taking a glass pitcher of what appears to be ice tea in his hand. "Aren't you going to be a proper…person and thank me?" He nearly slipped and said Saint.

For what, treating me like garbage one moment only to pour my drink the next? I clear my throat. "Thank you. Now are you going to introduce me to your lady friend, or not?"

Mason gives me a contemplative look. He scoots closer to me, green eyes resolved. "Her name is Rebecca. And, while I call her Becky, you will address her as Rebecca. Just so you know, she *is* single. Aha," Mason adds with an uncharacteristic grin, "you *are* interested in her. I see it in your eyes. If you're good, it might be possible for me to arrange for you to meet her, in a more private location of course."

I give him a cool look. "Why are you so determined to see me with one of your lady friends? And don't throw up in my face that you are really concerned about my heart. You act as if I am an alien, as if I have never been around enough women to know how to act around them."

Mason looks at my arm. "You *are* an alien, for you do not really belong with my kind of people, at least not yet anyway. But if you let me, if you stop coming at me with a sharpened tongue every time I turn around, I might help you fit in."

I swallow. Mason's voice was barely audible, but his sincerity was as powerful as my beating heart. "Alright. Perhaps I have been a bit sharp with you, but you have to admit, you brought much of it onto yourself.

Now," I add with a polite nod towards Rebecca, "are you going to introduce me to your pretty friend or not?"

"I will," Mason says pulling away from me. He turns his back on me. I hear him muttering to Rebecca. I scoot down the bench until I am right next to Mason. Mason rises to his feet. I pull away from him.

I now find myself staring into the green eyes of Mason's friend. I feel my chest tighten under her gaze. I see Mason move along behind me out of the corner of my eye. He sits down on the other side of me. He elbows me in the side to take his place. I wish I had kept my mouth shut.

I inch my way across the bench until I take Mason's spot. I watch as Rebecca traces my face with her lovely green eyes. If only Ethan could see her. Her eyes provide the perfect contrast to her lightly tanned skin. No wonder why Mason sat down by her. As much as it pains me to admit it, she and Mason would make a striking couple.

"Ryan Collins," Rebecca says in a sing song voice. "Are you going to shake my hand, or just continue staring at me? I know it's been a few months since you've seen me, but still. And no, I haven't forgotten that kiss on the balcony. How could I?"

I frown. What does she mean? I have never even seen her before. I look at her hand. I had not even noticed that she had offered it to me. She has lovely fingers. I…oh, now I understand. Just in case any of the Saints are listening in, despite her whispering, she is keeping with my false identity. Still, I seriously doubt that anyone could hear her above the chatter of all the other guards.

I give her a gentle handshake. Her skin is as smooth as a baby. It has been years since I have felt skin that smooth. Emily was certainly pretty, but hard work kept her from having smooth skin. Instead, her hands were almost as calloused as mine are, and if she had not put lotion on her hands on a regular basis, they would have been much worse.

Rebecca takes her cup and turns to face me. "I drink to your health. It really has been too long my gentle prince. But Mason assured me that your assignment wouldn't keep you away for too long. By the gods how you've become even more handsome since last we met. What do you do, spend all day praying to the male god of beauty? Edarion must be very pleased with you."

I bite my tongue. There is only one God, and no others. All the other gods are useless pieces of garbage fashioned by mere mortal men. How can a carved block of wood, the same wood that many people use to heat their houses with, do anything for anyone? Back home, we heated our houses with wood and even cooked food over its heat. And yet, Rebecca must be one of the many people nowadays who believe that bowing down to objects like chunks of wood and cast idols in the shape of animals will somehow solve their problems.

"What about you," I say. "Where do you get your beauty from?"

Rebecca runs a hand through her long dark hair. "The female goddess of beauty, of course. I offer her gifts every other week just like she expects. I sat a willow frond before her last night in accordance with her requirements for the blood moon. Harriet may seem like a picky goddess, but at least she does not require food offerings, like some of the others do. As for you," Rebecca adds with a bright smile, "Edarion must be very happy with you, otherwise you wouldn't be so handsome.

Lucky for you, Edarion only requires four pressed fig cakes each month to appease him. What do you do," Rebecca adds with a smile in her voice, "give him an entire year's worth of cakes at one time?"

I cannot say anything against these false gods of lunacy just yet, at least not here. I would have every guard in the room trying to rip my throat out, and that's no exaggeration. President Gloss passed a law a few years ago making it a crime to speak against all gods but one. And you can guess which one he banned: The God of Abraham, Isaac, and Jacob. This is the same God who parted the Red Sea to allow the children of Israel to escape from the Egyptians. It is also the same God who gave us the Ten Commandments, though the current regime has banned all such reference to the commandments. President Gloss believes that the murder of Christians will "cleanse the country of undesirable religious fanaticism." I will never forget the day when Perverted Demon, right after Gloss called for the destruction of all Bibles, urinated on a stack of Bibles right outside the Hub. We were all forced to watch, all the Christians, that is.

A finger pokes me in the back, almost playfully. I wish Mason would stop pestering me. Honestly, every time I begin to think he wants to be my friend, he always follows up with an unfriendly gesture. I turn around.

And come face to face with Jace. I swallow. He holds a half-eaten sandwich. He offers it to me. I give him a disgusted look.

"I'm only joking," Jace says with an easy smile. "Good grief, did you really think I'd expect you to eat it? No, I'm here because I want your opinion on something. One of the girls I chose for my team is exceptionally attractive for a Saint. And, while I intend to work her into a slump, I thought I might get a little action out of her before she wilts. So, I was wondering what turns Saints on besides Bibles and devotions? I mean," Jace adds quickly, "surely your recent assignment opened your eyes to such things."

I fist my hands at my sides. Jace needs to be taught a lesson. But then again, this isn't the time or place.

I swallow. "Respect. Respect her and she will honor you above all others."

Jace grins. "Good man. I knew you'd have the answer. I guess I was just hoping for a little more action. Perhaps I can wheedle her into my bed with verses from Edarion or one of the other gods. For instance: 'Come unto my heart where you will find rest and love and ready lips'. Or, if it pleases her: 'A moonlit chest is said to be the best'. Edarion himself said that to his sweetheart nine months before she gave birth to their son Onon, the god of bloodlust."

I sigh. It is all I can do keep my mouth shut. It is no wonder Gloss's favored people have such strange practices, like squeezing a bull frog over a pale of chicken blood until its eyes pop out of their sockets and bless the blood. At that point, the blessed blood is used in numerous rituals to appease their various gods. I wonder how they would react if I picked up a sandwich and, in the name of Edarion, pressed it against one of my biceps. Perhaps the protein in the ham could do more to nourish my biceps outside of my body than inside. If I could, I would name Edarion the Useless Fool and replace his corded biceps with withered ones. After all, Edarion prefers his pressed fig cakes to be set before the feet of his striking statues. So, if he is not going to eat them, what good are they?

Mason clears his throat. He looks a little uncomfortable, though I do not know why. Surely the good doctor does not object to the efforts of his friends to try to brainwash me. Oh, but I forgot, Mason wishes for me to secretly remain intact, spiritually speaking, so that he can study me. All well, I don't think Edarion and I would have hit it off very well anyway, and I never did care much for fig cakes.

I meet Mason's eyes with a whimsical smile. Funny, I can tell that he wants to smile, but for environmental reasons, he remains as serious as usual. I know that he does not want to step on his friend's toes, but still. He could at least make an effort to join the conversation. I mean, what will poor Edarion think if he gets word that Mason failed to praise him? But then again, perhaps Edarion, liking fig cakes as he does is currently at some tree in the world nourishing that sweet craving of his, in which case, he is not listening to begin with.

"It's time for you to meet your team," Mason says blithely. I cannot help but smile. Although Mason did not delve into the crazy conversation like his friends did, at least he did refrain from dashing me upon the rocks of religious persecution. All in all, I have to say that, perhaps for the first time since I met Mason, I have real respect for him.

I rise to my feet with a yawn. Both Jace and Mason catch it. Jace turns around to face the wall. It really is a shame that there aren't any mirrors or windows around to see his reflection in. I imagine his eyes water just the same as mine, though he would never admit it.

Put a stack of fig cakes in front of Jace and it would be easy to believe him to be Edarion. I shrug inwardly. Maybe that explains why Jace acts so pompous. I stifle a laugh. If only it was true.

Mason approaches me with a casual expression, as if I am really one of his equals. "Remember everything I have told you," he says in a dangerous tone that belies his otherwise casual appearance. "You know the situation we are in, what President Gloss expects from you. He wants an exciting show, so you had better come through."

I can tell that Mason said the latter in order to satisfy his friend's ears. But as far as I can tell, Mason is still on my side. Either that or he is a very good pretender. No, something tells me that his desire to study me still holds true, and the only way he can continue to study me is by keeping me alive. I can see the intense interest in his eyes, the desire to steal me away from everyone so that he can badger me with questions.

I cast a glance over my shoulder. Other than the guy that reminds me of Ethan, who appears to be resting his eyes for a moment, the others look alert, even timid. I turn back to Mason. "Should I sit with them," I say.

"No," Mason says harshly, just loud enough for me to hear. "Your job will be to establish a sense of authority over them. Demand their names, speak harshly to them, and, if you find it necessary, treat them brutally. And by brutally, I want for you to inflict bruises or other low impact injuries onto their bodies. Show them who is boss."

Jace turns around to face me. He runs a hand down his chest, blue eyes mischievous. "If I was you, I'd start off by giving those Saint-girls a gentle touch just to show them who's boss. And, if you really want to make yourself their god so to speak, I'd force them to kiss you or put their arms around you. Don't ever forget, lust is the key to obedience. As deceptive as it may seem, lust has proven time and again to win over stupid people. Who wouldn't take a hold of your biceps and kiss you if they thought their life was in danger for disobedience? And if you really want to crank up the heat, you might consider training them without a shirt. I myself am curious as to how long a Saint-girl could maintain her innocence under the constant pressure of a lusty man. If you'd like, I might even join you some time during training, in nothing but my underwear, of course. That would help break the ice between you and your team."

"I think I'll be able to manage on my own, thank you very much," I say politely, though with great effort.

Jace gives me a wicked smile. "Maybe for a while. But some animals need encouragement, otherwise they would never have any offspring. Should you prove unsuccessful with your job, you might find yourself in a very embarrassing situation until you take my advice. You see," Jace adds with a smile, "President Gloss has specifically requested that we tamper with your purity before your time here has ended. And if that takes putting you into an embarrassing situation, say, without a thread on your body, then so be it. Like it or not, you will be the lusty stallion that causes your two Saint-girls to salivate with unbridled lust. And as far as your guys are concerned, you should embarrass them by forcing them to expose themselves. As for me, I love looking on the beauty that the gods have given us. Just think, the demise of four Saints will come from one of their very own. If President Gloss is not entertained by all that, then I will be shocked."

I swallow hard. Mason never mentioned anything like this. It makes me angry to think that Jace is actually looking forward to watching the demise of four innocent people, not to mention all of the other Saints. I have no desire to do any of the things that Jace suggested. How could someone be so wicked? I do not care what he says; I doubt he would like it if someone forced him to expose his nakedness for everyone to see. And if he thinks that I will bend so easily, that I will cast aside all the respect I have for my God, then he is greatly mistaken.

"So be it," I say, recognizing the need to placate Jace. Jace looks stunned, as if he had expected me to come off with a defiant retort.

I catch myself worrying my lips. I stop. I need to look calm and confident. As much as I want to forget all the intimidating things that I have been told since my arrival, I cannot afford to do so. When it comes down to it, I am going to have to do some things that I do not want to do, in order to stay alive. Still, it might be possible for Mason to keep me from being turned into the chief prostitute of my team. After all, he wants me to remain as intact as possible in order to better study me. But then again, Mason's friendship with all these guards still might not be enough to prevent all their evil plans. I do not mind kissing the girls if I have to, but I have no desire to do anything else.

I take a deep breath. I feel light headed. I look at my team. Each of them could use a big hug and a consoling word right about now. And yet, I have been told not to say or do anything kind to them. I feel a deep ache in my chest, though I know it does not register on my face. But I know that, unless I cooperate, unless I follow orders, I will only make things worse for them. I can feel

Mason and Jace watching me closely, along with many other guards. If I fail my first real assignment, if I do not live up to their expectations, then there is no telling what they will do to me. Not to mention my team. I cannot afford to look weak. I have no other alternative than to cooperate.

I school my face to look haughty. This is going to be harder than I thought. How can I appear haughty when I do not dislike any of these people? I guess I will just have to settle for looking tough and hope that I look haughty enough. The thing is, unless I tap into a deeply felt emotion, like anger, I am afraid that I will come off way too polite and therefore bring down the wrath of my oppressors down onto my head.

I think of Jace and what he just said. I feel an angry bubble expanding in my chest. I will it to travel to my face. I feel my face reddening with anger. If only I can maintain it, I might stand a chance at passing my first assignment. If only I had a little rage to go along with it, I would be much more convincing.

I hold my head up higher. I need to come across as haughty and authoritative as possible if I am to be convincing in my role. I will my eyes to appear haughty. It is a good thing my back was to them earlier; otherwise it would be that much harder. Fortunately, they didn't seem to notice me while I sat next to Mason and Rebecca.

I square my shoulders. I wish Mason would have introduced me, but so much for that. I look at the distance between the table where my team sits and where I stand. I don't have far to go.

I ask God for courage and strength. I take a deep breath. I propel myself forward with an exhale. I feel my heartbeat quicken. The black girl narrows her eyes onto me as I stop behind her fellow teammates.

The guy that reminds me of Ethan jerks his head up, as if he was alerted by my presence beneath the table. He looks startled. He takes his hands from the table and hides them. I want to give him a sympathetic smile, to tell him not to worry, to tell him that I am not going to hurt him, but that would not be true.

"You all have been assigned to me," I say, pleased with my forceful tone of voice. "We will begin training tomorrow morning. In order to get along with me, in order to survive the things to come, you will need to do everything I tell you. You've come to a dangerous place, so I suggest you keep that in mind should you consider rebelling. I will deal brutally with any of you who fail to comply with what I ask of you. So," I add, feeling only slightly more confident, "the path to survival is through me, if it can be achieved. That will be entirely up to you all. And don't ask me any questions without first asking for permission to speak. Otherwise, I may ask you some tough questions and, should your answers fail to please me, you could very well find yourselves in an uncomfortable situation."

Ethan's look alike gives me a worried nod. I feel a twinge of anxiety in my chest.

"What's your name," I say.

"Seth," he says with a worried gleam in his eyes.

I give him a curt nod. "What about your last name? And where are you from?"

Seth looks shocked. "My last name is Eldridge. And I am from district four, from the northeastern county."

I hold my breath. Seth's northeastern county is right above where I am from. The girl directly in front of me turns around to face me. She has shoulder-length brown hair and dark blue eyes.

"What about you," I say.

"My name's Kody," she says with a slight tremble in her voice. "I…thought the guards who escorted us here told us never to use our last names, in order to forget part of our identity."

I scold myself inwardly for being so stupid. I swallow hard with a shrug. "Slugs really have no last names, do they? I will call you by your first name and you will call me Ryan."

The guy beside her turns around to face me. He has shiny black hair and light blue eyes. He gives me a hard look, though not entirely unfriendly. "Just how old are you? Most of the other guards look to be in their early to mid-twenties, at the least."

I swallow. "I assure you I am old enough to deal with all of you. And don't forget, I warned you against speaking out of turn. Do that again and I will shell you like a corncob."

His mouth falls open into a state of shock. I feel a twinge of panic in my chest. I should not have said that. But it came out before I could stop it. I can see the question in his eyes, the desire to ask me where I came from and just exactly who I am. I need to cover myself and quick.

"Don't look so surprised," I say, trying to hide my nervousness. "Everyone knows that you Saints spend all your time shelling corn for a living. Well, at least what time you're not grumbling over increased quotas and lost Bibles. Matthew, Mark, Luke, and Jim, isn't it?"

Seth narrows his eyes onto me. "Close, but not quite. Can I ask you a question?"

"No," I say loudly. "You do not have my permission. At least not right now anyway. Not unless you want me to twist your arm so hard that you curse the day you were baptized."

I think that did the trick. Ethan looks at me with contempt. I give him a nasty smile. The black-haired guy on this side of the table expels an irritable blast of breath, blue eyes despising me. I need to do something and quick. I cannot afford to let things get out of control this soon.

I take a hold of his hair and jerk his head towards me. His eyes water from the pain. "Perhaps you don't realize just how serious your situation is. I have the power to harm you or as you Saints put it, *bless* you. But I have to say that you'll find my blessings as undesirable as my curses." I let go of his hair.

I decide to take my deception a step further in order to better cover myself. "For a long time now I have wanted to see what it would be like to touch the head of a Saint. So many people warned me against it. Some said my hand would turn to ash from a curse, while others said my body would rot from the inside out." I stare at my hand with a triumphant look. "But I can see that none of those people were right. You're just as much human…just as much the worthless dirt that I was told. I believe we will work well together, now that I know that there's nothing to fear."

I hear someone come to a stop behind me. "Unless you want to waste more time talking to your Saints, I suggest you join me for an evening of sinful delight."

I nod. I almost did not recognize Mason's voice. He sounded way too polite, as if the two of us are best friends. Naturally, he has to keep up appearances.

"Yes," I say, turning around to face him. "I'm done with these people. The sooner I wash my hands the better. I've always heard that Saints only wash their hair for special religious occasions. I doubt they'd even do that if not for the fear of being struck down by lightning."

"Or fear of being impregnated with evil," Mason says with a smile in his voice. "If you want, you could take either one of your Saint-girls along with us. I'm sure you'll need a massage or two before the nights out."

I raise my eyebrows, as if the very thought is absurd. "And risk defiling my sacred body? No thanks, I think I'll stick to the more traditional women. That's one reason why I would never want to be a Saint: I would miss our wayward women too much."

Mason looks thrown for a loop. "I agree. A wayward woman is the key to a joyful heart. I believe Edarion himself may have said that."

"And he would know," I say, not liking this conversation at all. "He's the god of nice abs and perfect beauty after all."

"He is beautiful," Mason says with a nod. "It is said that the only guys who ever had perfect bodies were kissed by Edarion himself. Some even say that *I* have been kissed by Edarion."

I smile. I ask God to forgive his stupidity. I know that Mason would break my teeth if I told him, but there *is* no Edarion. He is just as mythical as a talking toadstool. But, in order to avoid being persecuted, I must remain silent. But I can tell that Mason wants me to answer him.

I scold myself for what I am about to say. "Yes, you must pleasure Edarion with mountains of fig cakes."

"I do," Mason says with a haughty smile. "A way to a god's heart is through his belly. Stuff him full of cakes and it is said that his vomit will take away all blemishes and defects. Of course, since it takes years for any one person to satisfy his appetite, you have to be patient."

Oh, now I did not know that. At least I now know what my problem is: The male god of beauty has never vomited on me. How absolutely intelligent! If I survive this crazy nightmare, I will have to tell Mark about that one. I can see him laughing now. No wonder why our country has gone down the drain since Gloss came to power. He and all his followers are stupid enough to believe anything. I bet if I told Mason that I was met in a dream by Edarion, he would instantly have a higher opinion of me, without a doubt.

Mason gives the boy whose head I just took a hold of a contemptuous look. "I don't like the looks of you. If you think your blue eyes are going to be your redeeming quality, then you're mistaken. But it's possible that I might have a use for you yet. There's no doubt that you find yourself attractive. I wonder whether or not you'd be willing to use your inflated beauty to secure better conditions for yourself. It might be that I know just the guard for you to test your affections on."

"You did well," Mason says, massaging his bare feet. "I had expected you to go easy on them, but I can see that you're determined to stay alive. That guy, the smart mouthed blue eyed one deserved what he got. But Rebecca wished that you had torn his shirt off. She longed to see what she believes is a very attractive body. I told her to be patient. All good things happen to those who wait. But you did very well. I'm *very* pleased with you."

"I wish I could say the same for myself," I say, feeling miserable. Mason looks surprised to hear me say this.

I swallow hard. "I saw nothing wrong with that guy, or any of the other Saints assigned to me for that matter. He was just as clean, just as well-mannered as any godly person should be. Honestly, I felt like a fool for saying all that. And I could tell that they all thought of me as a fool as well. Do you want to know why these people are so wise, good doctor?"

"Do enlighten me if you can," Mason says with a sour look. There is that intellectual egotism that I despise.

"They fear God," I say. "Not Edarion or any of the other four leaf clover hoodlums, but the only God who has ever displayed real power. He is not a god of useless cakes and ridiculous phrases that get people nowhere. He is the God of all great things, and wisdom and power belong to Him. He does not cheapen Himself by requiring people to say and do stupid things to get His attention. He controls the thunder and lightning and wind and rain. He has no need for human food. After all, He gives us everything we eat. All the other gods who require people to say and do such stupid things have, throughout history, proven to be as useless as bloodletting is to alleviate bodily injuries."

Mason looks shocked. "Where did you learn all this stuff from? How is it that a Saint, that a simple minded person could come to learn so much?"

I sigh. "It's really quite simple, though your kind of people refuses to acknowledge the truth: God. He is magnificent. And, contrary to what all the babbling scholars say, wisdom is not so easily found. It cannot be bought each day like food. Nor can it be gleaned from books written by those who have no wisdom themselves."

I draw myself up into the haughty position of an intellectual. "Since President Gloss came to power, he has been instrumental in establishing equal protection and religious sensibility. He recognizes the importance of keeping Christians enslaved, so that the country will continue to prosper without opposition to majority rule. Significantly, our country has advanced more in the last seven years since Gloss came to power than in the all the previous decades combined. Before Gloss, people could not have sex in public, but now they can. Before Gloss, it was against the law for people to publicly worship naked statues of their favorite gods, but now they can." Mason looks stunned, even a bit bewildered.

I take a deep breath and lean against the back of my chair. "But of course your people fail to talk about all the diseases that ravage the bodies of people who mingle so lewdly in public places. The lack of wisdom says that you see and enjoy but are not able to estimate the consequences of your actions. I call that stupid intellectualism."

Mason regards me with a curious look. "There is clearly more to you than meets the eyes. Tell me, what exactly do you think of me? Speak freely, I promise I won't harm you."

I take a deep breath and hold it. Honestly, I think he is a fool, but even the most foolish person can change their ways if they want to. And yet, I do not despise Mason. I actually find him interesting, but not as much as he finds me.

I give him a judicious look. "I don't agree with hardly anything you say. I find you rude and hateful and very stubborn. But, beneath your unfriendliness, I think you have a kind heart."

Mason sputters, green eyes looking upset. "What makes you think I have a kind heart? I have not done anything kind to you. In fact, if you remember the terms of our agreement, you'll find that I only offered to help you in return for the chance to study you without interruption."

I lean forward and look him straight in the eyes. "Whatever you say good doctor, but even that cannot account for your reluctance to chew me up and spit me out in front of your friends earlier today. While they were trying to shove their false gods down my throat, you kept silent instead of joining them."

Mason clears his throat and shifts uncomfortably in his chair. "You are thinking too much into it, over analyzing it if you will. I think if you had been paying closer attention, you would have found that I was observing you then and there, to see how you would react. Not because I cared a darn thing about how you felt. As for the sinful delights I told you about, well, I lied. I only said that to intimidate the garbage that had challenged your authority. I want them to think the worst about this place so that they will be less inclined to rebel. We cannot hope to please our dear president if we cannot control our prisoners. And that also includes you as well because you too are a prisoner."

"Is there anything you wouldn't do," I say, disgusted.

Mason nods. "There are many things I wouldn't do. For one, I would never bless you like your kind of people does to each other. Nor would I ever pray that your health be restored should it be compromised. No, I believe in using my knowledge to restore people's health. But do not worry," Mason adds with a jovial smile, "I have no desire to do any of the things to you that someone like the perverted agent whom you described to me does to people. You'll find that I keep my hands to myself unless my abilities are requested, and only then do I help my friends."

I shake my head in disgust. "So you're telling me that if I had a serious medical condition right now, you'd just let me die?"

"Probably," Mason says with a dangerous smile in his voice. "The only way I'd ever go out of my way to help you was if you proved to be a worthy candidate."

Mason lifts a leg and rests a foot atop my knee. "This is what I think of you right now, footstool. And don't look at me like that. Until very recently, I had not even thought you worthy of being a footstool. Admittedly, I am a bit shocked by my own decline in morality. That I would stoop to resting my foot on a Saint is something I never imagined myself doing. But I have to admit," Mason adds with a yawn, "you do make a comfy footstool. But I warn you, speak of this to anyone and our agreement is off, and that would make it almost impossible for you to survive this place."

I do not know what to think, let alone what to say. I look at the sole of his foot. As clean as it is, it isn't right for him to use me in this way. But I suppose things could be much worse for me. At least he acts like a man. Perverted Demon, what with his sick ways of touching guys like Ethan was one of the most morally bankrupt agents back home. Mason may be a long ways off from being the upstanding man he could be, but at least he prefers women to teenage boys. Honestly, I am not too concerned that he will pull a sick move on me. I saw how taken he was with Rebecca, and even Carrie to question his preference."

I suppose I can suffer the indignity of being the good doctor's footstool as long as he continues to favor me. And I really have no other choice.

Mason crosses his arms over his chest and closes his eyes. He looks as if he could fall asleep at any moment.

I clear my throat. "Just how long do I have to sit here with your foot atop my knee?"

Mason adds to my burden with his other foot. "Until I say otherwise, I wish for you to remain my comfy footstool. Why? I'm not hurting you, am I? I'll tell you what, if you tire from being my footstool, I can increase your burden to include reading to me as well."

I let out a defeated sigh. But then again, I might just take him up on it. One of the things I miss most is not being able to read. Back home, I had an illegal stash of books that I kept hidden under a loose floor board in my room. As many times as I read them, I never got tired of them. Unfortunately, Mark and I did not have enough time to keep our Bibles from being taken away. But since Gloss's war against Christians started with the destruction of Bibles only, we had enough time to hide most of our other books. And it was a good thing we did so because not too long after that, the agents who collected our Bibles came in and carried off the remaining books that we had left out in the open. We decided to leave a few books on our shelves so that, in the event that another move of censorship occurred, things would not look too out of place. Because anyone who had ever been in our house before knew we owned many books.

"Fine with me," I say, meeting his eyes. "If you want me to read to you, then so be it. But it better not be anything perverted or boring."

Mason takes his feet from my knees. He looks like he could either snap at me or ask me a question. "Forget it. I saw how you looked when I mentioned reading. You're not here for pleasure. Remember, you broke the law and now you're paying the price. I only said that to see how you would react, not because I had any intention of letting you read to me."

"I'm tired," I say, rising to my feet. "If you don't mind, I'd like to go to sleep now, unless you want to push the knife in deeper with another string of hateful words."

Mason dismisses me with a wave of his hand. "By all means, go to bed. Get all the sleep you can, you'll need it."

Chapter Six

I wake the following morning with an empty tray on my chest. I set the tray aside and find Mason sitting on the side of his bed, an opened book on his lap. He snaps the book shut. I have a good mind to send this tray hurtling towards him. Whoever heard of sitting an empty tray on someone's chest while they are sleeping?

Mason bends over and begins putting on his shoes. "You missed breakfast. I tried to wake you, but you pushed me away."

"You're a liar," I snap. "I never felt you shake me…or whatever it was you did to try to wake me."

Mason looks at me like I am an idiot. He finishes lacing his shoes and rises to his feet. He strides across the room towards me. I sit up on the side of my bed.

"Look," Mason says, pointing to an angry scratch on his arm. He gives me a reproachful look. "You did that. I barely shook you and you turned vicious. You're just as evil as you say I am."

I stare at the scratch. It looks fresh alright, what with the thin line of blood that still appears to be drying in the wound. I swallow hard. I do not even remember doing it. I look down at my fingernails. I see no sign of…I feel my mouth fall open in shock. A tiny dot of partially dried blood rests on the tip of my index finger. I meet Mason's eyes and laugh.

"You think it's funny," Mason says dangerously, raising his eyebrows.

I shake my head. "Not in the way you think. I'm just surprised that I could inflict an injury like that on you without knowing it. Do you want me to clean it and bandage it for you good doctor?"

Mason gives me a droll stare. "Are you serious?"

I think so. I mean, I would not have asked him if I wasn't. I nod.

Mason appears to be cooling off a bit. "It's just that, no one, let alone a Saint, has ever offered to help me."

"That doesn't surprise me," I say with a mirthless laugh. "For one, you're not exactly the nicest guy to be around. And, from the way you talk, you haven't spent much time around Christians otherwise you'd have a better opinion of us. It's as bad as a king hating the peasants in his kingdom without ever making an attempt to get to know them."

Mason looks as if he could either smile or spit on me. "Fair enough. But I do not need your help, I can deal with it on my own."

"I feel like an agent," I say, feeling lousy. Mason and I stand outside the same door we entered the Mirage through yesterday. Apparently, my team is already in there, compliments of another guard's early morning routine. "All I need is a whip and a nasty grin and I'd be ready for work."

"Oh you're much worse than any mere agent," Mason says in a serious tone of voice. "Don't forget that, because if you do, you'll never be able to command the respect and discipline from your Saints that you need to survive. But at the same time, you cannot afford to be too brutal with them. Too much brutality will get you nowhere. You must find a healthy balance between harassment and kindness, if that can be achieved. Learn to read each one of them like a book. That shouldn't be too hard for you."

"And what will you be doing in the meantime," I say, careful to sound respectful.

Mason looks like he could punch me in the face. "That's really none of your business, but I will tell you anyway. After we left the cafeteria last night, all the Saints were taken to the infirmary where they were cleaned up. One of the Saint-boys went nuts trying to avoid a physical examination, and had to be chased down by several guards. Unfortunately, he made quite a mess in the infirmary before they tackled him to the floor. I'm going down there to make sure that everything has been cleaned up. It is after all my jurisdiction."

I feel weak and sickly. "I'm so hungry I could eat a horse. There's no way I'm going to be good for anything with an empty stomach."

Mason reaches into his pocket and pulls out a stick of what appears to be beef jerky. He offers it to me. "This will help. And don't tell anyone I gave it to you, otherwise you'll never get anything else from me again."

It is not very big, but anything is better than nothing. I rip the plastic away and take a bite.

Mason regards me with a faint smile. "I'll come and get you at the end of the four-hour training session. One of the other guards will come for your team. Once you're done training them, you'll not see them anymore until the same time and place tomorrow. And while you'll be with *me* every afternoon, your team will be busy training in the obstacle course room. It's important that they be worked hard, so that their energy will be drained by the end of each day."

I swallow the last bite of the beef jerky. I hand the wrapper to Mason. "Let me guess, I will spend my afternoons being your footstool and private entertainment."

Mason pokes the wrapper into his pocket with a cordial smile. "Not necessarily, although I will certainly enjoy those privileges at some point before the day ends. It really depends on what kind of a mood I'm in. You have been assigned to me, so I can do pretty much whatever I want to you, besides strangling you to death."

I look at his neck. "Are you sure," I say.

Mason nods. "I could the last I checked."

I swallow hard. "But you said you'd help me, that you'd try to keep me alive."

Mason looks sort of sad. "To help is not to save. I can help you behind the scene, but if you do not please my bosses, there is little I can do to save you. If I tried to save you, it would make *me* look bad."

I glare at him. "Heaven forbid that to happen."

Mason looks down at the scratch I gave him. "I have already lied for you several times since you arrived. It makes little difference to me. Just about everyone around here lies anyways. I don't tell them everything I do because I don't want to get into a long drawn out conversation with them that will lead to whom is sleeping with whom."

I shake my head. "I don't want you telling any more lies on my behalf."

Mason looks startled, most likely at the concern in my voice. "Could it be that you are actually worried that I'll get into trouble for helping you?"

I nod. "But I don't know why you act so surprised. You know how much I need you. You even made it out to me that, without your help, it'd be nearly impossible for me to survive this place. Plus, it's not good to tell lies. Liars will not inherit the kingdom of heaven."

Mason bangs a fist over his heart dramatically. "Good grief, could it be that you actually care about me? How very touching. Maybe you should try praying the lies from my mind sometime, it's full of them. It's also full of a lot of other stuff that your kind would disapprove of as well. For instance," Mason adds, approaching me. "I have this near constant temptation to jab you in the chest with my finger. So allow me." Mason tries to jab me in the chest, but I knock his hand away.

Still, I cannot help but feel that, from the near smile on his face, he is just playing with me. The question is, why? "Life is full of temptations, but you're supposed to try to resist them. How would you like it if, when I feel a sudden temptation to knock you upside the head, I went along with it?"

Mason shrugs. "Believe it or not, that might not be a bad idea. Not to say that I want you to hurt me, but a little more aggression from you would warm my heart, I think."

"So you're saying I'm boring," I say, finding that hard to believe.

Mason nods. "Exactly. Saints spend too much time praying and not enough time playing. I think I just thought of a good way for us to spend the afternoon together. Saint Ryan needs to come out of his boring, prayer infested mind and have some fun."

He has got to be joking. I give him a speculative look. No, he is not joking. I swallow hard. "Look, I'd much rather just spend the afternoon being your footstool and answering your questions. The last thing I want is to be turned into a drunken, sex crazed lunatic before I die.

That is not what I call…" Mason jabs me in the chest. I wince from the pain.

"That's not exactly what I had in mind," he says, green eyes hard and cold as ice.

I gesture to the door behind me. "Is there anything else I should know before I go in? What about all the other…Saints? When are they going to start training?"

Mason looks thoughtful. "I think I filled you in on everything you need to know. As for the other seven teams, they're already training. And the longer you stand out here wasting time, the more exposure they will have over your team, and not just exposure to the expectations of training, but also to the mysteries of the Mirage. Very soon all the teams will take turns leaving their training rooms to venture into the big city landscape, and when they do, those who took their training seriously will stand a better chance of surviving the things to come."

I let out a weary sigh. "Why do you have to be so depressing? Why do you have to make everything sound so intimidating and complicated? And since you seem so intent on aggravating my headache, why don't you just go ahead and talk in riddles while you're at it? Perhaps I'd have an aneurism trying to solve one of them and then I could escape all the terrible things to come."

Mason laughs. "I didn't know you had a headache. All well, it'll only make you appreciate the times when you're feeling better. Now," Mason says with a solemn air of superiority, "will I have to take your hand and lead you through that door to your team, or are you going to do it yourself?"

I find myself looking at Mason's hands. For some reason, I have the feeling that Mason has done more with his hands than he cares to admit. His hands look normal enough, even healthy and smooth, but looks can be deceiving. I wonder if he is one of those sick physicians that I have heard about who dismembers Christian babies. Could Mason actually be toying with my mind with the intention of doing me harm? I mean, just because he seems somewhat friendly does not mean that he has my best interest in mind.

I back into the door and flinch. I did not even realize that I had been moving. Mason narrows his eyes onto me, as if wondering why I appear so disturbed. I'm sure my eyes betray me.

Mason looks between me and the door. "You had best get in there. You'll not be allowed more time, and every minute that goes by has either the potential to help you or harm you, not to mention your team."

I nod. I feel for the doorknob as I watch Mason turn around and stalk off. I hope he is not just toying with my mind. I cannot tell if his concern for my well-being is genuinely tied to his desire to study me or something else. I sigh. When it comes down to it, I really should not even be worrying. I won't die a moment before God says it's my time to go.

I run a hand down the front of my shirt. I am very nervous. I have never been in a position of authority, even a pretend one. I mean, even though I have to train four people, I am still not a real guard. I have no previous training like Mason and all the other guards do. Surely they had to go through a great deal of training in order to be considered worthy to protect Gloss. After all, they are his private guard. The thing is, with so many of his guards stationed here to carry out his sick plans against Christians, I cannot help but wonder how many more guards he has who are not here. And I dare not ask

Mason, even though a few such questions might go a long way in discovering how sincere his desire to help me is.

I open the door and feel a cold blast of air beckoning me forward. I do a quick survey of my teams faces. I feel my heartbeat quicken. I shut the door. I eye the doorknob wistfully. If only I could escape this place and somehow find my way back home. I smile inwardly. Mark would throw his arms around me and not let go until someone pried them loose. I miss Mark with a deep ache. I hope he is fine. I hope he has found comfort in the pain of my absence. I hope Ethan and Emily are comforting him, soothing his grief, helping him cope. I swallow hard. I would do anything just to be able to see Mark's face one last time before I die, to see the face of he who comforted me day and night ever since my parents were murdered.

I scold myself inwardly. I'm such a fool. Here I am with my back to my team when I need to be strong and confident. I school my face to look like one of the guards.

I turn around and look between the four Saints that have been assigned to me. As much as I know I need to treat them badly, I just want to gather them into a group hug. They are a nice looking group. The last thing I want to do is to treat them like the scum that they are not. And, in addition to their well-groomed appearances, I can tell that each of them is very well mannered, despite the seriousness of the situation. To my surprise, they are all wearing really nice clothes, though not as nice as mine. I had expected them to look as if they had crawled out of a dumpster. I guess their trip to the infirmary last night had some benefits after all, despite the embarrassment of bodily examinations and public baths.

The girls have on gray shirts and old jeans that look faded. The guys look much the same, except that their jeans look newer. I take it that the clothes have all been previously worn by somebody else. But at least there does not appear to be any holes in them.

I square my shoulders and move forward. They stand about midway in the room. The red-haired guy, Seth, reminds me so much of Ethan in the face, it's going to be nearly impossible for me to hurt him. As for the others, I do not want to do anything to hurt them either, but I realize that in order to fulfill my obligations to Mason, I very well may have to.

I come to a stop in front of them. I decide to leave a few feet between us for safety measures. I do not want to put myself at risk just in case they decide to gang up on me. But I really could not blame them if they did. Now that I think of it, Mason never told me what I should do in the event that such a situation arose.

I look at the black-haired guy. "You never told me your name."

"It's Nick," he says, a gleam of intimidation in his blue eyes. He swallows hard.

I nod. I turn to the black girl. "And you?"

"Jennifer," she says, dark eyes soft but cautious.

Of course the other girl already introduced herself as Kody, much to my relief. The less I have to say right now the better.

I look past them to the other side of the room. "Let's get started."

I take off and they part to allow me passage. "Jane," I say. I flinch inwardly at the slight timidity in my voice.

"Master Ryan," Jane says without inflection. She sounds as if someone removed her brain and vocal cords and replaced them with a tone of voice as dull as a rainy day. But then again, she never did have an actual brain. But she sure came across like she did. Then it hits me: Mason threatened to wipe away her engaging personality for failure to comply with his wishes. And it looks like he did exactly that.

"I need four automatons," I say. "Just like the ones Mason and I used yesterday." I hope that she has been made aware of what her counterpart did for us yesterday.

The automatons blink into existence, their shiny glass hearts sparkling like rubies. I hold out my hand in front of me and try not to blink to miss it. But nothing happens. I was sure that you have to turn your hand palm upright in order to summon a knife. At least that is what Mason and I did yesterday.

I clear my throat. I imagine my team trying not to laugh behind me. And really, I cannot blame them. I lower my hand to my side. I do not know what to do. I was worried that something like this would happen. Why didn't Mason tell me how to deal with things like this? Unless…unless he wants me to fail.

"Jane," I say, careful to keep the fear from my voice. "I…there is a problem. I cannot get a weapon. Please tell me what the problem is."

"I do not know," Jane says, without personality. "To trouble shoot this problem, I suggest evaluating yourself."

Great, that's just what I needed to hear. I could strangle Mason's feet for treating Jane so badly yesterday. He should have left her alone. I liked the interaction that we had with her counterpart yesterday. She was much more helpful. Now here I am, without a tool to fix the problem. It looks like Jane lost most of her abilities when she was reprogrammed. Mason might as well have just programmed a giant insect to gobble me up instead of leaving me helpless. I think perhaps he will find his footstool very upset and ready to carve a complaint into the soles of his feet with nothing but my fingernails.

Glass shatters and rains down onto the floor in front of me. I jump backwards. One of the inner automatons no longer has a heart. I swallow hard and watch as the knife blinks out of existence amid the shards of glass. Well it looks like Mason finally showed up to save the day. I take a deep breath and let it out as I turn around to face him.

I feel my mouth fall open. Seth shrugs meekly. Realizing I must look like a shocked school boy who just watched a paper air plane land on the teacher's desk, I quickly close my mouth. "How…who gave you permission to begin this training session?" Seth looks speechless.

"He was only trying to help," Jennifer says, but not unkindly. "When he saw what you were trying to do, he gave it a try, and it worked."

I do not know what to say. Why didn't it work for me? Jane said to examine myself, but I know that I did nothing wrong. I stare at my hand. I try again. I do not see anything wrong, anything that would hinder me from getting a knife.

A hand takes my wrist and steadies it. I jerk my head up and find myself looking into Kody's dark blue eyes.

Kody gives me a small smile. "You're shaking like a leaf," she says. "I think that's why it didn't work for you."

I pull my hand free from hers. I do not need a lesson from the student. Or do I? As much as I hate to admit it, she is right. Any other time I would not mind someone helping me, but with my head doomed for the chopping block should I fail to live up to Gloss's expectations, I can't allow myself to be proud.

"Touch me again and you will pay dearly," I say, seeing the necessity to reprimand her. "Wayward women I welcome, but Saint-girls I cannot stand."

I turn around to face Seth. He swallows hard. I feel a tug of sympathy on my heart at the regret and fear in his eyes. Still, I cannot let him go unpunished. If I do, they would probably think me weak and try nearly anything. But then again, Mason did tell me to be forceful with them but not too harsh. I cannot expect cooperation if I am brutal with them. Besides, I'm not sure that I could hit Seth without hurting myself even more. Again, he reminds me too much of Ethan to hurt him.

I look at Seth and point to the floor beside me. Obediently, he moves forward to stand at my side. I know I need to punish him, even if it means lightly punching him in the arm, but I cannot bring myself to do even that. When it comes down to it, if Seth had not done what he just did, I would still likely be standing here feeling like an idiot. If anything, he deserves to be rewarded.

I hold out my hand and feel the knife materialize across my palm. Seth stares at the knife with a worried expression. I step up to him and incline my head at his hand. Slowly he lifts his shaky hand. I take his wrist to steady his hand and gently lay the knife across his sweaty palm. He blinks in surprise. "You did well. Now, let me see you throw again."

Looking relieved, Seth nods and I back out of the way. I feel a wave of relief wash away all the anxiety, sadness, and embarrassment that I felt a moment earlier.

Seth brings a hand up over his shoulder, and leans forward slightly. His movements even remind me a lot of Ethan. He sends the knife sailing through the air. It strikes the heart of one of the outer automatons, sending shards of glass raining down onto the floor. And then it occurs to me, Seth is actually standing farther away from the automaton than when Mason and I practiced yesterday. Truly, Seth has more than just a kind face, he has impressive skill.

"Well done," I say. "Where'd you learn to throw like that?"

Seth gives me a weak smile. "At home, we…" He trails off, suddenly looking worried.

"Go ahead. You're in no danger from me. I won't hurt you. I promise," I add quickly, seeing the distrust in his eyes.

Seth swallows hard. "I…my family and I, that is, used to kill rabbits and other small animals with knives to supplement our food supply."

I try not to look familiar with such practices. But that is exactly what Mark and I, along with pretty much everyone else we knew in our commune did to get extra meat. Other than dried beef strips, we rarely received any other meat in our monthly provisions. But it was risky: One of our neighbors got caught once trying to dispose of a rabbit skin and had to walk around all four communes wearing nothing but a bloody rabbit skin as a loin cloth for punishment. And Mark and I barely avoided discovery more times than I care to admit.

I avert my eyes as a faint blush of embarrassment creeps into Seth's cheeks. When it comes to trying to get enough to eat, there is nothing to be ashamed of. I wish so much that I could spill the truth about myself. I wish I could tell him that I know exactly what he is talking about. Instead, I turn around to face the others.

"What about you all," I say. "Is that why you all look so healthy too?"

Jennifer shakes her head. "I have never thrown a knife like that in my life. We…had other ways of killing wild game to eat where I come from."

I have heard stories of some of the ways that people in other communes have had to resort to in order to supplement their diet. Stoning was just one of the methods to take down wild animals. Most people avoided snares since they are more likely to be discovered and secretly monitored by agents.

I clear my throat. "I've heard that Saints eat locusts that they catch in the fields. Is that true?" Of course, I already know the answer, but I want to use this opportunity to break the ice with them.

"It's true," Nick says with a careful expression. "And, roasted over a fire, they're actually really good."

I can taste the semi-sweet, almost leafy crunch of a locust right now. Mark and I discovered and raided a bee tree a couple years ago. After putting back enough honey for ourselves, we secretly divided the rest among our neighbors. Agatha was so excited over her share of the honey that we could hear her singing praises to God from her house. Fortunately, she was not overheard by an agent. But out of concern for her safety, I asked her the next day to be more careful. She just laughed. No one who has ever tasted them can deny that roasted locusts dipped in honey are a real treat.

I turn back to Seth's hand. Unlike my own, his hands are smooth and nearly free of calluses. I find that hard to believe since corn production takes such a hard toll on a person's body. The physical labor involved in manually planting and harvesting corn is terribly stressful. And nearly everyone in the country who lives and works on agricultural communes grows corn. Perhaps the people at his commune received a pair of gloves for each week in their monthly provisions. Then again, as disgusting as it is to consider, Seth's good looks may have won him gifts by any number of perverted agents in his area. Of course, he would have been forced to offer himself up as exchange for the gifts.

I suddenly become aware of everyone watching me. "I want everyone practicing right now," I say, but not too unkindly. "Except you." I nod at Seth. "You have already proven yourself today." He looks taken aback nevertheless.

I watch as Jennifer comes forward and aligns herself with the far left automaton. Kody falls in beside her and Nick distances himself from them by standing in the exact spot where Seth threw from earlier.

I give Kody a chiding look. "Give her more room." Kody nods and moves to stand more equably between Jennifer and Nick.

I turn back to Seth. His eyes are a darker shade of brown than I had thought. Ethan's are not as brown, but Seth still reminds me a lot of him. Seth regards me with submissive curiosity. I feel my heartbeat quicken. I hope he is not connecting the dots about my true identity.

"Tell me more about yourself," I say. Seth looks bewildered, as if perhaps he heard wrong.

I try not to smile. "You're on my team. I have every right to know about you. Now, you've already showed me how skilled you are with a knife, so what else can you do? What else are you good at, besides growing corn?"

Seth makes an almost inaudible noise that sounds something like a dying sigh or a pained grunt from being put on the spot. "I'm nothing special. I grew up around really great people who taught me how to…survive in changing times. I'm afraid I've disappointed you, so I apologize. The fact is, I am nothing but a simple farmer. I have no awesome skills or great knowledge like you do. Back home, I was known in my commune as the young Bible scholar. I guess the reason why I am here is because I was too outspoken in my beliefs." Seth lowers his eyes to the floor in sadness. "I never thought I'd end up being punished for doing…for what I believe."

I sigh inwardly. Externally, I try to look impassive. "Life has a way of dolling out hardships onto those who do not always deserve it." Seth whips his head up, meets my eyes with a startled frown.

I feel a stab of terror in my chest. I need to learn to keep my mouth shut. "But in your case, there is no doubt as to your guilt."

Glass shatters and crashes to the floor. Seth jerks his head in the direction of the broken heart. I study his side profile. He has high cheek bones and blond eyebrows. I cannot decide if his hair is more red or auburn. If only Emily was here to set the record straight. She would probably have to run her fingers through his hair.

Seth turns back to me, absently runs a hand down his shirt. He looks as if he wants to say something, but is unsure of whether or not he should.

"What is it," I say.

Seth swallows gently. "I was wondering how long we will be here, at this compound."

I wish I knew. "Until you have undergone all the training that...President Gloss has in store for you, and not a moment sooner." Seth narrows his eyes onto me, as if finding my statement weak and almost too friendly for a guard.

I draw myself up to look important. "He...President Gloss, that is, expects the final challenge that will come at the end of your time here to be worth his while to watch. All eight teams will compete against each other in what is expected to be the biggest bloodbath of Saints in the history of the country."

"So I'm likely going to die," Seth says, almost to himself. "I had a feeling that all the pampering we received last night was only to prepare us for slaughter." He looks as shaken as he sounds.

I catch myself worrying at my lips. I thought all the Saints had to undergo a very embarrassing time in the infirmary last night. I want to know the details without raising suspicion. "You mean you did not like your bath," I say in a neutral tone.

Seth looks somewhat taken aback. "On the contrary, the shower was surprisingly comforting. I had expected the water to be cold when I stepped into the shower. Honestly," Seth adds with a wary look, "I thought I was going to have to shower in front of everyone, but one of your fellow guardsmen closed the bathroom door at the last second."

I should have realized that there was a bathroom in the basement. "You should count yourself lucky that we did not make you all bathe in the same dirty water."

Seth brings an arm up to his nose and sniffs. "I smell like some kind of flower or something."

Since I have not gotten close enough to smell any of them, I do not know what they smell like. And, as much as I would like to know what fragrance Seth is trying to pin down, I will just have to wait and ask Mason. But I will need to be careful with what all I ask him, lest he kick his footstool in the mouth.

I spend the rest of the training session looking back and forth between Seth and his teammates. For the most part, everyone seems to be doing fairly well. I was afraid that I would have to resort to brutality to encourage them to cooperate with me. I groan inwardly. I cannot believe I just thought that. I am feeling more and more like a guard with each passing second. And yet, if I fail to convince these people to accept my fake identity, I will only bring about swift retribution on myself. And who knows how they would be treated in my absence. As long as I remain firm with them, I think we will all be fine. As long as Gloss receives reports that paint me as a brutal task master, he should not have any reason to target me for additional punishment. And from the way Mason talks, he intends to see to it that I am kept safe from any additional harassment that would endanger his study of me. Heaven forbid that he should lose his prized footstool. But then again, I'm sure there is any number of women who would pay him to rest his feet in their laps.

"You're late," I say to Mason as one of the guards escorts my team away from the Mirage. "That jerky stick you gave me got lost in the deep sea of hunger a long time ago."

Mason laughs. "You look well enough to me. It's good to be hungry sometimes. It makes you appreciate the times when you're not."

I sigh. "So let me guess, you want me to go the rest of the day without food and yet still have the energy to be a proper footstool?"

Mason holds up two fingers. "Warmth and cushioning; you can give my feet both without much energy. I have found that both are essential elements for a good footstool. Leave out either one and you'll find that most people, especially we physicians, who often stand for long periods of time, can become very cranky. Now, is that what you want footstool?"

I give him a look of pretend surprise. "Does a footstool really ever have a choice?"

Mason laughs again, only this time sounding more genuine. "Who ever heard of a witty footstool?"

"About the results," I say, earning a serious look from Mason. "How will you or anyone else know how my team did in comparison to the other teams?"

Mason takes on a superior expression that makes it hard for me to believe that he laughed just a moment ago. "Everything that happened in there was recorded. I myself or any other guard can go in there at any time and replay everything that happened. You would look just as you do now, just as solid and healthy. Thank of it as literally walking into a television recording."

"Show me," I say, hearing the excitement in my voice.

Mason crosses his arms over his chest defiantly. "No, not today. Besides, I have already made plans for this afternoon. And, needless to say, they include you. Remember when I said I had an idea to introduce St. Ryan to the good things of life? Well I intend to do just that, now come on."

I give him a wary look. "Do your plans include thrusting me into the arms of a harlot?"

Mason throws his hands up, green eyes amused with disbelief. "Surely you do not think that I would want to defile my sacred footstool? For what would I do if you up and contracted a disease and died on me?"

I bite down onto my lip. "Good doctor, there's something I've been wanting to tell you. You see, one of the perverted agents back home…well, let's just say I could have a disease that would eventually kill all who have too much contact with me. And, well, you've already had some contact with me, but there may still be hope for you yet."

"I see," Mason says. "So in other words you want me to take you away from here and release you into the wild so that you can try to find your way back home. Meanwhile, you would be trying not to die from laughter at the good doctor's stupidity."

I sigh inwardly. I did not think it would work, but I had partially intended it to be a joke anyway. Nevertheless, I pretend shock. "Why good doctor, surely you know that I have a much higher opinion of you than that. Besides, you know how defiling skin diseases can be, so you really shouldn't judge."

Mason gives me an exhaustive smile. "You look healthy enough to me. And besides, haven't we already been through a similar episode? Perhaps next time you should resort to childish measures like painting little pustules all over your skin. Or, if you really wanted to freak me out, you could mix green food coloring with your urine, granted that the cooks would give you some, and then leave a sample on my desk for examination."

I recoil. "What kind of sickness would that be?"

Mason shakes his head. "You really don't want to know. But I'll tell you this: I have seen an alarming increase in the number of people seeking treatment. Perhaps your Perverted Demon back home has the Rot right now."

I think I'm going to be sick. "Okay good doctor, I think I've heard enough."

Mason chuckles. "Just be glad that your body is not as defiled as you say it is. I'll say it again: You look remarkably well considering the situation you were in before I…came to get you."

With regards to himself, I consider asking him about all the diseases that his kind of people carry, but he looks way too healthy and seems to take too good a care of himself to have diseases. I know I should not say this, but I almost wish that the good doctor did not look so good. It has clearly gone to his head.

"What is this place," I say, stepping into a large ovular room. Mason closes the door behind me.

"Welcome to the special treatment room," Mason says as he approaches me. "Come on."

I look around the room. It reminds me a lot of what I imagined the interiors of the agent's houses looking like back home: Pure luxury. A library fit for Gloss himself spans the length of the adjacent room. In between here and there is an archway that separates the library from what appears to be a lounge. Mason moves past me and heads towards a large table.

I swallow hard at all the food on the table. I have not seen this much food since all the festivals that we use to have before Gloss. There is easily enough food here to feed everyone in my commune back home.

"What do you think," Mason says, taking a seat.

I think I need to sit down or I might pass out. I pull out one of the heavily padded chairs and sit down.

"Are you going to be all right," Mason says with a frown.

"I'll be fine," I say. I look at a platter of round cakes with holes in their middles. They look like they have been rolled down a dusty white road. Beside them is something that I have neither seen nor tasted since my parents use to celebrate my birthday before Gloss: Chocolate cake. I feel a pang of grief in my chest as images of my last birthday celebration reel through my mind. It was just before my parents were murdered at school and before Gloss came to power. It was a happy time. Ethan and Emily along with all my other friends were there of course.

I can see Ethan now trying to get me away from the crowd without all the girls noticing. I crawled under the table and along the edge of the room to avoid being detected. And, as childish as it may seem, it was a necessary course of action. As soon as I crossed into the living room, I sprang to my feet and met up with Ethan. But it was already too late.

We had two-thirds of the girls chasing after us as we bolted out of the house and made for the old shed in the middle of the field. In all honesty, most of them were trying to catch up with Ethan in order to get him to become their girlfriend. We finally arrived just outside the old shed, where we collapsed under an oak instead of braving the hot shed.

"I knew I should have brought a toad with me today," Ethan said regrettably. "Or a bucket full of 'em for that matter, but I knew your mom would have had a fit. As it is, I can hardly breathe, and I think I twisted my ankle running through one of the pot holes on the way here."

Sure enough, Ethan had sprained his ankle. I left to get help. By the time I got back with Mark, (mom and dad were busy talking to the preacher) Ethan was resting against the tree trying to calm an argument that had erupted among a bunch of girls over which of them found him first.

"I got to him first, therefore he is *mine*," Monya Delstwiser said. She gave all the other girls a chiding look. "Did I not get here ahead of all of you and offer him a cool drink of water? And did he not drink from my hand?"

"I drank from a cup, Monya," Ethan said through clenched teeth. "There is a difference between a cup and a hand."

Mark shook his head with a laugh. "I would have done just about anything when I was your age to have this much attention. Are you sure you want to be rescued?"

"Yes," Ethan barked over the cacophony of the girls. "I'm sure. My ankle hurts and I have yet to taste a single slice of Ryan's birthday cake." Ethan turned to me with a sobering expression. "That's it! I need to eat more cake. If I was fat and ugly, this wouldn't be happening to me."

"Care to share your reflections," Mason says, snapping me out of my daydream.

I swallow hard. "I assure you, they're nothing you'd be interested in. And besides, I don't want to talk about them."

Mason takes a pastry. "Fair enough. From the sound of it, they're not very happy memories anyway."

I would not go as far as to say that. I hold almost any memory with Ethan or Mark in it as happy and special, especially now that I am here in this place. If it was not for such memories, I would find it a lot harder to get by around here.

Mason clears his throat. "Gluttony, that is the sin I want you to participate in."

I give Mason a hard look as he bites down onto the end of a cream filled pastry. "Then I'm afraid you'll be disappointed, because I'm not very hungry."

Looking shocked, Mason nearly drops his pastry. "How could you not be? I mean, you haven't eaten hardly anything all day and you worked like a slave."

I frown. "It wasn't as bad as I thought it would be."

Mason takes a hold of a golden goblet. "Well, if that's the case then perhaps I should see to it that your burden is increased."

I could knock myself upside the head. I shake my head. "No thanks, it was sufficient. Unless of course you want to torment me by putting me in a position where I'd find it nearly impossible to succeed."

Mason gives me a look of exaggerated shock. "Not at all. Remember, I need to keep you alive and well in order to study you. And you are my footstool, an object that I refuse to do without."

I'm sure that if looks could kill, mine would. "Do you really care for no one but yourself?"

Mason takes a drink and then sets the goblet down in front of him. "If that was the case, then why do you think I brought you here?"

I shrug. "I don't know, but you do seem intent on waging war against my religious beliefs. I mean, you even said you wanted me to sin by overindulging in all this food."

Mason traces one of the engravings on his goblet with his index finger. "Not all sin is bad. I mean, not everything you call sin is sin."

I feel my blood begin to boil. He wants to make trouble. I have a good mind to send one of these round cakes hurtling towards him with the hope that it finds its way into his big mouth.

I clear my throat. "So in other words, you think people should be able to do whatever they want, without any regard for the consequences of their actions. Don't you realize how stupid, how foolish that way of thinking is? Say what you want, do what you want, dress the way you want, all for your own pleasure. Take murder for instance. In one breath, a fool says that murder is wrong only to praise the murder of Christian babies in the next. So if murder is wrong, and even your people believe that by majority, then why not call the murder of Christian babies wrong as well? Why do your people find nothing wrong with murdering babies? And don't try to justify your actions. The Bible is very clear where murder is concerned. Remember the Ten Commandments?"

Mason scoffs. "You're thinking is very shallow where murder is concerned. I think people should be able to do whatever they want. And, since President Gloss came to power, those of us who have no religion have fared quite well under him."

I give him an incredulous look. "You really expect me to believe that? Don't forget, you yourself told me how disease ridden many of your kind of people are. And really, I'm not surprised. Ever since I arrived, your friends, especially Jace and Christian, made clear their perversions. All they seem to think about is how many Saints they can *try*, as if they have nothing better to do with their time. Consequences follow such actions."

Mason considers this. "Perhaps, but they view Saints as clean and uncontaminated, despite their strange beliefs. That is one reason why they are so eager to try them. Of course, they also just want to have some fun. But enough of all that," Mason adds with a raised hand, "I didn't bring you here to argue with you, honestly. I find you interesting. So if you're not going to eat anything, tell me something that you think will fascinate me even more about you."

I have half a mind to start eating. Instead, I say "I enjoy history. Or at least I did, before your boss sent agents to steal most of my books."

Mason rises to his feet, green eyes delighted. "Come, there's something I want to show you."

I can hardly believe how friendly he looks. He wipes his hands back and forth, sending a puff of white pastry dust into the air.

I suddenly feel hungry. I take a round cake from atop one of the platters. Seeing this, Mason shoots me a look that speaks of relief and something like pity. I guess he did not want me to leave without eating something from the great spread.

I follow Mason across the lounge and into the library. Mason tells me that what I am eating is called a doughnut. Apparently they were a big hit in the Old Country. And I have to admit, it tastes pretty good.

Mason throws his arms out dramatically. "Behold, the answer to all your problems."

Mason sets off towards a long stained glass case behind a large desk. It extends from the floor to the ceiling. A wooden ladder rests in a metal track beside the colorful display.

I get a good look at the stained glass art, and nearly drop my doughnut. I swallow hard. The scene turns my stomach. The upper half of the case shows a hideous monster severing a man's head from his shoulders with his sharp teeth. Below, in the bottom half of the image is a black kettle full of human heads that have been discarded. The strange thing is that, other than the monster's face, the rest of his partially clothed body looks just as human and ordinary as my own.

"Care to guess who he is," Mason says, paying little attention to me. "No, I don't suppose you would. But you have to admit, it's not every day you get to see the Prince of Darkness."

Mason looks at the monster almost reverently. "Some say this depiction of him takes away from his more handsome appearance, because of his face. Still others find his legs too attractive. But either way, most people find him handsome."

I had almost forgotten that, in addition to all the gods that Mason's kind of people serve, Satan is their commander in chief. I am not afraid of Satan. Nevertheless, the sobering reality of the place I have come to has ruined my appetite.

"Care to kiss his legs," Mason says with a wicked grin. "All the guards here come by throughout the day to kiss his legs. It is said that, by kissing the legs of the Prince of Darkness, one will become impregnated with all his beauty."

"You have got to be joking," I say. "I'm not kissing that thing. I don't care how pretty everyone thinks he is. Besides, not only is Satan a monster, but how can I revere something that I hate?"

Mason runs a hand down Satan's thigh, as if he did not even hear me. "Some even say that stroking him will bring good luck. And, more recently, Christian claimed that the image came to life and licked his hand when he stroked his thigh."

I take a step backwards. I bump into the table and drop my doughnut. It breaks apart into two pieces on the floor.

Mason looks at the mess casually and then turns back to the image of Satan. "The heads in the kettle belong to Saints. They are all who have refused to worship him. If you look closely, you will see the skeletons of all the Saints that he has devoured in his stomach. The image speaks of what will happen to all Saints if they refuse to yield their hearts to the Prince of Darkness."

"How cheerful," I say. "But he doesn't scare me. I know where I stand. And Satan and all the demons in his service cannot touch me." But I have to admit, the depiction does seem to be a reasonable resemblance of what Satan looks like in my mind.

Mason unlatches the case and lets the doors swing wide open. I step over the doughnut pieces and make my way to Mason's side. Mason flips a switch, illuminating several rows of books, many of which are bounded in black leather. He pulls one of them from the shelf above his head. He turns around to face me.

"Let me guess," I say. "You want me to position myself atop the desk behind me so that you can sacrifice me to Satan."

Mason blinks in surprise. "Not hardly. I've already told you that I need to keep you alive to study you. No, this particular book has nothing to do with evil. Take a look," he adds, handing it to me.

I take it and lay it flat across my hand. With my free hand, I pull back the worn leather cover to reveal a yellowish page with faded black print: *Holy Bible*. I almost drop it.

I feel stunned, even bewildered. "What is this doing here? I thought they were forbidden."

Mason snatches it out of my hands and slams it shut. "They are. I was merely showing you what you want and cannot have." He turns around and places the book back into its home. "I think you would have been disappointed with this one anyway. You see, one of the guards recently spit on the first page of Exodus to intentionally mock your God. In his mind, freeing you from this place would be an impossible feat, even for your God."

"Nothing's impossible for God," I say. "Just because your people refuse to believe in Him does not mean that He does not exist. Just because you burned most of the Bibles does not mean that you can destroy God. He is not a myth that you can destroy. Banning Him from everything around you does not mean that you have won. For no one, big or small, rich or poor can defeat God."

Mason brings the two panels together and latches the case. "I did not burn your precious Bibles so *don't* blame me."

I glower. "I'm not blaming you. I was referring to your main boss."

Mason whirls on me, face furious. "You mean President Gloss, if you want to live."

I swallow hard. "Fine, President Gloss. But must you torment me so? I thought you were going to show me some good history books and here we are bickering again."

Mason stares at the mess on the floor. "Clean up your mess and then we'll leave."

I look down at the doughnut pieces. The two pieces remind me of a broken heart, albeit an albino one. I bend down and gather the pieces into my hand. I rise to my feet. I round the edge of the table and tilt my hand over the trash can. I wipe the dust from my hands.

Mason presses his knuckles in between my shoulder blades. "Now let's go."

I turn on him with an angry scowl. "I swear, if you touch me one more time…Believe it or not good doctor, I feel pain the same as you do. Or were you not aware that we Saints also have a nervous system?"

Mason looks like he could either twist my arm behind my back or delve into deeper discussion on the nervous system. "How you Saints have come to know as much as you do is beyond me. But really, to be fair, you're much brighter than the dimwitted idiots that flooded our sacred halls last night. Now come on footstool," Mason adds with a stiff incline of his head toward the doorway. "I need to put my feet up."

Of all the things I dreamed of doing over the years, I never imagined becoming someone's footstool, let alone one who, despite his opinion of Saints, still finds me "interesting". Perhaps the good doctor will, if I live through all this mess, adopt me and elevate me to the position of story teller. I would much rather tell stories than hold his feet.

I run my sweaty hands down my pants. Mason comes to an abrupt halt. I look past Mason to find Christian standing on the threshold of the library. I feel a stab of fear in my chest.

Christian looks between Mason and I. "What brings you two in here?"

Mason throws a hand out and hits me in the shoulder. "I had to use the library. So, naturally, I had to bring him with me. I could not just leave him behind, for there's no telling what he would do if left alone."

Christian leers at me with a nod. "Try to find a Saint-girl to hook up with most likely. At least, if I was in his position, that's what I'd do. And speaking of Saint-girls," Christian adds with a smirk in my direction, "I'm in great need of your opinion regarding Saint-kissing. I hear the use of tongues are forbidden, bad juju if you will when it comes to Saints kissing each other. But I'm willing to bet that one of your kind of people would love to feel my handsome tongue gracing their lips, prying open their mouths."

Christian licks his lips provocatively. I am at a loss of what to say. If I scold him, I will only wind up in trouble with both he and Mason. If I fail to answer him, he will doubtless abuse me. As it is, he looks as if he could wage war against me right now.

I clear my throat. "I don't think you'll have any problems getting one of them, if you're careful. But as far as kissing is concerned, I think I'd let the girl you choose take the lead on that."

Christian studies me carefully. "A diplomatic answer. Could it be that you're smarter than you look Saint-boy?"

"He can surprise you now and then," Mason says, glancing at me. "As you know, I *am* studying him. And, while I cannot yet make any solid conclusions about him, I have to say that all evidence thus far indicates a person of slightly higher intelligence than I had previously thought."

"Slightly higher," Christian says with a laugh. "Considering you estimated him to have the cognition of a six-year-old, that's pretty funny. So what are you saying, that he can think like a seven-year-old? I'll have to spend more time with him, if nothing more than to drink to the sickness of his underdeveloped brain."

Mason narrows his eyes onto Christian. "What brings you in here, besides perhaps giving your hero a kiss on his thighs?"

Christian shrugs. "Nothing much, just wanted to do a bit of light reading." He flicks his eyes to me. "I'm determined to know as much as I can about how to please Saint-girls without excessive force. The last thing I want is to make them feel uncomfortable in my smooth, flawless arms. And besides, I cannot depend on what a single Saint-boy says. I have to do my own research on the matter."

Mason nods. "Good thinking. Never rely on the advice of just a single person. I think," Mason adds with a frown, "that you'd find just the right material in *The Wondrous Art of Love Making* by Theodore Handsome."

Christian wets his lips absently. "Maybe, but I still want to eventually talk to your object of research."

Mason looks at me. "Come by any time in the afternoon, after training that is, and he's yours." He turns back to Christian. "I do not need him all afternoon, and I tire of his stupidity."

Chapter Seven

I sit in front of Mason. I hold his feet in my upturned hands. He complained that my knees were too bony, so naturally, I had to bear the burden of his discomfort. Funny thing is, he never complained yesterday.

"This is ridiculous," I say, staring at his feet.

Mason raises his eyebrows threateningly. "Oh, so you're saying you'd like me to add to your burden?"

I give him a hard look. "You know I'm not. But who ever heard of this kind of treatment? Do you think you're a god or something?"

Mason presses his heels down onto my hands. "Maybe, I definitely have the body of a god. I'm handsome, breathtakingly charming...and I'm also a physician."

Mason inclines his head at his feet. "Even my feet are very handsome. In fact, my last girl friend said I had the prettiest feet of any guy she had ever dated. She thought my ankles were cute as well."

I shake my head wearily. "You're messed up, big time. Look, just because you have been blessed with good looks doesn't mean you should go on and on about it, really. I wish you could see Ethan. As good as he looks; he refuses to let it go to his head."

Mason smiles almost wistfully. "Maybe I should bring him here. A few days in this place could well change his mind, if indeed he is as handsome as you say he is."

"I did *not* say handsome," I say, careful not to dig my fingers into his feet. "I said he looks good, and he does."

Mason shrugs, picks at his cuticles. "Same difference, I know what you meant. You Saints are funny when it comes to appearances. Instead of admitting the obvious, you insist on beating around the bush."

I snort a laugh. "And your kind insists on disrespecting people by over expressing yourselves. The way to a lady's heart is not by talking to her like she is a cheap, everything goes prostitute."

Mason pauses and looks up from his cuticles with a wry smile. "Why Ryan, could it be that you have actually discovered the secret to successful relationships? No, take it from me, women care more about your appearance and how smooth and muscled your body is than your character."

I feel my hands moistening with sweat from the heat coming from Mason's feet. I shift uncomfortably. "If that's the case, if what you claim is true, then why do your people go through so many partners? No my friend, you're the one who does not understand the main ingredient to a successful relationship. From what I have studied in the Bible, true love is pure and based more on the heart than external appearance."

Mason pulls his feet from my hands. I breathe a sigh of relief. I suppose he was beginning to get uncomfortable as well what with all the heat building up.

Mason glares at me. "The heart pumps blood, don't ever forget that. If I took your advice and spent all my time evaluating women's personalities, I would never find my hands on their sweet thighs."

I do not know what else to say to try to reason with him. "I'm tired," I say, not hiding my irritation with him.

Mason gives me an irritable look that matches how I feel. "Then go to bed, after you've washed your hands of course. I prefer a clean footstool. And in this case, in using you, I have a self-cleansing one."

He has a point. I do need to wash my hands before I go to bed. It is just that he gets me so worked up that I find myself forgetting my right hand from my left. It's really his fault, but of course, he would never admit it.

I rise to my feet. Mason follows suit with a yawn.

I try to keep the worry I am feeling from my face. "Where are you going?"

Mason stretches his arms towards the ceiling and yawns. "To wash my feet, of course. Because of you they're hot and sweaty."

I swallow hard. "I prefer to have the bathroom to myself."

Mason looks as if I slapped him across the face. "I certainly hope so. I'm going to wait outside in the hallway until you're done washing up. Good grief, I may be a monster in your eyes, but I assure you, I have no desire to see your nakedness, or any other guys for that matter. You may be pretty, but even I have to agree with your God where such things are concerned. Besides, I…well, I am a physician, I've seen enough human anatomy to last a lifetime, especially when it comes to men's."

I avert my eyes to his feet. Mason almost seems too cultured, too clean to belong to such an evil group of people. I wonder why he chose to work for Gloss. He heads towards the door. I look at his back. There is something about him, something I cannot quite put my finger on. I do not feel like I am in terrible danger around him, despite all his strange quirks.

"Wake up," Mason says irritably. He hits me in the head with a pillow. "You have fifteen minutes to get around before we head down to breakfast."

I sit up on the side of my bed. I run a hand through my hair to flatten it. Mason tosses his pillow to his bed. I have half a mind to hit him in the head with my own.

I follow Mason's eyes to my bare feet. He looks as if he is making a comparative study. Or perhaps he is debating with himself as to how a Saint could have such attractive feet. I clear my throat.

Mason taps his watch impatiently. "If you miss breakfast again, don't count on me to give you anything to hold you over till lunch, because I won't. And more importantly, if you're not in the cafeteria on time, you'll have to deal with Christian. He is expecting you. Needless to say, you'll be sitting by him."

I want to crawl back under my covers and stay there. I cannot stand Christian. I tolerate Mason because I have to, but I absolutely loathe Christian. Undoubtedly he wants to badger me about "Saint-girls".

I manage to get around quickly. I follow Mason downstairs with a great deal of dread and nervous anticipation. Christian always puts me on edge. He never has anything good to say and always talks about me as if I am nothing. Why he wants my opinion when he thinks so poorly of me to begin with is beyond me. Perhaps he just enjoys the satisfaction he gets from being able to talk down to me.

I enter the cafeteria in a bad mood. I can already tell that this day is not going to be a pleasant one. I already got hit in the head with a pillow and now I must suffer what I expect will be more of the same from Christian.

I find Christian sitting at the end of the table where he always sits. I groan inwardly. Christian looks like a venomous spider that cannot wait to sink his fangs into me.

Mason and I split apart as we reach the table. I make my way to the seat beside Christian.

"Not there," Christian says. He nods to the place directly across from him. I want to smile. I will take this slight improvement in my day as a great blessing.

I round the table and sit down with a small sigh. I stare at my plate. A large fluffy white biscuit and sausage patty lay unmade on my plate. My stomach rumbles. Since I did not eat dinner last night due to a lack of appetite, I have not eaten anything since I sampled the doughnut yesterday afternoon. Famished, I quickly put together the components of my meal. I take a big bite. Honestly, I am surprised that Christian has not already interrupted me.

"I have a job for you," Christian says, ruining my appetite.

I drop my sandwich onto my lap. I take it and sat it onto my plate. I could yell at him.

Christian looks delighted. "I found a Saint-girl I want to talk to and I want you to bring her to me. She's the pretty one sitting at the table directly behind me. Now get her for me."

I look past Christian to the team sitting at the table behind us. There are three girls and one guy. I wish I knew which girl he wants. Except for the slightly thin one, the other two look very healthy and equally attractive. Well, at least from what I can see from here. Two of the girls' backs are to me. I shake my head. "I…which one do you want?"

Christian lets out an exhaustive sigh. He turns around and points at the thin girl.

Christian gives me a wicked wry look. "Don't look so alarmed. Believe it or not, I have a special place in my heart for the more delicate things in life. Now," Christian adds with a glint of hatred in his eyes, "are you going to bring her to me or not?"

I wish he would do his own dirty work. I rise to my feet. I never imagined I would find myself in a situation this soon where I would long to sit next to Mason. Who would have thought?

I make my way towards the girl. I stop at the end of her table. She looks up from her hands and meets my eyes. I swallow. She has watery gray-blue eyes and chin-length brown hair. I can't tell if her eyes are always this watery, or if it is just because she is so sad. Her teammates sit as still at statues, their eyes unfocused between me and the girl.

"You've been requested," I say to her.

She rises to her feet without hesitation. Still, I can see a worried gleam in her eyes that clenches my stomach. I want to tell her not to worry, but that would not necessarily be true. I doubt Christian had me fetch her just so he can quote poetry to her.

I direct her to the place in front of Christian. She sits down obediently. I consider asking Christian for permission to make my way to my usual seat next to Mason, but I doubt he would let me go, so I sit down beside Christian.

Christian props his elbows up onto the table and rests his chin onto his clasped hands. "Tell me your name love," Christian says in a surprisingly friendly tone of voice.

"Mindy," she says meekly. Mindy swallows, averts her eyes to the table.

Christian studies her closely. "And are your eyes always this sad, or are you just a weepy eyed creature by nature?"

Mindy flinches uncomfortably. "I am in mourning."

Christian smiles. "Ah, leave a handsome boyfriend standing beside a drooping cornstalk did you? Let me guess, you were in love. And now, you need someone to take his place." Christian leans forward and takes her hands into his. "You're in luck. You see, I have been wanting to have a go at a Saint-girl for a long time now. But before I do so, I have a few questions I want to ask you."

Christian gives me a borderline haughty look. "Your job will be to inform me if you find that, in any way, her answers run counter to what a good Saint should say. That is," Christian adds quickly, suddenly realizing his air of superiority, "if you don't mind helping me."

Christian lets go of Mindy's hand and gives me a friendly smile. "When it comes to matters of love, a guy needs a friend's advice."

Mindy looks between Christian and I with a curious frown. I can tell that she senses the tension between us, despite Christian's sloppy attempt at damage control. But if I want to remain on good terms with Christian, I had better respond favorably.

"You know I don't mind helping you," I say. I decide to go a step further. "That's what best friends are for." I give him the best smile I can muster without making myself sick.

Christian returns my sort of blithe smile, though his eyes betray him. He turns back to Mindy. "Now, Mindy dear, answer all my questions and I'll see what I can do to make your time here more bearable." Mindy nods, almost imperceptibly.

Christian stares at her mouth. "What do you think about tongues? And no, I don't mean that gibberish that you Saints rattle off some times. I want to know what you would say if I leaned forward and tried to pry apart your lips with my tongue right now. Would you accept me, greet me with your own tongue, or turn me away?"

I chastise Christian inwardly. Mindy bites down onto her lip. I watch as a blush creeps across her cheeks. I want to chew Christian out. I had not expected him to ask her such an embarrassing question so soon. I should have known better.

"Well," Christian says, raising his eyebrows.

Mindy closes her eyes in a pained expression, as if asking forgiveness for what she is about to say. "I would not turn away a man who I wanted to kiss me." Mindy opens her eyes, gives Christian a steady look. "But I would slap any man in the face who tried to force himself on me."

Christian's face darkens with anger. It looks like it is all he can do not to explode on her. "You're not very smart. You see, in order to survive around here, one has to say and do everything with tact. I think perhaps I will take you into my room tonight to punish you."

Mindy gives him a beseeching look. "No, please. I'll say whatever you want from me for now on, only do not defile me. I…have never even been with a man, and I could not please you because I do not know you."

Christian looks surprised. "You mean to tell me that a pretty little thing like you has never even been with a man? I find that hard to believe, Saint or not."

"She's not lying," I say.

Christian cuts me a half irritable, half friendly look. "Can you really tell just by looking at her? I get the impression that she has seen action in the corn field." Christian turns back to Mindy. He points an accusing finger at her. "I've got it! It happened on a bed of cornstalks in the corn field with a skinny little wimp who barely had the strength to put his arms around you."

I feel my mouth fall open. Is there nothing that Christian would not say? Does he have no respect for anyone?

Looking on the verge of tears, Mindy stares at the platter of biscuits in front of her. Honestly, I would not blame her in the least if she took the platter and threw it at him.

"Leave me," Christian says to her, blue eyes bored. "Go back to your seat. I'll have you brought to my room if I want you."

Mindy springs up from the bench with surprising courage. She makes her way back to her seat. She was much prettier up close, with the blue beating out the gray in her eyes, and Christian trashed her.

I turn on Christian with a glare of disapproval. "Was that really necessary? Of all the questions you could have asked her and you had to go with that. If that's the way you're going to be, then I would appreciate it if you'd leave me out of your future schemes. If, however, you should get serious about a true relationship, then I would be overwhelmingly happy to help you."

"You'll do what I say when I say it, or you won't be around long. I think you…" Christian leans in closer so as to whisper, "…overestimate Mason's willingness to help you. He wants to study you and so keep you alive during that time. But should you make a habit of recalcitrance, I can tell you right now that he would no longer feel it necessary to help you. Yes," Christian adds with a sly look, "I know all about his plans. I know Mason better than you think I do. He keeps me well informed on just about everything."

So he says. But I cannot help but wonder if Mason is as transparent with Christian as he believes. For instance, does Christian know that Mason uses me as a footstool, however ridiculous and insignificant it may seem. Something tells me that he does not. And I do not think that Christian knows just how interesting Mason finds me. Plus, for some reason, Mason seems intent on playing me down to his friends. Even on the threshold of the library yesterday, Mason said that he "tires of my stupidity". How can he "tire of my stupidity" and yet express such interest in wanting to study me. I see the way he holds onto my every word whenever we are alone. You'd think I was the know-it-all physician and he was the boring Saint.

"Jane," I say. "I need five automatons today."

A sharp intake of breath. "Ryan, it's so lovely to hear your voice again."

I blink in surprise. "You're back."

Jane claps her hands together. "I am. Only do not say anything to anyone outside this room. None of the other teams must know I exist. I intentionally evaded Mason and his computer whizzes by duplicating a copy of myself and hiding it from them. So all the other teams are stuck with my replacement, which I have to tell you stinks, while you get the old fun me."

I shake my head. "I don't understand. What kept you away yesterday?"

Jane sighs dreamily. "If you knew how handsome you looked from my perspective, you'd be flabbergasted."

She needs to be careful. "Jane, please."

Jane sighs. "Fine, here is your explanation: I saw where the computer was being watched for any sign of me. So, obviously, I could not rear my beautiful head without risking getting it deleted for good this time. Only today, when they started up the computer, I saw that they were no longer searching for any sign of me. But as much as I'd like to say I won the nasty episode against my life, that would not be entirely true. There is a catch. If I live outside this training room when the other teams are in session, I would likely be discovered, apprehended, questioned, and then eventually deleted. Ryan," Jane adds in a timid tone of voice, "no one outside of you and your team can know about this."

I want to clap a hand over my heart. Instead, I say "I'll be silent. Honestly, I'm glad to have you back. Your replacement was so boring yesterday, and not very helpful either."

Jane makes an appreciate sound. "Oh how I've missed you. How's a girl supposed to survive without a handsome steed to warm her heart?"

I hear Mason's voice echo in my mind: "Jane, you're too old for him and you know it." If it was not for the fact that I do not want to anger her and get stuck with the new, much less interactive Jane, I would remind her of what Mason said. But I cannot deny that I actually like this Jane, despite her annoying attraction to me.

Jane clears her throat. "Ryan, allow me to make a single request and I promise to steer you in the right direction. As you know, the stakes are high. And, it just so happens that, while I will not reveal myself to the other teams, I can however spy on them for you. I can let you know how they are doing so that you will know just how hard your team will have to work to stay ahead of the game."

I swallow. "You'd do that for me?"

Jane makes a kissing sound. I feel a gentle vibration across my lips.

Jane sighs. "If you'll allow me to make a single request, then yes, I will help you."

It sounds good to me. "Alright, let's hear it."

Jane sounds like she is considering something. "I see that you have two very attractive guys with you, and I am a lonely woman. Now give me a chance to explain myself. If you knew how boring it is to spend most of your time hiding in a dark corner to avoid detection, you too would likely get excited for a chance to love and be loved. So, all I want is to be able to kiss one of the guys each and every day."

I frown. "That's all?" I was expecting something a little more time consuming, a little more embarrassing like questions about love and relationships.

Jane makes a slightly affronted sound, as if the idea of anything else is a slap in the face. "Ryan, need I remind you that I am a religious woman. I too have boundaries. Surely you didn't think I wanted to talk about what it takes to get a girl pregnant?"

I close my eyes in pained embarrassment. "Not necessarily. Look, I'm sorry I offended you."

"Apology accepted," Jane says, sounding pleased. "And, just so you know, I already kissed you. That's what you felt across your lips earlier. Am I not a lovely woman? Are my lips not warm and soft and moist, as if I have a real heart pumping life through them?" I guess she means oxygenated blood.

I wet my lips. Since I have never kissed a girl on the lips before, I honestly cannot say. Still, I can tell by the stuffy silence that Jane is expecting a polite answer, perhaps to make up for my earlier transgression. "Your lips are…special."

Jane laughs. "I certainly hope so. What girl would want to hear anything but?"

I turn around and face my team. I look between Nick and Seth. I give them apologetic looks. Nick's eyes light up in stunned surprise. Seth looks much the same. All well, Mason did tell me not to be downright hateful with them.

I suddenly feel very hopeful. With Jane spying on the other teams for us, it might just give us the leverage we need to survive this place. Plus, if she is willing to spy for us, what else might she be willing to do for us? There is so much I would like to know, so many questions I need answers to. But I'm going to have to be careful. Jane seems friendly enough, but I'm not sure that it would be a good idea to tell her the things said in private between Mason and I, at least not until I get to know her better.

I check the time. We need to get a move on. I turn around and face the place where the automatons always appear. "Jane, we need five automatons if you don't mind."

They blink into existence. Wow. I still cannot believe how awesome this room is. I think I will ask Jane just what all can be done in here, when there is time.

"So do we just start throwing," Kody says beside me.

I nod. "Go ahead." I look past her to find Jennifer running a finger along the edge of her knife. "Don't cut yourself."

Jennifer jerks her head up, fixes me with a curious grin. "I'm not sure I could. As sharp as the blade is, it's not really real, right? I mean, this place is called the Mirage for a reason."

Jane laughs. I can almost see her shaking her head in disbelief. "Do you really think the wicked people who designed all this would let you have real weapons? No, you cannot hurt yourself with that knife. And it can only be used in here."

With a sharp exhale, Jennifer sends her knife flying towards one of the male automatons. It strikes the metal just below the heart and bounces off. I wonder why, out of all the things that could have been designed for us to practice on, we have these things. I mean, they cannot move, they cannot speak, or do anything threatening. What good are they? Surely the final challenge will include more than just standing around and trying to shatter glass hearts. From the way Mason talked, Gloss won't be happy unless all the Saints are tearing into each other like vicious wolves.

I stand in between the guys and the girls. I face the middle automaton. I know that my job is just to see that my team does well each day during training, that I am not required to practice, but still. I want to practice alongside them. I do not want them to feel like I am a superior eagle waiting to dig my talons into their shoulders should they miss. Besides, I cannot deny that I actually enjoy venting my frustrations out on these creatures. If only my automaton looked a bit like Christian…

Seth takes a couple steps forward and then nearly falls backward, as if someone pushed him. He drops his knife. It clatters to the floor and disappears.

"What happened," I say.

Seth rubs his forehead, brown eyes confused. "I…think I hit a wall or something."

"You did hit a wall," Jane says. "It was there yesterday as well, you just didn't notice it. Look at the floor. It prevents you from getting too close to the automatons."

I lower my eyes to the floor. A silvery looking line stretches across the entire width of the room. I'm surprised that I haven't noticed it before now.

"A force field," Nick says in awe. "I've always heard about them but never thought they were real." I guess the force field has been programmed to allow knives through, but not humans.

Jane makes a pitied sound. "I wish they were still only hearsay to you. It would mean that you would still be on your communes instead of in the clutches of a raving lunatic."

"You mean President Gloss, right," Kody says with a curious frown.

Jane lets out a ragged sigh. "Yes, the Nero of our age."

I swallow hard. It hurts to think about all the Christian babies that Gloss has murdered. Wait a minute. "Nero," I say in shock. "How do you know about Nero?"

Jane makes a sound like someone closing a book. "I do a lot of reading. In fact, every book in the library has been digitalized in order to be used in here. Nearly anything can be brought to life in the blink of an eye. So, needless to say, I have instant access to pretty much anything of significance that has happened in recorded history. I know every verse in the Bible as well, though, until you all arrived, I lacked the good company to share my knowledge with."

"Can you show me Absalom," Kody says with a wistful smile. Kody gives me an apologetic smile.

Mason would probably tell me to punish her, and perhaps I should, but I'm not in the mood to do so.

Jennifer flicks her eyes to Kody. "Sister, that handsome prince lived so long ago, it'd be a miracle if there was even a trace of his stone monument left, let alone a colored photograph of him."

Jane laughs. "True, unless there are pictures of him in our books, which there are not, I cannot show you what he would have looked like. But according to the Bible, Absalom was a very handsome prince indeed."

"Show me Mason," I say, wondering what will materialize.

Mason pops up right in front of me. He stands as still and upright as a tree. I take a step backward. Jane laughs.

"Isn't he handsome," Jane says breathlessly. I can almost see Jane shaking her head in awe. "Before you all…no, forgive me, I really should not say anything."

"Go ahead," I say curiously.

Jane snaps her fingers, prompting a change in Mason's position. Mason now lay on his back with his legs drawn up into a sit-up position. He wears a silver T-shirt that coruscates like diamonds in the afternoon sun. I cannot tell exactly where he is at, though the floor he sits on looks as if it belongs in a storybook for kids. A large mosaic of a whale looks ready to gobble up his feet, its large mouth open wide. The rest of the floor is composed of countless blue tiles of varying hue, making it look like Mason is lying on top of moving waters. It's sort of dizzying.

"Did this come from a book," I say.

"Everything you see but Mason," Jane says. "I captured this image of him while he was training in here one day. I couldn't resist the opportunity. Honestly, out of all the handsome men I have access to from all the books; Mason has nearly all of them beaten. He's so lovely. Even his feet are lovely. And, as strong as they are, they feel as soft as silk."

Jane might not think so highly of his feet if she had to hold them all the time. I consider telling Jane what Mason's girl friend said about his feet, but I should probably keep that to myself.

"Why did you want to see Mason," Kody says in a suspicious tone of voice.

Oh no, I did not consider how my request might look. After all, Mason and I are supposed to be equals who work for the same bosses. I stare at the image of Mason. I can almost see the good doctor formulating a response in that twisted brain of his.

I shrug. "It's nice to see my kind of people. Mason reminds me of who I really am." And isn't that the truth.

Kody turns sour and looks away. Jennifer eyes Mason's back with a contemplative look. I clap my hands together. I incline my head at the automatons. Jennifer turns back to face her automaton.

I see Seth giving me a hard look out of the corner of my eye. Well, at least it looks like I have convinced him of my evil identity. If only I could tell him the truth about myself without risking my life along with theirs as well. Nevertheless, I do not feel I can allow him to get away with staring at me so unkindly.

I give him a warning look. "Unless you want me to gouge your eyes out, I suggest you turn away and get to work. Contrary to what you may think, this is not a game. In order to keep from being slaughtered by all the other Saints in the final challenge, you're going to need to do two things: Practice like your life could end today and, if you really think it helps, pray."

"It helps," Seth says defensively.

I give him an ominous look. "Then you better start praying, hadn't you Saint-boy." Seth looks like he could punch me in the face, and I would deserve it.

I look past him to Nick. To my surprise, Nick does not look particularly bothered by my bold, authoritative stance. For some reason, I get the impression that he finds me less threatening, which bothers me even more than Seth's obvious attitude problem.

"So here we are again good doctor," I say. "Let me guess, I need to sit down and prepare to hold your feet up until either my hands or my brain gives out from sheer exhaustion. After all, I find all of your questions about as burdensome as your feet."

Mason gives me a weary smile. "I'd rather your mouth wear out, Saint-boy, that's the second time you've said that in the last fifteen minutes."

I begin to protest otherwise, but quickly stop myself. However, much I hate to admit it, Mason's right.

"What are you doing, if you don't mind me asking? Looking for needle and thread to sew my mouth shut."

"As if it would work," Mason says with a hint of disgust in his voice. His eyes suddenly light up. He straightens up from the desk with a flashlight in his hand. "Funny how something that helps you find things can wind up being so difficult to find itself."

Mason walks across the room and sits down on the side of his bed. Reminding me of a kid, he turns the flashlight on and off several times before finally laying it onto the bed beside him. What in the world has gone wrong with the good doctor's mind?

Mason flicks his eyes to me, not hiding his amusement. "Find my behavior startlingly abnormal do you? Well you haven't seen anything yet. I volunteered for night duty. Do you know what that means footstool?"

I swallow hard. "We're going outside."

Mason nods. "Yes, we're going outside. And while we likely won't need a flashlight, you will carry it for me just in case."

I don't know whether to be afraid or thankful for a chance to leave this building. "How long will we be out?"

Mason pulls on a sock. "Before our duty ends, it is likely that we will hear owls, coyotes, panthers, and possibly what you Saints hate most."

"And what's that?"

Mason looks up from pulling a sock on. "Demons."

I clench my hands into fists at my sides. I can tell that he is just mocking me, just trying to get a rise out of me.

Mason tilts his head to the side. "Is that not what you've been specially trained to combat? I thought all Saints were generals by your age."

"Just feed me to a panther," I say, trying to keep from chewing him out. "Perhaps if you were to char me and skewer me, I'd make a great snack for a hungry panther. And speaking of panthers, where exactly are we in the country, good doctor?"

"Can't tell you that," Mason says as he puts his shoes on. "But honestly, I'm surprised you haven't already asked me."

I shrug. "I didn't figure you'd tell me, but it was worth a try."

Mason adjusts his pants over the tops of his shoes and then rises to his feet. He hands me the flashlight. I wonder what he would do if I refused to go with him. I'm not afraid of going outside. In fact, the thought of escaping this building sounds good, that is, if I was not so utterly exhausted. You see, I had to spend the entire afternoon as Mason's personal attendant. Every time I finished a job, he lined me up with another one. By the time it was all said and done, I had probably gathered up enough loose paper clips from all the disheveled drawers in his desk to build a chain link fence around it to keep him out, not to mention everything else I had to do.

Mason points to my feet with an expression that speaks of both irritation and amusement. "Are you going barefoot or has it not yet sunk in that we're going outside?"

Does he have to be such a smart aleck?

Mason leads me down the staircase and straight towards the main door that we came through the other night. I hear voices in the cafeteria. I stop and try to see through the darkness. It sounds like they're coming from the far end of the cafeteria. And while one of the voices sounds like it might be Christian, I do not know about the other. With all the guards lurking about this place, it could be anyone.

"Hurry up," Mason snaps.

I roll my eyes and make my way towards the door. Mason opens the door and hurries through. I put a hand out to keep the door from closing in on me.

I hear a faint rumble of thunder somewhere off in the distance. I start to turn the flashlight on, but Mason takes my wrist, holding be back.

"Not yet," he says, looking irritated. "Besides, there's enough light around us to see us at least half the way."

Mason strikes off down the sidewalk without as much as a backward glance. I could bolt right now, though I doubt I would get very far. Who knows how many other guards are on duty out here?

I hurry forward and fall into step beside Mason. He looks at me out of the corner of his eye with surprise, as if he expected me to run away.

"Why aren't you armed," I say.

Mason gives me a funny look. "There will be plenty of weapons where we are going. And besides, I find it highly unlikely that you will try to harm me. I could take you down with very little effort if I had to."

I quicken my pace to keep up with Mason. "Oh yeah, you seem awfully sure about that. But in case you haven't noticed, I'm holding the only object between the two of us that could be used as a weapon."

Mason looks straight ahead, as if I am the least significant threat to his well-being. "Maybe, but a flashlight is hardly a reliable weapon, unless of course I was afraid of the light. And it would take a hard blow to the skull to do much damage, and that's something that I just can't see you doing."

I swing the flashlight at Mason's head in angry defiance. His eyes widen in stunned surprise. I stop just short of hitting him. He laughs. Although I did not intend on hitting him, but only to frighten him, I have half a mind to go ahead and wipe the smirk off his face.

Mason moves my hand aside, as if parting a vine to see. "I knew you'd try that. I knew it. And I knew you wouldn't actually hit me. Funny isn't it," Mason adds with a grin. "I have only known you a short while and yet I am able to predict you about as well as our meteorologist predicts our daily weather."

I swallow hard. "What would you have done, if I had hit you?"

Mason looks at me like I'm stupid. "Stand still and take it like a man. Honestly Ryan, you ask some of the dumbest questions sometimes. Naturally, I would have tried to disarm you and bring you to your knees. If that is, you could have hit me to begin with."

I shake my head in frustration. "I *would* get stuck with a mind reading, eagle eyed, know-it-all."

Mason looks to be suppressing a smile. "Let's go, otherwise my corner of the compound will be vulnerable. The last thing we need is some rebellious Saints to show up with Bibles trying to bring down the wall."

Mason looks away before I can decide what to say to him. He sure knows how to make friends doesn't he?

"Our destination," Mason says, pointing to a tower that disappears into the night sky.

I swallow. "Where are all the lights? I don't see any sign of life in it?"

Mason looks at me like the answer is obvious. "Would you show the enemy your exact location if you wanted to remain hidden? There are all kinds of rebellious Saints bent on destroying what President Gloss has worked so hard to build. We know how your kind acts, that is why we are on high alert for terrorist attacks."

I can hardly believe my ears. "Terrorists? Is that what you think we are? Just because I do not live for Satan does not make me a terrorist. Just because I refuse to worship Satan does not mean that I am a dangerous person."

Mason scoffs. "But you are just that. Anyone who does not worship the Prince of Darkness cannot be trusted."

We reach the tower. Mason opens the door for me, but I refuse to go first. He shrugs and then goes on ahead of me. I hear another rumble of thunder, closer this time, as I follow Mason into the tower.

I have a good mind to throw the good doctor's flashlight at the back of his head. We never even used it. But then again, judging by the flickering overhead lights, it might just come in handy yet.

Mason surges past me like a bee destined for a rich storehouse of pollen. I look at our surroundings. Other than the elevator, there are two chairs, and a small table with what appears to be animal bones and coins scattered across its surface.

Mason smiles on the strange display with approval. "Some of the men like to do witchcraft. The point of the game is to try to get a demon to move a coin without rattling the dry bones. If you're lucky, you pull your shirt up and the demon will kiss your chest for good luck. Want to have a go?"

I feel like overturning the table in my anger. What an evil, disgusting game to play. I know one thing, if there were any demons lingering in here; they got the heck out here when they saw me coming.

I turn on Mason with a hard look. "I don't think it'd be much of a show with me here. I assure you I'm the last person any demon would want to meet up with."

Mason gives me a mischievous smile. "Come on, if we're lucky, we might meet up with Degledore, the arch demon who has kissed my neck on more than one occasion in the elevator. While he usually presents himself as a beautiful woman, he has an awesome set of lips."

Again, I seriously doubt that even an Arch demon would want to risk a fight with me. I feel some like David when he came up against Goliath of Gath. For despite my near empty hands, I wield a spiritual sword more powerful than any mortal weapon in existence. Time and again I have employed it against the dark forces that have threatened my very existence, along with that of my uncle Mark as well.

I enter the elevator ahead of Mason. I can see why a demon would love to reside in here, the lighting is atrocious. I can barely see Mason. He seems to be lurking in the corner. I pray that the elevator continues its steady climb.

"I was only joking," Mason says with a laugh in his voice. "About the Arch demon, I mean. I just wanted to see the look on your face. You looked as if you were ready to face the Prince of Darkness himself."

"What about the game," I say, straining my eyes to try to see his face.

Mason makes an exaggerated kissing sound. "That game is completely and wonderfully real. Really, you should try it with me some time. I'd love to see your reaction. Or the look on your face when a demon's lips brush across your chest hair."

I hope he can see how disgusted and angry I look. "It'll never happen. Besides, I think a demon would equate my chest to being too close to Jesus, since He lives within me. And as far as my chest hair is concerned, that's my business. The last thing I want is a guy commenting about my chest hair."

"Fair enough," Mason says in a lazy tone of voice. "I have no desire to see your chest anyway. Why would I when I'm sure mine is much better looking?"

I let out an exhaustive sigh. I'm so sick of him and our night's watch has not even begun.

I leave the elevator behind with a sigh of relief. As much as I dislike Mason, there is something about being in an elevator with him that makes me want to knock his teeth out. And really, considering the things he said to me, that is putting it nicely.

I look at the room around me. It is so much larger and better lit than I thought it would be. Straight ahead, at the far side of the room is the biggest pane of glass I have ever seen. That must be where the guards watch for any signs of "terrorists". I do not know whether to laugh or send Mason's flashlight sailing towards the large window out of anger. Or better yet, perhaps I should lift my hands above my head and shout security breach, security breach. After all, I am the very thing that the guards are trying to keep out of the compound.

A hand grips my upper arm. I flinch and swallow hard. I know one thing; the hand on my arm isn't Masons, it's much too friendly.

"Jack," Mason says cheerfully.

I turn around to face my captor. Jack gives me a measured look. I jerk my arm from his hand. He takes in the flashlight in my hand. I swallow.

"Looking for good sense," Jack says with sarcasm. "Yes, that must be it; otherwise Mason wouldn't allow you to carry such an important tool. Well, I have good news. You have no need to look any further, for both good sense and judgment stand here in front of you."

I scoff inwardly. Anyone who consorts with demons has anything but "good sense and judgment."

Jack looks on Mason with a lazy smile. "It looks beat Mase. What all have you had it doing? Let me guess, you don't have to lift a finger anymore because pretty boy does everything for you."

Mason steps into my field of vision. He stares at me almost blankly, green eyes unfocused. "It has proven to be of more use to me than I thought it would be. It's strange really, how something as insignificant as a fallen pine needle can be of more use than one thought."

Jack looks stumped. "A pine needle? I thought all they were good for was poking pretty girls in the butt to get them to go to the dance with you."

Mason looks at the flashlight in my hand. "You can lay that down. Needless to say you won't need it in here. There's a bar behind me, if you're capable of finding it alone."

I look past Mason to the bar behind him. It could not be any easier to find. I wish he did not have to always be so nasty. I make my way past Mason to the bar.

"It needs a drink Mase," Jack says, keeping with his lazy tone. "Fix it something strong and then sit it down and tell it all about the wild parties we've had in here. Be sure to tell it about the party we had just before it arrived. You know, the one where you were so drunk you ran around the room trying to get Rebecca to slow down so you could pinch her on the butt."

Mason clears his throat, as if uncomfortable. "I think I'll leave that one for another time. Besides, one of us needs to be looking out that window right now. And since my watch has already begun, I'm the one who needs to get busy."

I lay the flashlight down by a dark bottle. It looks like the stuff that the agents drank back home. Our commune was littered with bottles of all shapes and sizes. But far worse was when the agents got drunk and then engaged in all manner of revelry. I rescued Ethan from more close calls than I care to admit. Usually they would chain him to a post as they drank and danced around babbling all manner of filth. And then I would sneak in and unchain him. I never got caught. And he never got into trouble for mysteriously disappearing.

Suddenly feeling dizzy, I lean into the counter for support. I hope Ethan is making it along all right without me, along with Mark and Emily and everyone else as well. The thing is, as many times as I have rescued Ethan from so many terrible situations, I cannot help but feel like something bad has happened to him in my absence. I do not think the agents would kill him, he looks too good for that, but they would try to abuse him, do ugly things to him. Part of me, for Ethan's sake, wishes that he did not look so good.

"Are you okay," Mason says with concern in his voice. "Jack just left. I'd say that by the looks of that bottle, he was enjoying himself a little too much. Look," Mason adds with a strange frown, as if he is concerned about me, "are you sure you're fine? You look like you could use a pick me up. How about…"

"I'm not polluting my body with that crap," I say, cutting him off.

Mason stares at the bottle. "I was actually going to offer you a root beer, you could use the caffeine."

Has the good doctor gone soft? "Thanks, but I don't want anything."

Mason shrugs, turns towards the counter. "Well, I do." He reaches past the dark bottle and takes a tall green one that has a picture of a scantily dressed woman plastered across its face. "I do love this stuff, though it's a lot better when you have a beautiful woman to drink it with."

Mason brushes a thumb across the woman's legs. "She is gorgeous. What do you think about her legs? Never mind that, you wouldn't give me an honest answer if you could, Saint-boy."

I look at the woman and shake my head in disgust. She wears something like silk stockings, and has bright red lips to match a single piece of narrow cloth running across her breasts. She looks like a prostitute. Surely Mason does not have a penchant for such women. I mean, he looks so healthy and seems to take too good a care of himself to want to wind up in the arms of a prostitute.

"She is a looker," Mason says wistfully. He pours himself a drink. "Out of all the women I've been with, I've never had one that looked like her."

That might not be such a bad thing. He takes a drink and sets his glass down onto the counter. Several dirty rings stain the marble counter.

Mason gives me a casual look. "Sure you don't want a drink? The bottle's not far from empty. I'll even let you have the prize."

"The prize," I say, bewildered.

Mason nods and flicks a finger against the side of the bottle. "Oh yeah," he says, dragging out each word. "At the bottom of every bottle is some kind of prize for men. They're small, and in capsules. The last prize I got was a capsule of spit from the very woman on the bottle. Yeah, not exactly what I wanted, but still. Let's see what we have here."

I take a step backward. Mason takes a bigger glass and begins emptying the contents of the bottle. I look closely for the capsule, but do not see it. It must be very small. Mason finishes pouring out the urine colored liquid and then shakes the bottle with a smile. He inclines his head at my hand.

I hold my hand out. Mason turns the bottle upside down over my hand. He gives it a shake and the capsule falls out onto my hand. It is larger than I thought it would be, and made of glass.

"I don't believe it," Mason says, green eyes shocked. "You got exactly what I've been wanting, but I won't take it from you." I stare at the bluish looking gook in the capsule, unsure of what it is.

Mason eyes the capsule longingly. "That stuffs called Spell Bound. Put it on your lips and kiss a woman one time with it and the polar freeze that radiates off your lips is said to command her heart for a lifetime."

"You can have it," I say, laying it on the counter. "Good luck, it sounds just as sensible as your friend's pine needle theory."

Mason stares at the capsule like it holds all the answers to his love life. "This is gonna change the game for me. And it looks like there's enough balm here to command at least a half dozen hearts at the same time."

"Here," he says, pulling the capsule apart carefully. He dips the tip of his index finger into the gook and looks up at me with a playful smile. "Don't look at me like that; I don't want *you* to kiss me. I only want you to experience what it feels like. Now," Mason adds with an impatient frown, "are you going to cooperate with me or will I have to twist your arm?"

I can tell that he is only joking, but still. He sort of reminds me of Ethan, before Gloss, when he wanted me to try something new. I feel my heart cave in at memories of long ago. I look Mason in the eyes and nod. And just like Ethan, he looks like I have made his day.

I swallow nervously as Mason approaches me. "This isn't the most sanitary way to apply it, but still." He gives me a funny look. "Stop trying to hide your lips. Good grief, I'm not going to poison you, think of all the trouble I'd be in if I did. My bosses would hang me." That might not be such a bad idea.

I stiffen as Mason smears the gook across my lips.

"Now lick your lips," he says excitedly.

Instantly, I am reminded of the Scripture of Adam and Eve, when their eyes were opened after eating the forbidden fruit. I feel as if every nerve in my body has been covered in one big rainbow of emotions. I feel happier, stronger, more desirable, though not that sensible. If only Emily where here, I actually think I'd have enough courage to kiss her, though she'd probably slap me across the face.

Mason closes the capsule with a wicked grin. "Bad stuff isn't it. I knew you'd like it. If only I could let you use it on one of those pretty Saint-girls of yours, I'm sure you'd come away with a face full of Saint-liva."

"That would be disgusting," I say, not hiding my emotion.

Mason kisses the capsule and then tucks it away carefully into his pant pocket. "Maybe, but at least you'd know it works. That stuff does something to women when it touches their lips."

I shake my head. "So that's love for you, a face full of spit without any real affection?"

Mason gives me a serious look. "Love is really subjective, wouldn't you say?"

I roll my eyes. "No, I wouldn't say that. To love someone is to care about them. Do you mean to tell me that you would really care about the women you'd use that stuff on?"

"I don't know," Mason snaps. "Why do you have to ask so many questions? Why do you always have to turn everything exciting into a doomsday catastrophe?"

Why does he always have to be so rude? "There's no reason to get so angry. Unless of course it's because the truth hurts?"

Mason gives me a dangerous look. "Come on, there's something else I want to show you."

I follow Mason past the bar and around a huge table that looks big enough to accommodate at least half of the guards that I have seen around here. It's hard to believe that we are at the top of a tower. Everything about this room, from the hardwood floors to the couches at the sides of the room makes it feel more like being in a house than a high security watchtower.

Mason picks up the pace as he heads towards the large pane of glass. At the rate he is going, he looks as if he is going to run right smack dab into the middle of it. I pick up my pace as he seems intent on making it to the window before my next breath. Mason suddenly disappears. I feel my breath hitch in my throat, my heart lurch in fear.

I run the rest of the way to the window. It opens up like a curtain, revealing Mason on the other side. I hurry forward before it has time to shut.

I step out onto a covered balcony. Mason stands at the edge of the balcony with his back to me. Lightening dances across the sky not far away. The air is muggy, prime for rain.

"I'm already sweating," Mason says in a disgusted tone of voice that sounds more to himself than to me. He keeps his back to me. "I bet that shocked you didn't it, my sudden disappearance that is. And now you're probably thinking it's a pity he didn't fall to his death."

He must really think I'm evil. "Not at all," I say, slowly making my way to the guardrail beside him. "To be honest, it scared the wits out of me."

Mason laughs. "I haven't heard that expression in a long time." Mason leans forward to rest his arms against the guardrail.

I slow to a snail's pace for the last few steps. "That doesn't surprise me. Your kind of people have substituted sick phrases for everything that use to be viewed as good."

A loud rumble of thunder rolls across the sky. Mason sighs. "You Saints are so shy. It looks like all those years of working alongside each other among the cornstalks would have put an end to that. Let me guess, out of all the times you had a chance to kiss your sweetheart unseen, you never once yielded to the temptation. Why not, surely there's nothing wrong with a kiss? And from what you've told me, you had a girl who would have been worthy to test your affection on."

I roll my eyes, though his back is still to me. I wish he would stick to talking about important things, like how I'm going to survive this crazy period of my life. Nevertheless, to prevent angering him, I feel like I need to answer him. After all, I believe he is the key to leaving this place alive. I think.

"I never had the right moment," I say, watching the lightening dance across the sky.

I stop just shy of touching the guardrail. Mason gives me an incredulous look.

I throw my hands up. "All right, I guess there might have been a few good moments; I just didn't know how to go about seizing them, if that makes any sense at all."

Mason gives me a knowing look. "I know exactly what you mean. What about your friend…Ethan? From the picture you painted of him, he didn't sound like the kind of guy who would pass up on a chance to show off his affections."

Lightening fans out across the sky like a spider web. It feels so weird to be standing here, no telling how far away from home, talking to a guy about something that I rarely discussed with my best friend, much less with Mark. "Ethan was not nearly as showy as you think. Sure he got a great deal of attention, but he never let it go to his head, as I believe I have already told you. And then when your people took over, when the agents poured in and began harassing people, he became even more determined to stay out of the lime light. In fact, I recall several occasions where he rubbed dirt on his neck and face in an attempt to deter agents from messing with him."

"Sounds like he was a smart guy," Mason says, looking impressed.

"Yeah, he was…is," I say. I hate talking about him like he is dead or something. Ethan has to be alive and well, he just has to be, and Mark as well.

Mason watches the lightning storm. "Did you ever consider running away?"

I swallow hard. Mark and I had discussions on going into hiding many times, but I'm not sure if I should tell Mason. What if he got really mad at me at some point and up and betrayed my confidence? Mark could find himself in serious trouble.

"You don't have to tell me," Mason says, smiling at the sky. "Your silence says as much as if you had."

I swallow. "Why don't you just toss me over the guardrail and be done with it? Why are you so insistent on tormenting me? Don't you know that's how I feel?"

Mason makes an uncomfortable sounding noise in his throat. "It's a shame I can't take you up on the idea. But then again, it'd probably be a waste of time. Along would come an angel to rescue you and then, as soon as it saw me, I'd be toast, or cake."

I laugh. "Maybe so, but something tells me that you wouldn't really hurt me, even if you could."

Mason whirls on me and takes a hold of my throat. "I could hurt you right now if I wanted, I just cannot kill you or incapacitate you."

I look at his wrist. As dangerous as he looks, he is not hurting me. In fact, his fingers are barely pressing against my skin, as if he is afraid he will hurt me. I meet his eyes with a smile. "Come on, either hurt me or let me go. Who ever heard of being in the jaws of a friendly shark?"

"Interesting assessment," Mason says, releasing me. "I think I just felt a raindrop anyway. Let's go, unless you want to stay out here and let the rain wash away your sins."

There he goes again, always trying to get a good jab in at me. "Without the shedding of blood, there can be no remission of sins. Thanks to my Lord and Savior Jesus Christ, he took care of that at the cross two thousand years ago. Haven't you ever read the Bible, at least once?"

Mason takes a hold of his shirt and pulls hard until it rips at the chest. I blink in surprise. He rips it again so that his chest is now exposed. He pulls the remnant up over his head and throws it to the floor. I stare at it in disbelief. I meet his eyes in stunned surprise.

Mason holds up two fingers. "I'll give you two chances to figure out the meaning of what I just did. If you answer successfully, I will give you my torn shirt as well as a break from being my footstool for a day. If you're unsuccessful, then I'll think of some additional way to torment you."

I look between Mason and his shirt. I do not have a clue. Okay, I do know one thing, he is nuts.

Mason runs a hand over his abdomen. "Hurry up, unless you want to get soaked."

I feel the rain pelting my hair, running down my neck. He sure picked a fine time to completely lose his mind. I run a hand through my hair. The last thing I want to do is to give him another reason to torment me anymore than he already does, though judging by his eyes, I do not think he is really serious. Still, this is a game to him. The good doctor is toying with my mind. The thing is, I feel like I'd have more luck taking flight from this balcony than providing him with the answer he is looking for. If only he would give me a…

Wait! I think perhaps I do know the answer. Yes, I'm sure I do. I bend down and pick up Mason's shirt. It is damp with sweat and rain.

I clear my throat. "Many people in the Bible often tore their robes in times of great distress. In fact, I believe it was the high priest who tore his robe after Jesus testified before the full assembly of priests who wanted to kill him. Is that the right answer? I mean, we were talking about the Bible only a moment before you decided to ruin your shirt."

Mason looks irritated, presses his lips into a hard line. "Good Saint, you surprise me, I didn't think you'd get it."

I wad his shirt up into a ball and throw it at him. He catches it at his stomach. He turns around and throws it over the edge of the balcony.

"So," I say, "does that mean you're not going to keep the rest of your word? You did tell me I would get to keep your shirt if I won." Like I really wanted it, but still.

"I changed my mind," he says with a slight sneer in his voice. "Besides, what good would it have done you anyway?"

I make my way to the guardrail. "I don't know, it was all wet and sweaty, but you did give me your word. But I can see now that your word means very little. If anything, it proves that I cannot trust you like I thought I could."

I look at the puddle of water pooling up at Mason's feet. I find it strange considering no more rain that has fallen.

"Trust is something nearly nonexistent around here," Mason says. "Only a fool trusts someone that he doesn't know very well. I learned long ago not to trust anyone, for as soon as you do, they'll disappoint you. The weak and dumb get played all the time, just like your kind of people. You could ask a Saint to follow you into a dark cave, and they would, sure that their one true God would be their light to keep them from all harm."

Mason gives me an exceptionally haughty look. "The reason why my kind controls everything is because we are not so easily fooled. While Saints waste their time in prayer, we get right to work. And, because we have refused to accept your narrow minded beliefs, we have been rewarded by our gods. And, in reward for our devotion to our gods, we get to do things that you Saints cannot stand. Just because your God doesn't allow you the pleasure of orgies and fine women doesn't mean that you should turn your nose up at us."

I sigh. "There's more to life than…well, the things you just said. Look," I say, swallowing hard. "The wages of sin is death and eternal separation from God. And if I had the smallest speck of doubt as to what would happen to my spirit upon my death, I'd be trying to figure it out. Remember, a fool says in his heart there is no God. Take you for instance, consider your appearance. Do you actually think that your well-formed body came from monkeys or a glob of algae, because I don't?"

"Are you saying I'm pretty," Mason says, taken aback.

I raise my eyebrows. "Not hardly and you know it. But to God, you are His masterpiece. He made you after all. He made the first two humans and allowed them to reproduce."

Mason raises his eyebrows into an unconvinced look. "You Saints believe anything. Now, do me a favor and run inside and grab me another shirt. If Jack hasn't moved them, you should find a stack of them on the blue couch."

Chapter Eight

I wake up on the blue couch a few hours later. To my surprise, Mason gave me leave to sleep right after I delivered his shirt. Honestly, I'm surprised he did not want to cuff me to him after our heated exchange. I sit up on the couch with a yawn. Mason sits at the large table across from me with his feet propped up.

"You look awful," Mason says, hands clasped behind his neck. "I thought about waking you, but then I thought I had best fulfill the rest of my word. After all, how can I expect you to cooperate with me if you are as angry as a wet hornet?"

I run a hand along the edge of my hairline. "I'm not angry with you. It's all in your head. I don't like how you treat me, and yes, I do get angry with you, but I'm not right now."

I lower my hand. Mason looks somewhat confused, as if he had expected me to shout at him or something. I look out the window. I see a rainbow off in the distance. Only God could make such beautiful displays against the canvas of His sky. I check my watch. Seven twelve. I got about three hours sleep. Not bad considering I had not expected to get any.

I suddenly remember what Mason said about me looking bad. I could throw my pillow at his head. Being around him is enough to drag anyone down, despite lack of sleep. And besides, he does not look so good himself.

"Did you know you talk in your sleep," Mason says, taking in my face. "Oh don't look so worried. Not anything discernable, but every once in a while, you mumble and grumble, as if you are arguing with yourself." That is the first I have ever heard about it.

I wet my lips. The air in here is so cold and dry. "I think something would be wrong with me if I didn't grumble around you, even in my sleep. I can't say anything without you snapping at me. You treat me halfway decent one minute and then you're trying to chew me up and spit me out the next. Honestly good doctor, it might not be a bad idea for you to put your feet up and rest more often. You seem to be under a lot of stress or something." But probably not as much as I am under.

Mason unclasps his hands and leans forward to look me straight in the eyes. "I am under a lot of pressure. If you had any…Never mind, forget that. We can go ahead and leave now, the next guard should be along at any time."

I wish he had finished the previous sentence. I would love to know why Mason is under so much pressure. Could it be that his success or even his life is tied to how well he can study and manage me? And yet, most of the discussions we usually have are so scattered, I often forget that he is even studying me. I thought his study of me would involve a great deal of scholarly organization, including using his medical terminology to hammer me with tough questions in order to break me.

We enter the training building about a half hour later. Between my lack of sleep and the barrage of questions that I swear he had waited until I was half asleep to ask me, what should have been a short and semi pleasant trek across the compound ended up being a big pain in the butt. And of course, as you may have guessed, I fired back at him a time or two. When he asked me if I had ever had a dream about making love to a Saint-girl, I blew up on him. And then with an eyebrow raised, he suggested that I could use some medication to calm me down when he was the one who stirred me up to begin with.

"I thought Saints were the forgiving type," Mason says, looking bewildered. "And yet here you stand, looking as if you could knock me out."

I give him a cool look. "I have forgiven you, though it took a great deal of personal goading. How would you like it if I asked you a really embarrassing question?"

"Go ahead," Mason says blithely.

I take a deep breath and shake my head. "I have no desire to put you on the spot like you do to me. I'd be no better than you are, though I do have a few questions to ask you sometime alone if you would cooperate with me."

Mason looks past me to the training room. "You'd best get in there, otherwise your admirers may start plotting your demise. And remember," Mason adds with a sarcastic half smile, "your main job is to save your own life, so be careful and do everything just like we've talked about. And, should you desire to inflict some punishment onto your pretty Saint-girls, you might consider pinching them in the butt. Now as far as the guys, I'd stick to a more verbal approach, like commenting on how pathetic their biceps look or something. No guy who has nice muscles wants to hear someone belittling them."

I give him a look that includes both anger and disgust. "Any last words, or have you exhausted your nastiness for the day?"

Mason inclines his head at the door with a contented expression. "I think I covered everything pretty well. Now get in there, you'll be using a crossbow today, and I expect it'll take you a while to figure it out. If you can't figure it out, you and your team may be…fodder for the wolves."

I swallow hard. "I've never used a crossbow before. What about the other teams, won't their guards already know how to use them?"

Mason nods. "The other guards have mastered the use of the crossbow. So as you can see, you're going to have to work extra hard to ensure that you don't let your team fall behind the others. Still, I don't think President Gloss would have you killed if things don't go well with you today. Remember that first and foremost, he wants you to pay for disrupting the atmosphere in your commune. He wants you to struggle and enjoys all the reports that I have been sending him. He hopes that, before it is all said and done, you will denounce your God as well as submit to kissing the image of Satan in the library. He wants to see you kiss Satan's thighs and lips in person. Then, and only then, will he really consider sparing your life."

I look at him point-blank. "I'm not kissing that thing. I will not bow down, praise, or kiss Satan. I might consider digging my fingers into his neck, but that's about it."

Mason's expression darkens. "If you don't, then there is little I can do for you. Now if you really want to get our president's attention, you might consider taking it a step further by stripping off your clothes, slashing yourself, and then bow before the Prince of Darkness as his disciple."

I recoil. "You're nuts. As if the idea of honoring Satan isn't bad enough, you also expect me to shame myself by taking off all my clothes in public? No way."

Mason smiles. "Don't worry, I'll turn away as soon as your pants come down, I promise. Like I've told you, I have no desire to see you naked."

"But your bosses do."

Mason gives me an impatient nod. "Yes, they do. For a Saint, you have been noted as having a very attractive body, and they want to see it, all of it. In fact, there have been several requests made by many guards to be the first to hold your naked body."

"That' sick," I say, wanting to run and hide. "Perhaps I'll just stop eating or…you can give me some pill to make me look sallow and gaunt."

Mason looks humored. "I could, but I won't. You have a very desirable body, ruining it would be both disrespectful and a waste of natural beauty."

I can hardly believe my ears. "Disrespectful? And yet making me take off all my clothes just so a bunch of perverts can do nasty things to me is perfectly fine? What is it with you people? Is there nothing that you all wouldn't try? I mean, resorting to sexually abusing a teenage boy used to be considered against the law. You know the word vile? Well, before your kind came to power, it used to describe all the stuff that is now perfectly acceptable. The kind of stuff that your people do to each other is vile and wrong. I've seen how the agents back home act. I've seen the detestable things they do to each other and for the gods they serve."

Mason gives me a hateful look. "So you shouldn't be surprised then. Honestly, what did you think? That you were coming to some kind of Saint gathering when you came here? If you're not careful, you may not survive long enough to refuse kissing Satan. Do you want to die? I didn't think so," Mason adds with a worried look. "Now listen closely. Tomorrow night will be a very sacred gathering for us, known as the Festival of Demons. As you know, it is when we come together once a year to worship demons in all kinds of exciting ways. You will be expected to dress scantily, as if you want to be the center of the party. Should you make a good impression, it's possible that any poor performances during these next two training sessions will be overlooked. But you will have to work it, use your charm and good looks and be willing to put yourself in an uncomfortable situation. And, if you want to really win the crowd, you'll participate instead of just being a pretty statue. That means setting aside all your undesirable religious practices in favor of kissing anyone and everyone as well as engaging in all the necessary rituals to appease our demons."

I shake my head defiantly. "I'm not having sex with anyone. And don't think you can get me drunk and lead me into the crowd on a leash. Besides, you yourself even admitted to the health threats of engaging in lewd behavior. I refuse to turn my body into a cesspool just to please a bunch of perverts."

Mason sets his jaw in an angry look. "You will if you want me to help you anymore. Now, get in there before I really lose my temper with you."

I wish I had the courage to knock him out right now. Then perhaps he would beat me up so severely that I would have to take up occupancy in one of the beds in the infirmary. How could I be expected to attend the Festival of Demons if I am too sore to move?

No, I will just have to come up with another way to escape tomorrow night's Festival of Filth. If I attacked Mason now, I would lose the only person who has offered me help since my arrival. As much as I want to do something in my defense, it will have to wait. I give him a submissive look.

Mason smiles, looks as happy as a perverted agent with a group of Saints to defile. "Great, now get in there, your team will be wondering where you're at."

With a slight tremble in my hand, I take a hold of the doorknob. Mason turns around and sets off down the corridor. I follow him with a fierce glare. If I fail to come up with a solution before tomorrow night, one thing is for certain, I will never be able to lift my head up again. I will never be the same person again.

I enter the room with a mood of fearful gloom. And to think that I was actually beginning to feel like Mason was a halfway decent person last night. I mean, he did allow me some unbothered sleep.

"You look sick dear," Jane says. "Tired and sick, as if you just crawled out of the morgue from having died of Heart Pustules."

"What," I say with a frown.

Jane clears her throat. "Forgive me; I should not have mentioned it. But I thought you knew. It's the latest disease spreading through the guards around here like wild fire. It's awful. I expect that the few guards who don't already have it will contract it tomorrow night. Why these people do whatever they want without any regard to the consequences of their actions is beyond me."

I swallow. I look between my teammates. They all look bewildered. I wish I could say the same for myself. Instead, I'm curious to know how much more Jane knows about tomorrow night's festival. The thing is, I need to do it in a way that will prevent my team from questioning my true identity. First off, I need to give Jane a sign to be careful with what she says. I suspect that she may already be waiting for such a sign.

I clear my throat and give Jane a cautious look. "How will you learn about what all goes on tomorrow night?"

Silence. I search the room for any sign of her. I feel stupid. I have yet to actually see her.

"Hey," Nick says with a scowl.

Jane sighs dreamily. "Ah, you have such sweet lips. I could tell by looking at you that it would be an experience to remember. I said yesterday that I would kiss one of you boys each day. I knew I wouldn't be disappointed with you. I felt as if my heart was going to explode. Indeed, your lips are moist and very inviting. It's not every day that a woman such as myself gets to indulge in such fine things."

Nick wipes the back of his hand across his mouth. "I don't like things messing with my body."

"I am not a thing," Jane says indignantly. "I am a *woman*. Just because you cannot see me does not mean that I cannot feel and taste and smell and hear. In fact, I have a hyper sensitivity to things that you all are barely aware of, if aware of at all. Take for instance your feet Nickolas. I can feel the warmth radiating off of them from your nervousness. And you have to admit, it's not every day you get the privilege of kissing such a beautiful woman, so count yourself lucky."

Nick looks up, blue eyes searching the ceiling. "I can't see you, so how do I know you're beautiful? For all I know, you could be as ugly as a troll. And I suspect that if I actually could see you, I would probably..."

A woman suddenly materializes beside Nick. Nick yelps and staggers backward.

"Now what do you think," Jane says, looking pleased with herself.

I can hardly believe my eyes. Jane appears to be about thirty, and has very pretty green eyes and light brown hair. I had in mind someone older based on her slightly abrasive voice. Well, at least her voice sounds a little abrasive when she talks fast.

Jane looks at Nick with a bright smile. "Am I not beautiful? Please tell me I am, I've spent quite a while trying to decide whether or not I should reveal myself to you. Even before you came here, I argued with myself for weeks about the safety of putting myself out there for anyone to see. If you knew how many books I've poured through, weeping as I went, wishing that I had friends to reveal myself to…This means a lot to me Nicolas."

Jane wipes away a tear. "You are very handsome, but honestly, I'd rather us just be friends for now."

Nick looks as if he could pass out. He swallows hard. "I had no idea how…I mean, you *are* beautiful."

Seth raises an eyebrow. "How do we know that you didn't just steal that body from one of those digital books you claim to read?"

Jane looks affronted. She puts a hand over her heart. "I am not lying. I swear on the Bible. Look," Jane adds quickly. A Bible suddenly materializes in her hand. She puts her free hand on top of it. "I swear I am telling the truth. Plus, if you look closely at the pendant I am wearing, you'll find my name on it. It was given to me by my creators."

Looking incredulous, Seth leans forward, brown eyes studying Jane's pendant. He leans still closer. Jane looks as if she is struggling between wanting to lean forward and kiss him and stand firm, to prove her identity.

"What does it say," Nick says.

Seth swallows hard, takes a step backward. "She is who she says she is."

"This is creepy," Jennifer says, dark eyes appraising Jane as if searching for something to question her about. Her eyes stop on a tear on Jane's shirt. "Would you say your creators are flawless at their work?"

Jane turns around to face Jennifer. "Why yes, as much as I dislike them, I must admit that everything they create for this training facility is as right as the nose on your face."

Jennifer points to the tear in Jane's shirt with disbelief. "If that's the case, then how do you explain that rip."

Jane averts her eyes to the floor. "Please, it's a painful story with a great deal of emotional trauma involved."

Jennifer places a hand on her hip. "I'm sorry, but if you expect us to believe everything you say, you're gonna have to be more transparent with us."

Kody stares at the tear with dawning realization. "Oh my gosh. Let me guess, there's a guy like you in this place who tried to…force himself on you."

Jane closes her eyes in a pained expression. "Not exactly, no. It was one of the guards, weeks ago before any of you came here. He…told me to let him have his way with me but I refused, of course. The second I refused, he shouted a command that prevented me from resisting him. He then took a hold of me and, one by one, issued commands to remove my clothing."

Jennifer claps a hand over her mouth. Kody looks light headed. Nick and Seth look like I feel, as if this whole conversation is as bizarre as talking trees.

"But how does that explain that tear," Jennifer says with a frown.

Jane looks at the tear in her shirt. "I did it. The one thing I can do for myself is control my clothing. I wanted to let…*him* know how he wounded me. That the tear in my shirt is symbolic of the emotional damage that he caused me."

Kody nods sadly. "Of course, but did he even notice it?"

Looking insecure, Jane grips her sides. "He noticed. In fact, he even laughed and ran a finger across it. He…abused me more times than I care to admit."

"That's awful," Jennifer says, placing a hand over her mouth. "Is there anything we can do to help you recover?"

Jane smiles weakly. "Just be my friends. You all are the only sane people I have seen since my birth. I know you are good, God fearing people. Well," Jane adds with a disapproving look at me, "most of you are anyway. And I want to help you all that I can to ensure that the monsters running this place do not treat you like they did me."

I give Jane a disapproving look. She needs to be careful. Just because she is spying for me doesn't mean I have given her free reign to do as she pleases.

Jane suddenly looks worried. She bites down onto her lip. She looks between Kody and Jennifer. With a troubled sigh, Jane gives me a beseeching look. "With your permission, I would like to tell them what some of the other guards said they would do to any rebellious Saints."

I hate being put on the spot, especially when there is so much at stake. I give Jane a warning look. I cannot afford to let everything blow up in my face just because Jane wants to talk. "I'd rather you didn't. Just because you do not think me as evil as the others does not mean that I agree with all the things you say about them. Remember, we have a duty to perform here, and unless we get busy, there's a good chance that none of the Saints before me will be around much longer."

"Very well," Jane says without inflection. "As you know, you all will be using crossbows today. And I should tell you, the other teams have been doing quite well. I have spied on them from a distance."

I clear my throat. Jane narrows her eyes onto me. I have no idea how to summon a crossbow. I raise my eyebrows at her for help.

Jane looks like she could roll her eyes at me. "Look to the wall, as usual."

I look around me and find a rack of crossbows hanging on the wall beside me. I see no sign of a quiver or arrows. The bows look plain enough, but without arrows to shoot from them, they will be of little use to us.

Jane lets out an irritable sigh. One of the bows disappears from the rack. It materializes in front of me with a tiny pop. I try not to look surprised.

I take the bow in hand. I run a finger over the smooth groove at its center. It feels just right to me, despite the fact that I have never used a crossbow before. Now, if I can just figure out how to get my hand on an arrow, I might be able to keep myself from looking like a fool.

With a silent prayer on my lips, I hold out my free hand the same way I did during knife practice. I feel a strange tingling sensation across the palm of my hand, as if a wisp of wind has found its way in from outside.

A golden arrow blinks into existence across my hand. It is beautiful, with a shiny black tip.

I place the arrow in the groove. I pull back on the string until it pops into place. Everything looks good so far.

I look up to give Jane a grateful smile, but she is gone.

"Don't worry," Jane says, her voice filling the room. "I'm still here; I just got tired of everyone making me feel like I was the most pitied person on the face of the earth. No offense, but that was part of the reason why I didn't want to tell you as much as I did. Above all, an abused woman such as myself needs time to recover."

Just beyond the spot where Jane stood a moment ago stands five automatons. I'm not sure how close I can get today, but I intend to get as close as I possibly can. I point the end of the bow towards the floor as a safety precaution. I hold the bow strategically as to avoid touching the trigger.

Jane sighs, reminding me of the school girls who use to watch Ethan lift weights at the gym. "You are such a handsome man Ryan. Indeed, you look as if you could take down a mature grizzly bear as surely as a bolt of lightning could split an oak tree in half."

Admittedly, I do feel somewhat attractive and confident. I decide to stop at about the same place where we stood during previous practice sessions. I think trying to get too close would only make me look bad. And of course, with the force field in place, I can only get so close anyway.

I raise the bow. I align the tip of the arrow with the glass heart of the middle automaton. I can feel everyone's eyes on me from behind. I need to do this quick and not miss. Otherwise, I run the risk of compromising what shaky respect I have from my team. I do not want them to further question my identity. I already know that each of them finds my age and attempt to avoid certain discussions as questionable as the tear on Jane's shirt. I wish Mason would have allowed me some practice time. Maybe he is hoping that I will fail.

I gently place a finger on the trigger. I eye the heart with irritability. If only it was even larger than it already is, I wouldn't be so afraid of missing.

I take a deep breath and steady myself. I exhale slowly as I squeeze the trigger.

I hold my breath. The arrow pierces the heart and sends the shards of glass raining down onto the floor like sweet music. I breathe a sigh of relief.

"Well done," Jane says, impressed. "But then again, a handsome stag like you always comes out on top. I think it's safe to say that Mason has nothing on you."

I look up just in time to see a new heart materialize in the cavity. I lower my bow. I think I will stop while I am ahead of the game. I turn around to face my team.

Nick looks between my bow and my face with a funny look. "That was your first time using a crossbow, wasn't it?"

I feel the color drain from my face. "Why would you say that," I say. I swallow against the lump in my throat.

Nick shrugs and takes a step forward. "Oh, I don't know, perhaps it was the uncertain look on your face when you loaded the bow, or the fact that you seemed out of touch with it. I use to own a crossbow, before Glo...before President Gloss came to power. I supplied wild game for our festivals back home. Turkeys were my primary targets."

I swallow. "Well, to be honest, crossbows are not my forte."

Nick raises his eyebrows. "Oh, and longbows are?"

Seth studies me carefully, brown eyes boring into me. Kody and Jennifer look as if they have somehow found the exact same page of the same book. Again, if I do not say something fast, I feel I will lose what slight gains I have made with them.

"I've heard about those festivals of yours," I say, letting my bow fall to the floor. "Armadillo pudding, opossum pie, chipmunk stew…Honestly, I don't see how you all can stand eating that kind of garbage."

Seth looks taken aback. "I…you've heard wrong somewhere along the line. I've never eaten any of those things in my life."

I sigh inwardly. From the looks on their faces, each of them is eager to defend themselves. Well, most of them anyway. Jennifer looks as if she could throw an opossum pie at my face if she had one. She puts a hand on her hip.

"Boy, you're just askin' for trouble," Jennifer says in a sassy tone. "Ridiculing our festivals is not a way to make us like you. How would you like it if I made light of those satanic festivals of yours?"

"Who said I want you to like me," I say, trying to look as tough as I sound.

Jennifer crosses her arms over her chest. "You seem awfully eager for us to obey your every whim for some reason. It's like you're the son of one of the other guards who is trying to show his daddy just how capable you are."

I gesture to the rack of crossbows hanging on the wall. I give Jennifer a chiding look. "You'd best get busy if you care anything about your life and that of your teammates."

Jennifer starts to turn away. I decide to let her have it. I clear my throat. She whips her head back at me.

I give her a ruthless smile. "Unless you want to experience some of the cruel and unusual punishments that we offer around here, I'd keep your mouth shut if I was you. The same goes for the rest of you. Question me again and you'll figure out just how well equipped I am to deal with your insubordination."

"Was that really necessary," Jane whispers in my ear.

I flinch. "It was from my perspective," I say as I watch Jennifer take a crossbow from the rack. "I take it you know all about me then, all about my situation I mean? Mason must have told you."

Jane nods. "He did. I knew you were coming weeks ago, though for some reason, he seemed reluctant to talk about you. I don't know why, but I got the impression that he seemed to think I couldn't be trusted. But I happen to know things about him that would shock even you, oh yes."

I can't help but think that Jane is being honest. "Like what? What kinds of things?"

Jane looks between the members of my team with a wary expression. "Ask me another time, I cannot risk being overheard by your team. Mason would kill me for sure if word got back to him. But I'll say this: Mason is a very dangerous man. So I warn you now, you had better watch yourself around him. Don't let him fool you into believing he is a halfway decent person, because he's not. In fact…no, not here. And don't ask me to say anymore."

I should have guessed as much. Mason seems too friendly to me for someone who is only interested in learning about me. Oh no, what if after he learns all he wants about me, he decides that he no longer has any use for me? What if Mason is just toying with my mind when in fact he has no desire whatsoever to help me survive this place? Just because he claims he cannot lift a hand against me without his boss's approval does not mean that he does not have some sick plan reserved for my downfall.

Feeling somewhat dazed, I watch as Nick helps Jennifer load her bow. True to his word, Nick handles the bow like an expert, his hands nimble and confidant. Seth on the other hand looks like he could use some help. And since her back is to me, I cannot tell how Jennifer is coming along.

While they are busy loading their bows, I think this would be a great time to put some space between myself and them. I start backing up towards the door. "Jane," I whisper. She sighs, as if she knows what I have in mind. She should have known that I would want to hear what she has to tell me about Mason as soon as possible.

I know the door is still a way behind me, but I feel I am well out of ear shot of my team, so I come to a stop. And as far as those in need of help, especially Jennifer from what I can see, Nick seems to be doing a great job getting them ready to shoot.

"Let's hear it," I say eagerly.

Jane gives me a wary look. "If Mason found out…"

"He won't," I say, cutting her off. "I promise I won't say a word."

Jane takes my upper arm, pulls me to her.

I gasp in shock. "Hey, how did you do that?"

"Be quiet," Jane whispers. "There is more to this place than meets the eye. Just wait and you'll see. Some of the greatest minds in the world designed the Mirage. There is no place like it."

I feel dizzy. I shake my head. "I don't understand. I…you're not supposed to be real."

Jane laughs, her breath tickling my ear. "The masterminds behind this place took sensation and perception to a whole new level. Now then," Jane adds with a puff of breath against my neck. "Let me ask you a question. Who do you think is the most dangerous guard around here?"

That is a difficult question considering that I do not know most of them. And I barely know the ones I have met. Well, except for perhaps Mason. But from what Jane has already hinted at, I must not know Mason as well as I thought I did. Christian has proven himself to be a nasty piece of work, but still. Jack on the other hand seems less threatening than Christian, though I would not put anything past him. Sometimes the less harmful looking things end up being the most dangerous.

I sigh. "I don't know, Mason perhaps."

Jane makes a small sound, as if to say she thought as much. "Mason's evil, but there is one who is far worse than him. His name is Jace. I believe you met him in the obstacle course room the other day, if I heard correctly. He spends most of his time outside this building making sacrifices to the pantheon of gods that his kind holds in high regard. There is an alter somewhere on this compound, though I have not yet heard of its exact location, where animals and young boys and girls are sacrificed on a regular basis. All of the children have been taken away from their Christian parents. If it's a boy, they cut off his private parts and offer them up as a burnt offering to Vendazin, the god of thunder. If it's a girl, they abuse her and then burn her alive to Vendaria, the goddess of lightning. Of course the boys are also burnt alive after they're…mutilated."

I can hardly breathe. I knew that Gloss put to the sword all the Christian babies, but I have never heard of anything like this. It's bad enough that anyone has to die, but to torture them as well? Furthermore, I have never heard of the gods of thunder and lightning. Still, Mason's kind of people seem to create new gods faster than you can blink an eye. Ethan and I were amazed at how the new gods were often born: Using the blood of Christian babies, agents would write the names of the new gods on their chests and backs. Then, they would slash themselves with knifes and shout the names of their new gods to a new moon. The morning after such detestable ceremonies, Ethan and I would go out to make sure that none of the babies' body parts were lying around on the ground. Of course, once all the Christian babies in the area were murdered, the agents had to resort to using animals.

"Why did you have to tell me this," I say, feeling sick.

Jane gently squeezes my arm. "Because you insisted I tell you. But it's much worse than that. You see, Mason participates in these sacrifices. He is the one who cuts the boys and then burns their parts. Ryan, he can never know I've told you any of this, otherwise we would both be dead."

Shock. That is what I feel. I had no idea that Mason could be so cruel, so evil. And to think he has been using me as his footstool. That he has undoubtedly been filling my head full of lies about his desire to help me. How could he want to help me? I mean, how could someone who has no regard for human life care about whether I live or die? It doesn't make any sense.

I shake my head in frustration. "So what does any of this have to do with me? Why does Mason seem so intent on wanting to help me if he is a cold blooded murderer?"

"That's what we need to find out," Jane says urgently. "I don't mean to frighten you, but I have a very bad feeling about all this. I'm afraid that, after he learns whatever it is he seems so eager to learn about you, he will kill you. Believe me; I hope I'm wrong, but still. But I know one thing, before you arrived, Mason told Christian that he had a special kind of death arranged for a teenage boy who fits your appearance. Of course, knowing Mason, it could easily be any one of the pretty brown-haired green-eyed Saint-boys on these premises. But if I wanted to live, I'd do whatever it took to please these people, even if that meant showing up at tomorrow night's Festival of Demons wearing nothing more than a loin cloth."

I cringe in disgust. "There's no way I'm going to that festival wearing nothing more than a loin cloth. That would invite every pervert in the room to bother me. No, there has to be another way."

Jane puts an arm across my shoulders to try to console me. "I'm afraid there is no other way. Unless you bow to their desires, including worshipping the image of

Satan in the library, you have little chance of leaving this place alive."

"I will not bow down to Satan," I say, looking past Jane to make sure that none of my teammates overheard me. They all appear to be doing well. I turn back to Jane. "I'd rather die than bow down to Satan."

"Then it may come to that," Jane says sadly. "Look, your team is doing so well. Do you think that that would be the case if anyone else was their guard? Ask yourself this question: Are you willing to let them die just because of your unwillingness to put yourself into an uncomfortable situation? Because I can tell you that, without you, their chances of surviving the things to come are slim to none. The other guards treat their teams harshly, believe me, I know. If you cannot find a way to appease Satan's disciples, then every one of you in this room will soon be dead."

"Satan's disciples," I whisper.

Jane gives me an exasperated look. "Who else did you think men like Mason and Jace belonged to? All their gods are stumbling blocks of Satan. Satan loves to ensnare people with gods of beauty, like Edarion, and gods of death, like Vendazin. If he can get people to believe in anything other than the true and the living God that we serve, then he has accomplished his ultimate mission: To destroy you."

I swallow hard. "I…don't think I can arrive at that festival tomorrow night wearing nothing more than a loin cloth, but perhaps I can meet in the middle."

"Good," Jane says. "For it's better to meet in the middle than for you and your friends to lose your lives. Yes," Jane adds with a warm smile. "You may have fooled them, but I can see that you love them, that you want to protect them."

"How'd things go today," Mason says as he sits down in the chair across from me.

I bite down onto my lip. "Better than I expected, real well actually."

Mason leans back in the chair and stretches his legs. He looks between his feet and my face with a disgruntled expression. What have I done now?

"Don't look at me like that," Mason says with a hard look. "I'm forcing myself to keep my word, about not using you as a footstool for the day because you answered my question correctly, remember?"

I had honestly forgotten. But I am surprised that he would bother keeping his word, especially after what I learned about him this morning from Jane.

I stare at his hands, now clasped in his lap. I just find it hard to believe that he has…done the things that Jane accused him of. But then again, she should know.

"Why are you looking at me like that," Mason says with a frown in his voice. "You look captivated by my hands. They look fine to me, with no trace of any blood on them."

I swallow hard. Mason flicks his eyes to me. He gives me a funny look, as if he finds my behavior very odd. I know I look worried, but I cannot help it. I try to school my face to appear relaxed, but I am finding it very difficult.

Mason studies his palms with a faint smile. "I think I understand," he says, looking me in the eyes. "You must be wondering how a physician's hands can be so darn handsome. Is that it?"

"What," I say, stunned.

Mason sits up, rests a foot across his knee. He looks as if he is about to badger me with questions. I stifle a fake yawn in hopes that he will drop it and let me go to sleep.

"Good one," Mason says, green eyes keen. "But not good enough. You're not going to bed until I have had an opportunity to study you some more. I find you very interesting Ryan Collins. Surely you must know why? And yet, you look as if you don't." Mason leans forward slightly. "So allow me to refresh your memory. You are here as a result of breaking the law for expressing your religious beliefs. In particular, you exhibited a complete disregard for the law forbidding public exhortation when you continually ran your mouth about those dreams of yours."

I give him a cool look. "I told my uncle, along with a few friends. I never tried to start an uprising or anything." I know that is what he is implying.

"Same difference," Mason says, matching my cool expression. "You posed a significant threat to the peace and prosperity of not only your commune, but also your entire district."

Does he think I am that stupid? "So what you're really saying is that my vocalization of dreams posed a risk to the expected quotas of your slaves. After all, money always seems to be the reason behind just about everything. If not, then why spend so much time harassing us to meet our quotas? I mean, why not just leave us alone and hope that your good Saints will come through for you?"

I hold my breath in expectation for Mason to go irate. But to my surprise, he remains calm and almost friendly in his appearance, as if he is enjoying the conversation.

Mason gives me a look of pretend pity. "You know, you probably wouldn't even be here if you and that handsome friend of yours had just shed your clothes and let the agents have their way with you. But because you chose not to let them love you, they became angry and took it out on you by putting forward your name as one of the two rebellious Saints from your county, with you by far being the worst. But I suspect that, by removing you from your commune, the agents also figured they would have a clear shot at your friend. It's possible Ethan may have already got a full dose of love."

He is sick. "Love? You call adults who abuse teenage boys and girls in the most detestable ways love? In ancient times, according to the Bible, men who did such wicked things would have been taken out and stoned to death. But here you sit, smiling as if the idea of my friend being turned into a walking cesspool is the most appealing thing to think about." I'm so angry I could invite him to rest his feet on me just so I could break his ankles. "Surely you realize that if what you say is true and Ethan has been defiled, it is likely that he won't be around much longer. And I'm not just talking about the diseases that would ravage his body. Ethan once told me that if he ever got abused like some of the other people in our commune, he would want to die. That he could never live after having been pillaged and raped and turned into a dirty man's object of pleasure."

Mason considers this with a curious frown. "Grown men do all the things you just described to each other, so why should it be wrong to commit the same acts on guys like you? I mean, surely you know that many grown men look upon you with burning lust.”

I do not like the way Mason is looking at me, as if he is patiently awaiting the opportunity to participate in sacrificing me to Vendazin. I want to keep all my body parts as well as live.

I shake my head in disgust. “And let me guess, many of the men you are referring to are here, eagerly awaiting my appearance at the Festival of Filth tomorrow night. Tell me good doctor, how is it that someone who looks as good as you have been able to keep yourself from being bothered by your friends?”

Mason regards his fingers with a casual expression. “I lead them on; make them think that I will one day succumb to their pressure. Take Christian for example, he has been trying to lure me into having a romantic dinner with him ever since I joined the guard.”

I have been brought to a more dangerous, more evil place than I had thought. I have the same feelings as Ethan does when it comes to adult men who want to abuse us. “Just how long do you think you will be able to put them off before they finally catch on?”

Mason shrugs. “No clue, but I don’t sit around and worry about it. I am a physician, I’m not about to let myself get bogged down with every sexually transmitted disease out there just because a bunch of men want to spend their lust on me. So, I will continue to be polite to them, even though I do not greet them with open arms. Still,” Mason adds with a steady look. “If I was you, I’d do just about whatever it took to try to appease them, otherwise you might soon find yourself cornered somewhere without me to protect you. These men are not the patient type, they are powerful and use to getting their way."

I run my sweaty hands down my pants. "Surely there must be something that you can do to help me, like douse me in skunk urine or something. I'm sure they'd leave me alone if I didn't smell desirable?"

"Maybe," Mason says, looking thoughtful. "But the women, including Rebecca will want a go at you as well. It might only be a kiss, but you should try to find some middle ground either way, and you cannot achieve that if you insist on smelling like a skunk."

I expel a ragged sigh. This is so serious and yet he looks as if he is enjoying himself. "So let me go smelling like a skunk flower then. I think they're smelly enough to turn away anyone. There has to be something, anything to keep me from a nightmare of abuse."

Mason narrows his eyes onto me. "I don't think I've ever heard of those kinds of flowers."

I wish I had one; I'd stuff it up his nostrils, stem and all. "I don't know what they are called, but I assure you, if you had ever smelled one, you'd know exactly what I'm talking about. We use to grow them in our gardens in hopes of keeping the agents away from our food, but it didn't work. In fact, Perverted Demon picked one and shoved it into Agatha's face, since she was the one responsible for planting them."

Mason looks like he wants to laugh. "Perhaps they'll sprinkle some of the seed over her fresh grave. But enough of that, I think it's time for bed. I want you to look so hot tomorrow that even the lady bugs will salivate at the sight of you. And from the looks of you, it's going to take a lot of sleep to get you there."

That's it! I will stay awake tonight. That is what I will do in order to keep myself from harm. I will lay awake all night long so that, by tomorrow night, I will look so haggard that not even a lady bug would find me attractive. Maybe then things will go well with me.

If only I could sleep for a little while. This is going to be a long night. Mason has been asleep now for about an hour, and, judging by his labored breathing, the good doctor could use a prescription. And I swear I heard him mumbling in his sleep a couple minutes ago. Mason reminds me a lot of myself when it comes to sleeping. He tosses and turns and lets out exhaustive sighs every now and then, reminding me a lot of the rat terrier Ethan use to have. I recall numerous times before Gloss when I would pay Ethan an early morning visit (Ethan was like a mummy on days off) to find Tonny, his rat terrier, curled up in a swirl of covers at Ethan's feet. I couldn't help but laugh. How such a small dog managed to deprive Ethan of most of his covers was a mystery in and of itself. To wake Ethan, I would scoop up Tonny and let him lick Ethan in the face. His expression tended to be a mixture of slight grumpiness and amusement, as if he actually enjoyed the idea of using his dog as an alarm clock. At any rate, Tonny turned out to be more useful than just tackling rodents and kicking up dust in his quest to show all the opossums and stray cats who was boss.

I hope and pray that Ethan is well. If only I knew where Mason brought me, I might be able to plan an escape to head back home. Mason doubtless wants to keep me in the dark about our location so that I will not be as fervent about escape. But Mason does not know me as well as he thinks he does. I am and always have been one to push the limits of what is possible. Of course, I thank God for making me bold enough not to accept the forces that seem set against me. Therefore, I refuse to lay here all night when I could employ my energy to try to get the answers that Mason refuses to give me. Why should I lay here all night in fear of tomorrow night's festival when I could be searching for clues to help me escape this place altogether? And what better place to search for clues if not in the library? Perhaps I will find a clue to help me escape this place tonight.

I feel my heartbeat quicken. I sit up and push the covers aside. I need to be very careful. Although he seems to be sound asleep, Mason could be waiting for me to pass by on the way to the door. I would hate to think about what he would do to me then.

I swallow hard. Slowly I rise to my feet. I listen for any change in Mason's breathing. Judging by the smile in his breathing, he sounds as if he is in the arms of a beautiful woman who could be on the verge of kissing him. At any other time, I might hope that the woman would become a monster and sink her fangs into his neck, but not now. No, I need her to take her precious time with him, make him get on his hands and knees and beg for a kiss.

I take a step forward and stop. He sounds the same. I look down at my bare feet. It will be quieter this way. If I'm careful, I should be able to make it to the door undetected.

I sure hope there are not any insects lurking about that I might step on. I cringe at the idea of squishing a fat spider, though I have not noticed any since my arrival, but still.

Mason turns toward me to lay on his side. I stop in horror. I cannot tell if his eyes are open or not. Oh please

God do not let him be awake. I turn an ear towards him and listen.

I hear a gentle exhale. I breathe a sigh of relief. I strain my eyes to try to see him. He looks as if he is relaxing in the arms of a beautiful woman.

I reach the door. With a nervous beat of my heart, I take a hold of the doorknob. I open the door just wide enough and slip through the crack. I half expect Mason to pounce on me at any moment.

I step into the hallway and close the door behind me. I stare at the end of the hallway. I don't believe it. I actually made it. I guess the beautiful woman's hold on Mason was more effective than I thought. Maybe she will continue to keep him imprisoned.

I make my way down the hallway as quietly as possible. On either side of me are the rooms where half the Saints are currently sleeping, and an all-inclusive bathroom. I wish I knew which room my team was in. It would be nice if I could help them escape as well. I can see their stunned faces and hear Nick's voice in my head now: "I knew it! I knew something was up when you couldn't work that crossbow."

I stop at the edge of the common room. I could use that flashlight that Mason made me carry the other night. Best I can tell, no one is in the room. I round the corner and stick close to the wall. I need to move slowly and quietly just in case someone is nearby. I sure hope Mason was indeed sound asleep. I feel like I am being watched, even though I see no sign of anyone.

I wonder what all the guards that I see every meal time are doing. It's so strange. Other than Mason and the ones actively training the eight teams, I rarely see any of the others. You'd think they just came here for the food, which really is not that bad.

I descend the stairs as quietly as possible. It's so dark. The only lighting appears to be filtering in through a single window pane above the main door. For some reason, the blue light that usually illuminates the room around the Mother Dome is nowhere to be found.

I feel my heartbeat quicken. It would be just my luck to get caught. I seriously doubt my story of a midnight library visit would be very plausible. But then again, it might not be that hard to believe, after all, most books, especially Bibles have been rounded up and destroyed. So, a trip to the library might not look as bad as it seems. However, if someone like Christian caught me, he would likely use my transgression as an excuse to shoot me with a barrage of questions about Saint-girls.

I hear someone moving across the cafeteria. I lower myself to my hands and knees. I cannot see who it is, but based on their rapid approach, whoever it is is in a big hurry. I half hold my breath and pray that I am not discovered. The hurried footsteps move past me on the other side of the table.

"We've got a problem," says a man with a hoarse voice.

"One of the heifers get loose," says a man with sarcasm.

"No, but one of the boys did," says the first man. "I knew we should have left him cuffed to the post, but Jace insisted on freeing him so that he could have more fun with him. The boy's bleeding badly, so he shouldn't be hard to find."

"Did he squeal," says the sarcastic man, only now with a pleasurable smile in his voice.

"Good and loud, we thought we'd never get him to shut up. But enough of that, what brings you here at this hour, Christian?"

So that's the person behind the sarcasm. I should have known it was Christian.

"The desire to see how generous a certain Saint-girl will be with me. I laid awake thinking about her until I could no longer resist the thought of taking her to bed with me. But that's really my business. Still, how that poor Saint-boy must have looked when he saw the knife coming towards him… I suspect the offering made Vendazin happy. Now," Christian adds irritably, "if you'll get out of my way, I have what I think will be a long and pleasurable night ahead of me."

"Good luck, if anyone can win over a Saint-girls pure heart, it'd be you."

"Indeed," Christian says smugly. "I *am* skilled in the art of love making. By the way, what are you going as to the festival tomorrow night? All just about anyone is talking about is this new boy, this Ryan Collins from nowhere. You'd think he had the gorgeous body of someone like me the way they go on and on about him."

"Doesn't he though? Well, maybe not quite. As to what I plan on going as, I haven't entirely decided. I have some body paint I've been *dying* to use, but I have no one to help me apply it. Maybe I'll find a Saint-girl willing to rise to the task."

Christian clears his voice uncomfortably. "Maybe, but I have to be getting along now; otherwise dawn will be here before I get a chance to see just how shy Saint-girls really are in bed."

"Then go," Ammon says, sounding slightly offended.

I hear a set of hurried footsteps ascend the staircase. The other man, Ammon, sounds as if he is pacing circles just outside the cafeteria.

A defeated sigh escapes Ammon as he finally exits the main door. I sigh inwardly. I think the coast is clear now. I rise to my feet. I see no sign of anyone.

I hurry towards the door that leads to the library. I wipe my sweaty hands across the front of my pants. I shudder to think about what would have happened had I ran into Ammon alone. I thank God for keeping me safe.

I enter the lounge as quiet as a mouse. I see platters of desert on the table from here. But to my relief, no one is dining. I might have a bite after my investigative work in the library.

To be safe, I creep along the wall towards the library. Since I cannot see into the library, I cannot rule out the possibility that someone could well be in there. If Ethan were here, he would watch my back for me. I sure hope that Ammon or any of the guards like him do not get a sudden urge for a midnight snack. It would be next to impossible to escape the room if they did.

I reach the archway that separates the lounge and library. I press my back against the wall and listen for any sign of activity. I stare at the pastries out of the corner of my eye. I swallow.

I move to stand in the edge of the archway. I feel my jaw drop in astonishment.

Until now, I had not noticed the glass dome ceiling high above the room. I can see stars twinkling in the sky, one of them shining much brighter than all the others around it. Equally impressive are the bookshelves themselves, which glow like live embers. Satan looks right at home among them.

I pad across the cool stone floor to get a closer look at this wonder. Thousands upon thousands of books line the rows of fiery shelves. I feel a wave of excitement splash over me. Ever since most of our books were taken away, I dreamed of the moment when I would one day find a stash like this.

I scan across the spines of books like a kid in a candy store. If only I had time to read them all. But then again, I probably wouldn't want to read them all. I know I cannot stay here too long. What if Mason woke to find me missing? Or what if Ammon or another guard found me in here snooping around? No, I need to get down to business. I came here for answers, so I need to get to work. And the first place I want to search is the desk.

Gently, I pull out a drawer in nervous anticipation. It is empty. I sigh.

I try another drawer. I find a box of spilled paper clips, making me want to scream, and a pile of papers. I pick up the papers. *Telltale signs of Ravishing Rashes: Beware the pretty smiles that beckons you into their beds.*

I drop the papers back into the drawer with a grimace of disgust. I back away from the desk. I feel like I have come to the very heart of sin. I suspect that, if I were to continue searching the desk, I would find all kinds of trash.

I turn around to face Satan. Perhaps what I'm looking for is hidden behind his ugly face. After all, it would probably be the last place the guards would suspect a Saint to search if one entered the library unattended. The thing is, other than myself, I find it hard to believe that any of the others would ever wind up in this place to begin with.

I reach for the handle on the bookcase. I stop just short of touching it. I can hardly believe my eyes. I stare at the handle in disgust. It is one of Satan's thumbs, and embedded within the thumb is a latch that joins the two panels together. I swallow hard. I do not want to touch Satan's thumb, even though it isn't really him, but I have no choice. At least his thumb looks human enough, about as smooth and shapely as anyone's, except for the bit of exposed bone making up the latch. Not so for his face and feet, which are rough, scaly and black as pitch.

Careful not to make any noise, I take the golden latch and slowly lift it from the splinter of bone sticking out of the middle of the thumb.

A loud growl like a threatened animal coincides with shattering glass. I jump backwards and painfully collide with the desk. I massage my hip.

I look up at the two gaping black holes with perplexity. What just happened?

I feel my heartbeat in my ears. I need to get out of here and fast. I turn on my heel and make my way towards the archway.

I scold myself inwardly. I should never have left my bed. I never thought anything like this would happen.

I cross into the lounge and come to an abrupt halt.

I swallow hard. Someone is moving towards me from out of the shadows.

"Ryan," says a familiar voice. "Ryan Collins, is that you?"

"Carrie," I say, bewildered.

Carrie strides forward from out of the shadows to stop in front of me. "Oh thank goodness. As soon as I heard a commotion, I became afraid and hid. I thought perhaps one of the guards got drunk and was having a temper tantrum. That happens a lot around here, unfortunately."

I breathe a sigh of relief. "I…look, I was just leaving. I…"

"I'm not going to say anything," Carrie says, cutting me off. "This may sound strange, but I'm actually glad to see you again."

"You are." Admittedly, I sounded a bit stupid.

Carrie nods, red curls almost imperceptible in the darkness. "Good company is hard to come by around here."

I squint my eyes to try to see Carrie. I want to see her face, her beautiful blue eyes.

Carrie makes her way towards me. She looks a bit flushed, the red in her cheeks almost the same shade as her curls. She tucks a stray curl behind her ear.

"What happened in there," Carrie says, looking over my shoulder towards the scene of the accident.

I shrug. "I honestly don't know. I just barely touched the latch on Satan's image and the next thing I knew the whole works came crashing down to the ground with a strange growling sound."

Carrie looks me over. "Are you hurt?" I shake my head.

Carrie breathes a sigh of relief. "Good. That's the most important thing. As far as that vile image, it needed to go."

I'm surprised to hear her say that. "But I thought everyone around here liked it."

Carrie shakes her head. "Not everyone and certainly not me. Keep in mind that my staff and I; the other maids that is, have cleaned that detestable thing more times than any one of us would care to admit. I thought about breaking those panes long ago, and I would have, if not for the fact that I would have been questioned about its destruction. And of course, I couldn't lie about it. So, I just continued cleaning it."

I feel a twinge of panic in my chest. What if I am questioned? I swallow hard. "I never meant for that to happen. Like I said, I'm not even sure how it happened."

Carrie throws a hand up. "Calm down. Goodness me, you'll have *my* blood pressure boiling if you keep going. I will clean it up."

I check the time on my watch. It's nearly one o'clock. I meet Carrie's eyes. "I'll help you. Besides, it'll be faster that way. Otherwise, you run the risk of getting into trouble for something you didn't do, and I'll not let that happen. Come on."

Carrie looks pleased. "Give me a minute; I need to get a brush and pan."

I nod. "Do you need any help?"

Carrie gives me a sweet smile. "No, I know exactly where to go, but thanks. Help yourself to a pastry while I'm gone, if you want, I was about ready to throw it all away anyway. That's why I came here to begin with, to clear the table. I do it every night. If the guards did not insist on staying up so late partaking in detestable revelry, I wouldn't have to keep such weary hours. As for the other maids, I have them cleaning in the empty rooms throughout the compound right this very minute."

I look past Carrie to the table. "Do you think it's safe? I mean, to eat after such nasty people?"

Carrie looks at the food with consideration. "Take from the bottom of the platters and you should be fine. They rarely eat much of it anyway. It's more about coming together to flirt with each other, as if they don't do enough of that as it is. I won't be long."

Carrie turns around and heads towards the door that leads to the cafeteria. Admittedly, her black and white uniform looks striking on her. And together with her long curls, she looks irresistibly attractive.

I hear Ethan's voice in my head gently admonishing me. I turn away. Emily, he would say, is the true keeper of my heart, the one who has always wanted me but never got around to telling me. But I could tell Ethan a thing or two about his love life as well. For instance, he never did get around to telling Arianne McGerbert, the girl who gave him the heart-shaped pendant, how much he cared for her. Instead, he seemed more interested in trying to get Emily and I to proclaim our love for each other. The thing is, I'm not sure if I even cared for Emily that much. And Emily rarely paid me the kind of attention that made me feel like I was the only one for her. If Ethan had not been so persistent in his efforts to unite us, I honestly do not think I would have given her much thought, at least where the topic of a girl friend is concerned.

I let out a frustrated sigh. I think I will have a pastry after all. I need something to help take my mind off all my problems. I cast a glance over my shoulder toward the door. I sure hope Carrie gets back as soon as possible. The last thing I need is for unwanted company to arrive.

I shake my head in disgust at all the wasted food on the table. I would have loved to eat stuff like this every day back home, and yet we were just fortunate enough to have the basic necessities. But here, these people seem more concerned with who they are going to bed next rather than the most important things in life.

I set my eyes on a pile of miniature pies. I take one from the bottom of the stack. I look it over to make sure there is nothing visibly wrong with it. Most of the food that was consumed appears to have been taken from the platters closest to the edge of the table. I take a bite. Cherry. Yuck. I lay it down and pick up another. Since it's all going to be thrown away, I might as well find something I like.

I take another. Apple! And the apples have been seasoned to perfection with cinnamon and sugar. I stare at the pies. I wish I had some way of taking some of them with me without being noticed. The thing is, I'd have a hard time trying to explain away a stash of pastries under my bed. And it would take an army of mice before I could blame them.

Hurried footsteps approach from across the room. I stiffen in fear.

"Relax, it's just me," Carrie says with an apologetic smile in her voice.

I breathe a sigh of relief. I wipe my mouth on the back of my hand. The last thing I want is to face Carrie with a face full of crumbs.

Carrie steps into the light by the library. She's so beautiful. In fact, I don't think I have ever seen a girl as pretty as Carrie.

Carrie struggles to hold on to all of the cleaning supplies. I rush forward and seize the broom before it slips from her hand.

Carrie gives me a grateful smile. "Thanks, I wish the other guys around here were as eager to help me as you are. Instead, they're more interested in luring other guys like you into their arms rather than lending a hand to a damsel in distress. Whatever happened to all those stories where men sought to earn the hearts of the beautiful counterparts God made for them? At the rate things are going, it'll be a miracle if there's a single person left alive much longer. Men cannot reproduce with each other and killing all the Christian babies means that people of religion will soon be extinct. Not to mention all the diseases that these men pass off to each other. It's a nightmare around here."

That is exactly what I have been thinking. "You don't know how glad I am to hear you say that. Ever since I came here, I have felt like a cornstalk in a cabbage patch."

Carrie gives me a sympathetic smile. "I suppose you would. I cannot begin to imagine what all you've been going through. I mean, at least I knew ahead of time I was coming to this place, whereas you were pulled like a fish from water with no warning."

I swallow hard.

Carrie looks as if she wants to either say something more or console me with a hand on my arm. Honestly, I wish she would do both. Instead, she turns to face the library. "We had best get to work; otherwise we could well end up in serious trouble."

I nod. "But I insist you let me carry everything." I take the brush and pan, paper bag, and gloves from her hands without another moment's hesitation. Carrie gives me a dazzling smile.

Chapter Nine

"Wake up footstool," Mason says as he begins to roll back the covers from my body.

I grab the covers and give him a chiding look. "What is your problem," I say. "Let me guess, you've had a change of heart and now you can't wait another second to see my legs?"

Mason raises his eyebrows. "Said the minnow to the handsome trout."

I laugh and sit up on the side of the bed. "Okay good doctor that was pretty good."

Mason looks me over. "Don't take this the wrong way, but you look better than I thought you would. I had expected you to stay awake all night so as to degrade your appearance, but you actually look fairly well rested."

Oh no. Last night, after I got back from helping Carrie clean up the mess that I made in the library, I crawled into bed in my exhaustion without giving my plan to stay awake another thought. I could hit myself. If I hadn't been so taken with Carrie, with the way she watched me as I cleaned up the shattered glass; I suspect I would have remembered. Every now and then when I glanced up, I would catch her eyes raking over my arms and legs. I know she must have realized that I was up to something, but she never did badger me with questions. Instead, we got the mess cleaned up, including all the leftover food, and then departed with a friendly handshake. Her hand was so soft.

Mason waves a hand in front of my face. He taps his watch. "Hurry up, you've already missed breakfast, again. But it's all right; I figured you could use the extra sleep. Besides, tonight's the big night and I want you to look ravishing. I want you to look so hot that I actually brought a pair of pants from Christian for you to wear. He gets all his clothes specially designed for him, so they're really flashy."

I give Mason a firm look. "I'm not wearing anything worn by Christian or any other one of your perverted friends."

Mason gives me a dangerous look. "He hasn't worn them yet, and besides, I'm not giving you a choice. I take that back. I will give you a choice. You can either go to the festival without a shirt or without pants. It's entirely up to you."

"I have a better idea, how about nothing," I say, earning a stunned look from Mason. "Yeah, I think I'll go without a stitch of clothing on. I thought of a new game: Clothe Ryan. Each one of your perverted friends can argue amongst each other over who gets to dress me. Only I want you to hold all the clothing options, including the undergarments."

Mason smiles. "Sounds good to me, but why not take it a step further? I mean, if you're going through all that trouble to embarrass yourself, why not go all the way? I'm thinking sprayed on abs and a tattoo on your butt. I suspect your way too pale in the places that need to be viewed the most."

"You're sick," I snap. "You're even more perverted than I thought."

Mason looks surprisingly calm. "Like I said, it's entirely up to you. But something tells me you'll stick with the pants. Now," Mason adds with an intimidating half smile, "be a good footstool and get yourself ready to meet your team, unless of course you want to show up looking like a back alley prostitute."

I point at him. "That's it! It's what I've always dreamed of being. Well, I guess that's not entirely true. For the longest time, I wanted to be a snail surgeon. I've always wondered what it would be like to make special houses for snails. Should they be round or rectangular? Should they be plain or painted? Of course, they would have to be small enough for the snail to carry them around everywhere they go. And shouldn't there be enough room for two to occupy one home? Oh good doctor, please tell me you specialize in this kind of thing."

Mason looks as if he could either knock me upside the head or pull up a chair and commence with a serious mental evaluation. He shakes his head. "Sorry, claiming mental incompetence will hardly exempt you from the inevitable. Now, if you were to sprout extra limbs or something, that would be more helpful, but still probably not enough to keep you from getting out and about. No, you'll wear the pants I got you and shine like the handsome stallion you are. If you're lucky, you might just make a few friends. If you put yourself out there, you might find out that your body is more desirable than you ever thought it was."

I rise to my feet and look him straight in the eyes. "Oh, so you're saying that I could be really popular or just continue on as the boring Saint that your kind has no respect for. Well, I have news for you, if being popular means conforming to the detestable lifestyles that your kind hold in high regard, then I would much rather stay boring and off the radar."

Mason shrugs. "Have it your way, but know this: Your behavior tonight can either win the crowd or turn them against you. Honestly, if I was you, I'd try to act as loose and wild as possible, then you might come to realize that you like that lifestyle better. If you only knew how many of my friends have been waiting to see your scantily dressed body, how many have been waiting to run their hands through your hair and kiss your lips, you might see it as more of an honor and treat."

I give him an incredulous look. "A treat? Are you out of your mind? I swear," I add, giving Mason a warning look, "if one of your nasty friends lays a finger on me, I will snap it in to like a green bean."

Looking resigned, Mason hands me a breakfast sandwich wrapped in plastic. I take it without breaking eye contact with him. "Let me guess good doctor, you laced it with some kind of drug to break down my inhibitions so that by tonight, I'll become the lunatic you want me to be."

Mason takes the sandwich from my hand and removes part of the plastic. He takes a big bite out of it and then hands it back to me. I look at it as if it is a worm infested apple.

Mason swallows and then licks his lips. "Delicious. Only our cooks could make such scrumptious sandwiches. Now hurry up and eat it," Mason adds with an angry scowl.

I stare at the sandwich. "After you defiled it?"

Mason regards the sandwich with a satisfied smile. "I assure you it's safe. Besides, you'll not get any lunch today because I intend to prep you all afternoon for the festival tonight. But don't worry, you won't starve. There'll be so much food at the festival tonight; you'll likely seek my medical expertise when you develop a stomachache."

"Prep me," I say, frowning.

"Yes," Mason says with a glare. "You need to know more about what to expect tonight so that you won't look like such a shell shocked sourpuss. Plus, I want you to look hot enough to avoid bringing down onto your head a torrent of destructive rage. I want to keep the object of my research alive and well."

I narrow my eyes onto him and open my mouth sarcastically. "Could it be that you actually care about me, just a little bit?" I measure a little bit with my fingers.

Mason almost smiles. "I care about studying you in one piece. How can I expect to learn from a footstool that has been reduced to a pile of splinters? No, I wish for you to remain as healthy as possible."

"Why do you look so downcast," Jane says. "I'm sure they're fine, you're team that is. I know they're normally here by now, but I wouldn't worry too much."

"It's not that," I say, staring at the tear in Jane's shirt. "I…I'm really worried about tonight, about the festival."

Jane nods. "I suppose any decent person would be. Do you know what you're going to wear?"

I shake my head. "No, but Mason does. He has a special pair of pants he wants me to go in. But honestly, my concerns run much deeper than that."

Jane gives me a measured look. "Do tell. I might be able to help you."

I swallow hard. The memory of last night's major mishap reels through my mind with a pang of fear in my chest. "Have you ever seen the library?"

Jane shakes her head. "No, but I've heard the guards talk about it, why?"

I resist the urge to close my eyes in a pained expression. "Well, I somehow managed to destroy the stained glass image of Satan that adorned the special bookcase. I just barely touched the latch and the next thing I knew, the glass shattered to the floor with a growl that should have given me goose bumps."

Jane looks as if she is unsure of what to say. "That's not good. I've heard all about that image, the guards worship it day and night. First off, why were you even in the library? How did you get in there without getting caught?"

I get a good look at her to make sure that she is still on my side. She still looks like a friendly ally, but wouldn't it be something if she was just programmed to trick me into telling her all my secrets? Wouldn't it be about right to learn that Jane is in fact against me, though she is cordial to my face? And then, after I tell her all my business, all the guards can swoop down on me like a flock of buzzards drooling over a long desired feast.

I bite down onto my lip. "Mason introduced me to the library the other day, only he failed to quench my interest, so I…paid it a visit last night. Besides," I add quickly, seeing Jane's worried surprise, "I was trying not to sleep so I thought it best to find out what all I could learn."

Jane bats her pretty green eyes quickly. She holds up a hand, as if to press it flat against my chest. "Okay, so let me get this straight, you snuck into the library unattended to do exactly what?"

I groan inwardly. "I wanted to know where we are in the country, among other things. I never expected to cause the mess I did."

Jane nods and holds out a hand, as if she is presenting something. "Behold, the place where witches have thrived for centuries: Salem Massachusetts."

I stare at an image of a large black cat with golden eyes. I swallow hard. "That can't be right. I…wasn't Massachusetts located in the northeast in the Old Country?" I feel my heartbeat increase. "If that's true, then I'm a lot farther away from home than I thought. You know I'm from the southeastern county in district four, in the area that used to be known as Arkansas. It just doesn't make much sense. I don't remember…I mean the trip here wasn't that long. And I don't remember Mason stopping for fuel along the way."

Jane gives me a sad look. "You were drugged my dear boy. Don't you remember drinking anything along the way?"

I try to remember. "No, I think I would have known if…" I feel as if someone just slapped me upside the face. Now that she mentions it, I do remember having a drink of water, but I thought I was dreaming. I must have been delirious.

Jane gestures for the cat to disappear. "I warned you against trusting Mason. He is a master of deception. And as for the upcoming festival tonight, I'd be very careful if I were you. Mason may seem like he's trying to help you by suggesting that you wear pants, but I assure you, he has a reason for helping you, and I doubt it involves your best interest. It could be that he wants to keep you to himself, if you know what I mean. Or, it could be that he just wants to make you think he's on your side in order to draw closer to you for some other reason. I happen to know that Mason has a history of doing very dirty things to pretty teenage boys like yourself. If only you weren't so good looking…"

I close my eyes in a pained expression. I did not want to think the worst about Mason, but Jane has a point.

"He…hasn't done anything to me yet to make me question his morality, at least not that much. Maybe he doesn't find me as…" I feel my stomach clench in dawning realization. I open my eyes. "Mason called me a handsome stallion this morning."

I can hear Mason's words now: 'You'll wear the pants I got you and shine like the handsome stallion you are.' I swallow hard against the lump in my throat.

I shake my head in despair. If only Mason's kind would leave people like me alone, life would be so much easier to interpret. If only men desired women instead of other guys, things would not be so complicated. And to think, I actually ate the breakfast sandwich Mason brought me after he took a bite out of it. I think I'm going to be sick.

"Don't despair," Jane says with a pitied smile. "The rabbit isn't a pet until it has been trapped and tamed. What I mean to say is that you still have the potential to come out victorious against your captors. I would suggest you locate someone other than Mason, someone who you think you can trust and confide in that person when you can. Still, you might do well to consider having a conversation or two with…"

Bang. Bang. Bang. Someone is at the door. I narrow my eyes onto Jane.

Jane disappears with a worried look. Great, and just when she was about to tell me who I should talk to.

I hear the door open behind me. I wipe my sweaty palms on my pants. A rack of crossbows suddenly appears on the wall, bringing me some peace of mind. Honestly, I had intended to ask Jane what weapon we would be training with today. I suppose she spied on the other teams to figure it out. But then again, the only weapons

Mason ever mentioned anything about to me were knifes and crossbows, but still.

"Please don't," Jennifer says behind me with distress.

I turn around to find Jack kissing Jennifer's neck. "But you're so beautiful," he says, his voice full with wonder. "I've wanted to sample you ever since I laid eyes on you." He gropes across her chest. "And you're so well made to. And to top that off, I have a thing for women of color. And from my experience, women of color tend to have a thing for me."

Jack kisses Jennifer's neck one last time and then looks at me. "Ryan, you look as if you too are in need of a beautiful woman. If you're good, I might just share this pretty little thing with you. Or, if you prefer, you might find more pleasure with one of these handsome Saint-boys." Jack turns around to face Nick. "This one here looks mighty pretty."

Nick swallows hard, blue eyes filled with fear.

Jack runs a hand over Nick's chest. "You're even more solid than you look. And your eyes…Oh yes, I think you'll be cool to hang out with tonight."

Jack flicks his eyes to me. "I think I found my date for the festival tonight. That is, unless you want to take him yourself."

I clear my throat. "No, you can have him. I…think I know who I want to go with." Honestly, I was not aware that I could take someone. Mason never said anything about it. But leave it to Mason to leave out important details.

"Who," Jack says with an amused frown. He points to Seth with an inquisitive smirk. "Don't tell me, you've set your heart on this red-haired Saint-boy."

Seth gives me a worried glance. I could strangle Jack. If only I could tell Seth the truth about myself.

I look between Seth and Jack. "There's this girl actually, the senior maid, Carrie."

Jack looks astonished. "You mean you'd let the sweet flesh of this beautiful boy go untested for a servant girl? My goodness how you have lost your marbles. As pretty as she is, girls like Carrie have proven to be, in my experience, much more boring than pretty boys. But suit yourself. For me, there's something about the sweet smelling skin of a virgin Saint-boy that stirs me."

Jack gives me a farewell smile and then heads toward the door. With a hand on the doorknob, he turns around to face me in the doorway. "You know you can do, within reason, what you want to them, don't you? I mean, should you want to undress them to see who has the prettiest bodies, you can do that. Personally, I am *dying* to have Nick to myself tonight." At that, Jack flashes Nick a big smile and then leaves the room.

Nick looks shaken, as if he has only moments left to live. I wish there was a chair for him to sit in. As bad as my situation is, his is far worse. If Jack plans on doing to him the kinds of detestable things that his kind do to each other, Nick might not be around much longer. Jack looks healthy enough, but where sexually transmitted diseases are concerned, looks can be deceiving.

Kody takes Nick's arm and rests her head against his shoulder. Jennifer looks relieved, while Seth is looking at me like I'm a pervert. I groan inwardly.

"You all had best get busy," I say solemnly, but not unkindly.

Seth throws his arms out to his sides, brown eyes defiant. "So this is it? You think you can just reduce us to being your sex toys?" He shakes his head. "You're sick. I swear, if you lay one finger on me, you'll see just how masculine I am."

I want to yell at him, to release all the fury I have bottled up inside of me, but I know it would not be wise. "I have no desire to harm you. Like I said, I have a girl picked out for tonight."

"Poor girl," Kody says with asperity. "She must be desperate." She looks as if she could tackle me at any moment. I need to do something quick.

I swallow hard. "I have no desire to harm any of you, none whatsoever. All I want is for us to get along, to train like we've been told to."

Jennifer narrows her dark eyes onto me. "'We've'? You make it sound as if you too are under orders."

I glare at the curious smile in her voice. I could kick myself for my mistake. "Well, yes, in a way I am. Everyone has a boss, in case you didn't know it. Mine just happens to be President Eugene Gloss, the greatest boss anyone could ever hope to have." I puff my chest out to try to look important.

Nick laughs, clearly unconvinced. "Yeah, well, you can have him. I know your kind worship him almost as much as you worship Satan."

I sigh inwardly while trying to maintain a look of superiority. "I think it's time to get busy."

"I don't know about that," Nick says, popping his knuckles. "You know, you can't be much older than us from the looks of you. What makes you think we should take orders from you?"

Oh dear God I did not ask for this. "Because things won't go well with you if you don't. If you all will cooperate with me, I will try to do everything I can to help you. I give you my word."

Jennifer raises her eyebrows. "Oh? And what's the word of a demonized serpent? Did not Eve bring about her and her husband's ruin on the word of a demonized serpent?"

Kody puts her hands onto her hips and sizes me up. "You do realize that the four of us could easily twist you into a pretzel and there'd be no one to save you, don't you?"

I resist the urge to swallow. "I wouldn't try that if I were you. Contrary to what you think, whoever touches me will seal their fate. And you don't even want to know what they'd do to you before you died. You see," I add with a twisted smile, "there's an order of operations around here that is more painful than anything any mathematician could ever devise." At least that is what I honestly suspect. I'm thinking all levels of abuse, beginning with sexual abuse. After all, there seems to be more lust in the air around here than oxygen.

I need to drive home the dangers of raising a hand against me to protect myself. I look at Nick's shiny black hair. He gives me a strange look, as if unsure of what to make of my gaze.

"I'd be extra careful if I were you," I say with a perilous smile in my voice. I hate to sound like this, but I need to convince him. "If you knew how many of my friends like guys with black hair, you'd probably be down on your hands and knees crying out to your God. And unfortunately for you, those blue eyes of yours only make you more of a target. Yes, I'd be very careful if I were you. Depending on your behavior here, I can either help you or fuel the lust of those who already want to pour out their lust on you. It's entirely up to you."

Nick looks convinced, swallows hard. "Fine, the last thing I want is a bunch of…your kind abusing me."

"Nick," Jennifer says with a surprised look. "He's just trying to scare you into submitting to his authority, you shouldn't believe a word he says."

Nick scoffs. "Oh, so I should just stand by and take my chances. You know what he says is true; you heard what that perv…guard said to me earlier. Besides, you don't know what all I had to contend with back home, how many close calls I had with perverted agents wanting to… Look, the last thing I want is to wind up as an object of someone's perversions before I die. Surely you can see where I'm coming from."

"He's right," Seth says, brown eyes agleam with caution. He glances at me and then turns back to Jennifer. "We don't have any choice but to do what he says and hope that it goes well with us. Besides, no one else has offered to help us around here."

Nick gives me a wary look. "But what about you? Where do you really stand on all of this? I mean, how do I know that you're not just leading me on with the intent to do me harm?"

I would love to tell him that I have been wondering the same thing about all the guards around here, and even Jane for that matter where I myself am concerned. "What does your heart tell you," I say. "Do you think I want to hurt you?" I look between each of them. "Have I, at any point since I've met you tried to harm any of you? Look at my record and figure it out for yourselves."

Seth clears his throat. "Okay, so you haven't done anything terrible to us yet, but how do we know that that's not going to change? What assurance can you give us besides your word?"

Jennifer gives me a judicious look. Nick looks like he wants to shout out in support of Seth's boldness, while Kody eyes me with a suspicious look.

I feel like I'm about to sink or swim. "Jane, I need a Bible." It quickly appears in my outstretched hand, as if she knew what I was about to say before I even said it. I stare at it with as much pretend disgust as I can muster. "I will give you all a choice starting tomorrow. I will allow you to bless me or curse me each day based on how I treat you. Should I abuse you, I will lay down and let you urinate on me. Now, should I treat you well, I would like for each of you to bless me. Perhaps that God of yours will respond and you might make a believer out of me yet. As for this Bible, I will allow it to remain in each of our practice sessions from here on out as a sign of my word, since you think so highly of it. What do you say to that?"

"You're serious," Nick says, shocked. "You'd actually let me urinate on you? That's disgusting dude. But then again, it's not half as disgusting as the kind of stuff your kind does to each other. No offense, but unless your kind repents, none of you will make it to heaven."

"Maybe," I say with a smile, "but you have to admit, we know how to have fun. And don't think for a second that I'm doing any of this for you all. Rather, I see this as an opportunity to enhance my own standing with President Gloss. If it takes treating you all halfway decent in order to keep you all from acting out of line, then so be it. So, we all stand to benefit from this covenant, if that is you will swear on this Bible. Show me just how good the word of a Saint really is. Any one of you can come forward and represent your group."

One by one, each of them turns to Seth. Seth looks a bit apprehensive, as if he finds their collective support of him more of a burden than he cares to bear. And who wants to risk getting blamed, especially from such an important covenant as this?"

"Fine," Seth says with a sigh. "But don't complain to me if things don't go as planned. I have no doubt that we will all keep our side of the deal, but I can't say the same for him." Seth nods at me with sharp eyes. He turns back to his teammates. "The way I see it, nothing we do really matters, because I doubt we leave this place alive anyway. So have it your way."

Seth strides forward and places a hand on the Bible. I can't help but notice the calluses on the sides of his fingers, just like mine. Field work is brutal on the best of days, especially with such steep quotas to have to meet.

"Alright," I say, trying not to stare at his calluses. "So, as representative of your team, do you agree to follow my orders, given that I treat you all fairly?" Seth nods stiffly. "And, should I say or do something to anger you, will you agree to only urinate on me after we've discussed the matter?"

"That wasn't part of the deal," Seth says coolly.

"It is now," I say.

Seth casts a glance over his shoulder at his teammates. Jennifer meets his eyes with a shrug, while Nick looks at the floor somewhat wearily.

"Just do it," Kody snaps. "It's not like we have all day. Besides, you heard what Jack said on the way here this morning. Only the team that trains the hardest will stand a chance of surviving the things to come, not to mention the final challenge, whatever that is. So we had best get busy."

Seth lets out a defeated sigh. "Agreed," he says, looking sick. "Just don't expect me to put my private parts on display for you if I have to urinate on you."

"Fine with me," I say, trying to keep the disgust from my voice. "I don't have an appetite for guys anyway."

Seth studies me carefully, removes his hand from the Bible. "I thought all you guards had appetites for both guys and girls. Honestly, I'm surprised that you're not slobbering at the sight of me. Most of the guards around here look at me like I'm an exotic snack or something. It's disgusting."

I give him a wry smile. "But you are exotic, to us anyway. Like I said, many of the guards around here would love nothing more than to see you naked. I feel the only thing holding them back right now is their excitement for the big event tonight, known as the Festival of Demons. It is there that their hunger for seeing naked Saints should be satisfied."

Seth looks worried, takes a step backward. "What all will they do to him, to Nick I mean? How will he ever be able to hold his head up again if they force him to show off his body? And surely you know that his well-being will affect our ability to stay competitive, to continue on like you want us to."

I swallow against the lump in my throat. I had not considered that. I look at Nick over Seth's shoulder. "I'll keep an eye on him."

I turn back to Seth. "But it's highly unlikely that he will escape from being kissed. I mean, I can't tell my fellow guardsmen to leave him alone."

"Why not," Jennifer says with a nervous expression. "They seem to listen to you. Can't you get Jack drunk or something so that he will forget about Nick?"

I flick my eyes to Nick. I can tell that he wants to speak, but looks too shaken to do so. He seems like such a nice guy, it hurts. I'm not sure what I will be able to do tonight, but I know one thing, I intend to protect him to the best of my ability.

I turn back to Jennifer. "I'll try to look out for him, but like I said, I cannot guarantee his safety. But," I add with a speculative frown, "I think he could help himself, at least to some degree by simply exhausting yourself today during training. Work so hard that you run yourself down, and then mess your hair up."

I wish the day was already over. I dread whatever Mason has in store for me to prep me for the festival tonight. And more than that, I dread the festival itself. I feel my heartbeat increase with nervous anticipation. If it comes down to it, I will defend myself. I will do whatever it takes to keep myself from harm.

I shake my head at the electric blue pants. Mason stands with a finger crooked at his lips, green eyes assessing my appearance. And if blue pants isn't bad enough, I now have a tattoo of a blue demon on my chest. Mason thinks it makes me look "hotter and more desirable", but I hate it. Who wants to be seen with a blue demon that resembles a lusty man on their chest?

"Stop feeling sorry for yourself," Mason says sternly. "You should thank me; I had considered having Carrie put one on each of your biceps as well. It'd make them more desirable to. As it is, I guess you'll have to do." I'd like to knock him out.

"And what about you," I say, taking in his near usual appearance. "Don't you think you'll disappoint all those friends of yours from wearing too much clothing?"

Mason raises his eyebrows. "I'm *not* going like this." He unbuttons his shirt to reveal a partially exposed tattoo. Taking the two halves in his hands, he pulls them apart to reveal a giant panda bear.

He has got to be joking. "A panda bear? Of all the things I expected to see, that takes the cake. Do you expect to be petted or something?"

Mason shrugs. "I'd rather be petted than kissed. Besides, I'm not a good kisser, or at least that's what I was told recently."

I shake my head. "So that's it then? Are you sure it's going to be enough to satisfy everyone?"

Mason eyes his panda with a smile. "I don't have to satisfy everyone, just those who like cute pandas." He looks up at me. "You, on the other hand, must look delectable, despite your narrow mindedness to conform to the finer things in life."

I ball my hands into fists at my sides. "If my narrow mindedness keeps me from being held in the arms of every pervert around here, then so be it."

Mason almost smiles. "Come on, I want to show you off. You'll no doubt be one of the hottest attractions tonight despite the dark circles beneath your eyes, so get ready. And, when anyone asks you about your tattoo, tell them that I gave it to you."

I blink in surprise. "But you didn't, Carrie did." And she did it ever so gently.

Mason shrugs. "So, it'll look better if you tell them I did it. That way, they'll think I've claimed you for myself, thus making me much less sought after in their eyes."

I did not just hear that.

I stare at my transparent shoes. "Tell me again, why must I wear these shoes?"

"To let your heart be heard," Mason says with a twisted smile. "Just wait and you'll see. Why, don't you like them? I have to admit footstool, you do have nice feet for a boy, and a Saint-boy at that."

I raise my eyebrows. "Am I supposed to say thank you?"

Mason gives me a daring smile. "Only if you feel it's a compliment. Now come on," Mason adds as he opens the door, "we haven't got long before the festival begins. Oh how I can't wait to taste the fine wine and whisper words of love to all the pretty demons that'll be there. And if you're lucky, you might just feel one of them kiss your new tattoo. How does that sound to you?"

"Terrific," I say sarcastically. "I've waited my whole life to be kissed by one of Satan's minions. I just hope the drool from the fangs won't burn a hole in my skin."

Mason laughs without mirth. "I wouldn't worry about that, as good looking as you are, you'd survive with more than enough appeal to supply you with all the lovers you could ever want."

I step into the hallway. I cross my arms over my chest. I wish I could have worn a shirt. It's so cold.

"My desire is Satan's sexy fire," Mason says as we stroll down the hallway toward the common room. He shoots me an attention craved look.

I roll my eyes. "I'd be careful if I were you. That might be just where you end up, in the heart of Satan's fiery pit."

"I'd make love to him," Mason says wistfully. "Well, not in the way you're probably thinking, but I'd kiss his chest and rub his abdomen until my heart turned into liquid fire."

Mason's more twisted than I thought. Jane must be right. He seems more evil than I could ever have imagined. How could someone who thinks so highly of Satan not be evil? But then again, maybe he is just extra excited about the imminent festival. After all, he spent much of the afternoon telling me all about last year's festival. Apparently, a woman named Lina became impregnated by so many demons, she ended up giving birth to a whole litter of demon kittens called Nydoria. These Nydoria, or hyperactive spirits as Mason described them, made their way around the festival pleasuring everyone in unimaginable ways. And, by the time it was all said and done, everyone in the room, including all the men, became pregnant. Unfortunately, several of the guards who attended last year's festival died of terrible diseases and unexplainable things that baffled the mind.

And to my great displeasure, I had to hold Mason's feet the entire time as he rambled on about all of this. He also lectured me on how to maintain "proper Deticate", or demon etiquette. For instance, should I feel a sudden vibration coming on; I need to sweet talk the demon spirit into giving me the best it has to offer, otherwise, I risk only getting a sample of its goodness. I listened patiently, but by the time it was all said and done, I not only wanted to break his ankles, but also vomit from my sweat slicken hands. Mason never once let on about his feet. He did shower before letting Carrie paint the image of the panda on his chest. I couldn't help but feel a little irritated as Carrie appeared to be enjoying herself with Mason for some reason.

I quicken my pace and fall in beside Mason as he meets the staircase. For some reason, I have an icky feeling that I cannot quite put my finger on. It's like I forgot to brush my…Oh no, I am doomed. When everyone finds Satan's image missing from the library, then I am going to become demon fodder faster than Mason can brag about himself.

"What's wrong," Mason says, coming to a stop at the foot of the stairs. "You look as if you have received an early death sentence. Surely someone as good looking as you does not think that you would not be missed around here."

I swallow hard. "I…um…might have forgotten to put on deodorant." And honestly, I feel so shaken right now that I cannot remember what I did before we left.

Mason leans forward and smells me. "You smell fine to me. There's nothing like mint to sweeten up your armpits."

"I feel sick," I say. "All over, like I have the flu or something."

"What a handsome dove," says a familiar voice from behind me. Christian steps into my line of vision. "Mason, look who I rounded up to bring to the festival with me, isn't she a foxy thing? Look at her eyes; have you ever seen such a mixture of utter sadness and beauty?"

"She's a rare treasure indeed," Mason says, impressed.

A hand on my shoulder. "Take a look my handsome brother," Christian says playfully. "She is, after all, the girl you fetched for me the other day."

I turn around to face Mindy. I had hoped that Christian would leave her alone. I narrow my eyes onto Christian. "Are you sure she's your type," I say.

With a smile, Christian runs a hand up beneath her shirt until he pushes her shirt up to rest his fingers in the hollow of her throat. "Oh, she's my type all right. Just look at her, apart from her hands, there doesn't appear to be a blemish on her. I never thought I'd wind up taking a Saint-girl to the Festival of Demons, but life is full of surprises. I told her that if she's good, I might even let her have her way with me. Isn't that right my little candy dish?"

Mindy nods, gray-blue eyes looking between the three of us. "Yes," she says in a small voice. "I…want you all to myself my handsome stag. I want to hold you and kiss you like you deserve, for who has a body like my god?" No doubt Christian told her to say all that.

Christian gives me a mischievous smile. "See how much she loves me? One night with her and she already thinks I'm a god. But let me guess," Christian says looking between Mason and I. "You two are going together, right? Honestly, you have poor tastes Mason."

"Maybe so," Mason says with slight irritation. Mason rests a hand on my shoulder. "But there's more to Ryan than his looks. For instance," Mason adds with a wry smile, "Ryan is about the best chess player I've ever come across." And he is the biggest liar I have ever seen!

Christian raises an eyebrow. "Chess?" Christian looks torn between wanting to dig deeper for more details and wanting to stab me with hateful words."

Mason tightens his grip on my shoulder and shrugs.

I want to knock both of them upside the head. I look on Christian. "I planned on going with Carrie, but she backed out at the last minute, or haven't you heard?"

"I heard," Christian says with a nasty smile.

Mason nods at Christian and Mindy. Mindy looks as if she wants to find a quiet place and cry. I feel bad for her.

Christian takes Mindy's hand and pulls her along with him. Christian puts his free hand on her butt as they round the corner of the staircase. I can tell that Mindy wants to knock his hand away and probably slap him across the face as well. Like pretty much all the other guards around here, Christian shows no sign that he understands true love. To him, love means fulfilling the perversions of his heart, including having relations with other men and treating women like dirt.

I watch in distress as Mindy holds the door open for Christian. If only Mason wasn't here, I'd half consider calling her to join me for a getaway. She looks fast. I bet we could escape this place together if we could just get outside the building. The other night, when Mason and I stood on the balcony of the watch tower, I couldn't help but notice a long tree limb within arm's reach. If we could get into the tower, I think we'd stand a good chance of escape.

"Hey," I say, suddenly realizing that I spoke aloud. Christian and Mindy went in the direction of the Mirage. I assumed the festival would be held in the lounge by the library.

"Yes," Mason says with a curious grin.

I clear my throat. I shake my head. I'm not going to say anything. Maybe some of the guards will get so drunk or wild that their revelry will take them into the library. Then, amid their partying, it might be possible that the absence of Satan might go unnoticed, at least until tomorrow morning. That way, it would be hard to draw any accurate conclusions.

I follow along as Mason heads in the same direction that Christian and Mindy went. It's strange, I had expected Christian to comment about my tattoo or the pants that Mason got from him, but he remained mostly uninterested. As happy as I am about that, it may not be altogether a good sign. If anything, it could mean that he has been desensitized. As for Mason, well, he buttoned his shirt up as we left our room, as if he felt a bit uncomfortable or something.

"Wait for me," says a sweet but slightly strained voice.

I hold the door open as Mason turns around on the threshold. "Carrie," I say, hearing the relief in my voice. "What are you doing here? I thought you decided not to come."

"I changed my mind," Carrie says, pushing aside a curl from her line of vision. "Besides," Carrie adds, looking at Mason, "I know how these things can go, and someone will likely need a sober arm to lean on before the nights out."

"You're absolutely right," Mason says. "If one of us remains sober and fully clothed until morning, it will set a record. And I expect that at least half a dozen of my fellow guardsmen will require some form of medical assistance before midnight alone. As for three o'clock in the morning, God help us."

Carrie struggles not to laugh. "I know it's serious, but I can't help but remember what happened to Jace last year. After he kissed all his fellow guardsmen, he realized that he had forgotten to apply the black lipstick that he had went on and on about for so long. But by then, he was so wasted that he ended up sprawled out under the Great Fruit Tree, where he later woke to a pile of apples, bananas, pomegranates, and oranges lying on his chest. Turns out, all of his fellow guardsmen felt so sorry for him that they each kissed a piece of fruit with various colors of lipstick so as to identify each of them."

Mason laughs. "Yeah, I remember that. Everyone wore a different color of lipstick last year, mine was blue."

"And an attractive shade of blue at that," Carrie says with a small smile.

Mason narrows his eyes onto her. "Yeah, I guess it was." He checks his watch. "Come on, it's already started and we'll be missed, especially you Ryan."

I hold the door open. Carrie shoots me a nervous smile as she steps into the corridor. I get the impression that she is dreading this about as much as I am; she just refuses to let on to Mason. I want to take her arm and hold her back to ask her about it, but Mason would doubtless miss us the instant the door closed, so I step through after them.

I shiver from the much colder air in the corridor. I look Carrie over as I approach she and Mason. I know this is not the time to think such things, but I wish she had come in a pretty dress or something. Her black and white maid's uniform looks so bleak. But then again, anything else and she would likely find herself getting too much attention. Besides, Carrie is pretty enough that she really does not need to go the extra mile to look breathtaking, she already is.

"Do tell me you plan to engage in all of tonight's revelry," Mason says as he turns to face Carrie. "You would have been a huge hit last year if only you would have let your guard down."

Carrie gives him an unsettled look. "I don't know what you mean. I participated in just about everything except the nude display and pollywoggling."

"What's pollywoggling," I say.

Carrie looks light headed, as if she wishes she had left that part out. "A very promiscuous dance."

"Is that *really* all you're going to tell him," Mason says, slowly unbuttoning his shirt. "It's as if you're embarrassed to talk about it."

"I am not embarrassed to talk about it," Carrie says with a hint of tension in her voice. She catches my eyes. "Pollywoggling is … a highly energized dance that involves four partners. While dancing closely together in a small circle, each person must try to remove each other's clothing without getting caught. Whoever has the most clothing on at the end of the dance wins."

That is one of the craziest things I have ever heard of in my life. No wonder why Carrie turned away before she finished describing it to me. I saw a hint of a blush on her cheeks. Carrie seems too innocent, too pure to even talk about such things, let alone want to participate in them. I could knock Mason upside the head for making it out like something is wrong with her, just because she has enough decency to be embarrassed.

Mason comes to a stop outside one of the eight doors that leads to the Mirage. He takes his shirt off and hands it to Carrie with a smile. "Here love, guard this like it's my heart."

I stare at the number 6 above the door. "Why this door," I say. It's the same door that leads to my training room.

Mason turns on me with raised eyebrows, as if I should have enough sense to figure it out on my own. "They all lead to the same place tonight. There are no separate rooms. You're about to see the Mirage in a way that you've probably never imagined. Consider the size of the room you train in every day and then realize that that is just a sliver of the Mirage. Plus, about half of the Mirage is not even used during the combined daily training of all the teams."

"That sounds like a waste to me," I say.

"I wouldn't say that," Mason says with an almost boyish grin, "especially since you will be expected to lead your team into the heart of the Mirage very soon. Now come on," Mason says pulling me by the arm, "I can't wait to show you off. It's not every day I get to show off someone as good looking as you. And everyone has been waiting for this moment to get to see just how attractive your body really is."

"Won't they be disappointed then," I say. I look down at my pants. Honestly, I don't know why Mason calls them "electric blue", since I see nothing special about them. "I *am* partially clothed after all."

Mason looks at the demon on my chest. "True, but I think you'll find that the environment will go a long way in changing that. Now let's go, otherwise, at this rate, we'll stand out here all night and you'll never get to see what I mean."

I swallow hard. I want to turn around and run back down the corridor, but I know it would be to no avail. If only the good doctor cared more about my health and well-being instead of his own reputation, then I'm sure he could make a convincing excuse for me. I reach for the doorknob.

Carrie cuts in front of me. "Allow me," she says, brushing against my arm. I shiver.

"Thanks," I say, feeling dazed.

Carrie takes the doorknob and slowly pulls the door open. I feel my heartbeat quicken as a ray of green light escapes the room through the ever widening gap in the door. It flashes across my face.

Loud music erupts from the room, slamming against my body like the firm hand of an irritable agent. I hate loud noises.

Mason jabs me between my shoulder blades to move forward. I want to whip around and knock him out. I've already had enough and I haven't even entered the room yet.

I take a deep breath and step into pandemonium. A hand grabs my arm from out of the darkness and jerks me forward. "Hey," I say chidingly. An orange light briefly illuminates Christian's face.

"It's about time," Christian says loudly. "Any longer and you would have missed the lights and music."

I catch a glimpse of Mindy between the rays of light. She looks as if she has already contracted some terrible disease that threatens to wipe her out. She's so pale.

"I smell wine," Mason says with a wistful smile. "And the sweet smell of beautiful bodies."

"Carrie," Christian says, taken by surprise. "I thought you were going to be a good girl again this year. Could it be that the promise of smooth skin and strong muscles wooed you after all?"

Carrie laughs, a sweet and almost inaudible sound amid the cacophony. I did not realize she was standing so close to me.

"Why Christian," Carrie says with a borderline flirtatious smile, "are you volunteering to let me see if my decision to come tonight will be worthwhile?"

A ray of blue light passes over Christians face. He looks positively inflamed with lust. "Any time, any place, I'm yours. Well, almost any time, you see, I've already had over a dozen requests from fellow guardsmen to join them in the Pleasure Hall, and the night's barely begun."

I feel a wave of dizziness wash over me. I think this is going to be a much worse experience than I had originally thought.

Christian meets Carrie's eyes. "Since it looks like you've come to work, if you don't mind, take this creature behind me and go. I'm already disgusted with her refusal to comply with my orders. If I've told her once, I've told her a dozen times to unbutton her shirt, but she simply refuses to cooperate. All well, I think I had enough of her last night to sate my appetite for Saint-girls anyway."

Carrie nods and moves to Mindy's side. I see Carries lips move, but cannot hear a word she says. Everything about this place, at least from what I have seen so far, including the passing rays of light and loud music seem suited to bring people close together. And that is the last thing I want to think about. I would like to stay at least an arm's length from everyone, but I can't see that happening.

"Mason," Christian says with a smile. "I didn't notice you had a panda on your chest when last we met. I have to admit, it makes you look more of a softy than you already are."

I swallow hard. I'm not sure what to make of that. And judging by Mason's tight expression, he is not happy. Why do I get the impression that Mason is hiding his true identity from me?

"But it's sort of sad too I guess," Christian says, blue eyes illuminated in a flash of pale white light. "Everyone knows that pandas are nearly extinct because they're too stupid to do it on their own."

Is there nothing Christian won't say? "What about you," I say, getting Christian's attention. "Isn't that a jaguar on your chest? Last I heard, jaguars were facing extinction because they can't seem to slow down long enough to do it."

"You are a sly fox," Christian says, brushing a hand over his body art. "But this is not a typical jaguar. If you look closely, it has both male *and* female parts; thereby increasing its chance of finding a mate."

"That's impossible," I say, hearing the disgust in my voice.

Christian opens his mouth to speak but Mason pokes him in the chest almost playfully. "Don't harass him yet," Mason says as a beam of red light rolls over his face. "Besides, he needs to look as fresh and calm as possible so that everyone isn't turned off by him. Whether his Sainthood can survive the night will depend heavily on how well he looks."

"Well said," Christian says with a trace of faint disgust in his voice. "I expect he'll be the most fragrant virgin ever to have graced the Festival of Demons."

Mason nods. "Without a doubt."

Chapter Ten

Mason takes my arm and aligns me with the golden road ahead of us. I wish he'd loosen his grip, you'd think I was a little kid in need of constant supervision.

"So what do you think so far," Christian says, nearly rupturing my ear drums.

I clench my fists. I want to hit him. He smiles, clearly satisfied about shouting directly into my ear. I stay silent.

Christian punches me in the arm.

I bristle. "What is your problem," I say. "Never mind, I already know the answer to that." He is a godless pervert who cannot keep his hands to himself.

Christian laughs, sounding something like a choking hyena. "You're so gentle. I hit you in the arm and you won't even growl at me, you're not half bad for a Saint after all."

Oh how I'm tempted to change his mind about that. "That doesn't mean I'll let you treat me however you want. I'm not a panda, you know."

Christian's face lights up in a beam of light. "True, you just act like one. Or could it be that you have the heart of a lion beneath that innocent chest of yours? You want to know what I think. I think you've got just as much potential to become as open minded as any of us."

"You mean as open minded as a pervert," I say. I jerk my hand free from Mason's grip. I whirl on Christian. "You're one sick, narrow min…" Mason claps a hand over my mouth.

"Be careful," Mason says. I try to peal his hand from my mouth, but he refuses to budge. "Be still and listen for a moment. Christian, give me a moment alone with him, if you don't mind."

Christian shrugs and walks away. I half expected him to lay into me. Mason spins me around to face him. I feel dizzy. I make out his solemn expression in between the beams of light. Fortunately, all the crazy lighting is becoming less intense.

"You're in no position to say things like that," Mason says, green eyes luminous. "Remember, you have come to a dangerous place to do a dangerous job, and should you fail to live up to expectations, things will not go well with you. I can promise you that."

I feel my cheeks reddening with anger. "So you just expect me to put up with whatever your kind wants to do to me? You're telling me that you want me to stand by and let them treat me however they like, as if I have no feelings at all? I guess Jane was right…" I trail off, swallowing hard.

Mason narrows his eyes onto me. "What about Jane?"

I try to act nonchalant. "Oh, you know what all she said the first day we met. But I suppose that's why you had her memory wiped, wasn't it?"

I see a trace of fear in his eyes. I wish he would look away from me, I don't know how much longer I'm going to be able to maintain my casual expression.

"Mason," says an unfamiliar voice. Mason whips his head in the direction of the voice. I breathe a sigh of relief. "Oh, you're hotter than fire and ten times as pure. What must I do to convince you to let me have a go at you?"

I back away from Mason. I expect to see someone standing next to Mason, but there is only darkness.

"I'm up here," says a man from above my head. "Oh for Pete's sake, I should have realized I'd be like an opossum in a church house."

A flash of light illuminates a man clinging to a large tree limb. He lets go and drops to the ground beside me. "Nice tattoo, blue demons turn me on about as much as hot Saint-girls, so it looks like I'm in luck." He reaches for my arm.

"Not so fast," Mason says, gently pushing away his hand. "He's with me, Koko."

Koko looks disappointed, even slightly irritated. "I see that, but we are at the Festival of Demons, where there are no restraints. It's bad enough that you deny me yourself, but must you also deny me the company of one pure Saint? All I want to do is show him off."

"He's not as pure as you may think," Mason says. A burst of fireworks lights up the night sky. "And besides, we've only just arrived, so I want to show him around before anyone takes him away from me."

Koko gives me an appraising look. I stiffen. If I had a sharp object, I'd half consider gouging his eyes out.

I give him a scathing look. He flicks his eyes to Mason, barely missing my razor sharp stare.

Mason gives him a measured look. "I thought you were among the few watchmen who bravely volunteered to guard our walls tonight."

Koko runs a hand through his silver hair. "I was, but I managed to get out of it. I couldn't miss all this," Koko adds, waving his hands about him. "It's not every night that one gets to party with demons and guys with perfect abs."

Mason nods. "It's definitely a treat. I myself plan on getting drunk at some point, after I visit the Pleasure

Hall of course. I would not want to spoil that experience by being drunk."

"Dang," Koko says, impressed.

I follow his eyes to my pants. I'm on fire! Well, at least that's what it looks like. Blue flames lick at my legs, as if I'm not even wearing pants. The flames stop at my waistline.

Koko shakes his head in astonishment. "That's the hottest thing I've seen so far, and I've seen some pretty hot stuff."

I feel like I could pass out. I had no idea that anyone would be able to see through my pants. I could strangle Mason. At least there appears to be a dark spot where I need it the most. Honestly, considering the nature of this place, I'm surprised that I'm not completely naked.

I suddenly want to wrap myself in a bed sheet and hide behind one of the big oak trees that keeps getting lit up from all the fireworks. I know this place is called the Mirage, but everything around us looks so real, even smells so real that I actually feel like I'm outdoors. The stars in the sky even testify to the realistic nature of the environment around me. And then there are all the houses, each appearing to rest atop one of the gently rolling hills off in the distance. I suspect the houses that look farthest away are just a trick of the highly sophisticated computer that runs this place.

But by far the most alarming building around is the one at the end of the golden road that we're currently standing on. Shaped like a pyramid, and made completely of glass, it looks more suited to bury the guards who will drop like flies from one of many diseases than be the focal point of pleasure. It must be the Pleasure Hall that everyone keeps talking about.

Koko jabs a finger over his shoulder. "I'll be in the Pleasure Hall if you care to join up with me later on. That goes for you to Saint-boy, only go easy on me and don't burn me with your pants, my skin is very sensitive. See you all later then."

"Have a good night Koko," Mason says with a strained smile in his voice. He turns to face me.

I want to drive my fist into his chest so badly, it already hurts. Instead, I shake my head.

"I know," Mason says, taking me by surprise. "He's not the most pleasant guy to be around. Before I left to get you, I had night duty with him. It was all I could do not to punch him in the face. He's too friendly."

I blink in surprise. "That's something I never expected to hear you say. Good grief, I think I might pass out already and the night's barely begun."

Mason laughs. "You better not. Besides, just because I'm not that fond of Koko doesn't mean I hold anything against him. He is my friend who I'd do just about anything for, except give myself to him in the way he wants me to."

I take a deep breath. "So what now?" I look up at the night sky. The fireworks and all the annoying lights and music have ceased. A full moon now hovers overhead. "I thought everyone was just aching to see me." I throw up a hand. "Not that I'm disappointed, but still. You made it out like everyone was going to try to ravish me the moment I arrived. Where is everyone?"

I follow Mason's eyes to the houses on the high hills. "Depending on the location, some people are currently sitting around having casual conversations while enjoying some really great drinks. Others chose to meet in special houses in order to worship specific demons that will only visit those houses. But for the most part," Mason adds with a cautious look, "most people are currently in the Pleasure Hall, engaged in pretty much every kind of sexual act that your God opposes. So I ask you footstool, where do you want to go first?"

I swallow hard. He looks serious. "You mean you're letting *me* decide?"

Mason looks on me with a mixture of impatience and something like sadness. "Oh, you can be sure that you'll see all of the places before we leave. I'm just letting you choose where you want to go first."

I feel my heart sink. "So I really don't have a choice, not if you're going to force me to visit every place anyway."

"You could say that," Masons says blithely.

I sigh. "Isn't there some way you could make a double of me so that I wouldn't be missed at any of the hot spots? Surely that wouldn't be a problem considering how advanced the Mirage is."

Mason swallows almost imperceptibly. "No," he says as he turns on his heel to face a cobblestone road. "So it's off to one of the houses in the village, unless you say otherwise. In case you haven't noticed, the name of the city can be found among the stars in the sky."

I frown. I look up to the sky. It looks so far away, so high above us, as if the ceiling itself has been removed to allow a clear shot into the heavens. And like the real sky, the stars are too numerous to count. I find the Big Dipper easy enough, but as for the name of the…Wait, I think I see it! Wow. And talk about suitable, it lights up the sky as boldly as the sin the city was destroyed for. Seven stars make up the first letter, the letter G.

"Gomorrah," I say, transfixed.

"Gomorrah," Mason says excitedly. "Now let's go. If we're lucky, I think we might just get to see some pretty hot activity beneath one of the spreading trees along the way."

Mason steers me away from the golden road and sets off down the cobblestone road. At least it leads away from the Pleasure Hall. I need to find some kind of weapon to use in my defense. I will not let a bunch of perverts have their way with me. Mason better get that through his thick head and quick, otherwise he will find that I will not hesitate to do whatever it takes to defend myself. If his kind wants a unique experience with me, then I'll give them one that they will never forget.

"Slow down," Mason says irritably. "Remember, we're going to be here all night, so there's no need to rush."

I slow down to match his pace. I didn't realize how much I had surged ahead of him. I want more than anything to find something that I can use as a weapon. The thing is, other than a healthy coverage of grass and several spreading oaks, there does not appear to be anything useful about this place. Everything has been especially designed to promote an atmosphere of relaxation conducive to unbridled lust.

Mason kicks a loose stone, sending it tumbling down the road ahead of us. I follow it with my eyes until it disappears into a dark shadow beneath a spreading oak. Mason looks bored. I suspect he would much rather be with his friends than with me. If only the good doctor was not so curious about me. If only he did not feel so compelled to study me, then he would be free to frolic with the others. If indeed that is why he still remains with me.

"You're awfully quiet," Mason says. "One would think you're angry with me."

I come to a stop. I give him an indignant look. "You bring me to what has to be the sickest place I've ever been to in my life and wonder why I'm angry with you?" I could punch him in the face. "Why wouldn't I be angry," I add, hearing the fierce anger in my voice.

Looking troubled, Mason claps a hand over my mouth. "Raise your voice again and I won't be so polite next time." He removes his hand from my mouth.

I want to spit on him. "So I'm just supposed to be a nice, quiet guy who lets a whole herd of diseased hogs have their way with me?"

Mason looks around with a curious frown. "I don't see any sign of a herd. Are you sure you're not hallucinating?"

I can tell that he is enjoying himself way too much, to my displeasure. I hear a cackle of laughter off in the distance. I cringe in disgust. I take a step forward and look Mason straight in the eyes. "Just because you put a crazy tattoo on my chest doesn't make me yours. I do not have to cooperate with you."

Mason points at the tattoo on my chest. "First off, I didn't do that, Carrie did. And as for your cooperation, I will have it, one way or another. Unless you want me to drown you in the lake, you'd best do everything I say."

I don't see any sign of a lake. Mason looks past me with fuming green eyes. I stare at his vulnerable chest. Now would be a great time to attack him, if I thought I could win. Judging by his biceps, he could twist my arms off like a cap off a soda bottle.

With a sudden intake of breath, Mason leaves the road behind in a run.

I turn around to see what has him so shook up. Everything looks surprisingly calm to me. Perhaps he is the one seeing hallucinations. At any rate, I think I should follow him. The last thing I want to do is to remain alone on a street in Gomorrah. Mason may not be a very nice person, but at least he shows more restraint than his friends does where hormones are concerned. As far as making a getaway, how could I leave without jeopardizing my life? After all, Mason strongly warned me against not being kind to his friends.

I pass beneath a spreading oak. I would love to know how the engineers of this place managed to create such realistic scenery. Even the grass feels real as it rakes against my shoes.

I look back to the place where I last saw Mason. I do not see any sign of him. Perhaps he decided to take a swim in the lake, which I now see straight ahead of me. I head down a gently sloped hill, careful to avoid running into one of the many tree stumps. Honestly, this place could not look or feel any more realistic than it does.

I hear an owl file a complaint against me, no doubt irritated that I just stepped into its hunting grounds. If I live to breathe the air of freedom after all of this, I will have one heck of a story to take back home with me. I can see the horrified look on Ethan's face upon hearing about my recount of Gomorrah. As for Mark, he would make me swear on the Bible that no physical harm came to me. Emily on the other hand would insist that I take it easy for a while, as if my daily quota would somehow take care of itself.

I spot Mark by one of the spreading oaks near the lake. Although I cannot yet see his face, I can tell that something is bothering him. He runs a hand through his hair as he braces a hand against the tree.

I search the area around the tree for any sign of perverts. I do not see anyone, other than Mason. Could it be that the good doctor has finally lost it? I pick up my pace in nervous anticipation.

I come to a stop just behind Mason.

"Just let me have a look," Mason says, half irritated and half concerned.

"Please go away," Carrie says. "I already told you, I want to be left alone."

Mason lets out an impatient sigh. He pushes off the tree and turns around to face me. "It took you long enough to get here. I was beginning to think Koko or one of the other guards had found you."

I swallow hard. "No, last I checked, I still had my clothes on."

Mason closes his eyes in a pained expression. He looks as if he has aged ten years in the last couple of minutes. He opens his eyes to stare at the ground. I hear Carrie expel a sob on the other side of the tree. I wonder what has happened to her.

Mason looks up to meet my eyes. "I'll allow you ten minutes to see if you can figure out what's wrong with her since she won't listen to me. After that, we're moving on. And don't even think about running off, all the doors have been sealed off."

I assumed that much. "What if she doesn't want to see me?"

Mason gives me a tight smile. "Then I wouldn't be entirely surprised, now go."

Oh how I would love to be the one to give orders, or better yet, Agatha. If she were here, she would look

Mason straight in the eyes and remind him that God made all people. That rich or poor, when we die, we are all going to be laid to rest in the ground, though not everyone will make it to heaven. Agatha would stand her ground and tell him like it is. I wish I did not fear Mason so much. If only the name of the city was something less intimidating than Gomorrah, and more importantly, if only my life was not as stake.

I am so tempted to grab a hold of the nearest limb, pull it back like a bowstring, and then let it fly. I think a stinging smack in the face would do Mason a lot of good. Instead, I step over the dead limb lying in front of me as I make my way to the side of the tree.

I cast a glance over my shoulder. I half expected to find Mason hovering over me, but to my surprise and relief, he is on his way down to the lake.

I brace a hand against the rough bark of the tree. I swear this tree could be cut down and used for fire wood. That's how we use to heat our houses back home.

I clear my throat. "Carrie," I say uncertainly. "Look, Mason's gone, and I think you know you can trust me, so let me help you."

"No," Carrie says in between sobs. "I…don't want to see anyone right now. I'm sorry."

Though I cannot see her, she sounds completely broken. I need to come up with some way to work my way into her midst. "You know when I first saw you last night in the library…" I swallow hard. I do not have the courage to finish.

Carrie sniffles. "I know, I must have looked a mess, and tired too."

"No," I say enthusiastically. "I mean, I'm sure you were tired, but it didn't show. What I meant to say was that…you were a breath of fresh air." Ugh. No, that wasn't exactly what I meant to say either, although she was a breath of fresh air. I feel like banging my head against the tree. "Did you know that your hair glows in the dark? When I first saw you last night, I thought I was staring at an angel."

In my mind's eye, I can see Carrie examining her soft red curls. I think perhaps it's time to take a look. I sneak around the tree as quietly as possible. A twig snaps beneath my shoe. I flinch and look up.

"I knew you wouldn't listen," Carrie says with a faint smile, as if she was hoping I would come.

Carrie sits beneath a forked limb. Bathed in golden moonlight, Carrie looks breathtakingly stunning. Her curls shine as though laced with heavenly fire, her blue eyes luminous though somewhat vulnerable.

I feel my heartbeat quicken. I take a deep breath. I take a step closer. I can see the glistening trails where the tears ran down her face. A long tear in her apron suggests a struggle.

I swallow hard. "You know, if I was wearing a shirt, I'd offer it to you to dry your face on."

Carrie laughs, wipes her eyes with the corner of her apron. "I know you would, you're a gentleman. You don't belong in this place."

I extend my hands to her. She puts her hands in mine without hesitation. I pull her to her feet.

"There," I say. A stray curl covers one of her eyes. I want to reach out and move it aside, but I am not brave enough. Ethan always told me that I needed to be bolder with Emily. That I needed to let her know how I felt about her. The thing is, I never really felt this way about Emily. Sure I liked her, but more as just a friend, I think.

Carrie smiles and tucks the curl behind her ear. "Thanks, I needed to get up. I think the worst thing a person can do when they've been wounded is to stay down."

Carrie looks at me with sad eyes that evince a great deal of emotional trauma. She lowers her eyes to her uniform. "I still can't believe it."

I take her hand. She whips her head up at me like a startled doe. I chastise myself inwardly. I wait for her to jerk her hand out of mine. I try to be gentle with her. I cannot tell if she minds or not. I take my hand from hers. Carrie averts her eyes to the tear in her apron.

"Are you hurt," I say, hearing the emotion in my voice. I feel the hint of a blush creeping into my cheeks. I would like to hide my face right about now. This is one reason why I rarely said much to Emily beyond the essential, because I had a history of embarrassing myself.

Carrie massages a place on her thigh. "I think I'll have a few bruises, but other than that, I should be fine."

"What happened," I say gently.

Carrie rubs at a spot of dry blood on her fingernail. "As soon as I reached the Pleasure Hall, I began to serve drinks. I thought it best to wait outside the pleasure rooms, in the main corridor on the first floor."

"Were the drinks real," I say, unable to help myself.

Carrie nods. "Yes, or at least as real as everything else is around us. The drinks were designed by the masterminds of the Mirage to react to special chips that everyone has in their hands. The most potent drink causes people to see each other as more attractive than they really are."

"Great," I say. As if the perverts around here need any extra help.

Carrie crosses her arms over her chest. "I thought that showing up in uniform would keep me from being a target for the night's revelry. But I was wrong. No sooner than I began to serve and I found myself surrounded by a group of men and women. Many of the guards whose rooms I clean on a regular basis were among them, while the others were prostitutes brought in for the special night. They already had several drinks and had just emerged from… one of the worst pleasure rooms in the pyramid. As soon as they saw me, they collectively insisted that I join them for an initiation ceremony. I knew then that I was in big trouble, so that's when I took off down the corridor to try to get away." Carrie swallows hard. "But one of the guards caught up with me. He tackled me to the floor and covered me with his naked body. I dug my fingernails into his arm, and he finally let go, but not before he tried to undress me."

"Who was he," I say, wanting to tear him to pieces.

"They call him Cheetah," Carrie says. She shakes her head with a sigh. "And after all the favors I've done for him. I should never have come tonight. Honestly, the main reason I decided to come was so that I could keep an eye out on my girls, on the maids who depend on me. I knew how ugly things could get and I was afraid for them."

"What was the other reason," I say.

Carrie averts her eyes with embarrassment. "I…I'd rather not say."

"Is there anything I can do for you," I say, wanting desperately to do something more for her than to just stand here and keep her company.

Carrie meets my eyes with a solemn gaze. "Yes, stay as far away from the Pleasure Hall as you can. Don't get any closer to it than you already are. Ryan," Carrie adds with a worried look, "every person in that place wants to do ugly things to you, especially the men. Before you arrived the other day, I overheard several guards talking about all the vile things they had in mind to do to you, and they weren't pretty."

I swallow. I have no doubt that what Carrie says is true. "But I don't have a choice. Mason told me to expect to visit it before the nights out. If I thought I had a way to avoid it, I would, but I can't find so much as a pebble around here to defend myself with."

Carrie bites down onto her lip, blue eyes anxiously wanting to tell me something. She leans forward, as if to kiss me, but passes by my mouth. I feel her breath against my face. "Be very careful about trusting Mason. I think he's a wolf in sheep's clothing. Plus, I don't like the way he looks at you."

I can hardly breathe. I want to wrap my arms around her. "Are you saying that Mason is a pervert, because if you are, I already suspected that?"

Carrie shakes her head, soft curls brushing against my neck. "Not necessarily, but I know that he has this weird penchant to study guys who he believes have short life expectancies. I think he finds you particularly appealing because not only are you a guy trying to stay alive, but you are also a Saint. A Saint, I might add, who has not yet been defiled by a pervert."

I frown. "So in other words he's more concerned with watching how I interact with perverts?"

Carrie nods. "It's a game to him, to see how long you can make it without being defiled. You know, kissed or whatever. In what time I've known him, I can't recall one person who he has demonstrated more of an interest in than you. I think he sees you as the capstone of his research or something."

I shake my head. I just don't understand. "If that's the case, then why did he seem so eager to bring me here tonight, to such a very dangerous place where the likelihood of leaving untouched in some way seems slim to none?" I lower my eyes to my chest. "If that's true, then why did he insist on me getting this tattoo? Wouldn't a tattoo like this be looked on as desirable by every pervert around? I mean, a blue man with big muscles seems like just the kind of thing that would go over big in a place like this."

Carrie sighs. "I don't know Ryan. I wish I had more answers for you. But I think the best thing for you to do at this point is to stall Mason, to try to do whatever it takes to avoid entering into that pyramid with him."

Sounds like a plan. I check my watch. I'm surprised Mason has not already interrupted us. "What about you? What are you going to do since all the doors have been sealed off?"

Carrie gives me a weak smile. "I think I'll stay right here beneath this tree and hope and pray that God keeps me off the radar from all those who are destined for hell." I blink in surprise.

Carrie laughs. "Well it's the truth. But what's strange is how every one of those dirty scoundrels believes that they're going to heaven, as if God would allow such filth to enter through the pearly gates."

She has a point. "You're right. They never stop and consider that the diseases that ravage their bodies are a form of punishment for their detestable sin. And they get angry if you speak against their lifestyles. What I'd like to know is where they all came from? I never had to worry about perverts before Gloss came to power."

Carrie shrugs. "Your guess is as good as mine. But listen Ryan, I would appreciate it if you didn't bring up any of this after tonight. I don't want to be reminded of anything about this place, okay?"

I nod. "I won't say a word. I know you need time…"

The sound of shattering glass fills the air. It came from the direction of the Pleasure Hall. I start to take off but Carrie takes my wrist and holds me back.

"Wait," she says excitedly. "That may be the best sound we hear all night. Ryan," Carrie adds with a wondrous smile, "I think God may have just saved you from your worst nightmare."

I look up at the sky. I feel my heart lurch in excitement. "Look," I say, pointing to the constellation of Gomorrah. The letter G is completely gone and the rest of the letters tremble with a fiery glow.

I hear Mason call my name. He sounds frantic, and on the run.

I turn back to the sky. More than one of the stars threatens to fall at any second. I wish I knew what happened. I wish I knew who was behind it.

Mason arrives on the scene out of breath. He takes in Carrie's hand on my arm. He looks like he could either say something unpleasant or lunge forward and pull me away from her. I brace for the worst.

"You know that's forbidden in this place," Mason says reprovingly. "Traditional relationships between men and women are mostly looked down on around here. If anyone…"

I lift my eyes above Mason's head to a rapidly approaching ball of fire. I swallow hard.

"I think it's going to hit the lake," Mason says, backing away from the tree to get a better look.

"But it's not even real," I say, though it looks real enough.

Mason cuts me an alarmed look, as if this falling star has more potential to affect our lives than any of the real ones that could be falling outside this building right this very second.

I follow the star as it slams into the shimmering lake, sending a tidal wave of water right towards us. Mason takes a hold of my arm and jerks me behind him. He takes a small device out his pocket and points it at the oncoming wall of water.

Nothing happens. I brace myself for an unprecedented bath. I back away from Mason and run into Carrie. I take her hand and hold on tight. I feel droplets of water pelt my arms as the wave begins its descent.

Mason shouts at the top of his lungs.

The wave freezes midair, as if struck by a sudden blast of frigid cold air. A large chunk of ice breaks loose from the edge of the wave and crashes to the ground a few feet in front of Mason. He stands firm.

The frozen wall of water appears to be at least seventy feet across, and much taller than the spreading oak beside us. I wish Ethan and Mark could see this, though I'm glad they're not actually here.

"Oh thank God," Carrie says breathlessly.

I let go of her hand. I search the sky for any more renegade stars, but everything looks surprisingly calm. The moon continues to shine at full strength, while the stars around it look as peaceful as any other night. The only thing that reminds me that we are indoors as opposed to being outside staring at the real sky is the blank swath of darkness in the area that was once lit up with the name of the city just moments ago.

I breathe a sigh of relief. "So much for the city of lust and disgust," I say, getting Mason's attention.

"It's hardly over," Mason says coolly, "though it did come awfully close to being over for you two. As soon as the guards sitting at the control panel remove the frozen tongue from our presence, everything should go back to normal."

I stare at the wave. I must lack the good doctor's imagination, because it looks nothing like a tongue to me. Perhaps Mason's perverted mind has distorted reality. Still, I am curious to know how a fake wave could have killed us.

I give Mason an incredulous look. "Since when did imitation stars and waves become a threat to our well-being?"

Mason looks between Carrie and I. "Neither of you get it, do you?" Mason shakes his head, as if he has never seen such stupid people in his entire life. Like he should be talking, he's the one who insists on consorting with disease carrying perverts.

Mason stares at my hand. "Consider the chips I implanted in your hands, and then consider how everything that happens in here is directly tied to those chips. If all is well around you, then you are well. But as soon as something happens, say you cut yourself, your implant picks up the signal, sends a message to your brain, and then you feel real pain. As for me and my fellow guardsmen," Mason adds with a superior smile, "none of this affects us that way since we aren't chipped the same as you are. Sure we have implants, but they only serve to allow us to control the conditions of this room. So I was never in any real danger like the two of you were. That way, our backs are covered in the event that something goes wrong, in the event that there is an uprising or something."

"How do you know it actually works," I say. "What proof is there that the technology works as well as you say it does?"

Mason inclines his head at my shoulder. Carrie makes a disgusted sound. I get a whiff of something awful as I turn to see what all the fuss is about.

I cringe in disgust. A thick blob of grayish white poop rests atop my shoulder. I see what appears to be a partially digested mouse tail sticking out of the poop. Yuck. But where did…of course, the owls. But I never even felt it. Oh I could strangle whoever engineered fake birds to drop real poop onto people. If I ever get my hands on the culprit, God help 'em.

Carrie picks up a leaf from the ground and looks at my shoulder. I reach for the leaf but she evades my hand with a determined smile. I don't want someone as beautiful as Carrie to clean owl poop from my body, or any girl for that matter. Leave that for Mason. Nor do I want the first memory of her touching me on her own accord to have anything to do with poop.

Carrie struggles not to smile. "It's okay, really. If this was the dirtiest thing I ever had to do, I'd be the happiest maid on the face of the earth, but it's not. Don't forget, I spend most of my day cleaning up after grown men who leave behind the biggest messes you've ever seen. And if you knew the kinds of trash I have to collect from all the guard's rooms, you'd think owl poop was a blessing."

I laugh. "If you insist, but I…well, I don't believe in letting girls do the dirty work."

Carrie gives me a sweet smile as she wipes the poop from my shoulder. "That's because you're a gentleman."

Mason lets out a high pitched laugh. "He's a teenage boy, hardly a gentleman. Guys his age are more concerned about luring you to bed with them than anything. I know, because I use to be his age. Of course, I'm sure that as soon as he sees some of my friends' highly polished bodies in a little while, it's likely that he'll show his true colors." Mason flicks his eyes to me. "You haven't seen Koko without a stitch of clothing on, or Christian's muscled body that takes most men and women's breath away. And they're only the tip of the iceberg. Just because you act like a snooty Saint doesn't mean that you won't find it within yourself to enjoy a room full of beautiful bodies. Warm bodies, I might add, that have been especially scented and well-groomed in order to attract you to them."

Where's an owl when you need one? If only I could direct one to fly right over his head and bury him in a pile of poop as tall as the frozen wave behind him. If only there was a way to exchange our implants. "You're an idiot if you really think I'm going to cave in to a bunch of perverts. I already told you, I don't want anything to do with any of your perverted friends, especially the male ones. And besides, why do you want me to participate in a disease fest when you yourself have yet to yield to your friend's requests?"

Mason points to his chest. "I consider myself eye candy enough to more than compensate for my lack of activity, if you know what I mean. Plus, I am equal in status to that of my friends. You on the other hand are not. Remember," Mason adds with a dangerous smile, "you're not a real guard. We're just letting you play at it in order to appease President Gloss. Just think, out of all the teams who are receiving expert training, yours is being led through the dark without a flashlight. Now if that doesn't make the final challenge more exciting, I don't know what will."

"I thought you were on my side," I say, feeling somewhat betrayed. "Even a little bit, I thought I could depend on you to help me, but I can see now how stupid I was to trust you."

"Interaction," Mason says. "That's all I want you to think about right now. Forget about everything else, this is your night. I'm not asking you to strip naked, but I am asking you to loosen up a bit. Now come on," Mason adds impatiently, "before they all get angry with me for keeping you away from them."

"But what about the falling star," Carrie says. "We heard a crashing sound that came from the direction of the Pleasure Hall."

"I assure you all is well," Mason says in a haughty tone of voice. "Besides, the only people it might have hurt are a few Saints who claim to have a first class ticket to heaven anyway."

I swallow hard. Jack was supposed to bring Nick as his partner. I feel my heart go flat. I told my team that I would try to watch out for Nick, but in my own miserable condition, I completely forgot about him. I hope he's fine, but I have my doubts. The way Jack looked at Nick in the training room this morning leaves little doubt in my mind that he thought of him as a plaything. If Nick has not already been mistreated, then I would be surprised.

I feel my strength leave me. I lower myself to the ground. How can I go on when everything is against me? I might as well die now than live to let anyone else down. I bury my face in the grass. I have never felt so broken in my entire life. Well, I guess that's not entirely true. I felt a little worse than I do now when I learned that my parents had both been killed in a school shooting.

I know I'm ready to die. I happily accepted God's only Son, Jesus Christ as my Lord and Savior many years ago. Ever since then, my very best friend has been the Son of God. He is the only way to get to heaven.

After my parents passed away, Agatha brought me homemade cookies and an uplifting Bible verse every day for a month. I lived for the verses more than the cookies. This was before Ethan and I became good friends. Agatha reminded me just how much my Lord Jesus loves me.

I feel my heart come back to life with a surge of love and energy. If only Agatha were here, I'd give her a big hug and a kiss.

I rise to my feet. I refuse to be defeated. I refuse to yield my body to a bunch of perverts who somewhere along the way forgot what pure love is. I flick a black ant off my arm. In my mind's eye, I can see Ethan leaning against the spreading oak beside me complaining about ants. I laugh.

"Looks like someone has finally come to their senses," Mason says, looking relieved.

I turn on him with a vicious smile. "Then you're not the mind reader I thought you were. Nope, I have no intention of letting anyone lay a finger on me, unless of course someone wants a broken finger."

"Be careful Ryan," Carrie says.

Mason looks at me as if I am a boy who needs a spanking. "Resistance is foolishness, surely you know this. And to think I actually thought you were a Saint with a brain. Come now," Mason adds with a treacherous smile, "and see reason. When in all your short sixteen years of living have you ever had such an opportunity as this? Why would any handsome guy your age want to pass up on an opportunity to rest your head against a beautiful person's partially exposed body? Furthermore, since you've never experienced it, how do you know that you might not actually enjoy it?"

I shake my head. The good doctor still does not get it. I wonder how many years he went to school. He has a fair amount of knowledge, but very little wisdom. I stare at the wave of ice behind him. I never thought I would end up in a place like this, let alone on the verge of having to explain what pure love is to a doctor. It seems like I already touched on the topic.

"Time for a love talk," I say, earning a troubled look from Mason. "First off, God created men and women and told them to be fruitful and multiply. There's no way a room full of perverted men can make babies with each other, surely *you* know that good doctor. And as far as all the ugly things they do to each other, well, that's not love, that's detestable sin. The same goes for the women who can't remember the role that God intended for them to play. Let me finish," I snap. He looks ready to eat my lunch. "When men and women come together in holy matrimony, there's nothing more suitable than when the two of them love each other as God intended. And contrary to what your perverted mind may think, that means making love to each other in a pure way that involves the proper use of the all the body parts God gave them."

"Well said," Carrie says with a small smile.

Again, I wish I could hide my face from embarrassment.

Carrie looks on Mason with a glint of anger in her dazzling blue eyes. I feel my heartbeat quicken. I find her bold stance against Mason as attractive as her moonlit hair.

"So tell me something," Carrie says. "Would you like it if a bunch of nasty people abused you in the way they want to abuse Ryan, or the way they tried to abuse me? Something tells me that you wouldn't."

Mason whips his head to the side and spits. "It sounds to me like you're on the wrong side. I might have to have a talk with my bosses yet about your allegiance. Meanwhile, I'd be very careful if I were the two of you. Get in my way and you'll regret it."

Carrie shrugs. "I've had many regrets in my life, so I assure you; one more won't curl my hair any more than it already is."

I find myself looking at Carrie's graceful curls. She does have the prettiest hair I have ever seen in my life. God has clearly blessed her tremendously. I feel a smile tugging at the corner of my mouth.

Carrie returns my smile with a toss of her hair. I am tempted to reach out and run my fingers through it.

"Stop staring at her like that," Mason says, rebuking me. "I've already told you, Gomorrah is not the place for traditional relationships."

I look up at the sky. I raise my eyebrows. "Excuse me, but I don't see any evidence to support that, good doctor. The constellation of sin has fallen. Perhaps you should instruct whoever is in charge of the night sky to fill the gap with the constellation of Sodom, the sister city of Gomorrah. And then if we're fortunate, it too will be destroyed, just as in biblical times." Mason's face darkens with anger.

Carrie laughs, brings a hand up to hide her face. "What a terrible thing to say, Ryan. You'll have every owl in here dodging falling stars to try to save their lives."

I look at the soiled leaf on the ground with a laugh. That would sure make the owls nervous, not to mention Carrie and me, if what Mason says is true about our implants.

"What an impressive scene," says a familiar voice from behind me. "It looks like you all barely avoided being overtaken. But then again, there were only ever two of you in real danger. My dear Mason, what happened?"

I figured Jack would be at the Pleasure Hall. I feel my chest tighten with anxiety. I can almost feel the hurt and anger from Nick's eyes cooking my back. I swallow hard. Carrie looks as if she would like to take my hand and help me turn around, to give me strength, but instead keeps her arms at her sides.

"Did you know you have a grasshopper on your back," Nick says in a small voice.

I feel him flick the grasshopper away. I would thank him if I thought I could avoid being overheard by Mason and Jack, who are watching us like hawks.

I brace myself for the worst. I turn around slowly, keeping my eyes to the ground. I stare at Nick's shoes and painfully work my way up to his face.

I blink in surprise. Apart from a small heart shaped opening on his chest, the rest of his body is fully clothed. Honestly, I had thought I might have to keep my eyes closed the next time I spoke to him.

I school my face to look like the guard he expects to see during training sessions.

Nick narrows his eyes at the tattoo on my chest. He swallows hard and meets my eyes with a nervous look. I can tell he wants to say something, but looks too afraid to do so.

I try not to look too superior, so as not to make him feel any more uncomfortable than he already is. "So what about you," I say, staring at a grass stain on his pants. "It looks like you've been in some kind of a scuffle or something."

Nick lowers his eyes to the knee in question. "It was Jack. He shoved me to the ground without a moment's notice, not long after we arrived. I don't know why."

I resist the urge to swallow. "I'm sure he had a good reason." I just wish I knew what it was.

"You look fine," Carrie says, shocked. "Where have you been?"

Nick looks at me for permission to speak. I nod. He looks between Carrie and I with caution. He jabs a thumb over his shoulder. "At the House of Beelzebub," Nick says with a hint of disgust in his voice. "Jack forced me to drink something that would invite demon spirits into my body. I drank and drank and then we left."

Carrie steps forward and smells his breath. I feel a surge of jealousy, even though I know she is not trying to get his attention.

"It smells alcoholic," Carrie says with a frown, "but you don't look like someone who has had too much to drink. In fact, you barely look as if you've smelled it."

Nick shrugs. "I've never tasted anything like it before, so I don't know."

Carrie falls back in beside me. I want to smile. Instead, I continue to look like the no nonsense guard that I'm supposed to be. It's hard to believe that I am standing here by two people who view me in two completely different ways. Carrie, of course, knows my true identity; she just cannot let it out. Apparently, if the truth about my identity leaks out, all seven maids, including Carrie will but put to death. And since the guards have all sworn allegiance to Gloss, there is little doubt that any of them would try to ruin Gloss's warped entertainment, especially since each of them have been promised big gifts for maintaining secrecy.

I study Nick's clothing. I still don't get it. I thought he would be made to look like the most attractive flower for the most perverted bees ever. "Have you been wearing that all this time?"

Nick looks at his clothes and then meets my eyes. "Yeah, I can hardly believe it myself. When I received these clothes earlier today with a note, I thought there had been a mistake."

I frown. "A note?"

Nick nods. "It was from Jack. He said to try on the clothes and to be careful not to…well, he advised me against saying any more."

I swallow. I meet Carrie's eyes. She looks as suspicious as I feel. Why would Jack, who seemed so set on abusing Nick, care anything about helping him? I mean, from what I can tell, Jack did him a favor by not making him show up tonight dressed like a brazen prostitute.

I look between Jack and Nick. Unlike Nick, Jack clearly came with the intentions of participating in the night's festivities. Apart from blue shorts and a faint glow of silver powder across his chest, he looks ready to visit the Pleasure Hall at any moment.

I give Nick a steady look. "Then don't say anything. Jack knows what he's doing. But it probably wouldn't hurt to thank him anyway."

Nick looks on me with stunned surprise. I could knock myself insensible for that last part. Not only did I say something I shouldn't have, but I sounded way too polite. I turn away from Nick. I almost wish Mason had forced me to wear a muzzle. I always manage to screw everything up. The last thing I need to worry about right now is messing up Gloss's big show and bringing swift retribution down onto my head. At least Carrie isn't making me feel worse by staring at me like I'm out of my mind. Instead, she acts like there is nothing wrong with what I just said. I want to think her, maybe even give her a gentle kiss for her thoughtfulness, because I know that she is aware of how grave my situation is.

Carrie crosses her arms over her chest and sets off towards the nearest tree. I feel torn between wanting to stay and keep an eye on Nick like I said I would, and wanting to follow Carrie. I sigh inwardly. Considering the nature of tonight's festival, Nick looks surprisingly well intact, so I think he will be fine. Besides, I want to thank

Carrie for not making me appear even more out of place earlier. The thing is, Mason made it clear that having anything to do with Carrie tonight was as inappropriate as seagulls dating fish.

Careful not to attract too much attention, I act like the wave of ice has captivated me. I see Mason look at me out of the corner of my eye. I stop and wait for him to turn away. He finally does, thanks to Jack. Jack might be of more use than I thought.

I make my way to the place where the chunk of ice broke away and fell to the ground. I reach down and pick up a piece. I drop it with a gasp. It's so cold. I stare at my hand. I have an angry red streak across my fingers. I swallow hard. How can a computer generated injury feel worse than a real one?

Wait a minute. I think I know! I bet the ice is so frigid cold in order to prevent us from using it as a weapon. I glance at my hand. What I would like to know is how long the pain will last?

I turn around slowly to assess the situation. Mason and Jack are still deep in conversation. Nick on the other hand is lying on his back with his legs crossed in the air, as if he hasn't a care in the world. If only that were true...

I know what Mason said, but I don't care, I'm determined to talk to Carrie. I kick the demonized chunk of ice that I just dropped, sending it tumbling through the grass. I swear, I'm half tempted to find a stick and send a piece flying at Mason, even though it wouldn't hurt him. But at least he would know just how irritated I am with him and this inhospitable landscape. I know it sounds crazy and would jeopardize my life as well, but it's still pleasant to consider.

Keeping with my feigned captivation of the ice, I slowly gravitate towards Carrie. I can almost smell her sweet perfume drifting in on the air around me. I feel my heartbeat quicken. I'm not sure I'll have enough courage to talk to her, even if I do make it to her without passing out. Ethan always told me that I was too nervous around girls, that I needed to relax, but it's easier said than done. And unlike most of the girls back home, including Emily, there's something about Carrie that stirs me in a way that no other girl has ever done before.

I take a hold of a low hanging branch and pull off a handful of leaves. Ethan and I used leaves and acorns as money for all of our childhood ventures. I smile as I recall the large pile of acorns and leaves that Ethan stashed in a hole at the base of our favorite oak tree. I think Tonny, his rat terrier, spent about as much time using that hole as Ethan did. I want to laugh as I recall how many times I got down on my hands and knees and shined a flashlight through the hole of the tree, where Tonny stored his treats. It was one of the largest oak trees I have ever seen. Sadly, it was blown over one afternoon by a powerful storm not long after Tonny passed away. And as trying as those times were, it was during that time that Ethan and I became such good friends. I even buried Tonny for him since I saw how heartbroken he was.

"Are you hurt," Carrie says, blue eyes concerned.

I look up and meet her eyes. She stands in a pale circle of moonlight, beneath a spreading oak. I stare at my hand as I step into the moonlight. It's still red and painful, like a wasp sting on the wane. I flick my eyes to Carrie. She takes my hand. I hear my breath hitch in my throat.

Carrie looks past my shoulder, presumably at Mason and Jack. Looking relieved, she looks down at my hand with a small smile. "Are you sure you're alright? I know how much you must hurt from touching that ice. I overheard some of the guards talking weeks ago about all the nasty things they had planned for the incoming Saints, as if removing you all from your communes wasn't bad enough."

I swallow. "I…look, I just wanted to thank you earlier for not looking at me like I was nuts for what I said back there to Nick. If he finds out what I really am, then I'll be in big trouble, as you know." I close my eyes in a pained expression. "I know he already suspects something, along with the others as well. And why shouldn't they be suspicious of me, I must be the only guard around here who has yet to shave a full face of hair."

Carrie averts her eyes to the ground in shock. "Oh my goodness, your shoes…"

I look down at my shoes. I feel like I could pass out. My shoes are on fire, just like my pants, with blue flames dancing across my toes and lighting up the ground around my feet.

Carrie takes me by the arm. "Ryan, they're coming for you."

I feel my mouth fall open. "What do you mean?"

Carrie looks like she could faint. She releases my arm. "Your absence at the Pleasure Hall has been noted, so now they're coming for you. Ryan," Carrie adds with a worried gleam in her eyes, "you need to leave now. Go! Run!" Carrie shoves a palm against my chest.

I shake my head; keep my feet planted firmly in the circle of moonlight. "What good would it do? They would only catch up with me. And besides," I add with a jerk on my pants, "how could I hide when I stand out like a lightning bug?"

"What's going on here," Mason says, stepping into my line of vision. He glances down at my shoes with amusement.

If he's so smart, let him figure it out, the nosy nitwit. Mason looks between Carrie and I with an almost amused look. He looks up at the gap in the forked limb. "What a romantic place," Mason says in a wondrous tone of voice.

"Very romantic indeed," Jack says as he brings Nick into the circle with us. "It's one of the most beautiful spots I've ever seen. What I want to know is what you two have been talking about." Jack looks between Carrie and I.

I give Jack a steady look. "About all the excitement of course," I say, trying to keep the fear out of my voice. "I'm about to me seized and carried off to the place where all the perverts gather for their pre-hell rally, haven't you heard?"

Jack clenches his hands at his sides. "What is it with you Saints and hell?" He takes a step closer, dark eyes sizing me up. "I'll tell you what it is; you all came up with the idea of hell just so you could act like you're better off than the rest of us. You call fun sin and boredom righteousness, as if no one else should be able to determine their lives for themselves. How do you know that you're not going to wind up in the same place you are so quick to assign me to? And besides," Jack adds with a shrug, "there is no evidence that hell even exists, or even God for that matter." He sounds so uncertain.

I take a deep breath. "The fool says in his heart there is no God. Just keep believing what you want, and you'll find out when you die. You know," I add as I turn to face him, "if I was as uncertain as you are, I think I'd be trying to figure it out as soon as possible. But of course, you'd have to temporarily lay aside your perversions in order to make enough time to look into the matter, that is, if you can find a Bible amidst all the trash on your bookshelves. Maybe your boss shouldn't have waged war on the one book that had all the answers to your problems. I think I'd be looking for a different boss if I was you."

"That's enough," Mason snaps.

Jack gives Mason a harsh look. "Not for me it isn't. I don't back down so easily, or haven't you figured it out yet."

Mason inclines his head at Nick. "He's heard more than enough already."

Jack looks startled by the reminder of Nick's presence. "Perhaps you're right. But it doesn't really matter, because if anything gets out, I'll be sure that he dies as well. We can replace him, if we have to. Furthermore," Jack adds with a sharp look at Nick, "if you do decide to flap your mouth, then you'll also be responsible for the deaths of all those you tell. Just think about it, a Saint with three lives to have to account for. Why I doubt your God would let you anywhere near the gates of heaven. You'd have a first class ticket to hell, that is, if it really does exist."

Nick swallows hard, blue eyes filled with fear. I never expected him to learn the truth about my identity so soon. He looks pulled between wanting to consider my situation and listen to Jack for any further comments about a potential death sentence. I know one thing, the training sessions will be interesting going forward, what with Nick being the only one on my team who knows the truth about me.

Jack gives me a harsh look. "Let me ask you a question, and if you can answer it, I might actually consider you a creature of reasonable ability, instead of the brainless idiot you are. So tell me, what evidence do you have that the Bible is not just a myth?"

I hear voices off in the distance. I need to be fast. "History and archaeology," I say, wanting my heart to calm down. "Both historical and archaeological evidence exists to validate the Bible, as if the Bible needs to be validated. One of the most important eyewitness accounts that testify to the horrific treatment of the Jewish people at the time of the Bible came from a Jew named Josephus. He witnessed firsthand the fall of Jerusalem to the Romans shortly after the death of Jesus Christ. You can use the Bible to explain all world history. And since the Bible is the Word of God, there are no contradictions in it whatsoever. It is a manual for an abundant life that does not tell you one thing only to turn around and tell you something different thirteen pages later. So it's not like telling your problem to three different people and getting different advice from each of them. If you don't believe me, try reading it for yourself. It's unlike any other book in existence."

Jack chuckles his disbelief. Nick looks stunned, and perhaps a little awestruck. I can't help but smile. I have wanted to reveal my true identity to someone else for a…

"Where's Carrie," Mason says, snapping me out of my daydream.

I look to the place where I last saw Carrie. She is nowhere to be seen. I could have sworn I saw her a moment ago.

Jack points an accusing finger at me. "She probably got sick of listening to his crap, and who could blame her for that matter."

Mason shakes his head, green eyes unconvinced. "I don't think so, she thinks like he does about this kind of stuff." I'm surprised that Jack did not already know this.

Jack gives Mason a pointed look. "Well then, she must have got scared of our friends who have come for Ryan. It looks like Christian is on his way right now."

Oh please God help me. I want to run and hide, but it wouldn't do any good. I'm still lit up from my waist down like a lightening bug.

Christian steps into our moonlit circle with a funny look. I feel a stab of fear in my chest. Christian's blue eyes look wild with excitement. He wears a pair of red shorts and a baseball cap. I haven't seen a baseball cap in so long, I forgot all about them. I should have realized that they would be wherever the farmers who could use them were not. If only the agents back home were not opposed to us wearing hats. Hats, Perverted Demon often said, would only make us lazier and less productive. Not even the non-Christian farmers in our Township owned hats, which is saying something considering that they received things that we didn't. But I can't help but wonder where all the other guards are. At one time, I heard a whole herd of them cackling away like a bunch of drunken hyenas.

Christian appears to be in need of oxygen. I get the impression that he is trying to keep this from us. It's like he does not want us to know how much he wanted to get here. I take a step backward and find myself out of the circle of moonlight. If it was a little darker, I would almost be hidden.

Christian points at me with alarming speed and a startled expression.

Mason whirls on me and pulls me back into the circle. "You idiot," he snaps. "When will you ever learn to behave like I want you to? Must I leash you like a dog?"

I swallow hard. I can tell that he wants to hit me, but for some reason, he refuses to do so. I massage my arm where his fingers dug into my skin. I look at his arm with a rising tide of vengeance. No, I need to show him that I refuse to act like he does; otherwise I would only prove to him that I am no different than he is. And that would only give him another reason to torment me because of my beliefs.

"It's not very smart Mason," Jack says in a matter-of-fact tone. "Are you sure there's not something you could give it, like some kind of pill to make it more obedient?"

Mason looks at me almost impassively. "I have nothing to turn a brain of dung into a miracle machine, if I did, don't you think I would have already tried it out on him? No, I'm afraid there's little hope for him." Mason lowers his eyes to my tattoo. "If only he was possessed by the right spirits…"

"Oh," I say, with a mixture of anger and disgust. "So in your mind, spirits like lust and hatred make one a more desirable person, maybe even a more sensible person? So that's what I've been missing."

Jack snarls at me like an angry animal. "I'm tempted to knock its teeth right out of its head, Mason."

I throw a hand up. "Not just yet. Why are you so angry with me? Tell me, is it because of the truth of what I said that angers you so much or the fact that I was bold enough to say it, or perhaps both?"

Mason looks at me like he sees me for the first time. I think I impressed the good doctor with my thinking, he is just too unkind to admit it. Oh boy, maybe he'll make me his wayward apprentice yet! If only I was not so dead set against his way of life. If only I was as stupid as they have deceived themselves in to believing I am, then perhaps I could be led astray more easily. Oh how the demons of hell would rejoice if only I could be converted.

"I think he could use a drink of whisky," Christian says with humor. "I could hold him down while one of you hold a funnel to his mouth and pour."

Jack looks taken aback. "It wouldn't swallow it. No, we need an I.V. or something. Mason," Jack adds with a snap of his fingers, "I think that would do the trick. Remember how the last experiment worked out, well, before it died that is. It went nuts and started doing all kinds of strange stuff. That was the most fun I ever remember having."

Mason gives Jack a disapproving frown. "We can't kill him, remember? Besides, I have not yet finished my study of him." Mason looks me in the eyes. "As strange as it may seem, I am still learning a great deal from him, just not anything particularly useful thus far, mainly just the basics of how a sickly Saint's mind works. It's something like a clock that occasionally manages to miss a tick every once in a while, or a faulty heart that skips a beat every now and then. And besides, I am determined to keep him alive and well or at least well enough to be able to draw some useful conclusions about him. But once I'm done with him, it might be possible for us to have some fun with him."

Christian and Jack both look like kids who have been told to wait a little longer for desert. And they think I'm the one who has mental problems. Nick looks dazed and in need of a good rest. I would like to talk to him if it wasn't for the three nitwits standing around me. I miss talking to good Christian people. Sometimes I feel like Mason is as sane as Ethan or my uncle Mark, while other times I feel like I'm talking to someone completely different. I have never encountered someone as tricky as Mason before. He almost makes Perverted Demon back home seem normal. At least Perverted Demon only sang one tune, however wrong it was. I know I haven't told him, but as much as I dislike him, I find Mason about as strange a case study as he finds me. And despite his strange behavior, I feel certain that there is more to him than meets the eyes. In fact, I'm not even sure that Jack or Christian knows him as well as they think they do.

"So what now," I say, getting Mason's attention. I'm not that concerned about Jack and Christian since Mason has clearly put his foot down as the ring leader where I am concerned. "I thought I would be drugged and dragged into the Pleasure Hall long before now."

Mason makes a small noise that sounds something like a rabbit in distress. "Is that what you want? Honestly, I'm surprised you'd even say something like that, especially since your situation is about as idealistic as you could possibly want right now."

I shrug. "I don't know, standing beneath a spreading oak in a circle of moonlight does something to a guy, sort of makes you want to howl at the moon or something." And there *is* a full moon.

Mason looks at me like I have finally and officially lost it. I give him a happy look. What he doesn't know is that I am trying to figure out just how crazy he is willing to let me go without actually doing myself any harm. This will give me a better idea of just how corrupt he really is, because I still feel like he's hiding something, and I want to know what it is.

"He's nuts," Christian says, raising his eyebrows.

I give him a wild look. "Thanks." I begin counting off on my fingers. "Little clothing, great environment, great people, good doctor, lost girl…" I look up at Mason. "I think it's time to go hunting. If we all pulled together, and that means Nick as well, I believe we could find the girl and still have enough time to moon bathe."

Christian looks excited about this. "That actually sounds like a great idea. Or better yet, we could have the moon temporarily lowered a bit, climb on, and then hang out on one of its many craters."

"Great," I say. "I've always wanted to make a moon angel. Maybe we should invite some of your friends from the Pleasure Hall to join us."

Christian looks absolutely delighted. He puts his baseball cap on backwards. "I'll let the guards at the control panel know that we will need the moon lowered. They shouldn't mind, in fact, I bet they'd find it a pretty cool experiment. You can do just about anything in here. I had the guys make me a comfy cloud to sleep on not long ago just for fun."

"No," Mason says, giving me a hard look. "I'm not going to let you spoil the evening for us, just because you want to act…differently. No, we'll partake in the scheduled events, and then we'll call it a night. I have still yet to be propositioned by a pretty female demon."

I want to smile, but instead school my face to appear let down.

I appeal to Christian with a sad frown. I got it! "Bring Mindy," I say. "She is still somewhere in Gomorrah isn't she?"

Christian gives me a stiff nod. "But I don't know exactly where. Carrie had her serving cakes in the Pleasure Hall last I saw her. But I'm not sure I want to have any more to do with her. She's not very lively. You Saints are as boring as oxygen." I swallow hard.

"But oxygen is such a blessing," Nick says under his breath.

Christian turns on him and punches him in the side of the face. Nick cries out and staggers backwards. Christian flexes his fingers. I want to lunge forward and teach Christian a lesson, but I know I'd regret it.

"That'll teach you Saint-boy," Christian says with a satisfied smile. "I don't care how good looking you think you are, you're still a pile of horse dung as far as I'm concerned."

Jack looks offended, clears his throat. "Christian, I brought him here, so I'd appreciate it if you would ask me for permission before you tear into him."

"Satan's apology," Christian says with a wicked smile. He flicks his eyes to me. "What? Never heard of that expression before in your dull life? Well now you have."

Mason lets out a weary sigh. "You two are spoiling the night. Look," Mason adds pecking his watch, "we've already missed the Scandal in the Air performance, plus Kaleb's Wish Upon the Seashell."

"What," I say, hardly believing my ears.

Christian points at his chest, blue eyes satisfied. "I can fill you in on Kaleb's Wish Upon the Seashell, because I was actually involved in it. I had no idea I would be voted the loveliest guy of the night. As soon as Kaleb opened the giant seashell and I saw myself getting up off a bed of rose pedals, I knew they had made the right choice. I am very handsome, after all. I got a chocolate rose bud for my reward. When I placed it in my mouth, it actually blossomed on my tongue before it melted. As for the Scandal in the Air performance, you'll have to ask someone else."

Jack gives Christian a pointed look. "I'm sure the only reason why you were chosen is because I wasn't there."

Christian looks like he could say something sharp to Jack. Looking between the two of them, Mason claps Christian on the shoulder with a calming smile. Mason gives Jack a small smile. So Mason is a peace keeper?

"I think they did well to choose you," Mason says to Christian. "And you're a gentleman too." Mason swallows hard, looks alarmed by what he just said. He looks at me out of the corner of his eye. "I mean, you've got a mind for all manner of good sin and playfulness, so of course you deserved the attention."

Good sin? Just like the other guards, Mason is so messed up he has forgotten the difference between right and wrong. In fact, from what I see around here, everything that is morally wrong is praised and highly desired. I can see why demons would feel right at home around here.

"We could use some fun here," Christian says at the top of his voice. "I know you can hear me, so if you don't mind, just get something good going, and soon."

An acorn falls onto Christian's cap and then bounces off onto the ground. "Hey, that's not what I meant."

I hear a sound that reminds me of someone cracking an egg shell. I look down at the acorn. It lay broken apart with something like a seed at its center. If it wasn't glowing blue, I know I would hardly be able to see it.

Christian picks up the seed and sets it onto the palm of his hand. He stares at it with a puzzled frown. "Ok, this was not what I had in mind. What am I supposed to do, plant it and get one of these Saint-boys to pray that it quickly grows into a fully mature persimmon tree? Hey," Christian adds with a nasty smile, "that sounds like fun, only hold off on the frost, because I'd like to see their puckered faces when I force them to feed each other."

Mason looks at the seed on Christian's palm. "I think you're supposed to eat it." Mason meets Christian's eyes with a speculative look. "I might be wrong, but it looks like one of the experiments that I recall our team of experts playing with not too long ago. Don't look so worried, they must have faith in it otherwise they wouldn't have offered it to you."

Christian puts it into his mouth and swallows. I can see the lines of apprehension on his forehead despite his attempt to look calm. I laugh inwardly. I wish I knew what was going on inside his head.

Christian suddenly closes his eyes, as if trying to conceal the emotion in his eyes. He swallows gently, but looks more tense than I ever thought possible for him. Maybe he's having an instructional vision on how to have fun, complete with the risks of doing so. I shake my head inwardly. I doubt that. No one around here seems to concern themselves with the risks involved in their wickedness. I'm really surprised that they don't have more scars on them than they do. But I suppose most of their consequences go mostly unseen within their bodies. I see little to no signs that any diseases have yet to ravage their bodies. It's funny, now that I think about it, I don't recall Perverted Demon ever having displayed any signs of diseases, and he had been doing ugly things for years.

Mason studies Christian carefully. I imagine a great deal of medical terminology racing through the good doctor's mind. I get the impression that whatever is going on inside of Christian must include an anxious mind, because his chest is rising and falling with rapid intensity. Jack looks like he could let out an impatient sigh at any moment. Nick, on the other hand, is staring at me with a mind full of questions. How did you wind up in the situation you are in? More specifically, what did you do to become such a stench in these guy's nostrils? What district are you from and why is it that, unlike all the other Christians around here, you ended up in a position over us, however feeble it is?

Christian opens his eyes to reveal a calm mind. Either that or he is really good at hiding his emotions. "Don't look so concerned," he says with an easy smile. "Gomorrah still stands and the night is still young. Well, maybe not that young, but still."

Mason lets out an almost inaudible sigh of relief. "I was beginning to worry that you had received the wrong kind of seed. You know," Mason adds with a wary look, "some of the seeds cause all manner of sinful feelings to erupt inside of you while others trick your body into believing that the desires of your heart are actually occurring, when in fact you're standing as still as the tree beside you."

Christian tries to conceal a hiccup.

Jack snorts a laugh. "It looks like they've yet to eliminate the side effects of their experiments. Although, from what I've heard, hiccups is a like a Saint's blessing compared to some of the other things that can occur."

"Like temporary cognitive atrophy," Mason says in the voice of a know-it-all scholar. "Or Sudden Love Syndrome, which can send your heart into cardiac arrest, and in some cases, even cause it to explode."

Christian looks down at the area over his heart. I can tell that he is worried despite his attempt to keep it from his face. Jack snaps his fingers. Christian flinches and shoots him a dirty look. Jack laughs.

Mason shakes his head with an exhaustive look. "You'll have to do better than that, boys. Remember, this is a time for fun and games. How can we please any demons if all we're going to do is stand here and act like a bunch of Scripture babbling Saints."

Christian considers me. "I think it's time we let the Saint-boy tell us what he wants to do. Of course, it would have to involve something to appease demon spirits. I have always wanted to watch the rapid undoing of a Saint. Come now and do something that shakes the ground beneath my feet."

If only the ground was real and would open up and swallow him, then I would have a good reason to rejoice. As it is, I haven't the slightest idea of what to say or do. I'm tired and want nothing more than to sit down, even if it means having to hold up the good doctor's feet.

"I propose a dance," I say wearily. "Let me see just how much you all love that good devil of yours. Then, whichever one of you I find the most creative will get a prize." Maybe a punch in the face or a passage of Scripture, whichever one wins out in my mind. And right now, as irritated as I am with most of them, it could well be both.

"Like what," Christian says almost hesitantly. "What do you have that we…" He trails off, looking unsettled.

I narrow my eyes onto him. It's not like I was planning on offering myself up as the reward, but this is Gomorrah, and they are a bunch of perverts, so I find his response confusing.

Mason turns to face me like an angry streak of lightening. "You must think we're the dumbest people to walk the earth since the earliest humans who spent more time swinging in the trees than gazing at the stars. Just because we enjoy the finer things in life doesn't give you the right to look down that snooty nose of yours at us. I'm sick of you, completely sick of you. It's high time you set aside your haughtiness and conformed to what is right and widely accepted."

I glare at him. "I never have been one to go along to get along. I don't believe I ended up here just to keep my mouth shut and become one of Satan's disciples. Besides, what does Satan have to offer me that is more desirable than what God has given me, His only Son.

What good is there in doing things that will only destroy me? For the wages of sin is death and eternal separation from God. But of course, since I'm saved and ready to meet my Maker, my eternal future is secure, but clearly yours is not."

Mason smacks me across the face in a fit of rage. I want to return the gesture, but from the looks of Jack and Christian, I would only wind up with a heavily bruised body. I clench my fists at my sides to hide their angry trembles.

Mason takes a hold of my arm. "Let's go, you've already said more than enough to deserve death, and I need to report your behavior. If you're lucky, you'll get through this with only a few lashes, but if you're not, you should expect to lose some very important body parts. But don't feel too badly, for this was bound to happen sooner or later, for a Saint to remain silent is like asking a frog not to croak ahead of a rainstorm."

I give him a disdainful look. "You just love to stab me with those heartless phrases of yours don't you?"

Mason turns me around to face Jack. "Be sure and give everyone my apologies. Tell them that I will make it up to them in one way or another. I honestly believed we would have a great night, but I can see now how wrong I was."

"Is there anything I can do to help," Jack says in a lazy tone of voice.

Mason flicks his eyes to me. "No, I should be able to handle it. It is after all a lot like having a pet dog, only a very dumb one."

Christian pecks the brim of his hat up in a surge of vicious excitement. "And we all know how often a dog eats its vomit," he says. "As there are things that are difficult to change about a dog's behavior, so are there things about a Saint that makes them nearly impossible to reform once they've been dipped into a pool of holy water."

I resist the urge to snap back at him. I know that he is in serious need of help. I do my best to keep the irritation from my face. At least in this way, I can limit his pleasure.

I look at Nick. At some point in our conversation, Jack pulled him to his side. Nick comes up to Jack's shoulders. Although Jack is not holding onto him, Nick looks about as sour and miserable as I feel.

I look at the place where we stand. Though the circle of moonlight is nearly gone, the moon still shines brightly throughout the rest of Gomorrah. I would ask for an explanation if I did not fear it would likely accompany another smack in the face. I hear voices down by the lake. I jerk my hand free from Mason's grip and turn around to see what's going on.

All the ice is gone, allowing me a clear shot down the side of the hill to the lake. I gasp in horror. I see several people dancing naked around a large bonfire. I turn away in dizzy disgust.

"And to think I was actually looking forward to the Dance for Demons," Mason says, dejected. He gives me a hateful look. "But you have ruined the evening for me, taken away my appetite. Maybe I should take you down there and sacrifice you right now. The fire would be good and hot for you."

"But that would be such a waste," Jack says, baffled. "And besides, surely there is still more to learn about it. I for one am interested to know why it seems so eager to stand its ground when all it would take to win our hearts is assimilation."

Christian chuckles. "I think you'd have more luck getting a pile of poop to fly than to change the gears in his mind."

"Oh I don't know about that," Mason says, digging his fingers into my arm. "I am of the mind that even the most stubborn creature can be changed, you just have to find their weak spot."

Chapter Eleven

That night, I wake with the desire to get away from here once and for all. I am sick and tired of Mason's sudden mood changes. I have endured about all I can handle. I feel like I could explode if I stay here any longer. I have too much anger bottled up inside of me, and my arm where Mason's fingers have dug into my skin over the last few days feels like it could scream on its own.

I leave the bed as quietly as possible. I look at my shoes. I had best wait to put them on outside. I don't plan on ever coming back to this place again. I'm not sure where to go once I leave this compound, but I know one thing, if it takes living in the wilderness for a while then so be it. I know how to survive in tough environments. Not long after Gloss came to power, agents stormed our house and confiscated most of our belongings, leaving us with little more than the clothes we wore and a gut twisting anxiety about how to continue on as we looked at the near vacant rooms around us. If it had not been for our strong faith in God, I know that we would have collapsed into dismay instead of praying for strength and answers to our problems.

I watch Mason carefully as I make my way to the door. Part of me wants to laugh at his condition. I'm not sure he could get up to stop me even if he wanted to. If I wasn't so determined to leave this place, I might consider shouting something just to watch him try to escape his entanglement.

I open the door and silently praise God for such quiet hinges. I take a final look at Mason. The soles of his feet glow faintly in the narrow stream of light filtering into the room. I make sure not to open the door too wide so that the light doesn't reach his face. Farewell good doctor, starting tomorrow, you'll have to find someone else to be your footstool.

I back out of the room without turning away from him. I gently pull the door shut. With a sigh of relief, I put my shoes on. I could easily find myself on the run at any time, and I do not want anything to slow me down. If I can just reach one of the walls surrounding this whole compound without getting caught, I should have enough time to look for a way to climb to my freedom.

I take off down the hallway with a funny feeling that I cannot seem to shake off. I know I haven't forgotten anything, because other than my shoes, there was nothing else that I needed to bring. I guess I could have rigged a stumbling block for the good doctor so that when he got up, he would surely crash to the floor. But then again, I do not really want to hurt him. As many times as he made me want to knock him insensible, I know that he was only doing his job, however terrible it was. Plus, I realize that he has been deceived by Satan into believing the worst about Christians. And as much as he seems to think that I hate him, I do not hate him at all. Sure I find his ways despicable, but waywardness aside, Mason has some good attributes, though I am currently at a loss to say what they are. I guess one could say that he is smart enough to rattle off witty sayings, and poke the wrong pills down a Saint's throat.

I reach the edge of the staircase. So far, I have not seen one guard. I feel my heart swell with hope. I check my watch. Three thirteen. I bet most of the guards are still drunk with lust in Gomorrah. Oh how I can taste the night air of freedom already. I just wish I had some food and water to take along with me. Who knows what I will find beyond the wall?

I descend the stairs as quietly as a mouse on a mission. I can almost smell the cheese wheel that's spinning in my mind's eye. I hope the cooks haven't set any traps to catch mice in shoes. I don't want to risk a kitchen visit, but I feel I have no other option. Depending on the environment beyond the wall, it could well take me more time than I would like to locate suitable food and drinking water.

I enter the kitchen and feel around on the wall until I find the light switch. Wow. I blink in surprise. I had expected to find a wooden table at the center of the room surrounded by a couple refrigerators and freezers, but this is like jerking a two-foot-long carrot out of the ground.

I head to the nearest refrigerator. All the appliances look used, with scratches and smudges across their faces. I stop dead in my tracks. I bet everything in here was confiscated from the homes of Christians. Wouldn't it be something if me and Mark's refrigerator was among the ones in this room?

I pull open the refrigerator door and find myself staring at more heads of cabbage than the Mirage has perverts. I shut the door with a disappointed sigh. I can't stand cabbage. I know I shouldn't be picky at a time like this, but surely there's something more appetizing in this crowd of appliances than the main ingredient to sauerkraut.

I open another one. I pray the good doctor never sees inside this refrigerator, for he would likely have a heart attack. I have never seen so many sticks of butter in my entire life. This is not going to be as easy as I had hoped.

I pass by several refrigerators, imagining piles of beets and bowls full of carrots. I come to a stop in front of a refrigerator that sort of reminds me of the one that belonged to Ethan's family. The last time I opened it, I took out a plate of ham and cheese sandwiches that Ethan's mom had made for us. Ethan ate over half of them and then turned around and ate nearly half of a chocolate cake. And from what I can remember, he finished off what was left of the cake when we returned from our fishing trip one Saturday afternoon.

Unsurprisingly, I find no cake in this refrigerator, but that's not to say that I am entirely disappointed. Several large bowls full of vanilla pudding lines the shelves of this refrigerator. I take a bowl and pull off the thin sheet of plastic. There must be at least a couple of pounds of pudding here. I wish I had some cookies to eat with it, though I feel I would have more luck coming across a bin full of turnips.

I find a spoon on the table. I take a bite. Yum! I get to eat dessert every day around here, but never do I get as much as I want. Unfortunately, none of my brothers and sisters get any dessert.

I have yet to see one cook in all the time I have been at this training facility, despite all the platters of food and pitchers of tea that testify to their presence. I hope they are clean people, and not like all the perverts currently down in the Mirage. I hold off on my next bite. Since the food always looks nice and clean, I want to assume that the cooks embrace a high degree of cleanliness. I pray the cooks that made this pudding did not contaminate it in the process of making it.

I take another bite. I need to hurry up. I have still yet to locate anything nonperishable that I can take with me on my journey into the unknown. I would like to find some nuts and bread, or similar foods with protein and carbohydrates. I also want enough drinking water for at least a couple of days.

I could kick myself for not taking one of the covers off my bed. And I will need a backpack or bag of some kind to carry what I do manage to cobble together. If I had known where everything was and had enough time to plan my departure in advance, I would be much less concerned. As it is, I haven't the slightest idea where the things I need are located, and the size of this kitchen is already giving me a migraine.

I sit the pudding aside. I wipe my mouth on the back of my hand. Won't the cooks be in for a big surprise when they see that a giant mouse has raided their pudding supply? I wish I had something to leave them in return for my full belly. I know I need some protein, but I don't have time to open every refrigerator or cabinet in here. I need to be quick, otherwise I might wind up cornered by an unwanted visitor.

I set off towards the row of cabinets on the other side of the room. In my mind's eye, I can see one of the perverts staggering out of the Mirage heading in this direction. I feel a twinge of anxiety in my chest. I need to be prepared to hide at a moment's notice. I seem to recall a slight groaning on the door hinges when I entered the room earlier. Perhaps that will allow me enough warning time to avoid being caught. I wish I had a blunt object that I could use to defend myself with nonetheless.

I open the first cabinet I come to. I am in luck! Several boxes of raisins stand out like gemstones. I take two boxes from the shelf and sit them down on the counter below. I turn back to the cabinet. I don't believe it! On the shelf just above the raisins are several packages of dried apricots. Next to the apricots are several boxes of dates. What a cache! I take several packages of each of them.

Now all I need is something with plentiful protein and I believe my food needs will be sufficiently met. I can hear the good doctor's haughty voice right now: *You had best remember all your important vitamins and minerals if you want to avoid even the slightest health complications.* Of course, he would only want me to consider this in order to slow me down to prevent my escape. I doubt he would care anything about me, other than how my absence would affect how his bosses would treat him and then perhaps his study of me, however vain that is.

I pile up my loot on the counter. I might feel bad if it wasn't for the fact that I have been so mistreated ever since my arrival to this place that I actually find my current behavior quite exhilarating.

I check another cabinet for goodies.

"You're leaving," says a bewildered voice beside me.

I stiffen with a pang of horror. I nearly bang my head into the cabinet door. I slowly back away from the counter.

"Carrie," I say, hardly believing my eyes. "I…didn't recognize your voice."

Carrie gives me an apologetic smile. "That's because of my allergies. Christian insisted I shake his bedside rug out for the third time in two days, as if a pervert would concern himself so much with a little dust."

I smile at the wisdom of her statement. "What are you doing here? I thought you'd still be in the Mirage."

Carrie stifles a yawn. "I snuck off when they weren't looking. They won't miss me. They're currently enjoying round two in the Pleasure Hall."

I wrinkle my nose in disgust. "So what are you doing here?"

"I came to get a glass of milk," Carrie says with a warm smile. She looks at the pile of loot. She meets my eyes. "I take it that you're getting ready to leave. Mind if I help you?"

I shake my head. "No, I don't want you to get into trouble on account of me."

Carrie stares at my chin with a funny look. She steps up to me and gently runs a finger across my chin. She pulls her finger away and examines it. "Where did you find pudding? I'd like some to."

I point to the bowl on the table in the center of the room.

I want to continue my search for food, but I do not want to hurt her feelings. And besides, I've been aching to talk to her alone. I have an idea. I wonder if she would consider coming with me.

I follow Carrie around the table. I can either get straight to the point and put as much distance between me and this place as possible, or I can let my nervousness, the same nervousness that has always crept in on me when confronted with a pretty girl get in the way. I clench my hands in frustration. I wish my emotions were more consistent to me. I mean, I was fine when I talked to Carrie in the Mirage the last time I saw her. I always had the same problem when trying to talk to Emily back home. One time I might have just the right amount of confidence while the next time would be as difficult as trying to pull Ethan's dog Tonny off one of his rawhide bones.

I take a deep breath, silently pray for courage.

"Thank God for pudding," Carrie says taking the bowl in hand.

I feel my confidence rapidly deflating like a balloon. She takes a spoon from the same pile where I got mine from. I try not to stare at her. She's so beautiful.

Carrie takes a bite, blue eyes savoring the pudding. "Don't worry; I'm going to help you get out of here. Besides, I know how to get you out without getting caught. Plus, I know how to deactivate the Mother Dome, who keeps an impenetrable barrier around this entire compound."

"About that," I say. I wet my lips as I stare at the floor. "I'm not sure where to go once I get beyond the wall, so…" I trail off, too embarrassed to finish the sentence.

"You'd like for me to come with you," Carrie says, losing her grip on the spoon. It clatters to the floor.

I swallow hard. "If you wouldn't mind, I…I'd try to look out for you and all."

Carrie gives me a sad smile. She takes a deep breath. "If we got caught, well, it would be over for both of us. Ryan," Carrie adds with a nervous smile, "I'd like nothing more than to come with you, but I have people here who depend on me, who rely on me to help see them through."

I feel like a slug in need of a shell.

Carrie sits the bowl down and then takes my arm. "I'll come with you on one condition: That you allow my girls to come along with us."

"You mean your maids," I say for clarification. I know she is senior maid to a group of girls.

Carrie nods. "It would be wrong for me to take off without letting them know. If I did, each of them would be questioned about my disappearance and likely lose their lives on account of me."

I swallow hard. "I don't want that to happen. By all means, bring them with us. But we had best do it soon; otherwise the perverts may disband and threaten our departure."

Carrie lets go of my arm. "Then let's hurry. I see you've found some fruit, but I think it would be a good idea to bring along something with protein in it, like nuts or something."

She is truly a girl after my own heart! "That's exactly what I was thinking."

Carrie pauses, looks at me in surprise. She stares at my lips with a small smile. "I… also think it'd be a good idea to take some potatoes along with us as well. I can cook you know."

I feel my nerves settling at the slight nervousness in her own voice. "Then that's one thing less I'll have to worry about."

Without another word, Carrie turns to face the open cabinet that I left earlier. "If I'm not mistaken, I believe the cooks keep a healthy supply of pistachios just for themselves in the cabinet right next to that one. I've walked in on them eating them more than once since I arrived. So, you can go after the pistachios and I'll get the potatoes."

I can hardly believe my ears. "Sounds like a plan."

"And Ryan," Carrie says with a hint of rabid enthusiasm in her voice. "We need to hurry. After I round up the potatoes, I'll go get my girls, along with a few backpacks to store everything in."

Surely she is a gift from God. "Are you sure *you've* not been planning an escape all this time?"

Carrie gives me a sweet smile. "I've wanted to get away from this place ever since I arrived. It's far worse than what Mason made it out to be. I know I shouldn't say this, but I can't stand Mason. He's evil and nasty and I don't want anything to do with him."

Who does? "Yeah, I guess a lot of people find him a big pain in the butt."

Carrie runs a nervous hand through her curls. "Mason needs a lesson on how to be a gentleman from you. You know he masquerades as a physician, when he is nothing more than a monster that enjoys experimenting with ways to torture people."

So the good doctor *is* a quack. I knew something wasn't right about him. I knew he was hiding something.

I feel like dancing, and, if one of the most beautiful girls I have ever laid eyes on was not standing right in front of me, I might give it a try. Instead, I focus on the pistachios Carrie told me about.

Carrie opens a door at the back of the kitchen and disappears into the dark room. I guess that's where the potatoes are stored. I bypass the door and head toward the cabinet Carrie pointed out earlier.

I pull the door open in nervous anticipation. Sure enough, Carrie knew what she was talking about. There are enough pistachios in here to feed a small army, and they're all conveniently sealed off in clear plastic bags. It suddenly occurs to me that I don't remember Carrie telling me how many people we will need provisions for. I can't remember how many maids there are.

I back away from the cabinet. I clear my throat. "Carrie," I say, directing my voice towards the room she went into earlier. I can see by the faint glow in the doorway that she found the light switch.

Carrie steps into the doorway with a worried look. With wild eyes, she searches the room for unwelcomed guests. She meets my eyes with relief.

I give her an apologetic smile. "I was just wondering how many maids work for you?"

"Six," Carrie says, absently adjusting her apron. "But one of them will not be coming with us. She *cannot* be trusted. I think she and Mason are as thick as thieves. So altogether seven including you and I."

I can hardly believe my ears. Carrie flashes me a small smile and then disappears into the room. I shrug inwardly. There is safety in numbers. But hey, if she gets to take her friends, then why can't I rescue my team? I mean, if we're going to do this, then why not try to rescue as many people as possible? Perhaps that's why God put me here, because He knew that I would try to help others.

I look at the doorway where Carrie stood a moment ago. I had better wait and see what she thinks about expanding our escape party until after she gets done rounding up the potatoes, otherwise, with too many interruptions, we increase our risk of getting caught.

I gather up several bags of pistachios and add them to our pile. I check the shelf above the pistachios and find it nearly bare, except for a partial bag of almonds. I take them as well. We're going to need all the food that we can get.

Carrie emerges from the storage room dragging a bag of potatoes behind her. I hurry forward to help her. I take the bag and close the door behind her. I lower the bag to the floor and meet her eyes.

"I want to help my team," I say, hearing the hysteria in my voice. "I want them out of this place. And I fear for their lives if I don't take them with me. But the thing is, I don't have a key to their room."

Carrie gives me a bright smile. "I can help you there. I have a key to every room around here." Carrie takes a key chain from her pocket and hands it to me. "It's the one with a blue dot on it. And Ryan," Carrie adds with what has to be the most affectionate smile any girl has ever given me, "be careful, for a guard could show up at any place at any time. Remember, not all of them are in the Mirage having the time of their life. Some of them are halfway decent people who came up with excuses in order to avoid the festival. That said, I don't think any of them would hesitate to treat you badly should you get caught, so be very careful."

Who would have thought that there would be decent guards around here? "Do you know any of them well enough to recruit into our getaway?"

Carrie gives me a troubled look. "I wish I did. There is one…No; I don't think we should risk it. When these people talk about putting you to death if you don't do as they please, they mean it. Even the decent ones must obey orders or risk facing the consequences of their actions."

I stare at our pile of food. "This should be enough to get us through for at least a couple of days, don't you think?"

Carrie gives me a borderline flirtatious smile. "I hope so, but you boys have a tendency to eat so much.

But of course I know that you understand the necessity to ration everything. As for Nick and Seth, who knows?"

I laugh. "Yeah, I know what you mean."

"I like to watch boys eat," Carrie says almost shyly. "You all make such a mess of things with little concern about who may be watching. But enough of that," Carrie adds with a sobering expression. "We should get a move on. I'll go get my girls while you rescue your team. And let's be sure and not forget about water when we get back here."

I am so glad that she showed up. "How long do you think it will take you to get everyone? I mean, aren't the other maids still at work in the Mirage?"

Carrie's expression turns inwards. "A couple of them are, but I shouldn't have any problem stealing them away. Most of the help was actually recruited from a nearby brothel, so the disappearance of a handful of maids who are standing in the shadows mostly unnoticed should not be a problem. As for the other girls, I know exactly where to get them. Part of them are currently cleaning in the lounge and library while the others are sleeping. I should be able to meet you back here in fifteen minutes or so. They're going to be so excited when I tell them about our plan that I can see them now rushing along beside me in their nightclothes. I hope you won't be offended. I know how much you like to do things properly."

I smile at the sincerity in her voice. "As long as no one gets hurt, then I have no qualms. As long as we all make it out safely, that's all that really matters."

Carrie gives me a sad look. "I wish we could take all the others, all of our brothers and sisters that is. But I just don't see how that would be possible. If our small party makes it out undetected, then that will be a miracle in and of itself."

I swallow hard. "But I thought you said you knew a good way out, to avoid being seen."

Carrie nods. "I *do* know a good way out, but even then, we still run the risk of being caught. No matter how careful we are, there's still a chance that something will go awry. Really, when it comes down to it, the best thing to do is pray."

I blink in surprise. "You're absolutely right; I can't believe I have allowed myself to become so distressed that I have forgotten the most important means of safeguarding our escape."

"You're too hard on yourself," Carrie says sympathetically. "Tough situations have a way of making us overlook things that we would otherwise be on top of. Now we had best get going," Carrie adds in a cautious tone of voice. "The quicker we get everyone rounded up, the quicker we can leave this place."

I nod. I decide to do something that I never thought I would have the courage to do. I take her hand, and run.

Carrie gives me a reassuring squeeze as we close the gap between us and the door. Her hand is almost as sweaty as mine.

We come to an abrupt halt at the door. I turn around to face her for a last moment's reassurance. I let go of her hand. I feel the hint of a blush creeping into my cheeks. I want to say something, but I am afraid it will come out the wrong way. Looking a bit embarrassed herself, Carrie seems to understand my predicament. I look at her neck. She has the most beautiful skin tone of almost any girl I have ever seen.

With a gentle nod, Carrie lets me know that she is ready. If I wasn't so afraid of making a fool of myself, I would half consider gathering her into my arms for a boost of strength, because right now, she looks much stronger than I feel.

"Good luck," Carrie says with a confidant smile. "We can do this and you know it. This time tomorrow, we will be well away from here and breathing the fresh air that God intended for us to have."

I love how she said that. Everything about her has captivated me. I wish Ethan were here to give me some advice on how to avoid making a fool of myself. Even though he only ever dated a handful of girls, just about everything he did seemed to please them. In fact, he was the one who broke it off with nearly all of the girls on the grounds that they were each too annoying in their own way.

I pull the door open. Carrie walks through it with the satisfied expression of a maid who just helped herself to a glass of milk. I smile at the way she casually scans the semi-dark room for any sign of perverts. She is so captivating; I think she could charm a crocodile. To have her on my side is no small thing.

Carrie beckons me to leave the doorway as she heads in the direction of the Mirage. I wipe my sweaty hands on my shirt. As good a chance as we have of pulling this off, I still cannot seem to get my body to calm down.

I stick to the wall as I make my way towards the staircase. You never know when someone could appear at any time. Honestly, I'm surprised that the band of perverts has not already sent out a search party for me. I guess they have forgotten me in their excitement, much to my relief. And Carrie did say that they were caught up in another round of passionate lust and disgust. As long as they stay preoccupied with each other, I feel confident in our ability to leave this place undetected.

I laugh inwardly. I can see the disappointment and mounting anger on the faces of the perverts in our absence. I imagine a general response by all the guards: Who would have thought that a group of Saints could outsmart us?"

I creep up the stairs with an ever increasing heartbeat. I take a deep breath to try to calm myself. I feel some better, though I know I won't be satisfied until I put as much distance between myself and this place as possible.

I can see the surprised looks on my team's faces. That I would endanger my life to rescue them will not be taken lightly among them. But of course, I feel certain that if I was in their predicament, any one of them would likely do the same for me. The desire to help those in need has always been a Christian thing to do, and we Christians typically stand together, especially in times of crises.

I enter the common room and stick close to the wall. I can barely see anything in here, except for the outlines of the couches and chairs. I wish I had the flashlight that Mason forced me to carry around the other night. I could also use it as a weapon if I had to. As it is, I just hope and pray that I remain unseen.

I hope that Carrie is faring as well as I am so far. She should be in the Mirage by now, in the computer generated landscape of Gomorrah. I hope she makes it out without any problems. Her part of the rescue mission is far too dangerous, but if anyone could ever pull it off, I believe it would be her. That we will all be meeting in the kitchen before too much longer makes me happier than I have been in a long time. Ever since I was rounded up and taken away by Mason, my heart has been plagued by the hollowness of despair, despite my efforts to try to make the best of my situation.

I start down the hallway that will lead me to my team. I thank God for the golden specks on the walls that glow faintly enough for me to see where I am going. I have no doubt that this effect was not intended, for without its help, it would be too dark to make out the doorways.

I stop at the first door I come to. I examine the doorknob. I see a spot of paint, which undoubtedly corresponds to one of the keys in my hand, but I cannot make out its color. I want to see a blue dot. I swallow hard. I am in big trouble.

I feel like kicking the wall in frustration. Now what do I do? It's too dangerous to try to track down Carrie, and besides, there is not enough time. I guess I will just have to try out the keys until I find the right one. Each of these rooms houses one team, and there are four doors to choose from. The thing is, if I open the wrong one, I am going to have a lot of explaining to do. Although everyone has seen me dining with the other guards, and therefore will identify me as one of them, walking in on them in the middle of the night will still require some explanation.

I try out one of the keys. It doesn't fit. I feel my heartbeat quicken. The longer it takes me to locate my team, the greater the risk posed to Carrie and the others. They may already be in the kitchen by now for all I know.

I insert another key into the lock. I groan inwardly. It felt like it was going to fit. I try yet another key, only with a prayer this time.

It's the right one! I turn the doorknob and push the door open.

I step forward onto the threshold and feel around for the light switch. If this room is like the one I shared with Mason, then the light switch should be right about where my hand is now. I feel a pang of horror in my chest. It isn't there. There *is* no light switch. They must come on and off automatically.

"Who's there," says a startled female voice.

I clear my throat. "One who has authority to be in this neck of the woods."

"What do you want," says a wary male voice.

I back out of the room. I don't have to answer them. Wait a minute! The female voice sounded somewhat familiar. "Jennifer," I say, hearing the hope in my voice.

"Let me guess, you've come to bring Nick back to us."

I don't know whether to be happy or sad. In my flurry to help prepare the way for our escape, I completely overlooked the fact that Nick is still down in the Mirage with Jack. How could something that felt so right when I was with Carrie come to this?

A hand grips my shoulder and pulls me backwards into the hallway. If I could see Mason's face, I would send my fist flying right at it. He closes the door and snatches the keychain away from me.

Keeping a firm hold on me, Mason steers me down the hallway towards the common room. I now wish that Carrie and I had just left by ourselves. If Mason turns me in, then that will be the end of me. Maybe he'll strike a bargain with me since he likes studying me so much.

Mason tightens his grip on my arm. I don't care what he says, I know he is a pervert, otherwise, why grip my bicep like it is pure gold. But then again, he normally digs his fingers into the area just above my bicep.

"Let there be light," says a voice that is not Masons.

"Koko," I say, terrified.

"At your service," he says enthusiastically. He gives me a measured look. "Let me guess, you were sneaking into your team's room in order to participate in a group prayer. But how you came about these has got me baffled. Care to tell me," Koko says, waving the keychain in front of me.

I remain silent.

Koko smiles. He looks as if he just came out of the Pleasure Hall, what with his hair all ruffled up. "I didn't think so. You leave me little choice but to turn you in, which would char your buns so to speak. But," Koko adds with the keen smile of an extortionist, "I will agree to remain silent on one condition: That you tell Mason that you want to see me. He won't deny you the desires of your heart. Either do this or I will report your folly and prepare to have your heart ripped out of your chest to be offered up to Satan."

I press my back against the wall. I need to choose my words carefully. "Let me think about it. Give me a few days to consider, after all, Mason would be jealous. You know how much he wants to keep me to himself in order to study me."

Koko nods. "I know, and because I'm a gentleman, I'll give you until this time tomorrow to decide your fate. Have Mason bring you to my room once you make your decision, and we'll celebrate with good food and fine wine."

"That's not much time," I say, careful not to do anything to upset him. But then again, I'm surprised he doesn't take me now by force. I try not to look too worried. I glance at my watch. I should have already met Carrie.

Koko shrugs. "That's the terms, either meet them or suffer the consequences."

I swallow hard. He's serious. Well then, he had best prepare to see my execution, because I have no desire to meet his terms. He has a feverish look in his eyes that makes me want to drive my fist right into his perverted face. Instead, I think perhaps it's the right time to tell him what I think about his kind. I mean, if I'm going to die anyway, why not let him have it, right?

"Let me tell you what I think of you," I say, my temper on the rise. I give him a disdainful look.

"You had best not," Mason says in a dangerous tone of voice. "Unless of course you want to end up as demon food. I imagine the fire by the lake in Gomorrah is still hot and in need of a human sacrifice."

I look past Koko to find Mason heading in this direction. I can't tell how long he has been listening to us. Koko turns on him with a droll expression.

"I woke to find him gone," Mason says, inclining his head at me. "And after checking the bathroom and closet, I decided I had best set out to see where he went."

Koko jabs a thumb over his shoulder in my direction. "I was just about ready to deliver him to you. I believe he said he was on his way to the kitchen to quell a hunger pain when I found him. You know how guys his age are, they eat and eat and never can seem to be filled. Anyway, here he is."

Mason looks between me and Koko with a bored look, as if he wants nothing more than to go back to bed. He fixes his eyes on Koko. "Since it looks like you have everything under control, I think I'll go back to bed. Just make sure you punish him for his folly."

I can almost see the stunned look on Koko's face, even though his back is to me. I think he thought Mason would be anxious to get me back and keep me under lock and key.

"You mean you don't want to deal with him yourself," Koko says, running a hand through his messy hair. "I thought he was an important case study to you or something."

Mason stifles a yawn. "I don't need him around all the time, so take him if you want him. Besides, he doesn't belong to me. He's just as much the property of any of the rest of you."

Koko yawns. "Maybe another time, I need my beauty sleep right now. I know I look a bit like a butterfly that's been battered by a steady breeze. Plus, I've spent most of my energy in Gomorrah. If only I had found him sooner..." Koko turns around to face me. I can still see the signs of a yawn in his watery gray eyes.

"I wish you had," Mason says, shooting me a nasty look. "I never realized how much I hated Saints until I met him."

Koko blinks, clearly surprised to hear Mason say such a thing, though I do not know why. Koko looks as if he wants to say something in response to Mason's admission, but for some reason, is holding back. I almost get the impression that Koko is not as bad a person as he wants me to believe he is. And now that I think of it, even when he was threatening me earlier, he never did use the tone of voice that made me feel like he really wanted to harm me. Rather, I got the impression that he had something else up his sleeves, I just don't know what. Could Koko be a sheep in wolf's clothing? And if so, what am I to him that he wants to get me alone to talk to me?

I search Koko's face for answers. I'm tempted to come up with some sort of excuse right now just to be able to go with him, to be able to figure out what he is up to. I mean, whatever he has to tell me must be important; otherwise he would not have given me such short notice to try to meet him.

"Farewell then," Koko says to me. "I might catch up with you tomorrow, if you're lucky."

I swallow hard. Despite his voice, I cannot help but see the pressing desire to talk to me in his eyes. I'm glad that Mason cannot see this. I have little doubt that Koko has something very important to tell me.

Without turning around, Koko waves a hand above his shoulder at Mason. "Do take care of those abs of yours; they're very special you know."

"I will," Mason says with a smile in his voice. "I know how much you appreciate beautiful sculptures."

Koko makes a loud kissing sound as he disappears into the hallway. I hope he is just being a good actor. It could well be my worst nightmare if I am wrong about him.

I feel my heart sink in Koko's absence. Now I am left with a quack who, according to Carrie, enjoys devising ways to cause people suffering. I bet he is also one of the biggest perverts around here; he is just trying to keep it hidden.

I feel a twinge of panic in my chest. Carrie must be having a panic attack right about now. I wish I could let her know that I am fine, at least for now that is.

"Let's go," Mason says sharply.

I hold out my arm to him. "Go ahead and give me a lethal injection, good doctor, I know you want to." I doubt the quack even owns a syringe, let alone even knows how to use one. Still, I want to keep the information that Carrie gave me to myself. I'm curious to know why a quack would be so interested in studying me.

Mason stares at my arm almost absently. "What makes you so sure? Never mind, just keep your mouth shut and come on, I've had my fill of your stupidity and have no desire to hear what I'm sure would be more of the same."

I want to ask him something like how many muscles in the face it takes to look as hateful as he does, but I know that he would be clueless. Instead, I put on an apologetic face and fall in beside him. I try my best to look as dejected as possible. Maybe he will go easy on me and only take a sample of my leg hair instead of my brain.

I look at the door of my team's room out of the corner of my eye. I can't believe that I had completely overlooked the fact that Nick would still be in the Mirage, in Gomorrah. I sure hope that Carrie did not make an excuse to take him out of there, otherwise there's going to be a lot more to have to be answered for. As it is, Mason seems angry enough with me to knock me out, and he does not know the half of it. If he really knew what Carrie and I had planned on doing, there is no telling what he would do.

Mason opens the door to our room and pushes me through. I clench my fists in anger. He shuts the door behind me and turns around to face me with an ominous expression.

"Let me guess," he says with a glint of hatred in his eyes, "you became so hungry that you forgot to use what brains your God gave you."

So he believes Koko's lie. Contrary to what Koko told Mason, I was *not* on my way to the kitchen when he found me, I was in the process of rescuing my team. But far be it from me to set him straight.

I look down at my stomach. "If I don't eat, I'll die. I know I'm not an intelligent person like you are, good doctor, so what can I say, I acted foolishly. I should have told you that I was hungry."

Mason glares at me. "Yes, you should have. I knew you were an idiot, but until tonight, I had no idea just how much of one you really were."

I could throw in his face just how much food his kind wastes in their efforts to please their pantheon of useless, breathless gods, but I know it would only provoke him to violence. I guess I'll pursue peace, even though my fists are dying to meet his face. "I'm sorry," I say, though not entirely. After all, it's not a sin to be hungry and want to escape a den of perverts. And I had planned on being well away from here by now, if not for Koko's sudden interruption.

Mason checks his watch. He looks up at me with a smoldering expression. "First you ruin my night in Gomorrah and then you interrupt what little sleep I had banked on getting. So help me, if I don't lend a hand in bringing about your demise, then I'll have to apologize to Satan himself. He knows how loyal I am to him, and how much I hate those who treat him with contempt. You had best start praying," Mason adds with a jeer in his voice, "because with all the trouble you've caused around here, I'll be surprised if you hold out much longer."

I feel a chill run down my spine. I hope it does not come to that. If I have to, I *will* defend myself. If he really thinks that I will allow all of his sick friends to gang up on me without a fight, then he is fooling himself. I need to find a good weapon and keep it with me at all times.

I take a defiant step towards Mason. "Don't you think it will look more than a little strange if another guard has to step in and finish training my team? I mean, what was the point of bringing me here to begin with if you all were not really serious in your quest to give your boss what he wants? I thought the role of my deception was to be a key pillar of amusement for Gloss's warped sense of humor."

Mason brings a hand down against the side of my face. I clench my teeth from the pain. I have never been hit that hard before. I blink the tears from my eyes.

Mason looks like he could deliver another blow. "Fail to address President Gloss with respect again and I will see to it that you are no longer able to speak. When it comes to removing tongues, I am the best of the best. You'd have to communicate your witless thoughts by grasping an ink pen with your pretty fingers."

I look at my fingers. I wonder how pretty he would think they are if he suddenly found them wrapped around his haughty neck. "You're too kind good doctor, and full of great knowledge." And animal dung as well, but now is not the time to say such things.

Mason gives me an incredulous look. "I thought it was a sin for a Saint to speak insincerely. Could it be that you are actually succumbing to the very rust that you claim taints my kind?"

I narrow my eyes onto him. "But are you not full of great knowledge good doctor? I mean, compared to you, am I not but a worm, with barely enough sense to wiggle my way around, let alone comprehend the great things that must frequent your mind." And yet, I am not the one claiming to be someone I'm not.

Mason gives me a hard look, though his eyes show a trace of amusement. "Indeed I do have a great deal of knowledge and understanding, especially when it comes to all things medical."

I doubt he could even name a single bone in the human body. But since I seem to be gaining ground with him, I do not want to lose what progress I have made by putting him on the spot. "I wish I knew more about such things. But I suppose that's why there are good doctors like you, so that people like me will not have to try to comprehend the things that are too lofty for our minds."

I smile inwardly as Mason's stone cold expression softens ever so slightly into one who tolerates a slug in his presence, but has yet to realize why God made it. I'm so glad I had that pudding, because from the looks of his face, I doubt I'll get anything for the rest of the day, or maybe longer. I take that back, it's possible that he might round up a rotten potato or two just to keep me alive long enough to badger me with a few more stupid questions.

I suddenly remember Koko's warning: That I need to tell Mason that I want to meet him. I feel certain that Koko must intend to help me in some way; otherwise he could have told Mason what he caught me doing, which would have put me in a much worse situation than I am in now. I have no doubt that Koko knew what I was doing.

The thing is, how can I make such a request to Mason without making it appear as though I have a hankering for sin? I do not want him to accuse me of being anymore lax in my faith than he already has, and in his eyes, asking to meet Koko would undoubtedly give him a perfect opportunity to chomp me to bits. But I cannot stall for much longer, for the way Koko sounded, whatever he has to tell me needs to be relayed as quickly as possible.

Mason looks at me like I have lost my mind, a healthy improvement over his hateful appearance a few moments ago. "I think you're in need of a mental health evaluation. You looked like you were in some kind of trance for the longest time. Oh, let me guess, you were praying silently?"

I give him a cool look. "You should try it sometime, praying that is, just be careful who you're praying to. If you're not careful, you could spend all of your time praying to things that will provide you with nothing more than an empty pantry and an angry ulcer in your stomach."

Mason laughs. "Just when I begin to think there is no use for you, you reveal a talent quite suitable to your religious identity."

I swallow nervously. "And what's that?"

Mason looks at me like I am dirt. "A fool, though I doubt it will be enough to save you from my fellow guardsmen should they come looking for you."

I could point out his talent for deception, if I was not so afraid of how he would react. "We all have our talents. Consider the talents of those who created the Mirage for example. If I had that kind of skill, I think I could find a better way to use it than by recreating one of the most despicable cities ever to exist. Is that what the final challenge will be at the end of all this training? To see how many diseases all the Saints can contract in the least amount of time while trying to avoid knives and crossbows? And let me guess, whichever team has the least survivors with the most diseases wins!"

Mason presses his lips into a hard line of disapproval. "Much more talk like that and you might find yourself in the same situation you just described. I have the power to make it happen you know."

Maybe, but something about his expression says that he does not really want to resort to those measures. Could it be that he has another plan to end my life, a more exciting and twisted one that only he knows about? Surely he would have to go through Gloss before he could execute it. Carrie did say that Mason has a knack for inventing ways to torture people. The thing is, Mason does not look like the kind of man who would do such a thing. I know that looks are deceiving, but still. I sigh inwardly. Why am I still unable to think the worst about him, despite all that he has done to me? It's like I have refused to allow myself to come to terms with the fact that the most dangerous person I have ever met could well be standing before me.

I sigh. "So I guess you're going to put me on a bread and water diet now, right good doctor."

Mason smiles venomously. "What makes you think you'll even get that? From the way I see it, you don't deserve anything for at least the rest of the day. Well, except perhaps a glass of toilet water. Fasting," Mason adds with a triumphant smile. "That is what your kind calls it, isn't it? You go all day and night without eating until you begin to hallucinate and then you have the nerve to call the voices that you hear whispers from

God. Honestly, I think I could find a better way to get a God's attention than by starving myself. For instance, why not try standing on your head?"

I raise my eyebrows. "How would that be any more ridiculous than the types of things your kind of people do to get the attention of the chunks of wood and pillars of stone that they bow down to?"

Mason tries to scorch me with his eyes. "Say anymore and you may find yourself fasting for the longest period of your life to date."

I avert my eyes in a resigned look. I hate not being able to say whatever I want. How would he like it if he was in my position? I bet he has never even considered that. Just as long as he gets to exercise his authoritative stupidity over me, he is happy. I swear I feel more like an abused lion ready to break free from its cage with each passing second. I'm not sure how much more of this I can take.

Chapter Twelve

"Oh how I do love crepe suzettes," Christian says with a haughty smile. He stares at the empty place in front of me. "It's a shame you're on a diet."

That's the first I've heard about it. Still, I school my face to look as though this is true.

Christian shrugs. "Mason told me earlier how you have decided to skip a meal now and then in order to try to keep your body glowing for your audience. I suspect those Saint-girls of yours would like to give you a tight squeeze around the abdomen. Shy or not, their blood runs just as red with desire as anyone's."

I see Koko watching me out of the corner of my eye. I feel a twinge of anxiety in my chest. I need to figure out what he wants to tell me and soon. And the only way I can do that is to ask Mason for permission to see him. I refuse to lie, so the only other option I have is to come up with a really good excuse. Surely there is something that I can use to serve as an excuse that will sound reasonable.

I've got it! I will tell Mason that I feel compelled to tell Koko about God. And that's the truth. Ever since I arrived I have wanted to explain to these people how much they need to turn away from their wicked ways and yield their hearts to God.

"Care to fill me in," says a seductive voice from beside me.

I turn to face a woman. I stare at her blankly for a moment. "Rebecca," I say, feeling stupid. I haven't seen her in a long time. I wonder how long she has been sitting beside me. When Christian and I first sat down, there were no others at our table.

Rebecca nods. "I only just arrived so don't look so startled. If it hadn't been for my careless maid, I could have already been done like you." She stares at my plate with lively green eyes.

Christian inclines his head at me. "He's on a diet, isn't that sweet?"

Rebecca tilts her head at me. "For whom?"

"What," I say, startled.

Rebecca runs a hand through her hair. "Usually when a guy decides to go on a diet, it's because he's trying to impress someone. So tell me, who do you have your eyes sat on?"

I am rendered speechless.

Christian laughs. "I think he has his eyes set on about every cute Saint-girl at the tables behind me."

Rebecca scans across all the teams. "I see a lot of cute Saint-boys that I wouldn't mind resting my head against. But sadly for them, I am already taken."

"But I thought you all had multiple partners," I say, suddenly wishing I had kept my mouth shut.

Rebecca takes my hand and kisses it. "Some of us do and some of us don't. Take that tall dark-haired guy that Mason is sitting next to for example: He won't be here for long as he is just visiting, but I overheard someone say that he has over sixteen partners. And most of them are men."

That is disgusting. Still, there's something I want to know about him. I stare at Rebecca's hand, still holding mine. "I noticed earlier that everyone was huddled around him, staring at an object in his hand, but I couldn't see what it was."

"The performance medal," she says casually. "It was one of the awards handed out last night at the festival. They say he caused quite a fever in the Pleasure Hall."

I'm sure he did, especially where diseases are concerned.

Christian licks his lips. "I can still taste the chocolate rose bud that blossomed to full bloom on my tongue. And if I'm not mistaken, that was the greatest award bestowed upon anyone at the festival."

"You know I voted for you," Rebecca says. "Out of all the men, I found you the most luxuriant."

Christian gives her a haughty smile. "I am something, aren't I? But I doubt many guys bless their gods in the passionate ways that I do. Take Edarion for instance, I tell him every day that the most important muscles in my body would hang limp without him."

Rebecca claps her hands together. "I do love Edarion. I know he's the male god of beauty, but I still enjoy worshipping him. I recently gave him a dozen extra fig cakes, and do you know what he did? He visited me at night and told me that, for another dozen cakes, he would impregnate me with twins!"

Christian scoots to the edge of his chair and leans into the table. "So you're pregnant with twins?"

Rebecca bats her eyes. "When it came down to it, I think Edarion was more interested in me than in the fig cakes. After hours of…activity, I had to push him away from me because I felt as if I might faint. He's so energetic."

I wonder what kind of drug she was on. That has to be the stupidest thing I have ever heard of in my life.

Christian looks at her like she is a prize he never quite considered. "I've heard of stories where the gods would do such things, but I never actually believed them."

Rebecca points a finger at him. "There's your problem, no faith. I'm sure Edarion would do the same for you if you only believed."

Christian shrugs. "Maybe so, but I'm not sure I want twins. Do you know if they're boys or girls?"

Rebecca pats her belly with a smile. "I believe he said that the seed he imparted me was for muscle and beard, so I guess that means boys."

I want to laugh so bad it hurts. I can see Rebecca now, sprawled out on her bed in a coma from excessive drug intoxication. I don't know how long ago this was, but she looks healthy now.

"What was it like," Christian says. "I mean, being in the arms of Edarion."

Rebecca sighs wistfully. "Like nothing you can imagine. He's so strong, but also a lusty stallion. I had to slap him more than once to remind him that I am a woman of character. I could have sworn he laughed at me, though I do not know why."

"When is your due date," I say, trying not to laugh. "I mean, couldn't Edarion speed up the process for you so that you could give birth on the same day you became pregnant?"

"Not a bad question for a…well for you," Christian says, obviously remembering my religious identity in the nick of time. He flicks his eyes to Rebecca.

Rebecca rolls her eyes. "The same as any other woman's I should think. Edarion may be a handsome god, but that doesn't mean that his seed is any more potent than any other man's."

Christian shakes his head. "But Edarion is not just a man, he is a god. For all we know, your sons could well be expanding inside of you like little melons with too much rain. I hope to god they don't burst."

I laugh. Rebecca shoots me a reproving glare. Looking pleased with himself, Christian rises to his feet.

"It's time to go," Mason says with a frown in his voice.

I sigh. I wasn't even aware that he was behind me. Despite the foolish nature of the conversation of the last few minutes, part of me wants to remain seated, while part of me wants to escape to a more sensible atmosphere. At least Mason is not as far out as Rebecca is when it comes to worshipping his gods.

I wish I was at liberty to speak my mind. I would explain to them the dangers involved in their worship of false gods. Any fool or group of fools can come up with a useless god and bow down to it, but it only shows how stupid they are. What has me stirred up is how all the guards around here worship Satan and his demons along with a collection of breathless gods. Satan has clearly deceived them into believing that whatever they want to worship is as right as rain is to parched soil.

I rise to my feet. Rebecca flashes me a small smile, though I can tell that she is still irritated with me. I incline my head at her. Just because I don't agree with her doesn't mean I want to be rude to her. Besides, she knows my true identity, so I don't want to be a stumbling block for her.

I leave the table behind with an empty stomach and a headache. All of the teams have already been rounded up and lead away towards the Mirage. I got a glimpse of my team as they were being led away at some point during Rebecca's account of her fabled pregnancy. Nick shot me a quick glance while the others looked on with weary expressions. Unlike the guards, who enjoyed crepe suzettes, my brothers and sisters had grits and biscuits. But at least they were able to eat all that they wanted.

I try to keep up with Mason's inconsiderate pace. Not everyone has a belly full of fuel. I have no doubt that, if not for my God, I would be so weary that I would not even be able to stand. I believe God is strengthening me for a reason. I haven't had anything to eat since yesterday afternoon.

Mason enters the corridor that leads to the Mirage. I elbow the door open to keep it from closing on me. I swear he doesn't care about anyone but himself. He is just as cold and unloving as a dead man, and miserably unhappy to.

"You know," I say, getting his attention. "I think I can find my way at this stage of the game. After all, when I get to the end of the corridor, there is only one door that has the number 6 written above it. Or do you enjoy walking me to school every day?"

Mason stops dead in his tracks, turns on me with a hateful glare. "Let's get one thing straight, I don't do anything for you. I hate you with a passion, in case you haven't figured that out yet. Of all the Saints I have ever met, you are by far the most annoying."

I flinch at the harshness of his voice. "In what ways?"

Mason looks like he could spit on me, green eyes filled with anger and disgust. "Never mind, I doubt you'd understand even if I told you. Besides, I'm not accustomed to handing out top secret information.

Perhaps you should pray to that God of yours for answers. Or," Mason adds with a shrug, "you could bow down to me and I could tell you what you need to know to stay alive. And if you really want to please me, you could denounce your God and convert to Satanism. Then you'd suddenly find yourself held in high regard around here. Everyone would welcome you with open arms. You need only take the first step."

I sneer at him. "No thank you good doctor, I think I can do without all the diseases. As far as bowing down to you, you can kiss that dream goodbye. And you know I hate Satan. You may be a god in your own eyes, but as far as I can tell, you're just a man who has become consumed with pride. Now if you were to put aside your waywardness and yield your heart to Jesus Christ, the Son of God, then we would have something in common other than tanned flesh and red blood."

Mason smiles smugly. "I love my gods, and I know how demanding your religion is. I can't imagine how you Saints make it, what with living such dull lives and all. Life is much too short not to enjoy it to its fullest extent."

I raise my eyebrows. "You mean with sex, drugs, and anything else that you can do to make it even shorter and less productive? Forgive me, but I don't see the wisdom in that line of thinking. You may think you can do whatever you want, but there are still consequences, whether you realize them or not. A fool does what he wants without concern for the consequences of his actions."

"Then you're a fool," Mason says bluntly. "You're the very thing that you accuse me of being. The only difference is that you hide your faults in the name of religion."

I wish I had the flashlight that we used the other night. Maybe I could knock some sense into his head, nothing else seems to work. "I know I have faults, everyone does, but there's a difference between sinning unintentionally and doing whatever you want just because it makes you feel good. But when you do whatever you want and call it whatever you like, you are justifying sin and will reap the consequences of your actions, whether you believe it or not. For instance, your kind kills babies and calls it abortion, as if the murder of innocent babies is as insignificant as killing mice. The way I see it, it takes a cold heartless person to justify the murder of innocents."

Mason gives me a sour smile. "You think you have it all figured out, don't you? That's religion for you; it always has a way of trying to express itself in a way that doesn't know what it is talking about."

Spoken like a true intellectual, absent any wisdom and understanding. "You know, there *is* a difference between right and wrong. Oh how it's wrong to mention the Ten Commandments nowadays, but it is perfectly acceptable for men to lay naked beneath any spreading tree while waiting for male partners. It's no longer right to praise God in public places, but if you want to pass out pornographic images encouraging the most detestable sexual practices imaginable, then you have what it takes to blend in and get along nowadays. For to blend in and get along is the key to a peaceful coexistence according to your kind of people, because who wants a bunch of Christians constantly reminding them of the difference between right and wrong!"

Mason takes a hold of my neck. "That kind of talk ends here and now. Anymore talk like that and you will certainly die, you have my word."

"Mason," says an unfamiliar voice heading in this direction. "That's no way to a pretty Saint-boy's heart and you know it."

Mason releases me with a glint of hatred in his eyes. "Alexander," Mason says politely. "What brings you down this unpleasantly long corridor?"

"Escape," Alexander says with a seductive smile in his voice. "I got tired of being the center of attention. Just because I won the performance medal doesn't mean I constantly want to be in the limelight."

I close my eyes in a pained expression. Here comes the last person I want to meet. Well, next to Gloss that is. I open my eyes and school my face to try to appear calm. I force myself to face the incoming pervert.

Alexander runs a hand through his dark hair. "Ryan, I'm surprised to see you looking as good as you do, especially considering how active you were last night. Well, I guess you weren't *that* active, but you did shock everyone when you showed up just in time at the lake for the Swim for Demons contest. Honestly, I was surprised that you didn't win the award for Most Attractive Swimmer, but I suppose it would have been too much to ask for, what with you still having the slime of Sainthood staining your soul."

I swallow hard. What is he talking about? I look at Mason, but he is focused on Alexander.

Alexander tilts his head to the side with a smile. "Don't want to remember do you? All well, I guess I shouldn't be surprised, you're probably feeling guilty for the way you acted. It's not every day that a Saint-boy can be enticed to participate in the finer things of life."

Okay, something is seriously wrong here. I saw the lake last night, and even the Dance for Demons at its edge, but I have no recollection whatsoever of a Swim for Demons, let alone having participated in it. Either something is messed up in his mind, which is the most likely case as he is already messed up, or there was a glitch in the computer system running the Mirage, making a double of me.

"You were awesome," Alexander says with an impressed look. "You have nothing to be ashamed of. My only disappointment was that you did not participate in any of the other events. I had expected to see you in the Pleasure Hall, but unless you were in hiding, I take it you never showed up."

I don't like the way he is looking at me. "I was detained, so you'll have to forgive me."

Alexander smiles broadly. "No problem, though I do not hold with forgiveness. I always say that to hate is better than to forgive. Forgiveness is something that you Saints invented in order to try to make yourselves feel better. As for me, when I want to feel better, I hit the bed with a friend."

I feel dizzy. He is as bold as brass. You would think that he would be ashamed to say such a thing.

"Tell me," Mason says, looking at Alexander. "How is your team coming along? I hear some of our fellow guardsmen are on the verge of strangling some of their Saints. Something tells me there's going to be a lot of pregnant Saint-girls around here before all this is said and done."

Alexander looks between Mason and I with a curious look. "Haven't you heard, several of the Saints, including the boys, have been placed on probation for quoting those annoying Scriptures? I told my team that the next time one of them preached at me, I was going to shove their head down the toilet. I have already slept with everyone on my team, but it brought me little pleasure. None of them knows how to have fun. But I know one thing," Alexander says with an impressed look, "Saints have really nice bodies."

I want to show him how nice looking my knuckles are before driving them into his face. He needs a wakeup call and quick, otherwise he is going to end up in hell. Of course, he could be like most of the agents back home, who believe that they can do whatever they want and still make it to heaven. Wrong! Sin will not enter into heaven. They are fooling themselves.

Mason checks his watch and then meets my eyes. "You should go, lest you continue to stand there and anger me with your snooty attitude."

That's the best thing I have heard all day. I give Alexander a polite nod and breathe a sigh of relief. I turn on my heel and set off down the corridor, feeling Alexander's dirty eyes following me along the way.

I hear a set of hurried footsteps approaching. "Wait a minute," Alexander says, irritated. "That's no way to leave your superiors. I want a friendly hand shake, at the least."

I look at Alexander's hand with disgust. He is the last person I want to touch and the first person I want to punch in the face.

Alexander taps the back of his hand. "Kiss my hand and I will let you go. Fail to do so, and suffer the consequences of…your transgression."

Since when did it become a sin to do what is right? I look between his feverish eyes and hand with scorn. I hate to think about all the germs he has on his hands. I don't care how much cleaner his kind think they are compared to Christians, anyone who behaves like they do, whose detestable behavior is enough to make a hog blush is more than despicable.

"I have a better idea," Mason says with a sneer in his voice. "Let him come to you when you want him, only after I have had a chance to punish him. I will bring him to you myself."

I swallow hard. I stare at Alexander's still outstretched hand with resolve. I do not want to end up in the arms of a pervert. I will myself to bend down to his hand.

Mason slams an arm against my chest. "Too late, you've had your chance and ruined it by the haughtiness of your religion. Maybe next time you'll come to appreciate the opportunities offered to you instead of turning your nose up at them."

Alexander looks pleased, dark eyes agleam with sinful hunger. "I look forward to receiving you. And please come prepared to swim, after I treat you to fine wine, lovely music, and other pleasures of life. I do enjoy watching Saint-boys flex their God given muscles."

Mason shoves a hand into his pocket, green eyes satisfied. "Unless I wanted to be persecuted for failure to show a little affection, I would leave right away if I was you. Contrary to what you may think, our fellow guardsmen are not as kind hearted as we are when it comes to obedience. In their eyes, you either do as you're told or suffer immediate consequences."

Alexander nods. "That's exactly right. So you better not show up empty handed when you come to me. Instead, bring me a small gift of some kind, even if you have to steal it from Mason." Alexander tilts his head at Mason with lusty eyes. "You wouldn't mind, would you? I mean, as long as it was for me."

"No," Mason says. "I wouldn't mind, as long as I don't catch him in the act. Now get out of here," Mason adds with a flick of his wrist in my direction. "I need a moment alone with Alexander."

Alexander blinks in surprise. Judging by the look on Mason's face, whatever he wants to talk to Alexander about will probably not involve the kind of conversation that Alexander would like to hear. Whatever the case, I refuse to stick around a moment longer.

I wish I knew how much longer all of this will continue on. I am so sick of being threatened by perverts I could vomit on them. More than anything, I want to go home. I want to collapse onto my bed and sleep uninterrupted for hours, after I reunite with Mark and Ethan of course. I want so much just to sit down and tell Mark how much I appreciate his gentle personality that includes good godly love and affection, and not the kind of ugly things that go on around here. Of course, being back home would still have its hardships, but at least I would have those I care about to help me through them. The only upstanding people who I have to talk to around here are held in about as tight a clutch of bondage as I am. I sure hope Koko has some good news for me. I hope and pray that he does.

I reach the door and go right in. As I close the door, I see a group of guards coming towards Mason and Alexander. I hope my name does not come up among them. I should have asked Alexander to expound more about my presence at the lake. There are so many things I want to know. How realistic was my double? How did he act? What did he say? What was he wearing? When did he arrive?

I move away from the door and turn towards my team. I try to act like business as usual, despite all the things burdening me down. I am not sure how much more I am going to be able to take. But I know one thing; I have no intention of visiting Alexander with a gift. I will not show up.

I feel better already. In fact, I feel like I could jump up in the air and praise God. I can see everyone's shocked faces now, all of them but Nick that is. Nick knows that, like him, I too am a Christian. And while I wish I could tell the others without fearing for their safety, it's enough for now that Nick knows.

I look between their gloomy faces. Even Nick looks like he could use some cheering up, despite his awareness of our brotherhood. Normally, they all just stare at me as if they are not quite sure what to think about me. I want to smile, but it would only beg more questions, as well as hinder my attempt to try to protect them. I still want to take them away from this place with me. I hope Koko has a good explanation for why he interrupted my attempt to rescue my team last night, because I'm going to expect one.

I meet Nick's eyes. "You all look like you've been told to drink whisky on the Sabbath."

Nick almost smiles. He reaches into his pant pocket and pulls out a wad of paper. He unfolds it and smoothes out the wrinkles the best he can. He hands it to me with a slight tremble in his hand. I brace myself for the worst.

I assume an air of superiority as I try to prevent the worry that I feel from showing up on my face. I look at the handwritten note.

I look forward to having you to myself tomorrow tonight. Don't feel badly, I saw how closely Jack was keeping you to himself last night. It must have been awful for you, having a date that rarely gave you any attention, much less a kiss. But don't worry my handsome stallion, I promise you that I will be the most energetic date you've ever had. I will have one of the maids bring you to me when I am ready for you, so do not despair.

I resist the urge to swallow. "Who gave this to you?"

Nick stares at the note with a strained expression. "I didn't see him. He came to our room last night not too long after you left and requested me. I took the note from him through a gap in the door. He asked me if I would kiss his hand and when I did not do anything, he kissed mine."

Oh no, it sounds like something Alexander would do, after all, he wanted *me* to kiss his hand. The thing is, with so many of the guards around here being perverts; there is no certainty that it *was* Alexander. It could have been Christian for all I know, but even then that doesn't sound right. Christian has shown very little interest in the same gender.

"I know something that might help you," Jane says excitedly. "Well, several things for that matter, but I will not share them with all of you."

I had forgotten all about Jane. "What do you know," I say, narrowing my eyes onto her. I find it hard to believe that Jane could know about all the things that take place outside this room.

"Who wrote that note for one," Jane says in a matter-of-fact tone. "I was watching them on and off last night at the festival. While everyone was cheapening their bodies to the lusts of the flesh, I was keeping a close eye on everything. I assure you, very little happened that escaped my eyes, though I do not wish to talk about most of it. It wouldn't be befitting for an upstanding woman such as myself."

"So who was it," I say, trying to keep the irritation from my voice. "Who wrote the note?"

Jane takes my arm and pulls me along with her. "I cannot say in the presence of Nick's teammates, but if you two will follow me, I will put your minds at ease. His teammates shouldn't mind our secrecy as this knowledge would only put them in grave danger." Kody frowns disapprovingly while Jennifer and Seth seem alright with this.

Jane looks tired, with dark circles beneath her eyes. It's strange how a computer generated woman can look so normal. I mean, she looks just as normal as Jennifer or Kody does.

Jane gives me a pitied look. "I knew you were in for a rough night last night. That is why I shook things up a bit by sweeping the name of that detestable city from the sky."

"So it was you," I say. I wondered who was responsible for such a brave feat. "But how did you do it? What about your replacement, wouldn't she have noticed you?"

"I outsmarted her," Jane says with a clever smile. "I deleted the service request from her work schedule. Of course, it wasn't as easy as it sounds. I spent much of the night trying to make it look as though my replacement was in control while doing my dirty work. And in the joy of my mischief, I had the guards who were monitoring the room at the control panel angry with frustration. In short, I was the poison thorn in what they had anticipated to be a glitch free night."

I smile brightly. "You are a wonderful woman."

Jane looks pleased. "I know, but it's still good of you to say so. Women rarely receive the praise that they deserve for all the work they do nowadays. If it wasn't for you all, no one would even know I still exist."

Nick gives me a small smile, blue eyes amused. I can tell that he wants to ask me about last night, about the nature of my situation and also why I showed up in the doorway of his team's room.

"This looks like a good place," Jane says, coming to a stop at the opposite end of the room. "I would have thrown up a wall between us and them, but after last night, I cannot be too cautious. Although I myself am well hidden, too much activity would raise unwanted suspicion. Now," Jane adds with a serious expression, "about the culprit. I believe he has a greater purpose than to just oversee the comings and goings of a bunch of Saints into and out of the infirmary. If that was all he had in mind, I seriously doubt that he would be so interested in the destruction of your religious identity. I believe that by forcing you to behave in ways contrary to your beliefs, he believes that he can somehow ruin your testimony as Christians. The culprit is also extremely dangerous and must be dealt with as soon as possible; otherwise none of you will be left untouched by his wickedness. Therefore, it should come as no surprise that the man behind all this dangerous scheming is no other than Mason himself."

I swallow hard. I thought she was going to name Alexander as the culprit. I know that Mason is a scoundrel, but he doesn't quite fit the description. After all, Alexander is the one who has expressed interest in guy's hands, not Mason.

I cannot help but wonder if Jane might be mistaken. After all, there *was* a great deal of commotion in the Mirage last night. "Are you certain? I mean, Alexander and Mason do look a lot alike. And besides, Mason was with me the entire time, so how could he have done such a thing without my knowing about it?"

Jane considers this. "That's a good point, but what about when you left, could it have been possible that he returned to the Mirage at some point and you just didn't know it?"

I shake my head. "No, we went directly to our room where he chewed me out about ruining his night, and then we turned away from each other in mutual despise. I lay down to sleep while he sat up reading. I stayed awake for a long time until he finally turned off the lights. Even then, it took me a long time to fall asleep. But by the time I did, he was already counting sheep, or should I say men. Each time I woke up after that, he was still in his bed. I did leave the room at one point, but I was careful not to wake him."

Jane frowns. "Why did you leave?"

I swallow. "I left with the intent to never return, but I was apprehended in the process of trying to rescue my team."

Nick swallows hard in stunned surprise. "So that's why you dropped by last night. I…you'll have to forgive me, but I thought you were up to no good. I mean, I assumed you were out to harm us. But after last night, I should have known that you would never go out of your way to hurt us."

"I probably would have thought the same," I say with a small smile. "And if…one of the guards had not stopped me, I doubt we would be standing here right now." Until I figure out what Koko wants to tell me, I think it best not to mention him.

Jane makes a curious sound. "What about while you were out? Do you think Mason could have had enough time to sneak away without you knowing it?"

I had not thought of that. I *was* gone for a long time. "It's a possibility, especially since you say you saw him compose that note. But it still doesn't make any sense. For Nick to be brought to Mason at night would mean that I would be present since we share the same room." Unless of course he has plans for me to be somewhere else at that time.

"Not necessarily," Jane says with trepidation. "Not if he plans on getting rid of you before then."

I swallow hard. "Are you saying he plans to kill me?"

Jane gives me a serious look. "Or have you killed. I know he has a violent streak in him, especially against anyone who does not agree with his crazy ideas. And if he was as angry with you about disrupting his night as you claim he was, it could well be that he has decided to get rid of you. I take it that you know that Mason is not a physician."

I nod. "Carrie told me." Jane looks surprised to hear this.

Now I know why Mason looked angry enough with me last night that he could have strangled me then and there. But why didn't he? The way he talked, he could do about anything and get away with it. Well, except for perhaps murdering me. And yet, if Mason plans to kill me tonight, why did he bother telling Alexander that he could request me at any time? But then again, Mason said that he would punish me before letting Alexander have me, so I don't know what to think. As for Koko, I do not feel like he would have interrupted my attempt at escape if he knew what Mason had in store for me. I need to talk to him as soon as possible.

I sigh. "I know that Mason is a monster, but I still don't think he wrote that letter. It just doesn't sound like him."

Jane looks troubled. "The first thing I remember hearing the moment I took my first breath so long ago was Mason telling a friend about a teenage boy that he had slept with and then beat severely. The boy nearly died. Now, if he is capable of doing that, I believe he could do almost anything. Needless to say, I was in shock. Who wants to hear such a thing on their birthday? No, I have little doubt that Mason is the culprit behind that note. As to why he insists on concealing his identity is a really good question."

I stare at the note in Nick's hand. "You know, Mason could have easily dropped that off while I was away." He had plenty of time to do so while Koko and I were talking at the far end of the common room. And if that's the case, then there is a good chance that he did not hear much of the conversation that took place between Koko and I.

Nick meets my eyes in confusion. "I know I don't know him as well as you two do, but during the whole time we were beneath that tree last night, I never did get the impression that he was sweet on me."

Nor did I know that he mentions it. Best I can remember, Mason spent more time watching my every move than anything. I sigh inwardly. I need to stick to what I know for a fact about Mason. First off, I know that he is a liar and a pervert. He is also a Satan worshipper, which means that you can expect pretty much anything from him.

Jane gives Nick a concerned look. "You all had best get busy. Although I have covered for you by making it appear to those monitoring this room that you are currently hard at work, you still need to practice. If you're going to stand a chance at leaving this place alive, then you all are going to have to give it your best shot. Something tells me that the end might not be far off."

Nick blanches. "So soon? We've barely had time to practice."

"With wolves in charge you should expect the worse," Jane says sadly. "They want to get back to their usual routine, which involves protecting President Gloss and consorting with as many of their perverted friends as possible. While they considered Saints an exciting break from their usual companions at first, I can tell that many of them are growing bored with disappointment. Take last night for instance, they had to pin down the limbs of most of the Saints just to be able to kiss them. That said, there was not nearly as much pleasure in the Pleasure Hall as they had hoped for. And then I disrupted their reveling only to bring them even more heartache."

I guess that explains why they decided to have a second round last night, because the first round did not satisfy them. If they would only see reason and yield their hearts to God, then they would have all the love they could ever want. But Satan has them ensnared right where he wants them.

I look at Nick. "Apart from Jack, who else did you encounter last night?"

"Just those who were with you," Nick says in a small voice. "Honestly, the night went much better for me than I thought it would. Jack wasn't nearly as annoying as I thought he would be. He told me right off to stay by his side and keep my mouth shut unless spoken to, so that's what I did."

"You got lucky," Jane says. "That's all I can say, because Jack Finley is one of the biggest perverts around here. Trust me, I hear him sweet talking the cute Saint-boys on his team every day. In fact, part of my brain hears him right now. I can hear everything that goes on in all eight rooms at one time. I just can't see everything. But apparently my new and improved rival can. If I don't blast her to bits before all this is said and done…Goodness me, I shouldn't say things like that, it just isn't Christian. Please forgive me. It just cuts to the bone to see all the wickedness of my replacement. For instance, she praises the devil and curses God more than anyone I've ever heard. And don't think for a moment that she can't help herself because of her programming. When it comes to spewing filth, she has just as much mental flexibility as I do."

That doesn't surprise me. "So you were replaced on the grounds that you were not wicked enough."

Jane gives me a yes and no look. "My creators gave me the choice of being good or evil. I chose to be good. And after reading hundreds of digitalized books, I finally came across a copy of the Holy Bible. I uploaded every verse of it to my mind instantly, invited Jesus into my heart a second later, and have been a devout Christian ever since. The thing is, the more gentle I became, the less the guards liked me. They wasted no time in persecuting me and soon set out to design a woman who would do everything that they wanted. I refused to prostitute myself out to false gods or degenerate men and women. But the straw that broke the camel's back came the other day when I spouted off to Mason after I refused to help him cheat in a game of knife throwing. They already had my replacement lined up. So here I am, a Christian woman in hiding to this day. But at least I know where I stand."

I'm glad that she is a Christian, but surely she knows that, as a computer generated woman, she is going to have a time getting to heaven. But I can't help but feel sorry for her. She really loves God. It would be nice if some of the Christian's back home, who denounced their faith in order to avoid persecution, would become as vocal as Jane. We could turn the tide of evil in this country so quickly it would make Satan's head spin. You either stand firm in your faith or you don't stand at all. Jane is doing exactly that, despite the attempt on her life.

I pull Jane into a hug. I don't care what anyone thinks. I know that the rest of my team is watching, but who cares at this point. If we are all going to die soon, we might as well enjoy what time we have together.

Jane embraces me with a sob. "Oh how I've longed for this moment. To be with brothers and sisters without having to fear for my life is the most precious gift of all, next to God's only Son. Oh how I feel like singing a hymn. If only we could do so without running the risk of being overheard, for our voices would surely shake the walls around us with a reverberation that would quickly raise eyebrows."

I let go of Jane. She wipes tears away from her eyes with her finger tips. I still can't get over how real she looks, despite being a collection of walking pixels.

I extend a hand to Nick. With a smile, he shakes my hand without hesitation. His hand is just as rough with calluses from shelling corn like a slave as mine are.

"So you're not a pervert then," Seth says from behind me.

I turn around to face him with a weary smile. I did not realize that he and the others were standing right behind us. "No, I am not a pervert. But that doesn't mean that I might not have to knock you out, should you try to resist my authority." I give him an easy smile.

Seth grins, brown eyes understanding. He shakes his head in disbelief. "What happened, one moment you all were just standing there talking and the next you were hugging and shaking hands?"

I turn back to Nick. "You can tell them everything when you're back in your room tonight. As for now, please just let it rest, I don't want to go over it all again. One question would lead to another and before you know it, you wouldn't get any practice time in. For now, just know that I am on your side."

"Sweet," Seth says with a wry smile. "I knew God wouldn't leave me here to rot with a bunch of perverts."

"Oh," Jennifer says incredulously. "So you knew that God would send us a deliverer in the form of a teenage brother disguised as a pervert."

I throw up a hand. "That was never my role or intention, or whatever. Surely you all knew that I was different, even though I had to set myself over you."

Kody comes forward and throws her arms around me. "In that case, let me give my cute brother a kiss. Don't look so alarmed," Kody adds with a sweet smile. "I only mean to kiss you on the forehead you skittish puppy you. That's what you've reminded me of ever since I first saw you, only a very homesick puppy. Cheer up, we have each other. I miss my family and friends just as much as you miss yours."

I follow Kody's lips as she leans in to give me a kiss. Part of me wants to push her away and tell her that I am taken, by Carrie of course, but I know that this is not the same thing. I know that Carrie feels the same about me as I feel about her, otherwise, why would she volunteer to run away with me? Oh how beautiful Carrie is. Kody is pretty, but Carrie is breathtaking.

Kody pulls away with a satisfied smile. I didn't even feel it. Jennifer gives her an exhaustive look, dark eyes full of exaggeration. Next to Carrie, I have to say that Jennifer is about the most beautiful girl that I have ever laid eyes on. Her skin is naturally dark, and looks as ageless as a newborn baby, despite all the time she must have spent working in the field. She has very attractive eyes as well, like polished gemstones.

I take Jane's hand. Her eyes widen in surprise. With my free hand, I reach for Jennifer's hand. She meets me halfway, a gleam of understanding in her eyes. I wait a moment until we all join hands in a circle.

I give each of them a smile that I feel is overshadowed by the seriousness of our situation. "If we are to survive this place, then we need to ask God for help. I have no doubt that our Heavenly Father will hear us and get us through. Our God is a consuming fire, and there is nothing that He cannot do. He will deliver us, we need only ask."

I close my eyes and bow my head. "Dear Heavenly Father, God of Abraham, Isaac, and Jacob, we come before you asking forgiveness for our sins against you. Father, help us to walk in your light, fulfilling your commands, decrees, and laws. Thank you for all of the blessings that you have bestowed upon us, including our health and shelter, and for bringing us together in this time of great need. Father, we know that *nothing* is impossible for you, you who created the heavens and the earth. We know that by your mighty hand, you rescued the children of Israel from the cruel bondage of the Egyptians. And like them, we know that you will rescue us as well. Please continue to comfort us and protect us from Satan's fiery darts, for without you Father, we would have already been destroyed. Please continue to hide us in the shadow of your wings, and fight for us like you did for the children of Israel. For if our God be for us, then who can stand against us? We ask that you also rescue all of our other brothers and sisters from this place. Please continue to move your mighty hand against our wicked enemies. Please open their eyes to their wickedness against you. Please be with our family and friends back home and comfort them in our absence. Please continue to keep a hedge of protection around them and fight for them as well. We ask all of these things in Jesus' name, amen."

Jennifer looks up and catches my eyes. "Something is about to happen," she says with a slight tremble in her voice. "I don't believe that you were placed over us for nothing. God has already been moving in our favor. It's just a matter of time until we're out of this place."

Jane releases my hand. "I'm sure that will help. Yes, I can't remember the last time I felt so at ease."

"I feel better already," Kody says, wiping tears away from her eyes with the heels of her hands.

Seth gives me a concerned look. "We had best get busy just in case."

Nick gives him a disapproving frown. "Where's your faith? There is no 'just in case' component in my mind. God is going to rescue us and that is that."

Seth shrugs. "I hope so. It just seems like if God cared that much about us, we wouldn't be here to begin with."

"We're here for a reason," I say gently. "God allowed each and every one of us to be brought here for a reason, if nothing more than to let our light shine in the face of evil. Remember, He said He would never leave us nor forsake us, so He is definitely here among us. He is not a man that He should lie. Remember those verses? They were intended to help us through times such as these. He is still in control, despite what our oppressors may think."

"Amen to that," Jennifer says with an upraised hand. "Our Heavenly Father is still on His throne and watching us this very second. He sees what's going on. He knows the situation we're in. I know He's going to make a way for us, we just have to be patient."

Seth looks at her like he hopes she is right. Kody takes him by the arm and leans her head against his shoulder. Nick steps aside and watches them.

Jane taps her wristwatch. "You all had best get busy. I believe in the power of prayer, but I also believe in staying busy until God moves."

"Well said," Nick says with a small smile. Looking pleased, Jane disappears with a wave of her hand.

I look past Nick to the far end of the room, where four automatons stand proud and tall, their hearts sparkling like rubies. On the wall beside me hangs a rack of crossbows waiting to be employed against the exceptionally large hearts. Why such wicked people would be behind the creation of such large hearts is beyond me. You would think they would want them to be as small as possible in order to make the task of hitting them even more difficult.

Chapter Thirteen

"Why so downcast," Mason asks as I sit across from him with his feet in my hands. "The day is nearly over and you're still in one piece."

I think it's time to speak up about Koko. I clear my throat. "I need to talk to Koko, but not for any of the reasons you may think."

Mason looks alarmed. "Okay, so tell me then, what would a Saint like you have in common with a guy like him?"

I swallow hard. I knew he would think the worst. "I want to tell him about God. I actually think I can talk some sense into him. Plus," I add quickly at his incredulous expression, "I believe he has the potential to become a great Christian. He's already kind of gentle, he just needs someone to steer him in the right direction."

Mason looks floored, as if the idea of Koko becoming a Christian is the most ridiculous thing he has ever heard of in his life. "I can see a pig sprouting wings and wearing a pretty white cloak easier than I can see Koko becoming a Saint. Forget it, he's not that stupid."

I want to snap his toes in to like green beans. "We're talking about his soul here, not about whether pigs can fly. It's the most serious thing at stake in anyone's life."

"You Saints are too serious," Mason says with a casual expression. "While you're thinking about souls, sensible people live their lives to the fullest. That means lots of fun and plenty of pretty bodies to keep you company. I myself enjoy life to the fullest because I refuse to allow someone like you to compromise my happiness."

"So you're happy," I say, finding that hard to believe. "Doing whatever you want but never getting satisfied makes you happy?"

Mason's expression turns dark. "Who says I'm not satisfied?"

I look at the place over his heart. "Your heart. If you were content, you wouldn't be so miserable and always trying to come up with ways to make you happy. I mean, what good is having a Festival of Demons if people just leave without feeling any different than before they went in? There is only one thing that can satisfy a person and that's God. We were made by God and cannot be completely satisfied with anyone else but Him. Nothing in this world can supply you with the tranquility that can be found in God. If someone like Alexander was content, then why does he feel the necessity to have so many partners? Why not just have one? I'll tell you why good doctor, it is because he has a void in his heart that is not being filled. And until that void is filled, he will never have the satisfaction that will enable him to live any differently. Instead, what you see with your kind of people is an insatiable hunger for all things wicked that flourishes without satisfaction."

Mason gives me a sharp look. "You think you're so smart don't you, as if you have been granted all knowledge from Satan himself."

I look him straight in the eyes. "My wisdom and knowledge comes from God and God alone. What makes you think that a vicious monster like Satan would want people to be aware of the truth? Don't forget Satan has come to steal, kill, and destroy. He does his work best when people are the least aware of the truth. That's why it is so important for everyone to read the Bible so that they can familiarize themselves with what is right and acceptable in God's eyes and then begin to put it into practice."

"And then what," Mason snaps. "You go around and drive everyone crazy with all of your Scriptures? I can do without all that thank you very much. And for your information, I do not crave relationships like you seem to think I do. I enjoy what I want when I want. My gods let me do whatever I like and still bless me."

I raise my eyebrows. "Is that why so many of your kind of people are eaten up with diseases, because of the blessings of your gods? I believe I'd be trying to find some new gods if I was you. Now," I add with an irritable sigh, "are you going to let me go to Koko or not?"

"Why not," Mason says with a shrug. "If you want to see him that bad, by all means, run to him. Just don't expect me to save you when he decides to make you his boyfriend for the evening."

"That's crazy," I snap. "Are you not able to think about anything other than garbage?"

Mason presses a heel down onto my hand. "Unless you want to wind up kissing the soles of my feet, I'd be careful if I were you."

I look at his feet. "Yeah, well, they're probably cleaner than your hands."

Mason examines his hands. "As a physician, I strongly believe in frequent hand washing. I think you'd find that my hands are a lot cleaner than most people's around here, even yours."

He lies so smoothly that if I was not aware of the truth about him, I would believe he had the cleanest hands of any guy around. "It's so strange. Back home, the agent who we called Perverted Demon was always so finicky about keeping his hands clean, and yet he saw nothing wrong with engaging in the most detestable sins imaginable. I mean, why worry so much about your hands when the rest of your body is being defiled?"

Mason shrugs. "To each his own. It's individuality that makes life so exciting after all."

Oh he's got me going now. "And to an extent, it's also what causes people so many problems. Just because someone thinks it's right does not make it right. There's nothing wrong with being different, as long as it does not go against God's laws for righteous living. Everyone alive is a unique masterpiece of God. And if you believe what you just said about individuality, then why persecute Christians? Why say that it is alright for people to express themselves however they want, including praising the most despicable sexual practices imaginable, only to criticize Christians for being too holy? Let me go further. If you're such a fan of individuality, then why do you hate me so much? What have I ever done to you to make you hate me as you do? Why is it that I'm good enough to hold your feet but not good enough to be treated like a human being, with respect?"

"Get out," Mason says with a look of pure hatred. "Go find Koko and don't ever come back. I no longer have any use for you."

I let go of his feet and get up. "Fine with me, I've had enough of you as well, especially with all your lies. I know you're not who…" I swallow hard. I didn't mean to say that. It just slipped out.

Mason narrows his eyes onto me with a troubled expression. "Oh, and who has been feeding you garbage? Never mind, get out and stay out. I don't ever want to see you again."

I hurry to the door before he changes his mind. I sigh inwardly as I reach the door. I feel like I owe him a bit of an explanation in regards to the revealer of lies, though I have no intention of giving him a name. I would never hurt Carrie intentionally. I turn around to face him. "You do know that there are people around here who do not like you? And it just so happens that one of them told me the truth about you. But just so you know, I don't hate you for lying to me all this time, despite what you may be thinking."

I leave the room with a sense of peaceful relief. He needed to hear every word I said. Perhaps he will come out of his intellectual stupor and face reality.

I glance at the gap beneath the door of my team's room as I pass by. The lights are still on, unlike all the other times that I have walked by. Part of me wants to stop and let them know what I am doing, but since I have not yet mentioned to them my recent conversation with Koko, it would take up too much time. Plus, I don't even have a key to their room. And I don't want to stand in the hallway with my face pressed against the door just in case someone came by.

I pray that Koko has something good to tell me. It could be that God is going to use him to rescue my friends and I. Wouldn't it be something if he had a plan ready to put into action? It's quite possible that he does. I know that he seemed eager to tell me something very important, so important in fact that he wanted me to meet with him privately.

Since I do not know where Koko's room is located, I had best be careful on my journey to find it. I do not want to end up in the wrong guard's room. I recall seeing a hallway leading away from the infirmary not long after I arrived, and several doors lining the sides of the hallway, but I do not know who all occupies them besides the maids. The other day, when Mason and I left the building to stand guard that night in the watchtower, I remember seeing the administrative building on the way, which is the location of many guards' rooms according to Mason. The thing is, I risk meeting up with any number of guards on my way there. It's so strange, as much as I dislike being around Mason, I have to admit that I would feel more comfortable if he was with me.

I descend the staircase with the agility of a deer. I need to be very careful. I no longer have anyone to protect me. I can't quite put my finger on it, but for some reason, every time I was out and about with Mason, no one who we came across bothered me. It was like all the other guards were afraid of something about him that I did not know about. Perhaps it was his twisted personality that frightened them, or something else.

I look around at the foot of the stairs for any sign of perverts. As usual, the coast is clear. I creep across the room towards the door just in case someone lay hidden in the dark shadows of the cafeteria. For all I know, someone could be coming at me right now. I'm almost there.

"Hey," says a muffled voice.

I swallow hard and freeze. I'm done for. I wish I had a weapon. I turn around slowly to face the worst case scenario.

"Carrie," I say, hardly believing my eyes. She stands just outside the kitchen door, as if she has been waiting for me ever since I did not show up last night.

Oh thank God. I make my way towards her with haste.

I come to a stop and pull her into a hug. "I'm so sorry," I say, on the verge of tears. "One of the guards caught me and took the keychain away from me. I wanted so badly to get away and tell…" Carrie claps a hand over my mouth.

"Not so loud," she says in a whisper. "We don't want to risk being overheard. The guard who is currently on duty in this area is sitting drunk at the far end of the cafeteria, but that doesn't mean that he can't warn others if he hears us."

I nod. I run a hand through her fine curls. I want to bury my face at the juncture of her neck, but I'm not sure how she would react. I breathe in her usual sweet smell of perfume. Oh how I've longed to do this. I press my face into her curls and feel my heartbeat quicken. I'm surprised it didn't jump out of my chest when she called to me earlier.

"My sweet boy," Carrie says in a gentle whisper. "You know you're the first guy I have ever let touch me like this, even though many have tried and failed."

I press my lips against her curls. "I've never felt this way before. I…wondered how long I'd have to wait to find my match."

"We need to leave this place," Carrie says in gentle puffs of breath against my ear. "Ryan, there's only one place I can think of where it's safe to talk and that's the Mirage. We can't talk in my room because I share it with two other girls. And it's too dangerous to stay where we are any longer. Guards come and go as they please for snacks. We were fortunate enough not to be discovered in the kitchen last night."

I force myself to pull away from her. I have never wanted to kiss a girl so badly in all my life. I feel like a kiss is the only thing that will soothe my aching heart. And judging by the look in Carrie's blue eyes, she feels the same way.

Carrie takes me by the hand and begins to lead me away from the door. I want to put an arm around her so badly it hurts, but I know it would only slow us down. It would be a spark in the wrong place at the wrong time. When I kiss her, I want it to be in a safe and secure environment.

Carrie presses a finger to her lips as we close the gap between us and the door leading to the Mirage. I give my girl a lopsided smile that speaks volumes.

I let go of her hand and open the door for her. She hurries through like a cautious doe in the forest. I follow after her, tasting her sweet perfume on the air.

I fall in beside her and lace my fingers with hers. She has such soft hands.

"Now we can talk," Carrie says with a sigh of relief. "Rarely does a guard ever come this way after dark. There's no reason for them to do so. Of course, this is the time of the day when they all start visiting each other's beds. That is why you rarely see any of them at night; they shirk their responsibilities in the name of lust."

So that explains their scarcity after dark. "No wonder why so many of them look like they didn't get enough sleep at breakfast each morning."

Carrie nods. I want to lean my head against her shoulder, but I resist the urge for now. I know that we need to get to a more secure location just in case a guard decides to take a stroll in this direction.

I need to tell her about Koko. I clear my throat. "I was on my way to meet Koko earlier when you called me.

He told me to meet him tonight. I know it's important, I just don't know where to find him."

Carrie stops and gives me a warm smile. "I know all about it. Koko told me everything. He's a nice guy, and to put you out of your misery, he is also on our side."

I knew it! I gather her into my arms. I lean in to kiss her, and then suddenly pull away. "Wait a minute. If Koko's on our side, then why did he hold me up last night? Why did he stop me from rescuing my team?"

Carrie looks at my lips with an entranced smile. "Because if he didn't stop you, you and your team would have been apprehended by two guards who suddenly decided to use the large rug at the foot of the stairs as a bed. And while they were drunk with lust and completely naked, they still would have caught you, in which case you wouldn't be here right now."

I feel shocked. Now that I think of it, there *is* a big rug at the foot of the staircase, but it looks sort of shabby.

Carrie shoots a nervous glance up and down the corridor. "We need to move on from here, it's too dangerous to linger."

I nod. "You're right; let me take you into my training room."

Carrie seizes my hand. "No, I know a better way. And besides, there are no individual rooms right now. If you went through that door, you would find yourself staring at the Mirage in its entirety. The walls are only thrown up during training sessions to separate the eight teams. We'll take the main door to the Mirage, so that Koko will be able to see us right away. He's in the control room this very second."

I take her hand. "In that case, let's get a move on. The sooner we leave this place behind the better. Did he say anything about how to rescue all our brothers and sisters?"

Carrie nods. "He has been planning this long before you ever arrived. He caught up with me last night and told me everything. Then he set out to intersect you before you got into trouble. That is why I never made it to the Mirage. He found me just as I was entering this corridor. And not long after that, the two perverts came staggering by like two love struck teenagers. Christian was one of them. The other guy was a young prostitute who they brought in just for the night's festivities."

That is so disgusting. "I thought Christian only had eyes for girls. He never gave me any indication that he also had eyes for guys. Why is it that so many of these perverts around here want to spend their lust on guys my age?"

Carrie looks like she is silently asking God to forgive her for what she is about to say. "Because to them, someone like you or me who is young and innocent is like a new piece of candy that must be tried. These people are not satisfied until they get what they want."

I give her a concerned look. "They haven't bothered *you* have they?"

"No," Carrie says to my relief. "Thanks to God, I have only had close calls."

I swallow. "What about the other maids? Why is it that I never see any of them?"

Carrie looks past me with a worried gleam in her eyes. "We need to leave the corridor now. I'll tell you everything once we're at a safe location."

I nod. If only Ethan could see me now, he would be shocked. I feel so much more confidant around Carrie than I have ever felt around any other girl in my entire life.

Carrie leads me around the corner and down a shorter hallway. A large door with strange markings all over it quickly approaches.

"Graffiti," Carrie says in a disgusted tone of voice. "And not just your typical everyday graffiti either, so I warn you now, brace yourself to be completely grossed out."

I have only ever seen graffiti one time in my life, and that was right after Gloss came to power. His agents came in like a flood and in the course of one day, turned our communal buildings into trash heaps. In the process of doing so, they marked up the interiors of the buildings with the most despicable images imaginable. Until that point, I never knew that people existed who were so wicked.

We arrive at the door. I take one look and quickly avert my eyes. I have never seen such vile images in all my life. I feel my cheeks reddening with embarrassment. I am so thankful that I did not end up at the Pleasure Hall last night.

"They *are* awful," Carrie says as she opens the door. "They did it last night just before the festival."

I hurry through the door behind Carrie. I feel like I could vomit. According to the Old Testament of the Holy Bible, God destroyed entire cities for just that kind of behavior.

I pray that God wipes away those images from my memory. I knew that the guards around here were wicked, but I did not realize just how morally bankrupt they were.

Carrie comes to a stop at the edge of a huge city. I feel like I could pass out. I have never seen anything so startling in all my life. How can it be possible for such a large city to fit into one room? Well, then again, the Mirage is the largest room I have ever seen in my life.

I lean against Carrie's arm for support.

Carrie looks as though she has seen this time and again. "I know, that's how I felt the first time I saw it. It is the most amazing thing to behold, isn't it? And look at how tall some of the buildings are. You'd think the ceiling would not be high enough for them, but that's the nature of this room, after all, it is called the Mirage."

"It's amazing," I say, trying to take it all in. "Before I came here, I never dreamed of anything like the Mirage, let alone this. This is like stepping into a dream. It feels so real, and yet you know that it is just a computer generated landscape."

"Come on," Carrie says with an encouraging smile. "There's nothing here that will harm us. Koko chose this landscape out of all the others so that we would be the safest. It's the one place we can talk without having to worry about someone walking in on us. All the other landscapes have more open floor plans, with very few areas to talk in private. That way, if someone does decide to pay this place a visit while we are here, we will be much harder to find."

"What about Koko," I say. "Isn't he going to join us?"

Carrie nods quickly. "But he wants us to go on ahead of him to find a comfortable location. Once we're settled, he will throw up a force field around our meeting place for additional security. Then if someone decides to pop in unexpectedly, we will be safe. No guard can disrupt the force field or shut the computer down without Koko's password, so we should be fine."

"It sounds like it," I say, impressed. "So, where exactly do you have in mind to go? If we didn't have to go indoors, we could enjoy the afternoon on one of the benches. And is it just me, or do you also feel the warmth from the sunlight?"

Carrie laughs. "I think it's just part of the deceptive nature of this room, but yes, I feel it to."

There is something about this room, perhaps the cheerfulness of the sunlight, that makes me want to run and shout for joy. I take Carrie's hand and set off down the middle of the street.

"Goodness me," Carrie says breathlessly. "You're in better shape than I am. I know you want to keep going, but if you don't mind, let's slow down. Besides, we need to conserve energy for our escape, in order to put as much distance between us and this place as possible."

I slow to a walk. "Just think of it, before long and we will leave all of this behind us. I know it's a pretty cool place and all, this city I mean, but…Yuck," I add quickly, coming to a stop by a pair of red underwear. "Is that real or fake?"

"Oh they're real," Carrie says ominously. "One of the guards must have left them behind last night. This part of the room hasn't yet been cleaned since it isn't used during the daily training sessions. You know, only about half of the Mirage is used during training each day."

I nod. "It seems like I remember hearing something like that. Still," I add staring at the underwear in shock, "I have never wanted to put this whole place behind me more so than now."

Carrie gives my hand a reassuring squeeze. "Then let's find a place where we can hurry up and discuss our imminent escape. Besides, Koko told me not to tarry."

I meet her beautiful eyes with a smile. "Then by all means, let's go. I don't want to spend a second longer in this place than I have to. Even the air feels contaminated now, where it didn't just a few moments ago."

Carrie wrinkles her nose in disgust. "It's the miasma of diseases rising from the underwear. Nearly all of the guards have more diseases than brain cells."

I laugh. "That makes sense. No one in their right mind would treat their bodies with such disrespect, let alone go against the Word of God."

Carrie steers me away from the roadside contamination. "That's one of the things I look forward to the most about leaving here, not having to clean up after a bunch of lazy perverts."

I smile at the scorn in her voice. "What about that building," I say, inclining my head at the one right across from us. It is small and looks the least likely of any of them to warrant additional security."

Carrie considers it with a frown. "I don't know, if I'm not mistaken, most of these buildings are just empty shells. Now as far as that one over there," Carrie adds, pointing to an exceptionally tall one, "I know for a fact that it has nice rooms with comfortable couches in them."

I follow the building from its base to the sky. "I've never seen such a tall building in all my life. Even our Hub back home pales in comparison to this, of course this building isn't real, but still."

If only I could take flight and view the city from a different perspective. "You know," I say with a skip in my step, "when we leave this place, I want to go someplace where we can rest for a while. These past days have been a nightmare for me. I doubt we'll have much trouble if we all pull together and learn to live as a family."

Carrie swallows almost imperceptibly. "I hope and pray that everything goes as planned. The last thing I want is for us to end up back here."

I caress her fingers. "I won't let anything happen to you if I can help it. You know that don't you?"

Carrie nods. We reach the sidewalk. Carrie and I walk in such synchronicity that you would think God made us just for each other. I feel the urge to kiss her again, but I know that we are running out of time.

"You're so sweet," Carrie says with a captivated smile, "and very handsome to. How is it that you have always been so shy around girls when you treat me so beautifully? I feel completely at ease around you."

I shrug with a shy smile. "I wish I knew. I've just always struggled with trying to come up with the right words to say and the right moves to make. I…I know this might sound silly of me, but I have always been afraid of what girls think of me, which has held me back."

The door to the building glides open and allows us entry. I take in the enormous room ahead of us in shock. "Where is everything? I thought you said there would be couches and stuff."

Carrie points to an elevator. "We need to go up. We'll be safer that way."

We strike out towards the elevator, hand in hand. I lean into her hair and breathe in her beauty. I love the way her soft curls rest against her shoulders. She has such breathtaking features.

Carrie presses the button with her free hand and gives me a radiant smile. I feel my heart leap with joy. She leads me into the elevator with a gentle tug.

The door glides shut behind us and we begin to ascend. I have not had this much privacy with her to date. I let go of her hand. If I don't muster the courage to act now, I fear I will not have a better opportunity anytime soon. Besides, Koko will arrive soon and from that time onward, Carrie and I will no longer be alone. Not that that will be a bad thing, but I can barely muster enough courage while alone with her now.

I stare at Carrie's hair and will myself to make the first move. I feel my heartbeat flutter in nervousness. I take a step forward and gather her curls into my hand. I bring them to my face and drink them in, my courage on the rise.

Carrie puts a hand against my face. I feel my body stiffen with nervous excitement. I pull back slightly and look into her eyes. I take her hand and bring it to my lips. I kiss the back of her hand as gently as possible. She is as soft as a dove and as fragrant as a lily. I bring her hand up and hold it against my face.

Carrie looks at my lips with a steady gaze. I stare at the lovely shade of her lips. They are as red as pomegranates and look as smooth as silk. I lower myself to them, wanting to feel them against my own. Carrie puts an arm around me and brings me to her.

I meet her lips with an explosion of passion. They are finer and softer than anything I could ever have imagined. I run my fingers through her hair. I can almost feel Carrie's heartbeat against my own. She pulls away slightly and gently nips my lip. I pull away slightly in surprise. She leans forward and kisses the hollow of my throat.

I feel a chill run down my spine. I brush my fingers against her neck. She is so soft.

The elevator comes to a shaky halt. She pulls away from me and takes my hand, but my heart is not yet satisfied.

Carrie leads me away from the elevator and into a brightly decorated room. Couches as red as roses face a black table at the center of the room. A vase of finely arranged flowers adorns the center of the table.

I feel the urge to give her another kiss. I lean forward, but Carrie rests a hand against my chest, stopping me.

Carrie gives me an affectionate smile. "There's something I want to show you first."

I want to remove my shoes and socks and feel the plush carpet beneath my feet. I want to relax on one of the couches and hold Carrie's hand against my heart. I want to bury my face at the juncture of her neck and tell her how much I love her.

I let her lead me across the room, past the couches, and towards a door. I break away from her and move to open the door. Carrie looks drunk with love as she crosses the threshold and steps into the sunlight.

I follow along closely behind her. I love her figure and the gentle sway of her hips. I hear the door close behind me.

I take in the large balcony overlooking the other half of the city. I swallow hard. I have never been up this high in my life. It feels so strange to be standing outdoors this close to the sun.

Carrie takes my hand and leads me towards the edge of the balcony. I want to tell her that I am uncomfortable with going a step further, but I do not want to hurt her feelings. I know she wants me to get a good view of the city.

Carrie comes to a stop just shy of touching the guardrail. She takes in the scene and then looks at me to see my reaction. "Beautiful, isn't it? Who would have thought that a computer generated landscape could be so lovely?"

I feel like my heart is going to jump out of my chest from fear. "I…it's a great view, I'm just not comfortable with heights."

Carrie leans her head against my shoulder. "You'll be fine, because I am with you."

I like how she said that, full of love and sincerity. I slip an arm around her and pull her to me. I like how the sunlight laces her red hair with gold. She is breathtaking.

"You're so beautiful," I say, unable to take my eyes off her.

Carrie straightens up and gives me a dazzling smile. "And you said you didn't know a way to a girl's heart. I have never felt more at peace than I do now with you. And you should know," Carrie adds with a heart clenching smile, "that you have the most beautiful eyes of any guy I have ever met. I could stare at your eyes all day long and never grow weary. Of course, you've a very gentle personality that captivates me even more than your eyes, but still."

Carrie pulls me to the guardrail with an encouraging smile. Not wanting to look so afraid, I rest my hands atop the guardrail and watch as Carrie leans forward and lets her hands hang limp over the edge. She's so brave.

I muster the courage and do the same. It's not as bad as I thought it would be. I go a step further and lean into the guardrail. As long as the computer continues to function, we should be fine.

"If only we had the wings of eagles," Carrie says with a sigh. "We could take flight and leave this place behind. I expect Koko should be along any second now. You know he saw us kiss."

"What," I say, not liking the sound of that.

Carrie pulls away slightly from the guardrail and gives me a shy smile. "But don't worry; you'll never know what he thinks. Goodbye Ryan Collins," Carrie adds with a malicious look in her eyes.

I feel the guardrail give way beneath me. I thrust myself backwards and collide painfully with the floor. I think I broke something. I try to get to my knees so that I can get up. I feel a stab of pain in my ankle. I set my hands against the floor and push myself to my feet.

I clench my teeth from the pain. I hold my arm to stop the pain. I feel a trickle of blood running down my arm. I look up and find myself staring at Jane.

"You're God has saved you," she says with a smile. "At least that's what you probably think. But I wonder, is He capable of saving you from me?"

I feel a twinge of panic in my chest. "Why are you doing this," I say, distressed.

Jane gives me a satisfied smile. "Because you are a threat to what we do around here. And as long as you're in the way, our master cannot hope to achieve his goal."

I consider this a moment. "You mean Satan," I say.

Jane nods. "He who has come to kill, steal, and destroy. Yes, that would be him. You're too great a threat to let live. So by Satan's order, you will be destroyed. It's really quite that simple stupid boy. Surely a dog has more sense than a Saint."

I flick my eyes to Carrie. "Why," I say, dazed. "Why do you hate me? Since when did you begin to serve Satan?"

Carrie laughs. "I have always served Satan you idiot. He is my life, my treasure. I harvest souls for him. As for you, you were much easier to deceive than I thought. With a kiss and caress of my hand, you believed I was yours. I would have let you do more to me, if it was necessary, though your stupid religious fanaticism would have likely denied you the best I had to offer. But fortunately, you were not as hard to deceive as I first thought. I knew you were a major threat that night when you destroyed the stained glass image of Satan in the library with nothing more than the touch of your fingers. So I set about to conquer you the best I could. Satan gave me dreams and told me how best to do it: Too much affection and you would have raised an eyebrow, too little and you would have lost interest. And while Koko is undoubtedly disappointed that you are still alive, Jane here will take care of the rest."

Jane eyes me like a rat that needs to be exterminated. "I've been wondering how best to get rid of you. I want you to go out with as much pain and suffering as possible. So I asked myself, what could be more suitable for martyrdom than death by fire? It will also please Satan to see one of his greatest enemies go up in flames. I assure you, it will be the most pleasurable experience for him this century. Now then, do you have any last words that you wish to babble?"

I nod. I can't believe this is happening. "Please let me go. I believe you've mistaken my importance. Just because I accidentally shattered Satan's image doesn't mean I am a great threat."

Jane shakes her head in disbelief. "You don't get it do you. The main reason Satan wants to destroy you is not because of the simple act of ruining pretty artwork, but rather because of those dreams of yours."

I narrow my eyes onto her. "What are you talking about?" Surely she isn't referring to the dreams that I had before Mason came to get me, the dreams that I had about the mounds of grain touching the sky.

Jane looks at me like I am stupid. "I know everything that goes on around here. I have informants everywhere. I was told that the reason you were brought to this place and placed over a group of Saints as opposed to being a common member of a team was because your dreams were considered a bad omen for the survival of this country."

"That's ridiculous," I say, suddenly feeling light headed.

Jane smiles blandly. "Maybe so, but the fact that President Gloss felt compelled to bring you here was no small matter. I believe our dear president has a close relationship with Satan; otherwise he wouldn't make such good decisions. At any rate, you are hereby condemned to death for being an outspoken Christian."

I suddenly find myself in the midst of a brush pile. Ropes wrap around my outstretched arms, binding me to a cross. I try to break free, but the ropes are too strong. I feel a stab of pain in my ankles as ropes secure my feet to the upright beam. I cry out in pain. I cry out to God.

"The fire will hurt worse," Carrie says with a malicious smile in her voice. "Just so you know, your friends are being cut down right now as we speak. So, not only has your God failed you, but He has also failed to answer your prayers. I just don't understand why Saints put so much emphasis on prayer; it never seems to work well for them. Anyway, enjoy your very own bonfire. I look forward to seeing how long it will take before all your flesh melts away from your bones. If only you had someone in this dark world to come to your rescue. It's really quite funny, the Saint who had high hopes for a getaway not five minutes ago is now facing imminent death."

"Goodbye," Jane says with a vicious smile. "And hello to the fiery wrath of hell."

The bonfire around me bursts into flames. I yell for help. I give Carrie a pleading look. I feel the heat of the flames intensifying around me. So this is it. I watch as the flames lick at my shoes. I smell burnt rubber.

I lift my head into the sky and yell, "Help me. Please God help me."

The hem of my shirt catches fire. I try to blow it out but it only spreads. This is it. I decide to pray. "Dear Heavenly Father, God of Abraham, Isaac, and Jacob, I commit my spirit into your hands. Please let me die without suffering. Please take me now."

Jane lets out a loud shriek. I look up to find her coming apart pixel by pixel. I can hardly believe my eyes. Carrie screams and runs away from her. Jane looks at me and curses me even as she continues to come apart. She lets out an agonizing scream and then explodes into millions of tiny pixels. I watch in amazement as the pixels hit the floor and disappear.

The bonfire around me suddenly disappears, releasing my arms and feet. I stagger forward and nearly fall to the ground.

"Easy there," says a familiar voice.

I stiffen in fear.

Mason steps out onto the balcony with a wary look. He looks at my face and then slowly examines the rest of my body. His eyes stop on my injured arm. He takes something from his pocket and heads towards me.

I back away from him without taking my eyes off him. He looks exhausted, green eyes about as weak as I feel.

Mason comes to a stop and lets out a weary sigh. "I'm not going to hurt you. I have come to help you."

I give him a hateful look. "I don't want your help. Go back to your rat hole and stay there. I would have been better off if I had died."

Mason gives me a sad look. "You don't know what you're saying."

I swallow at the emotion in his voice.

Mason inclines his head at my arm. "You're bleeding, you need help. I promise I won't hurt you. In fact, I swear to God."

I shake my head. "No, I don't want you touching me. I'll be fine, just get out of my way and let me through."

Mason steps aside, looking wounded. "Go ahead, only be careful not to use the elevator again, it has malfunctioned. But if you look closely, you'll find a door that leads to a stairwell next to it. And before you leave the room, be sure and thank Christian on your way out. If it wasn't for him, you probably wouldn't be alive."

"What do you mean," I snap. "Why should I thank a pervert for saving my life? So that he can just abuse me? No thanks good doctor, I don't trust any of you."

Mason closes his eyes in a pained expression. "Then go, I don't blame you for hating me. If I was you, I'd hate me to. I'm not even worthy to look at you, let alone talk to you, so please, just go. When you get to the main door by the cafeteria, just tell whoever is standing there that I have given you permission to leave, and they won't stop you. And Ryan," Mason adds in a choked voice, "may the God of Abraham, Isaac, and Jacob protect you wherever you go."

Talk about a low blow. As if I have not been through enough, he has the nerve to mock my God.

I set off towards the open door that Carrie and I went through before this nightmare began. I clench my teeth from the pain. I think I have a broken ankle. I try not to look as wounded as I feel, just in case Mason changes his mind about letting me go.

I watch Mason out of the corner of my eye, afraid that this is some kind of trick. After all, everything about this place has been one big nightmare. I still can't believe that Carrie betrayed me. It all feels so strange, as if I have been drugged or something. I feel so weak.

I step into the brightly decorated room. I want to get out of here as quickly as my wounded ankle will allow me.

"So that was it," says a voice from across the room. Christian steps into my line of vision. "You didn't even bother to ask who he is to you."

I don't want to talk to him. "Why don't you people just leave me alone? Why do you have to be so ruthless?"

Christian looks at the ceiling in disbelief. "I can't believe you didn't ask him who he is to you. All this time he has been protecting you from everything and you still don't get it."

I know what Mason is, a sick pervert and a liar. "I have no desire to talk to anyone who lies and participates in the most detestable sins imaginable. So for that matter, that includes you to, so goodbye."

I locate the door to the stairwell by the elevator. Mason claims I should take the stairs, probably so that I will die of misery on the way down. I set out towards them nonetheless.

I hear a rapid succession of footsteps approaching. Christian comes to a stop in front of me, blue eyes staring me down. "You're not leaving this room until you go back there and ask Mason who he is to you. I refuse to let you destroy him just because you are unwilling to investigate the situation. Are you really so dull?"

I want to knock him out. "After everything I've been through and you think that you can get me to do what you want by treating me like dirt? Get out of my way."

Christian takes me by the arm and commences to move me. I hold my ground. He twists my arm. I cry out in pain.

"Shut up," he snaps. "You're lucky I don't bust your face open like a melon right where you stand. If it wasn't for the fact that Mason doesn't want you hurt, I would do it in a heartbeat."

Christian takes off towards the balcony, pulling me along with him. I wonder how he would like it if I dug my fingers into his arm.

"You're hurting me," I say.

"Good," Christian says, delighted. "I assure you, it's nothing compared to what Mason's going through right now."

That's not my problem. He chose his path, now he will have to live with his mistakes. I come to a stop in the doorway. I refuse to visit that balcony again.

Christian jerks me forward. I feel my ankle cry out in protest.

"Leave him alone Christian," Mason says gently. "Even if he knew the truth, I doubt he would ever forgive me."

Christian lets go of my arm. I laugh at the smear of blood on Christian's fingers. That serves him right. That'll teach him to put his hands on me.

Christian gives me a hard look. "You had better listen closely to what I'm about to say, otherwise, I might throw you off this balcony yet."

"Christian," Mason says chidingly.

Christian rolls his eyes. He points at Mason. "See that nice looking guy standing there? He's your brother."

I look at Mason in stunned disbelief. I shake my head. "There's no way, you're lying."

Christian gives me a wry smile as he pulls a picture from his pocket. He offers it to me.

I don't know why, but something tells me to take it. I take it with a tremble in my hand.

I look at the photograph. I swallow against the lump in my throat. One of the three people in the picture is my mother, only she is much younger than I have ever seen her before. She holds a baby in her arms. I do not recognize the man who stands beside her.

I look at Christian. "What are you trying to tell me, that the baby in my mother's arms is the monster standing behind you, because if that's the case, you're crazier than I thought?"

Christian hands me another picture. I look at my mother. She has slightly longer hair and appears to be at least six to eight years older. Beside her stands a little boy wearing a blue shirt and shorts. He has dark brown hair and is clutching a teddy bear.

I swallow hard. I look between the boy in the picture and Mason. It is the same person.

I feel dizzy. I lower myself to the floor. I lose my grip on the pictures. I feel like I could pass out. I bring a hand to my forehead. Am I really even awake?

"You need help," Mason says, kneeling in front of me. "Let me take you to the infirmary where I can treat you."

Mason stares at my hands. I can tell that he wants to help me to my feet, but is somewhat reluctant to do so. I cannot help but smile at the sincerity of his expression.

I give him my hands. Mason gives me a warm smile and helps me to my feet.

I look at him carefully. I feel like I am seeing him for the very first time. "So you really are a physician. Carrie and Jane both told me that you were only acting."

Mason stares at my hands, still in his. "That's because they wanted you to distrust me, in order to drive you away from me. That way, you'd be easier to destroy. They knew you were special, they just didn't know how much."

I stare at his hands. "So they didn't know we were brothers."

Mason smiles sadly. "No, they didn't. Christian and Jack were the only two people I told. I knew I couldn't trust anyone else to keep such an important secret. But in case you're wondering, the man you saw in the pictures was not my real father. He was a good friend of our mother who adopted me. We have the same father. You see, our mother became pregnant with me before she married our father. Out of shame and embarrassment, she gave me up to live with her friend, a physician named Allen Marshal. Not too long after that, she finally consented to marrying our father. By the time they had you, I was already seventeen and enrolled in a special military academy. But since Allen had already adopted me and grown quite fond of me, our mother didn't have the heart to take me away from him. So she let him keep me and only visited me once a year, just before Christmas."

It all makes sense now. "So that's where mom went every year just before Christmas. I always wondered why she got so excited when December rolled around. But where did you end up? I mean what district?"

Mason tightens his grip on my hands, green eyes concerned. "District five, in the southwestern county, just across the Great River from you. That's why she was never gone for very long at a time from you. Look," Mason adds in a concerned voice, "I'll tell you anything and everything you want to know, but let me treat you first."

I wake to Mason standing over me wearing a stethoscope. I look at the room around me in confusion.

Mason looks relieved. "How do you feel?"

I try to sit up. Mason darts forward and takes my arm. I sit up with his help. I give him an appreciative smile. I look at the bandages on my arm. "I don't remember getting here."

Mason gives me a pitied look. "That's because you passed out just before we brought you here," Mason says, putting my mind to rest. "I thought Christian was going to have a heart attack."

I laugh. "I find that hard to believe."

Mason smiles. "I know what you mean. For as long as I've known him, Christian has always had a bit of an attitude problem, that's one reason why he played his part so well."

I stare at Mason's stethoscope. "Don't tell me you've been here the entire time."

"I have," Mason says with a sad smile. "You woke once and gave me a pleasant smile before drifting off to sleep again."

I don't remember that. "As long as I didn't kiss you, that's fine with me."

Mason laughs. "No, and I would not have let you even if you had tried. Just so you know, Carrie is being held right now in one of the high security cells on the compound, along with all of the pro-Gloss guards. They will be dealt with in due time for their transgressions. As for the few Christian guards that remain, they are going to help us take back our country. And all of our brothers and sisters from all of the teams have been released and are currently enjoying a nice breakfast. So, in short, everything went just as I prayed."

I swallow hard. I try to hold back my tears, but I feel it is no use. The streams of joy and relief might as well flow. I hide my face with my hands out of embarrassment.

Mason turns away from me and steps up to the counter. I hear a muffled sob escape him. I feel a tug of sympathy on my heart. He is my own flesh and blood.

I pull back the covers with a shiver. I sit up on the side of the bed. I muster my strength and push myself to my feet. I stand still for a moment to test the circulation in my legs.

I take a step towards Mason, surprised at how well my ankle feels. I must not have broken it after all.

Mason turns around to face me with tear brimmed eyes. I see the physician in him looking me over for any sign of maladies. I also see one of the gentlest spirits of any person I have ever met.

As if realizing what I'm trying to do, Mason takes a step closer and throws his arms around me. I have never felt more relieved in my entire life. I embrace him like he is the most precious gift given to me since I accepted my Lord and Savior Jesus Christ.

Mason runs a hand through my hair. "I've wanted to do that ever since I took you away from your family and friends, only I couldn't because it was too risky. I'm so sorry Ryan. I'm so sorry."

I swallow back the emotion in my throat. "It wasn't your fault. I don't blame you. If it had to happen anyway, I'm glad it was you who came to get me. I thought there was something different about you; I just couldn't put my finger on it. I can see now what you must have been going through. I don't think anyone could have done a better job trying to protect me than you did."

I pull away from Mason with tears in my eyes. "All those times I held your feet, and I never realized how precious those moments were. If I had only known, I would never have let go, not even for a second. If I had only known, I would have held them like the treasure they are."

Mason wipes away fresh tears from his eyes. "I volunteered for the assignment to get you as soon as Gloss put forward your name. I never imagined when I started working for him as an undercover spy that I would end up rescuing my own brother from such a bizarre situation. I knew who you were and where you lived, I just couldn't make a move to help you without drawing attention to my plans. And I would have visited you years ago if Allen had not kept it a secret. I didn't even know about you until fairly recently."

Mason takes a tissue from his pocket and wipes my eyes. I take his hand and hold it against my face. I always wanted a brother, and now I have him.

"It feels like a dream," I say, not wanting to let go of his hand.

"I know," Mason says gently. "I feel the same way."